Queen of Aces

To my great friend Stephanie

Aaron

Dedicated to my children:

Brandon & Madris

Queen of Aces

by

Aaron Masters

Top Publications, Ltd. Co.
Dallas, Texas

Queen of Aces

A Top Publications Paperback
First Edition

Top Publications, Ltd. Co.
12221 Merit Drive, Suite 750
Dallas, Texas 75251

ALL RIGHTS RESERVED
Copyright 2000
William Brownell
ISBN#:1-929976-02-X
Library of Congress #00-133685

No part of this book may be published or utilized in any form or by any means, electronic or mechanical, including photocopying, recording or information storage and retrieval systems without the express written permission of the publisher.

The characters and events in this novel are fictional and created out of the imagination of the author. Certain real locations and institutions are mentioned, but the characters and events depicted are entirely fictional.

Printed in the United States of America

PROLOGUE

The sun beat unmercifully on my shoulders as my aching, ancient feet hobbled along the sea of moist, warm grass with a book tucked under my arm. Using a hand to shield my eyes, I squinted, trying to read the solemn epitaphs, looking for one particular fallen comrade. Finally, my long journey had come to an end.

I never thought there could be something romantic about someone buried six feet under. But there I was, smiling, yet gripped with grief, staring at an inconspicuous grave marker bookended by miniature American flags. As I reached up to remove my black homburg, I could almost hear the sound of the cheering crowd as a powerful fighter roared overhead, executing a high-speed fly-by. I snapped my head back trying to spot it, but the sky was empty.

I often regretted the promise I had made so long ago. When she gave me her diary, she made me promise never to publish her story until she was gone. She always said that she never needed to be a hero. But I had feared she would out-live me, and that I would go to my grave without having told the World about this gutsy, freckled-face gal from New Jersey.

A tear traveled down a deep, tired crevice of my leathery face. I watched it fall--it splat on the toe of my right shoe. There was a time I could have leaned over and wiped it dry with a handkerchief.

As I panned upward, an eerie chill stiffened my neck. I shuffled the last few steps and slumped to the moist, green carpet to rest and pay tribute. I could hear my raspy efforts to catch a breath.

It seemed like a million years since I penciled the notes for my first feature story about her and aviation. It was about her. I reached into my suit pocket and pulled out a note pad, its pages yellowed with time.

I then took out a small gold cross and chain, kissed it before leaning forward, and strained to loop it over the right side of the marker.

Suddenly, I could feel the pattering of youthful footsteps behind me. I leaned back, craning my stiff neck to see whom it was. A small blond boy wearing blue shorts and blazer, stood eye-to-eye with me, blankly staring. His attractive mother hustled to catch up to him, apologizing for the intrusion. I smiled politely then turned back to read the epitaph.

Megan Kathleen Reilly
Women's Auxiliary Ferrying Squadron
1919-1999

All of a sudden, I was exhausted. I looked down at the book about her life, resting on my lap, reflecting back to the first time we met.

CHAPTER 1

The faint, distant grind of a plane's engine sounded, broken and distorted by a periodic gust of wind sweeping across a massive blanket of green grass, rustling the tops of trees as far as the eye could see. Above was a deep blue sky, hindered only by the slightest of cirrus clouds. God had created a perfect day.

The grind became more pronounced as a small black dot appeared, gradually growing into the form of a blood-red Fokker triplane. Suddenly, it exploded past, engine roaring. The pilot was wearing the insignia of a German officer. His head rotated left and right then up and down like a hawk searching for its prey. Behind the goggles were wild eyes, calculating, confident.

A cold steel machine gun with a belt of full-metal jackets gleamed in the sun, awaiting its calling. It was a good day for fighting.

An imposing German Cross decorated the wings and both sides of the fuselage. Under the open cockpit was the name: von Richthofen. Forty-plus skull-and-crossbones marked the Bloody Red Baron's kills. A master gunfighter. A killer of the skies.

The Baron focused on his next victim, an American Spad XIII biplane, marked with a circular red-white-blue decal, cruising at 3 o'clock below. The Fokker peeled off then plunged into a steep dive. The Baron's eyes burned with concentration as he zeroed on his prey then opened fire. His machine gun crackled like a jackhammer on a metal roof.

The rookie American pilot broke a hard left then foolishly circled around to take on the Red Baron. Both planes approached one another, guns blazing. At the final second, the American executed a hard turn to avoid a collision. The Baron maneuvered behind the

Spad, mirroring every loop, spin, and rollout. The Baron's gun sounded again and again. Smoke began to trail the Spad as it sputtered then died behind a nearby knoll. A second later, a fiery explosion rocked the countryside. The red Fokker zoomed through the billowing smoke then climbed.

Suddenly, a second American Spad appeared at 2000 feet above the Baron, eclipsing the sun. It, too, was distinctively marked with a red-white-blue decal. The side of the biplane was filled with German Crosses, representative of the pilot's combat skill.

Behind the goggles was a rugged, handsome face. A four-leaf clover was tattooed on the back of the hand clutching the joystick as it masterfully directed the Spad warship. Patrick "Rye" Reilly's untrained, gravelly voice punched out the words of the early-1900's Stutter Song, K-K-K-Katy, timed to his aerial moves.

K-K-K-Katy, beautiful Ka-ty,
You're the on-ly g-g-g-girl that I a-dore...

Rye spotted the red Fokker and went into a dive. Any normal man's stomach would have been churning as the Spad plunged toward its mighty foe like a rocketing roller coaster.

When the m-m-m-moon shines o-ver the cow-shed,
I'll be wait-ing at the k-k-k-kitchen door...

He fired his machine gun.

K-K-K-door!

The Red Baron instinctively executed a chandelle that failed to rid him of the pesky American ace who was shadowing every flick of the Baron's controls. A series of soars and looping circles resembled falcon-like aerobatics. Finally, the Fokker went into a half-loop and rollout at the top, positioning the Baron in a commanding position behind and above the Spad. Now he was hot on the American's tail.

Rye broke left then a hard right. Glancing over his shoulder, the Baron was still behind him, his eyes glowing like hot coals as he zeroed on his prey. Rye took a deep breath and shoved the stick forward. The nose of the Spad immediately pointed at the earth, and soon, he was in a deadly vertical dive, his face distorted from the G-force.

The Baron was determined. He crammed the joystick forward and dove. Within seconds, he was in Reilly's vacuum, just feet from kissing the Spad's rudder. Rye's knuckles turned white from fighting with the stick. The vibration from the dive was teeth-jarring.

Grabbing the control stick with both hands, Rye pulled back with all his strength. Objects on the ground were growing at an alarming rate. With a final jerk, he finally managed to pull up. He sighed with relief as he executed a half-loop and rollout at the top. Now the Spad was coolly attached to the Baron's tail with a large barn staring at them.

"C'mon, make your father proud," Rye paused then resumed singing. "K-K-K-Katy, beautiful Ka-ty. You're the on-ly.....g-g-g-girl that I a-d-d-dore..."

The massive doors were open at both ends. The Baron had no choice. It was too late to pull up. The Fokker screamed toward the open doors, rotating his wings vertically to navigate the narrow, tall opening.

"That's it," Rye mumbled. "As easy as threading a needle-- with a one-inch rope!"

The Baron navigated the mouse-like opening, his right wingtip dusting the earth foundation.

With intense eyes, Rye followed suit, belting. "When the m-m-m-m-moon shines o-v-v-ver the c-c-c-cowshed...."

The Fokker exited the rear door, rotated its wings level then pulled up hard, narrowly avoiding a tall tree. The Baron then roared skyward toward the cirrus clouds, trying to gain an altitude advantage. Rye wasted little time accelerating. If the Baron got above the clouds first, he would be able to look down through them. Rye would be a proverbial sitting duck. His adrenaline pumping like a gushing fire hydrant, he raced to catch up, staying on the Baron's tail, singing, "I'll be w-w-wait-ing at the k-k-k-kitchen door," timing the rat-ta-tat-tat of his guns with "K-K-K-door!"

Suddenly, the Fokker emitted a smoke trail. The Baron broke right, climbed, rolled left then went into what appeared to be an uncontrolled spin. Soon, he disappeared behind a small woods, followed by a gigantic gasoline explosion.

Rye shrieked with victory as he rocketed through the billowy black smoke.

"Ladies and gentlemen," bellowed a golden-throat voice, "let's hear it for America's King of Aces, Captain Patrick 'Rye' Reilly!"

Rye looked down as he emerged. A cheering crowd was pointing excitedly. He executed a fly-over, tipping his wings to acknowledge their applause. Finally, he landed and taxied to the front of the grandstand where he performed a stylish pivot, stopped, and waved at the appreciative air show crowd.

"Let's hear it again for America's top ace of The Great War, winner of two Silver Stars, the Distinguished Flying Cross, and our nation's highest award, the Medal of Honor."

The applause and whistling climaxed as the handsome war hero stood and waved at thousands of people and children. He climbed down slowly to the ground with a noticeable limp, evidence of a damaging war wound. He reached up and extracted a crutch from the cockpit.

As the cheering crowd began to quiet, a red-white-blue motorcycle rumbled toward Rye. It was the pilot of the red Fokker, wearing a German leather flying jacket, dress uniform trousers, and saucer-shaped, German officer's cap. Playing along, the crowd booed the Red Baron.

The announcer's voice commanded attention once again. "Let's hear it for the very talented pilot of the red Fokker."

The crowd booed more.

The Red Baron stopped the motorcycle and removed the service cap, unleashing a mane of long auburn hair that slapped her buttocks.

"Sixteen-year-old Meg Reilly," the announcer continued, "Rye's lovely young daughter."

The square-shouldered tomboy flashed a brilliant, youthful smile as she climbed off the motorcycle and waved. She was tall for a girl, measuring five-foot eight-inches, and plain, yet devastatingly attractive with a sprinkling of freckles across her nose and cheeks, a gift from excessive sun exposure.

A short, young boy in a red T-shirt, faded blue jeans, and New York Yankee ball cap, crumpled his pudgy face. "A girl!" he sneered.

She comically stuck her tongue out at the boy. The spectators laughed more.

* * * * *

I was both infatuated and intrigued that day with Megan Reilly, an unpolished, airport rat, quite different from the other kids whose rich fathers had let them dabble in their aviation hobby. She was the feisty daughter of an Irish Catholic American soldier, a hero of The Great War--the man who had shot down the feared Bloody Red Baron.

And who was I? A recent journalism grad from Yale on my first assignment for *Aviation Life* magazine. It was 1935, and I was covering a story about the air show at Bendix Field, New Jersey.

* * * * *

Swarming spectators of all shapes and ages roamed about the flight line blanketed with canvas lawn chairs, picnic baskets, and colorful blankets while dozens of youngsters and aviation hounds swarmed like ants about the array of vintage aircraft and high-tech prototypes. Two young boys played tag about the legs of their parents, killing time till the next event.

Bendix Field was comprised of an irregular assortment of wooden buildings and corrugated metal hangars freckling the circumference of the grassy airfield. A number of military vets, some still wearing their overseas caps and dress jackets with all their colorful ribbons, medals, and patches, stood about, busily offering stories about The Great War to anyone willing to give them an ear.

"I direct your attention to the left side of the grandstand area," the announcer said. "More Reillys!"

A red-white-blue flatbed truck appeared from behind a row of planes. Sitting on the back were two high school boys. One was wearing a red-white-blue scarf and a leather flying jacket. The other was dressed in a clown suit. The children stopped playing tag and looked up, pointing with frenzy, their eyes bursting with excitement.

"Give a warm welcome to Sean and Garrett Reilly, Rye's two sons."

Sean and Garrett joked with the crowd then climbed onto Rye's biplane. Sean Reilly, tall, lean and very handsome like his father, slid into the cockpit while the clown climbed onto the wing and clutched the supports, waving and joking. In seconds, they took off, zooming almost vertically.

Several wide-eyed children, some on their father's shoulders, shifted their attention, shielding the bright sun with a cupped hand over their eyes. Flying overhead was the bright biplane. The clown had climbed up the wing struts and was in the process of fetching a bright red scarf tied to a rod. He waved it at the crowd then slipped and fell, drawing a chorus of oohs from the bug-eyed spectators. The clown snared a wing strut, waved the scarf at the crowd, and pulled himself back up, settling for a safe perch between the upper and lower wings. The spectators in the grandstand below leaped from their seats, cheering.

"Let's hear it for the Flying Reilly Brothers."

They soon landed, returning the Spad to the front of the grandstand. Nearby spectators gave a standing ovation. A small boy who was sitting on his father's shoulders leaned over, pointing toward the clown, excitedly telling his parents about the clown's incredible antics. Grinning fondly, his mother listened, nodding.

Meg and their father joined Sean and Garrett. Arm-in-arm, the smiling foursome waved at the applauding, whistling spectators.

"Another hand for the fabulous, stupendous, fearless Flying Reillys," bellowed the announcer. "A hint for you young fellas, the Reilly's operate a flying service at the end of the field. Just two bits can get you a ride with Meg."

A teenage boy, patches on both knees and socks crumpled at the ankles, planted both hands on his hips as he turned to one of his friends. "Not in a million years. I ain't flyin' with no dumb girl.....not if she was the last pilot in the universe."

"Yeah, me, too," chimed the other boy.

Several nearby spectators snickered at the boys' humorous reactions.

A pudgy woman in her late-forties turned to her pot-bellied

husband. "That Captain Reilly ought to be horse-whipped for exposing that daughter of his to such danger. Shirley told me that he lost his wife because of his drinking."

"Shirley? That old gossip?" her husband came back. "She's the last one to talk. Ralph's her third marriage, and he's been sportin' the idea of chuckin' her over the Burlington Bridge in a gunny sack since their wedding night so mind your own damn business, Gladys.....'fore I start gettin' ideas of my own."

Shocked by her husband's verbal attack, Gladys puffed her chest and looked away.

By now, admiring spectators were swarming the Reilly aircraft, gazing inside the cockpit and running their hands over its smooth skin, admiring its strength and power.

The announcer again broke the silence. "I again direct your attention to the west and Amelia Earhart."

The spectators masked the brilliant afternoon sun with a variety of objects, trying to spot Amelia's bright-red and gold aircraft. Slowly, it appeared out of the horizon, blazing at treetop level.

"Ladies and gentlemen, the infamous and lovely Amelia Earhart, in her 500-horsepower Lockheed Vega," the announcer shouted. "Amelia is the first pilot, woman or man, to ever solo from Hawaii to California–that's over 2400 miles!"

Hundreds of admiring spectators and a horde of reporters and photographers, including myself, began to converge on the Vega as it landed and taxied toward the grandstand area. Two sheriff's deputies managed to part the crowd to give Amelia enough space to disembark. She emerged smiling, wearing khaki slacks, a plaid shirt, and a seasoned leather flying jacket. She conversed with pressing reporters.

Considering it was my first assignment, I must have looked pretty green compared to the other reporters in my fresh Brooks Brothers suit, nervously holding a new, pocket-sized spiral note pad.

Meg was among a flock of teenage girls and autograph hounds rushing toward Amelia. The deputies were quick to react, allowing only Meg to pass.

"Amelia!" she called out.

Amelia stopped talking and searched the crowd. Her eyes

brightened as she spotted Meg.

"Meg?.....Meg Reilly?"

Meg grinned widely as she glided into Amelia's open arms.

"My gosh, Megan, you've grown. You look terrific in that jacket."

"It was Mom's."

Amelia looked more closely. "I know." Amelia took one of her hands and patted it.

A tear fell from Meg's cheek. "I miss her awful," she confessed.

Smiling compassionately, Amelia quickly changed the subject. "So how's that handsome father of yours?"

Meg regained her composure. "As ornery as ever.....He'll be back in a bit." Meg leaned closer. "Guess what? Dad let me fly the Fokker. Garrett and Sean think it's great. They know a female is the key to the act. The spectators freak when they realize I'm a girl.....Their eyes damn near pop out."

Amelia drew her head back. "So your father let you Thread the Needle, huh?"

"Yes," Meg answered, beaming with pride. "Oh, I wish you could've seen it, Amelia." Meg placed a hand on over her left breast. "My heart is still pumping."

"I'm sorry I got here late," Amelia apologized. "I ran into a nasty thunderstorm near Pittsburgh."

A flurry of questions erupted from my fellow reporters.

"Miss Earhart!" shouted an obese reporter. He was stuffed in a light-yellow seersucker suit, soiled black and white wingtips, a plaid bow tie that hung crooked to one side, and a tan, brimmed straw hat pushed back on his head. "Why are you--"

Amelia held up her hand, cutting him off. She leaned toward Meg and lowered her voice. "I'll be through here in a few minutes. Keep me company, will you?"

Meg nodded with a flashing smile.

With her arm under Meg's, Amelia turned back to me and the other reporters. "Gentlemen, I'm very tired and hungry. Please, just two more questions."

I stepped forward with my pad and pencil in hand, shaking.

"Aaron Masters, Aviation Life magazine. Now that--"

"How are you today, young man"? She asked.

She must have sensed that I was pretty fresh out of the chute.

"Just fine, Miss Earhart." I said. "Now that you have soloed the Atlantic, broken the sex barrier in the '33 Bendix Race, finished fifth in this year's Bendix, and the only pilot to solo from Hawaii to the Mainland, what's next?"

"I was thinking of having a Coney dog.....You buying?"

The other reporters laughed. I blushed like a five-year-old kid. Looking over at Meg, I noticed that she was staring into my eyes. I bashfully glanced back at Amelia.

Amelia winked at me. "I plan to solo around the world, either later this year or next year. It all depends on how quickly we can prepare."

That was a catalyst for another barrage of questions. The obese reporter dabbed at the perspiration rolling down his fat face with a drenched red handkerchief. "The Pacific. That's a 4000-mile stretch of ocean. Why do you, a woman, think you can do it? Sounds like a publicity stunt to sell yet another book."

Amelia smiled kindly. "As most of your colleagues already know, I am a writer by trade. In fact, I have written a number of books, and since I am a female spokesman for aviation, some of them naturally pertain to flying. In fact, that's how I met my husband George. You seem to forget that I managed to fly from Hawaii to California back in January. That's over 2400 miles. Jackie Cochran's husband has offered to sponsor the trip. I plan to fly a twin-engine Lockheed Electra. It will be equipped with a Sperry gyroscopic auto pilot, giving me an occasional break to check my bearings, have a decent meal, and a few naps."

A tall, thin reporter wearing a brown suit too baggy for his frame raised his hand. "George Putnam is your publisher. Isn't that true?"

"I almost forgot. Thank you for reminding me."

The reporters chuckled, except the fat one who stood to the side, writing.

"George and I met each other some time after Putnam & Sons became my publisher." Amelia looked at Meg for help. "After my fourth, wasn't it?"

Meg nodded, "That's right." Looking at me, she added, "Amelia's got the only books on aviation worth reading."

Amelia continued, "As some of you may know, I am a consultant for Transcontinental Air Transport to illustrate how safe flying can be."

A thin reporter in a wrinkled, charcoal suit and a loose striped tie took a half step forward. "Mike Brown, Trenton Herald. Don't you mean that you are nothing more than a salesman to lessen women's resistance to flying?"

"First of all, I am not a salesman, Mr. Brown. I've been touring the country for several years now as a passenger. I interview women during flight and often speak to women's groups about the industry's safety record."

"You mean that flying is so safe that women should do it?" Brown persisted.

"Of course!" Amelia flashed one of her classy smiles. "Flying 'round the world is part of that responsibility. I have no plans to write a book on it. I'm just sneakin' in a vacation."

The gallery chuckled briefly as the reporters' pencils again swung into action.

The obese reporter jumped back in, going for the jugular. "You are a woman pilot."

Amelia glanced down at her chest. "I can see there's no puttin' one over you."

More laughter ensued. The obese reporter turned and bolted through the crowd, almost knocking several on-lookers off their feet before they could make way. His face was beet-red with anger.

Amelia turned her attention back to the other reporters. "I pray that I have been able to open the eyes of the world to the abilities of women. Please, gentlemen, I am quite exhausted. Thank you."

She turned to Meg as the sheriff's deputies herded off the reporters, some still pressing to ask questions. "Now, get me to a Coney dog. I'm starved."

Meg snickered as she surveyed the crowd for familiar faces, motioning for her friends and me to join them. I trailed along like a good reporter, pencil and pad ready.

A gravelly voice suddenly shouted from the back of the crowd. "Well, if it ain't proof that angels really know how to fly."

Amelia stopped then backed up. A big grin had just gotten bigger. Rye hobbled toward her on his crutch.

"Rye! Give me a hug, you big lug." Amelia flew into his outstretched arms.

"For awhile there, I didn't think you'd make it," Rye confessed.

"No thanks to the storm clouds over the mountains." Amelia paused as she pulled back for a second admiring look. "Rye, how could I resist flying your prototype."

The trio walked toward the snack stand with the crowd buzzing at their heels.

Amelia leaned against a weathered picnic table and was immediately surrounded by Meg and her friends. Fifty or so spectators gawked from several yards away.

Amelia glanced at me. "Did you know that this crazy Irishman was the King of Aces during the Great War"?

I nodded affirmatively. "Quite an impressive war record--21 bogies, I believe."

"That was a long time ago," Rye added, looking down. "And it cost me a limb. He tapped his wooden leg with the crutch.

"That's nonsense, Rye." Amelia turned to the group of youngsters perched about her. "Captain Reilly single-handedly shot down the Red Baron."

"Rickenbacker taught me everything I know," Rye was quick to note, embarrassed with the accolade.

"Nonsense!" Amelia snapped. "It was the other way around, kids. Rye taught Eddie everything he knew."

Eyes bulging, the kid in the Yankee ball cap piped up, "Eddie Rickenbacker! Wow! You knew Eddie Rickenbacker? Gee whiz!"

Rye blushed. "Yeah, I knew Eddie. He was the best."

I glanced at Amelia who was fondly beaming at Rye.

It was very apparent that Amelia was romantically attracted to this rugged hero. Her admiration was as subtle as a sledgehammer.

Meg's eyes were luminous. As I was to find out later when I read Meg's diary, Amelia was her godmother and had been her mother's best friend. Meg would have liked nothing more than to have had Amelia as a step-mother.

"Now I just operate this little ole flying service to scrape up enough money for designing military aircraft," Rye humbly added, "and pay the rent."

I turned to Amelia. "Do you think women will ever get a chance to fly in the military?"

"Girls?" Blurted a deep voice from outside the ring of admirers. "Not a chance. War is men's work."

Suddenly, everyone turned, gawking at the late arrivals.

CHAPTER 2

Sean made his grand entry with a football teammate Dave Cummings who was the tallest and largest center in the conference. Dave "the Demon" had been bailing hay since he was eight, giving him the strength and temperament of a Brahman bull. Both he and Sean were in high demand. Nearly every girl in school had plotted to get laid by "Demon Brothers," a nickname ungratefully attached to Sean and Dave by the opposing teams who had suffered through four long years of domination by their team, the Red Devils.

Without prompting, the youngsters in Dave's path stepped aside, cocking their heads almost straight up to the point of snapping. All they could see was a massive chest and a jaw that could crush elephant bones.

"Never say never, young man," Amelia uttered, still gazing up at this modern-day giant. "You might end up eating crow some day."

"Hi, Miss Earhart," said Sean, smiling. "How have you been?"

"Just fine, Sean. It's great to see you again. You're such a handsome young man."

Sean blushed. "Thank you, Ma'am."

"Stop that!" Amelia snapped. "Call me Amelia, please. Save that ma'am stuff for your grandparents. Besides, I've known you since you were in diapers."

"Okay, okay," Sean conceded. "This is a buddy of mine, Dave Cummings. Dave, this is the famous, Amelia Earhart."

She mindfully pointed at Sean, grinning.

"Hi, Miss Earhart." Dave reached out with his right hand. "Glad to meetcha."

He pumped her arm a bit too rapidly, drawing snickers from

Meg and her friends.

Vibrating in her tracks, Amelia said, "Well, it's a pleasure to meet you, too, Dave."

Dave just stood there, trying to say something else, pumping her hand. He was the epitome of a male airhead.

Amelia fought the urge to laugh. "Was there something else, young man?"

"I...I was wonderin'," Dave stuttered, "if ya could use your influence with Meg to get her to go to the Senior Prom with me."

Meg's hands covered her face. "David Cummings! How could you?"

Her friends began to cackle.

Amelia reacted to save the situation. She leaned in close and spoke softly, "Dave, have you tried asking her yourself?"

Meg separated her fingers, enough to pan the expressions on her friends' faces. And mine. Some were laughing hysterically, slapping one another, pointing. Meg reacted with several hefty punches to their upper arms. They pulled back, rubbing the soreness. She blushed when her eyes met mine.

"Three times, at least, Miss Earhart," he answered.

Glaring at him, Meg growled so only he could hear. "David, I'm going to kill you."

He stood up straight and addressed her. "I'm not going to give up till you say *yes*."

"Over my dead body," Meg stammered, glaring at him with eyes to kill.

One of Meg's friends, a short, stocky ash blonde with a pixy hairdo, jumped into the conversation. "Meg's chicken to wear a dress."

Meg's upper lip twitched at one corner. She turned as she stood, ready to do battle, pointing at her chubby friend. "I ain't afraid of nothing.....but you better be.....of me, slug!"

The entire gathering roared louder.

Amelia came to Meg's rescue. "Is that true about dresses?"

"They look dumb. Besides, I don't have one."

Garrett stepped forward. "That ain't so, Amelia. Dad got her one for Christmas, isn't that right, Dad?"

Meg appealed to Amelia for help before Rye could answer. "Amelia, I never saw you in a dress before."

"I wear them quite often. I find them a nice change of pace."

"Amelia looks very elegant in them," Rye added.

Meg planted her hands on her hips. "Can we change the subject?"

Dave moved closer to Meg. "It's settled. How 'bout I pick you up at six?"

"Don't hold your breath, David!" Meg snapped, thrusting out an arm, trying to snare the hair of the blonde who was making faces.

Rye turned to Amelia but spoke to everyone else. "We better let Amelia get down to business here before we lose the daylight. Besides, she's had a long day."

"Please, I've gotta question I've just been dyin' to ask Miss Earhart," the blonde stammered. "Why's your plane red and gold?"

"For ultra-visibility.....in case I go down at sea," Amelia answered. "Search parties would be able to spot it more easily from the air."

A pudgy girl in a printed dress, sitting at the end of the table raised her hand. "Amelia, got any advice for a girl my age?"

"Learn to cook and sew!" snapped Garrett who joined the group, grinning.

"Shut up, smarty pants," Meg growled at her twin brother.

Amelia laughed as she stood and hugged Garrett. She then answered the girl's question. "Aviation is a career of the future. You and your fellow students have the first chance in history to train yourselves and become a part of it. We've come a long way in aviation since the war in Europe."

Sean nodded. "Dad said that by the end of the war, giant bombers were being constructed with metal and wood, some with 100-foot wings wide enough to carry three 500-lb. bombs."

"That's true," Amelia agreed. "The Army burned over a thousand planes after the war."

"The war to end all wars," added Rye facetiously.

Amelia smirked as she continued. "The rest were auctioned off for a few dollars."

Rye pointed at his small fleet of red-white-blue biplanes.

"Those are testimony to what Amelia is saying. Folks about these parts thought I had taken a bullet to the head instead of the leg," he quipped, tapping his wooden leg. "Considered it a frivolous investment."

He reached over and gave Amelia a friendly squeeze as I continued to jot down every word.

"It just shows that being a pilot has nothing to do with being a man, or a woman," Amelia added.

Dave rolled his eyes. He wasn't buying any of this talk about women.

Amelia continued, "But for the love of flying and individual skill and determination."

Rye nodded in agreement. "She's absolutely right, kids."

Amelia looked at the young people around her. "I see the faces of aviation's future right here."

The blonde spoke up again. "So what was it like to fly the Atlantic"?

Amelia thought for a moment before answering. "At times like ridin' a bucking horse."

"C'mon," the blond girl pleaded. "Tell us about it....please."

"First things first. I came here to fly Rye's new prototype." Amelia turned to him. "Is it prepped?" she asked, her eyes full of adventure.

"Like a thoroughbred snortin' at the gate," Rye drawled.

Amelia stood. "Then let's see how she does."

Rye offered the way with his hand. "After you."

Amelia walked alongside Rye who crutched toward the sleek prototype. Sean, Meg, Garrett, and the rest of the entourage scuffled alongside.

"Amelia, these high-performance aircraft tend to have hot landings. You'll have to come in 'bout twice the normal speed."

Amelia winked. "I'll remember that, handsome....Thanks."

Garrett helped her board then stood over the cockpit, briefing her on the instrument panel and the prototype's peculiarities.

The powerful engine turned over, caught, and slowly gained RPMs. The roar was deafening. She later confessed that it was like wearing a giant vibrating suit.

Amelia's adrenaline raged as she signaled a thumbs-up. Sean jerked on a length of heavy manila rope attached to the wooden wheel blocks then signaled a thumbs-up.

Amelia taxied to the tarmac and revved the growling engine. The grin on her face said it all.

The prototype lurched forward, quickly gaining speed. She pulled back on the stick firmly, and the nose pointed skyward. The out-buildings were speeding by at a blur. She knew in an instant that this prototype would be the future of military aviation.

The reporters and spectators stood about the Reillys, craning their necks, looking upward as Amelia circled around and raced past, drowning all other sound.

I panned the faces around me. Amelia had everyone spellbound.

"Nobody can put a bird through its paces like Amelia," Rye noted.

The prototype went into a climb, performing precision loops, rolls, spins, a chandelle, and finally a stall.

Suddenly, Amelia aimed it at the ground and plunged into a steep dive, pulling out at the last second. I finally took a breath myself. It was the first in minutes, or so it seemed.

The crowd below screamed and whistled its approval. Amelia waved during a breath-taking fly-over. The crowd fell into a thunderous ovation, continuing as she landed and taxied to the edge of the snack area. The Reillys greeted her just as the prototype came to an impressive stop.

Rye turned to me. "Well, Masters, what do you think?"

I found myself unable to describe it. I had been writing news since I was ten years old, and suddenly found myself unable to find the right words. "This is one hell of an aircraft, Captain Reilly. I should think the military would take great happiness in subsidizing its mass production."

Rye smiled at me. "Let's hope they share the same view."

I could tell by his sincerity why he was so revered by everyone with whom he came in contact. I sensed the same leadership qualities in his daughter, Megan.

Arm-in-arm, Amelia and Meg walked toward the red Vega.

A spectacular sunset silhouetted their bodies. Their shadows stretched to the edge of the runway as I observed from a distance.

"Tell your father that I love his new design," Amelia said. "I wrote down a list of suggestions." She handed a piece of folded paper to Meg who deposited it in her jacket pocket.

"I'm sure he'll appreciate it. He has nothing but respect for you, you know."

Amelia stopped and faced Meg. "Your father's a wonderful human being, and so are you. You know, you've got your mother's eyes and..."

Meg bordered tears. She glanced upward at the sky, sniffling.

"I'm sorry," Amelia apologized. "It must be painful for you. If you ever need anything or want to talk, call the house. They know how to get a hold of me."

Meg pulled Amelia into a hug. "When will you be back?"

"As often as I can," Amelia said, holding back the tears. She knew she had to be strong. "Keep writing. I always look forward to reading your letters when I return from my trips."

"Take care of yourself, Amelia."

Amelia released from the hug. "I almost forgot." She took off her long white silk scarf and placed it around Meg's neck.

"Amelia, what's this?"

"My lucky scarf. I wore it in the Bendix Race."

"For me.....I love it. But won't you be needin' it?"

"Your mother gave it to me before she--" Amelia was at the brink of tears.

"Dad won't talk about it," Meg related, still admiring the scarf.

"Make him proud of you, Meg. It's always the best healer."

Meg finally looked up. "I will. I promise.....I'm gonna be a famous pilot some day. Just like you, Amelia. You'll see. I'll be better than any man."

"Fly because you love it, not because you're trying to be better than a man," Amelia paused. "It's a thirst for knowledge beyond the horizon....beyond the stars." She gazed up at the sky and sighed.

Meg looked back down at the scarf, caressing its elegance. "Thank you, Amelia. Now, don't you go off and--" Meg stopped herself short. "Just be careful, okay?"

Amelia began to board the Vega then turned. "Okay." She winked then climbed into the cockpit.

Meg watched tearfully, clutching the scarf. Amelia started the engine and taxied to the runway. She flashed a smile and waved.

Soon, the Vega's tires sang along the grassy runway.

I watched from a distance, leaning against my '29 Ford, arms folded. That moment touched me as no other. I sensed it would be the last time I would see them together.

Meg stared long after the Vega became a dot in the horizon, reflecting back on that terrible day and her mother.

* * * * *

A firm knock on the door brought Meg to a sitting position. She seemed disoriented, somewhat frightened as she pushed back the bedspread and swung her legs over the side. Again, a rapid, authoritative knock startled her, followed by the scuffle of a slipper and thump of a crutch passing by her bedroom door and down the creaky, wooden stairs.

Five-year-old Megan hopped down and took the eight tiny steps toward the light coming through the cracked door. She peered through but could not see the foyer. Her father was talking to someone with an official voice. Meg slipped into the hallway and silently stood at the railing.

Her father was conversing with a heavy-set policeman. Behind them, outside, was a flashing red light of a patrol car, swirling round and round. Clothed only in a pair of mechanics trousers, Rye ran his fingers through his disheveled hair.

The policeman talked then listened, writing on a small notepad. Her father was having trouble with his balance. The cop closed his pad and slid it in a breast pocket, reaching with the other hand to reassure her father with a compassionate pat on the upper back. The patrolman then turned around and walked to his car.

Rye just stood there with one hand on the door, staring for a long moment after the police had left. He reached up and wiped tears from his face with the back of a hairy, muscular fist as he closed the door and slumped against it like a little boy, crying.

* * * * *

As I turned toward the tower, Meg spotted me and quick-stepped to my side.

I ceased walking and faced her. "Beautiful sunset."

"Mr. Masters, you were watching, weren't you?" Her wet eyes struggled to sparkle.

"Yes," I answered clumsily. "Amelia's an amazing woman.....and a pilot." I peered at the scarf. "Did she give that to you?"

"Yeah, my mother gave it to her a long time ago. They were best friends, you know. Amelia thought I should have it now."

I could tell that Meg was hurting. I wanted to ask what happened to her mother, but I felt it best to wait. This was not the time.

Meg was staring into my eyes. "You have beautiful blue eyes, Mr. Masters."

"Thank you," I said uncomfortably. "Please, call me Aaron. I'm not use to this mister stuff. I just got out of Yale two weeks ago."

"Do you always wear a suit, Aaron?" Meg asked, sizing me from bottom to top.

Embarrassed, I looked down and touched my lapel. "Oh, this? My folks got this for me at Brooks Brothers for graduation."

"You look very dashing in it."

I blushed. This was just a 16-year-old. I resisted the urge to admire her gorgeous hair and freckled face. She read me like a book. I must have been squirming.

"Let's go down to Ernie's and play darts or somethin'."

"Well, er, ah....I've got to get some work done on my article tonight," I responded awkwardly. "Besides, I rather doubt your father would approve."

"Na," she blurted, gazing into my eyes. "I can tell he likes you."

"Meg, I'm six years older than you."

"I know," she flirted, hooking my arm with hers. "Come on, Brooks Brothers."

CHAPTER 3

Bendix Field, two years later:

A brilliant moon danced off the dew blanketing the airfield. A chorus of crickets was harmonizing with the smooth Harry James trumpet emitting from a '34 Chevy coupe parked at the end of an old dirt road dead-ending at the airfield fence. It was a spot often used by young lovers to gaze at the stars.

Meg, her long hair tied back in a ponytail, was slumped in the passenger seat with her bare legs propped out the right window. She was wearing a sleeveless summer shirt and shorts. Dave Cummings was behind the wheel. A massive elbow that grew out of a tight T-shirt, protruded from the left window. Cigarette smoke flowed past it.

Dave leaned over and kissed Meg. Before long, they were necking ferociously. Dave soon implemented a sneak attack, slowly inching a hand inside her sleeveless shirt, trusting that she wouldn't notice, but as his bulky fingers began to fumble with her bra clasp, she pushed his hands away.

"David Vincent Cummings, ease up on the throttle."

Dave was perplexed. "For cryin' out loud," he whined. "Give me a break, will ya? Hell, everybody knows we're gonna get hitched, anyway."

"Whoa there a minute," she crackled. "I'm not gettin' married to no one, no how, especially you."

He pulled back with hurt eyes. "Why not? You're not going to do any better than me 'round here, and you--"

"You're right," she interrupted. "I'm not."

Dave puffed his chest in triumph. A sly grin appeared.

"That's why I don't plan to stay around here," Meg added. "There's a whole big sky out there and real gentlemen like Aaron Masters."

Dave's mouth dropped open. "What, that wimp writer from Harvard?"

"Yale, David. Yale!" Meg snapped angrily. She started putting on her shoes. "David, you've been out of high school over two years now, and you ain't held a steady job worth a slug of cheap whiskey. All you ever want to do is go out with the boys, down longnecks, belch and fart all night, bitchin' about how you got screwed out of playing football for Notre Dame, and braggin' about your sexual exploits."

"But I can ex--"

"It got back to me 'bout the tall tales you've been tellin' your buddies 'bout us," Meg countered, "so don't BS me, you sonofabitch! You're still livin' with your folks. You ain't got any goals, and I'll be damned if I'm gonna replace your mom, cooking and picking up after your lazy ass. In short, David Cummings, we ain't got a future."

"Then why in the hell did you come out here with me?"

"When you said, date, I thought you meant a movie or darts or something. No, not you. You pulled up in front of the house, honked that stupid horn of yours, and burnt rubber gettin' here. You thought I'd just lay back, pop my legs open, and let you jump my bones."

"Goddam! Relax for Christ sakes," Dave stammered. "God, you can be a bitch." He reached over and turned off the car radio.

"Yeah, where you're concerned," Meg countered as she reached over and spun the radio knob back to the one position. "You're such a beast, I swear!"

"See what I mean?" Dave bellowed, pointing at the radio. "You're stubborn. You and me, we're just alike. We both like sports. We both like to party.....We both like makin' love."

"Love?" she laughed facetiously. "Is that what you call it? To you, it's more like notches on your gun butt. No, about the only thing we got in common, David Cummings, is that we're both stuck in this.....this little town."

Dave sat back, pouting like a little boy, his fingers tracing the steering wheel. "I told you I love you. We're gonna get hitched, and you damn well know it."

Meg broke out in laughter. "Says who?" She reached for the door handle. "I'm never gettin' married." She quickly opened the door before his hand could reach out to stop her. "Least of all to you." She slammed the door shut.

"Where do you think you're going?"

Meg stooped enough to see through the open window. "Home"! Meg snapped.

"How ya gonna get home?"

"I'll walk. It wouldn't be the first time. I told you, hugging and kissing is one thing. Gettin' P.G. is another."

A streak of fear suddenly swept his face. Dave got out of his car and leaned on the top. "Relax," he shouted. "Lot's of broads get P.G. It's what a real woman is supposed to do."

Meg threw up her arms and shook her head in disgust. "Not if you want a career.....to fly." She spun around to walk away, looking briefly over her shoulder. "I'm gonna live my life the way I want to. I'm gonna be famous some day, just you wait and see."

"You don't care about anyone but yourself and your stupid planes, Megan Reilly," Dave shouted after her. "You're selfish and spoiled.....That's what you are! You ain't ever gonna get that twirp from Harvard. You're not his type.....You can fly all the planes you want, but you ain't never gonna be able to do everything a man does. You're a woman and--"

Fuming, Meg plodded faster and faster, briefly turning her head to counter his words. "We'll see about that, smarty pants.....You'll see."

A loud teletype sound interrupted the music, followed by Water Winchell's voice. Dave ducked his head inside to lower the volume.

"This is Walter Winchell with a news flash. America's First Lady of the Air is reported lost at sea. Amelia Earhart's plane has failed to arrive at Howland Island in the South Pacific. The greatest air-sea rescue mission ever has been combing the flight route for some sign of Miss Earhart's Lockheed."

"God Almighty!" Dave started the Chevy and crammed the

shift in reverse.

The auto lurched backward, kicking up stones.

"The State Department has denied to comment on any foul play by the Imperial Japanese war machine massing in the South Pacific." Winchell paused. "Hat's off to America's First Lady of the Air, Amelia Earhart.....missing at sea."

Dave turned off the car radio and increased pressure on the gas pedal. The Chevy sped toward Meg who spun around in surprise just as Dave slammed on the brakes, stopping just inches from her knees.

Meg rotated her head without turning around. "What?" she growled.

"Climb in!" Dave prompted.

"I'll walk, I said."

"It's Amelia," Dave said, his voice softening. "Her plane's missing at sea."

Meg's hands went to her mouth, and her eyes flooded with tears.

"C'mon, get in," Dave prompted her, leaning over to open the door. "I'll take you back."

Meg apprehensively slid onto the passenger side and meekly pulled on the car door, leaving it ajar to rattle and squeak with each bump and chuckhole. Normally, Dave would have bitched at her, but this was not the time.

"Drop me off at the hangar," she sobbed.

Without responding, Dave turned onto the airfield road and accelerated toward the Reilly hangar. As the Chevy came to a screeching halt in front of the large double doors, Meg jumped out. She dashed toward the darkness of the hangar and disappeared inside. Dave started to follow then stopped. He released the door handle then sped away.

A single light above the door leading to the adjoining office dimly lighted her presence. She opened a small leather Gladstone bag and took out a cigar box. In it were some small sentimental items, jewelry, a number of newspaper clippings, and a photo of two women standing next to an old biplane. One was a younger Amelia Earhart. Meg's eyes shifted to the other woman. She touched her likeness with a forefinger. It was her mother, a raving beauty with long red hair too thick to comb. Both were wearing leather flying jackets, clutching flying caps and goggles in their hands. The cut-line read: "Daring Femme Duo Omen Set Records."

Meg's forefinger moved lightly over the faces before setting the picture down and picking up another. It was a photo of a very young Meg sitting in the cockpit of the same biplane. Her mother was standing alongside. Meg was smiling as only an excited child can, when they are safe and secure next to a parent.

Meg then extracted the scarf Amelia had given her. She held it to her heart.

"Meg"! It was her father. "Is that you?"

Meg turned away, trying to hide the tears. Rye placed a hand on her shoulder. A sense of helplessness gripped him. It was a moment of pain for both.

Struggling to clear his voice, "I just heard the news about Amelia. I can't tell you not to feel what you are feeling. She was like a.....a sister to me. God knows that I went through this so many times in France, and it doesn't get any easier." He paused, afraid the emotion would stop his words. "I only know that it's just part of flying. Life, too, I guess. Sometimes planes go down when you don't expect them to. You learn to live with it.....That's all you can do." His voice was softer than usual.

Meg finally lost her poise and began sobbing. She turned and clamped onto her father like a vice, trying to pull him through her. Rye tried to hug her firmly but couldn't. His hands danced lightly about her shoulder blades, never quite settling. He looked down. His hands were shaking like a shavetail pilot's going up for his first solo.

When they finally stepped back, Rye noticed it. Meg had stopped crying and was staring straight through her father. It was eerie.

"We've got a lot of work to do," she announced with a new strength.

Five days later, the Japanese invaded China, kicking off the Sino-Japanese War. Of course, Tokyo denied any wrong-doing in the disappearance of Amelia. Regardless, she was gone. Who would step up to claim the title of First Lady of the Air?

In the months that followed, I found myself dividing my reporting time between this new war and two gutsy speedsters, Jackie Cochran and Megan Reilly. Such words as lunch, vacation, and golf disappeared from my day-to-day vocabulary, as I covered an endless array of speed events, often covering thousands of miles. I spent many a sleepless night flying from country to country and city to city to cover these events. I later realized that my editor knew something about me that I didn't.....or wasn't willing to admit to myself.

* * * * *

The Reilly Flying Service had re-marketed itself, shifting from barnstorming, crop-dusting, and excursion rides to the research and development of pursuits. Rye sold off the red Fokker triplane and three of the Spads, using the money to perfect his lightning-fast pursuit for the Army Air Corps. After many hot, humid days, Rye and Sean had improved the design of their sleek aircraft such the world had never seen, incorporating many of Amelia's suggestions. Sean had begun to modify an existing Packard engine block, boring and stroking it to leave the competition in its prop blast.

Two days later, Rye received a telephone call from Howard Hughes.

"Reilly Flying Service," Rye answered.

"Hello, is Captain Reilly there?"

"Speaking."

"This is Howard.....Howard Hughes. How have you been, Captain?"

"Up to my neck in work. How about you, Mr. Hughes?"

"About the same.....Captain, do you have a minute?"

"Yes, Mr. Hughes." Rye was unmoved by the power behind the Hughes name but was respectful.

"Please, call me Howard," he said unpretentiously.

"What can I do for you, Howard?"

"I'll get right to the point, Captain. Your reputation as a designer is second only to your ability as a combat pilot. Congressional Medal of Honor recipient and a fistful of other commendations. The King of Aces. That's why I called you. I need you because you're the best, and I know that you need operating capital to finish perfecting that prototype of yours."

There was a bone-stiffening silence.

"Why am I not surprised that you know about my prototype and my.....situation, Howard?" Rye stammered in a nervous yet cool tone.

"Captain, it's my business to know. I'd offer you the money to complete your prototype, but as you are quite aware, it won't be welcomed by the military, at least at this point in time."

Again, there was silence. This was the manner in which Howard always got his way--to shock you with his knowledge.

"Why's that?" Rye stammered.

"It's an offensive weapon. The Administration would be afraid it'd offend the Japs. The military only purchases short-range pursuits. Look what happened to Billy Mitchell."

Rye knew full well that General Mitchell had made public statements about the Japanese warlike aims in the Pacific. He was ultimately censored and court-martialled.

"What can I do for you, Howard?" asked Rye, somewhat impatiently.

"I want to commission you, Captain, to develop a small transport for corporate executives and the Top Brass."

"Hold on, Howard. I'm honored, but I'm pressed for time. I....There must be fifty other designers that would jump at such a chance."

"Not with your credentials." Howard paused. "I want you to put the development of your prototype on hold. I'll pay you $100,000 plus labor and materials. Half now, and half when it has crossed the finish line. The plane has to be sleek, yet comfortable, able to climb above bad weather, travel non-stop across the Atlantic, achieve greater cruising speeds than any cargo or passenger craft in existence, and make "cool" landings."

"No sweat," Rye uttered facetiously, rolling his eyes. "Simple as crop-dustin' a volcano."

Howard ignored the sarcasm. "Another thing, Captain. I would like your daughter Megan to fly it in the Bendix."

Another silence. "Why Meg?" Rye questioned. "She's never flown more than a couple hundred of miles."

"Because it will show that the plane is safe and simple to fly," Howard replied. "It would also challenge male pilots afraid to cross the Atlantic, which till now has been deemed downright venturesome. Besides, she's your daughter. And I've seen her fly. She's got your raw talent."

Rye had no choice. Every penny raised through the sale of the biplanes and the Fokker had long been spent developing the prototype. He needed money to continue. "Okay, Howard."

"Good," Howard roared enthusiastically. "I'll have a bank draft in your hands by noon Thursday. Oh, by the way, I want to keep this project a secret, especially my involvement. I'll make an announcement when the time is right."

Rye was no dummy. If the project turned out to be a failure, Hughes would deny any involvement. If it won the Bendix, he would claim full credit.

Many of my Fourth Estate colleagues covering the aviation beat in those early years often traveled by train, bus, or automobile. Although I often got air sick, I personally flew everywhere. I felt it necessary to earn the respect of the pilots and aircraft designers in order to get exclusive interviews and inside tips. Believe me, the word got around fast when you didn't. It was still a one-dog community.

The test flight from Bendix Field to Minneapolis and back was a huge success. My notepad and camera ready, I was at Bendix Field with Rye and Sean, anxiously awaiting Meg and Garrett's return. We stood on the tower deck, craning our necks for the slightest glimpse, listening to the radio chatter in the background. Suddenly, powerful engines bellowed from behind the tower, shaking the concrete beneath our feet. I felt a muscle pull in my neck as I swivelled my head to see the streaking aircraft just meters above our heads. The deafening fly-by rattled the windows, causing the flight control personnel to flinch, covering their eyes with a forearm and uttering their displeasure. I grabbed a fistful of suit coat, pulling it up to protect my face against shattered glass, but none came flying. I stole a glance at Sean who was smirking at my reaction. I quickly dropped my arm with embarrassment.

Meg executed an eight-point roll as the Hughes craft rocketed past, executing a sharp 180-degree turn before landing.

Rye appeared irked as Meg pulled up and executed a snappy, show-stopping maneuver. Before the propellers had stopped spinning, Meg opened the door. Garrett hustled over to assist with the portable steps. She spotted me as I assisted him.

"Hey, Brooks Brothers!" Meg shrieked, bubbly-eyed. "Wow! What a blast! You should've been upstairs with me."

"I don't think so," I thought to myself. "Gee, sorry I missed it," I remarked facetiously.

Rye caught my sarcasm as he pointed a crutch at Meg. "All right, young lady, this better be good."

"Dad, I did it! The altitude record," she beamed wildly, removing her leather flying cap. Her beautiful hair unraveled as it rolled off her shoulders and bounced off the small of her back. "I broke it"!

My heart raced with emotion. I immediately looked down at my notepad to record their comments.

Garrett and Sean looked at Rye for his reaction. Her father's face was filled with pride, yet nervous concern. He started to say something then simply spun around and limped off, leaving the rest of us behind.

"That calls for a celebration," Garrett said jubilantly.

"But no Coneys"! I joked.

Meg giggled. "Ah, c'mon, Brooks Brothers. Don't be a such a stuffed shirt."

Her brothers heehawed at me as they leaned over and pinched a patch of my lapel. I laughed along. "Smart asses."

Every strand of her radiant hair glimmered in the sunlight as she again lunged into my chest. I found my hands dancing briefly on her shoulders, her firm, modest points pressed against me. I suddenly felt my blood rushing through my veins like a white-water rapid. I tried backing up a step, but she had me in her grasp like a vise.

Sean winked at me as he spoke. "There's a great place to eat just down a bit from the airport. C'mon, let's catch up with Dad." He grabbed his gawking brother by the shirt sleeve and pushed him toward Rye who was headed for the airport terminal. "Kids!" Sean mocked, shaking his head.

Meg latched onto my arm with both hands and pulled me along. I feared Rye would turn around and see us.

"I'm so glad you're here, Aaron," she said romantically, gazing into my eyes as she plodded along like a tomboy.

I quickly changed the subject. "Ah, er. I'm starved for a big juicy steak. How 'bout you?"

"Ooh, and a big baked potato with lots of butter," she added, eyes beaming. "It's so good to see you."

The first floor of the red brick building was the home of O'Shannon's Pub, complete with a green awning. The smell of steaks sizzling over a charcoal grill grabbed our senses as we climbed out of a yellow cab.

Meg's long hair and flight jacket were drawing a lot of attention as we entered the smoky bar and grill. I tried to stay a step behind her, but to no avail. In the back, two men in ball caps were playing pool. Two others were throwing darts.

Her eyes glowed. "Darts"!

"Later, young lady," her father barked. "Let's get some chow first."

Meg cut loose with a disappointed sneer.

The New York strips were superbly charbroiled, but the wine selection left much to be desired. Meg and her brothers wolfed down their food before I was half-finished.

The men who had been playing darts departed.

Meg grabbed my hand. "C'mon, Brooks Brothers, I'll stand you in a game of darts."

Still chewing, Garrett's eyes perked up. "Hey, I will." He lurched from his seat and raced to beat Meg to the dart board.

Rye turned to me. "You'll have to excuse their manners. It's been like this since their moth....." he ended abruptly, his face suddenly bordering tears.

I finished chewing a bite of steak. "There's no need to apologize, Captain Reilly. I can remember a time or two when my siblings and I escaped the dinner table to play baseball. Besides, I've eaten quite enough."

As Sean excused himself and joined the twins, Rye offered me a Panatela. I sniffed the cigar from end to end. The aroma was rich and moist. I bit off the end and leaned forward as Rye struck a match. My fingers rolled the expertly hand-crafted cigar until the entire end was glowing red. We then sat back in our chairs and watched the game. Meg and Garrett were locked in a boisterous duel.

"Megan is quite a competitor," I noted.

"Yeah, she does like to win," Rye offered, grinning proudly. "You ought to see her hit a baseball. Lobs a pretty good pigskin, too."

"It doesn't seem to affect her relationship with Garrett and Sean."

"Oh, they used to get in some pretty nasty arguments, believe you me. But any time some kid tried to get rough with her on the playground, Garrett or Sean would box his ears." Rye blew a smoke ring then watched as it floated upward. "They're pretty close." Rye looked down at his lap and brushed off the spilled ashes.

Looking back at the dart game, Meg was chiding Garrett as he concentrated on his throw. When it was Meg's turn, she stepped up to the line with her left foot forward and tossed the first dart with her right hand, lurching forward, kicking backward with her right leg, up and back. She scored and let out a rebel yell, cheerfully bouncing up and down on the balls of her feet like a little girl who has just been presented a birthday cake. She was the life of the pub. Every young man there had an immediate crush on her. Some of the older ones, too.

"She has an unique delivery," I observed.

"Yeah. She picked up the habit as a little girl. Had to kick out just to get the dart to the board," Rye chuckled. "Don't ever get behind her. You might lose your family jewels."

I laughed, almost choking on my cigar.

Another dart sailed true, landing dead-center in the 5.

"I win," she taunted.

"God, you're lucky," Garrett grumbled, grabbing the sides of his head with both hands.

Rye, Sean, and I laughed at his reaction.

"No luck about it, Gar," Meg spouted. "Another game?"

"I've had enough," Garrett relented. "Why don't you get Aaron to play you one."

Meg bounced over to our table. "Hey, Brooks Brothers, want a shot at the title?"

I rolled the end of my cigar on the glass ashtray, knocking off the ash. "You're too good for me."

"Oh, come on. Don't be such a drag," she pleaded. "I'll take it easy on you," she added jokingly.

Sean stood. "Come on, Sis. I feel a win in the air." He turned to me and covered his mouth as he spoke. "Another lamb to the slaughter."

I snickered.

Rye blew another smoke ring and watched it flutter my way. "You're a smart young man, Aaron. Meg has scared away most the young guys around Bendix Field. They don't relish getting beat by a girl."

"Except Garrett and Sean," I reminded him.

"Yeah, well, they're family." Rye leaned back and puffed his cigar. "I just can't imagine her ever being with anyone that isn't a challenge."

I caught his point.

CHAPTER 4

Sean was stooping under the port side wing, pointing up, with Rye looking on over his oldest son's shoulder. "General, we positioned our fuel tanks inside the wings so we could trim down the fuselage for less wind resistance," Sean explained.

Army Air Corps Vice Chief of Staff General Robert "Shotgun" Thomas nodded then squatted. "Sean, what about fuel capacity?"

"More fuel, fewer refueling stops," Sean said, matter-of-factly.

Thomas turned toward Rye. "Very impressive. Very impressive, indeed."

"Thanks, Bob," Rye answered quickly, confidently. "We've experienced no problem, regardless of the humidity or temperature."

"Who will fly it?" asked Thomas.

Rye motioned toward Meg whose head was buried in a welding job. Garrett was busily mounting a radio antenna to the belly of the fuselage.

Reaching down, Rye massaged his right knee. "I'm afraid Howard insisted on Megan. Besides, it's time for new blood. About all I can handle these days, Bob, are the short hops and a bit of crop-dustin', if ya get my drift."

Three stars, precisely positioned on Shotgun's collar, reflected light from the hanging lamps. He raised his eyes to meet Rye's. "Megan? I rather doubt that Bo's staff will share my respect of her prowess in the cockpit. Most of my colleagues perceive barnstormers as nothing more than reckless daredevils, but I know you and your ability to teach others first-hand. God knows I wouldn't be standing here right now if it hadn't been for your tutelage back in France....and the bullet you took for me." The graying, slightly pouching general, feet spread, began to count down with his fingers. "I need to know how the average male pilot is going to perform. Can it climb in cold, dry weather? Can it clear a mountain range immediately after take-off with a full load? Can it fly at high altitudes to conserve fuel? Can it pull out of a spin with a full belly? As you know, we demand the most out of our pilots every time they take off. We push our payloads to the max. Don't forget. Across the board, I have to deal with average pilots, guys fresh off the street. Most have little or no cockpit time before enlisting."

Rye smiled. "Good point, Bob." He panned the inquisitive faces of his children over his shoulder with proud eyes. "Those questions will be addressed and answered."

As I spun around, I noticed Shotgun Thomas eye-balling a large object covered with a tarpaulin at far end of the hangar.

"Another project, Rye?" Thomas asked inquisitively.

"Affirmative. It's a long-range pursuit I had hoped to race this year, but we need more money to finish it. I'm hocked up to my ears. Thanks to Howard Hughes, we'll be able to continue its development."

Shotgun looked at me. I was busily scratching down notes as he made a beeline for the covered aircraft. Rye, Sean, and I quickly fell into step with Thomas and his aide who checked the time on his wrist watch.

Thomas grinned after Sean pulled back the tarp. "You're something else, Rye. I know it will be a real hummer with you behind it."

"Bob, would you like to hop into the cockpit?"

The very businesslike general's aide, Major Bernard Beatty, leaned toward his boss, pointing out the time.

Thomas shook his head. "I wish we had time, Rye, but we must get back to Washington." He then looked at me and smiled kindly. "Nice to meet you, Mr. Masters. Tell Bill Livingston I said 'Hello.' He's done a hell of a job with that magazine. I've known him since he was a shavetail correspondent in France."

"I will, General. It was a pleasure." I shook Thomas'

outstretched hand.

He had the grip of Hercules.

Thomas spoke as he turned to depart the hangar. "Good luck, Rye. It was great to see you again. We'll see ourselves out."

Beatty turned to Rye. "It was an honor to meet you, Captain Reilly." Beatty pivoted on a heel to face me. "You, too, Masters. I'm sure we'll be seeing more of you in the future."

I smiled as I nodded. "Major, have a safe flight back to Washington."

Shotgun and his aide walked briskly in step toward his staff plane. Thomas climbed into the pilot's seat and started the engine. A high-pitched whine echoed throughout the hangar.

Meg looked up and pushed the safety shield back on her head. A giant grin filled her face when she spotted me. "Brooks Brothers!" She turned off the welder and headed our way.

She surprised me with a big hug. I looked around to see if anyone was looking. Rye was grinning. I sensed my face turning scarlet.

She nodded toward the Hughes prototype. "What do you think, Brooks Brothers?"

"Incredible.....I like it." I looked back at Rye who had noticed his only daughter's attention toward me. "It looks like a real performer," I added.

"Yes, she is," Rye stressed, "Someday."

From the tone of his voice and the expression on his face, I knew that Rye was referring to his daughter. Embarrassed, I quickly nodded that I understood.

* * * * *

The first time I covered a Bendix Transcontinental Air Race was in May 1935, a few months after meeting Amelia Earhart and the Reillys. Before professional football came into being with its modern-day television hype and tailgate parties, the Bendix Race equaled the excitement and hype of today's Super Bowl. It was the hallmark of the National Air Races that featured three days of exciting exhibition flying and robust speed trials. It was also the first year women were permitted to compete in the Bendix.

Thousands of cars and trucks and tens of thousands of spectators choked the streets and major routes leading to Burbank Airport, the starting point of the annual Labor Day classic. It was the Indianapolis 500 of flying. It was an impressive site, one I shall never forget.

America was excited over its fledgling industry of the future, equaling the excitement surrounding the first space launch with Alan Shepard. The future pilots of America, the world for that matter, were congregated here in the form of prototypes and modified stock aircraft that would become tomorrow's routine airplanes and fighters. Tens of thousands of dollars of technology and the reputation and future of aero-engineers were at stake. Winning the Bendix Transcontinental opened the door to lucrative government and commercial contracts.

Amelia Earhart and a daring new speedster, Jackie Cochran, had entered as contestants. Looking around, I spotted nearly every notable photographer and journalist west of the Mississippi. I was like a kid in a candy shop. It was hard to know what story to cover first, but something riveted me to the female entries, the obvious underdogs.

Contestant after contestant took off into the night, escaping car lights and portable floods illuminating the field. Cochran's Gamma failed to finish forced to return because of mechanical problems. Amelia would go on to finish fifth, a significant accomplishment, considering the field of accomplished men pilots.

In 1936, Louise Thadden and Blanche Noyes won the Bendix with Laura Ingalls finishing second. Women flyers had competed evenly and performed better the men, but would continue to be treated as novelties, second-class pilots as far as industry was concerned.

I decided to embark upon a crusade to change people's minds about the abilities and feats of female pilots. And it was not my intention to over-glorify, just give them their day in the air, so-to-speak. Their courage and skill deserved that much.

Labor Day Weekend, 1938:

Southern California was suffering from a sweltering heat that had everyone cooling themselves with newspapers, hand fans, and a wide array of fashionable straw hats. A number of young men had who had taken off their shirts were sporting dark tans. Some guzzled longneck beers and six-cent bottles of Coke as they stood in clusters, flirting with pretty girls passing by in shorts and colorful sundresses.

The crowd grew enormously as the day transformed into night. It was almost impossible to move about the milling enthusiasts. I miraculously spotted Meg. Considering her youth, she was all business, conducting a pre-flight inspection like a seasoned pro. Garrett was by her side, discussing the engine as I approached.

Sensing someone behind her, she turned. "Brooks Brothers," Meg shrieked. She leaped at me, thrusting her arms around my neck. "You missed our birthday."

"I didn't know."

"I'm eighteen," she boasted. I'm legal now."

"Looks like you're a had man," Garrett joked.

I swallowed hard as I reached out to shake Garrett's outstretched hand. "Ah, er, ah, well.....congratulations, both of you."

"Thanks." Garrett then grabbed Meg's jacket sleeve. "Come on, Sis. We need to get through this stuff."

Meg latched onto my hand and pulled me along to review the flight route.

I studied their youthful faces, glimpsing down briefly at the map. Except for Meg's long hair and Garrett's heftier build, they were duplicates in their flight jackets.

Meg was still an unknown commodity to the majority of reporters who were glued to the traditional male contestants and upstart Jackie Cochran, the only other female entry. Once again, I had an exclusive story.

I learned that Sean had been sent ahead to Kansas City where Meg was to refuel. He would facilitate the resources necessary to provide a swift pit stop. Meg and Garrett then completed the pre-flight and reviewed the map one last time, going over the flight route, checkpoints, refueling strategy, and emergency procedures. Nothing had been left to chance.

While Garrett loaded several thermoses of hot coffee and a

bag of sandwiches, I interviewed Meg. She was unbelievably relaxed for this, her first major race.

Meg glanced at Cochran's prototype setting three parking spots away. Jackie was busily being interviewed by the Fourth Estate. The tall, moderately attractive ash blonde smiled warmly, excused herself, and sauntered over to Meg who was genuinely appreciative of the gesture, but I sensed that Jackie was sizing up the competition.

A gasoline truck loaded with aviation fuel arrived at Cochran's plane, a Coke bottle-shaped prototype. She excused herself and hustled back to coordinate with the driver.

Garrett finished loading the supplies and food then walked over to us. "She's quite the pilot," he noted.

"She set a new altitude record," I noted.

"We've got a better plane," Meg said defensively.

Garrett spun around. "Look, Sis, you better shift your attention to beating the bird on Cochran's far side. I got a pretty good look at the engines earlier today. They rate out maybe 400 more horsepower than ours."

Meg stood and looked in that direction. "But that also means more fuel, right?"

"Valid point, but don't think for a moment the designer hasn't allowed for that." Garrett paused, shaking his head. "Trust me, that plane will haul ass."

Meg stood on her toes. "Who's the pilot?"

"A newcomer by the name of Hub Martin," Garrett answered. "Couldn't get any stats on him. I understand that he has raced cars in the Indianapolis 500 and the Grand Prix circuit. I hear he's pretty cocky."

Meg snickered, "Hub, huh? She moved around, trying to spot him.

A handsome, slender young man who didn't look old enough to shave was boasting up a storm for several Army Air Corps officers, including General Thomas and his aide. Martin was wearing a brown leather flight jacket and khaki riding pants tucked into a pair of highly polished brown boots. He used a swagger stick to point at key features on his prototype.

"Looks like a real hotshot," Meg sneered.

"Don't underestimate him, Sis.....You best get ready. You're up after him and Denton."

Meg slipped on her leather flying jacket, leaving it open. She then draped the white flying scarf around her neck. "What about Cochran?"

"She takes off after you," Garrett answered. "Now listen up. Sean's in Kansas City, ready to refuel you. Dad's already at the finish line in Cleveland, pumping the Top Brass."

Soon, General Thomas and the other military officers shook hands with Martin and walked toward us.

"Good luck, Megan," offered Thomas sincerely. "And please tell your father I said hello."

Meg smiled politely. "Thank you, General. I will."

Major Beatty stepped forward. "Mr. Masters...Garrett." He then faced Meg. "Best wishes for a safe flight, miss."

Meg took a deep breath and smiled. "Thank you, Major."

As Thomas and his party continued on, Hub Martin began to walk our way. There was a cocky, macho swagger to his stride. He lighted a Lucky Strike clamped tightly between his teeth as he came to an abrupt halt in front of Meg. His penetrating brown eyes caused Meg to look away. I waited with great anticipation to hear this exchange.

"So you're Rye Reilly's little kid," he sneered.

Meg came to a quick boil. The muscles in her neck were pulsating. "What's Hub short for, Hubcap?" she snapped with razor sharpness.

Martin kept his cool. "Oh, someone in the press nicknamed me that after I won the Monaco Grand Prix."

"Maybe you should stick with what you know best....driving station wagons."

Now it was Hub Martin festering with frustration. "This ain't some 10-minute act in some barnstorming circus, little girl. This is man's work."

"Then why are you here?" Meg fired back with the coolness of homogeneous steel. "Shouldn't you be taking off about now, Hotshot?"

Hub was seething. "I was going to wish you luck, but--"

"Ain't no luck about it," she spouted, cutting him off. "We'll be downin' Coneys and ice-cold longnecks by the time that tripod clears the Mississippi River."

Frustrated, Hub pointed at his plane. "That there tripod, as you call it, Dollface, was aerodynamically designed by the one and only Ferdinand Pasternak who just happens to be the top designer in the world."

"Then why are you flying it?"

Hub's face turned purple from anxiety. I hid my laughter as he threw down his cigarette and stalked back to his plane, muttering to himself. Meg had won the first bout, but I sensed that another man had just entered her life. Was I being protective or just a little bit green-eyed?

Meg turned to face me. "Aaron, how would you like to fly this one with me?"

I quickly examined her expression for sincerity, and although I had a fear of flying, I got the sudden urge to call her bluff. "My editor would love it--a first-hand report"

"Aaron's riding with me," Garrett announced.

"Maybe I'll take Meg up on her kind offer," I blurted. "My editor will love it." I couldn't believe I had just agreed to this crazy idea.

Garrett's mouth dropped open. He was quite aware of my flying phobia.

As Hub taxied past Meg, he flashed a cocky smile then winked.

Meg reached over and took my arm, twisted her face like putty, and rolled her eyes. "Jerk!"

While I sensed a grudge match brewing between Meg and Hub, I was keenly aware of the shift in attention, no matter how negative it seemed. She was no longer the freckled-face tomboy in the red, white, and blue flying suit.

"I better get the co-pilot's seat cleared off," Garrett announced, "so you've got a place to sit." He turned and entered the plane.

The race announcer's voice then grabbed our attention. "A heavy fog is rolling in from the mountains, headed westward."

I stood on my tiptoes, straining to focus on the end of the runway where a Dracula-like fog had blanketed the last hundred feet and swallowing more as each second passed. I took a deep breath, wondering if I had lost my sanity.

"C'mon, Brooks Brothers," Meg prompted. "We don't wanna get caught takin' off in the soup."

Hub powered to maximum RPMs then let up on the brake. The nose of the fuselage lurched upward, and roared toward the menacing cloud. His wheels lifted off briefly then touched down again, screeching his tires. The wings of his plane moaned, as they struggled with the heavy load of high-performance aviation fuel. Hub held his breath as the plane built enough pitch to attempt one last shot at lift-off, knowing that he had but a few more seconds before obliteration.

The swept-wing beauty blasted into the fog, disappearing. The crowd gasped.

Gritting his teeth, Hub pulled back hard on the stick with both hands, yelling at the top of his lungs like a charging Sioux warrior. The wheels lifted off a few inches then touched down again. Then, like some great power had grasped his powerful prototype, the nose lifted.

Hub immediately banked toward the Pacific, spiraling upward to gain altitude, until he had enough elevation to clear the mountain peaks to the immediate east.

The sleep-weary crowd applauded with relief, anguished for what peril lay ahead for the rest of the contestants. Meg prepared to take off after Robert Hyselmann who was already on the ramp, revving his powerful engine. His tires bulged from an overload of fuel. Race officials had already voiced their opinion--it was suicide to take off in such a fog.

The nose bolted forward as Hyselmann accelerated, trying to build enough speed to take off. His plane disappeared in the dense, vile soup half-way down the runway. The anxious, silent crowd grasped at one another, some clutching hands of complete strangers awaiting the outcome. Suddenly, a shaded flash of light and a thunderous explosion sent muted shock waves rifling through the clustered gathering.

Dozens of horrified reporters, ground crewmen, and contestants dropped everything and began charging toward the muffled light at the end of the runway. Meg spotted Cochran backtracking toward her parked car. Meg broke into a full stride, grabbing a fistful of Garrett's sleeve as she passed by, almost jerking him off his feet. The three of us raced toward Cochran's accelerating Cadillac and leaped at the running boards as it passed by, grasping the door frames, slamming into the body. Somehow, we all managed to hang on, Meg and Garrett on the left and I on the right.

Cochran's stylish Caddy raced alongside airport rescue vehicles and fire trucks toward the crash site. The ends of Meg's long, velvet-like hair whipped her face as Jackie out-raced the others, abruptly arriving at the security fence cloaked with blind fog.

"Hold on!" Jackie screamed as she jammed her foot down hard on the brake.

The Caddy stopped just short of colliding with a hefty fence post, hurling Garrett against the front fender. Meg and I miraculously managed to hang on to our respective doors but not without some tissue damage.

The four of us zigzagged back and forth at break-neck speed, trying to find a break in the barrier fence. Garrett found a small hole often used by children and small animals. With all his strength, he widened the hole for the rest of us to slither through. Once through, I held it for him. We raced to catch up to Meg and Jackie who were at full stride, stumbling here and there on small rocks and holes en route, arriving at the crash site ahead of the rescue vehicles that had taken the service road.

"Stay back!" Garrett snapped as he bolted toward the burning wreckage.

Shielding his face with his left arm against the intense heat, he tried to free the screaming pilot.

Ignoring his warning, the rest of us raced to his side to help.

Another explosion spun us around, knocking us off our feet, tumbling backward over and over. Flames and debris spewed in every direction. Meg and I rolled to avoid being struck by a piece of fiery, twisted metal.

Bruised and lacerated, I looked up as the fire trucks and a

truckload of airport workers came to a skidding halt. Everyone was standing mute, staring. It was the first time I had been on hand to witness an air accident, one that has haunted me nightmarishly to this day.

Jackie's eyes met Meg's. Their shocked, distraught faces were full of horror, yet mutual respect.

No one uttered so much as a word as we rode back in Jackie's Cadillac to the flight line. I didn't need to ask Meg if she was planning to continue the race. I could see it in her eyes.

Unfortunately, race officials did not share her desire, placing a hold on any take-offs while they pondered continuance. Of course, she and some of the male contestants hounded the officials to continue. A year of development and preparation dangled in the balance. Meg later confessed that it was the longest fifteen minutes of her life.

It was also the longest fifteen minutes of my short life. Now, I really had mixed emotions about flying with Meg in the race. Looking around, I spotted Garrett draining off some of the fuel into a 55-gallon barrel. Weight was a problem. She would need all the fuel possible. That meant something had to go - me! Whether it was out of pride or not, I outwardly exhibited my disappointment.

Glancing over at Jackie's pursuit prototype, I spotted her evading toward the shadows of a nearby hangar where she buckled over with nausea. Out of respect, I looked away but recorded the event in my notebook. Looking up, I heard Meg and Garrett replotting their flight strategy, allowing for the reduction in fuel. I couldn't help but notice the respectful, professional manner in which they worked together as a team.

I glanced back toward the hangar where Jackie had ventured. She was nowhere in sight. She later told me that she had searched out a telephone to call her husband Floyd Oldum to ask if she should continue with the race.

Floyd paused thoughtfully before responding, "There's a fine line between a course of action determined by logic and one dictated by great emotional urge. No one can draw that line for another. It simmers down to a philosophy of life."

CHAPTER 5

The rich baritone voice of the race announcer broke the tense, tomblike stillness. "A moment of prayer for Robert Hyselmann."

Everyone bowed his or her head in reverent thought.

Two minutes later, the announcer's voice crackled again. "Ladies and gentlemen, race officials have decided to continue the race. Pilots wishing to continue, prepare to take-off."

I turned to see Jackie Cochran returning to her plane, her chin high with courage.

Tens of thousands of spectators stood silently in place like pillars of granite, only their eyes moving, waiting tensely for the next take-off.

I turned to Garrett and nervously cleared my throat. "I saw you draining off some of the fuel. Is it still possible for me to accompany Meg."

Garrett shook his head. "I'm sorry, Aaron. We can't afford the extra weight."

Meg leaned toward me, grabbed the sides of my face with both hands and gave me a firm kiss, embarrassing me to no end. "I wish you were going with me, Brooks Brothers."

"Your safety comes first," I noted.

Garrett patted me on the shoulder, thanking me with a nod. "You best get ready, Sis."

Within five minutes, Meg was taxiing in the pea soup toward

the ramp where she pivoted the prototype and shoved the throttle forward, revving the engines. Looking out, she could barely see the navigational lights mounted on the wing.

Meg sat coolly in the pilot's seat, zeroing on the tachometer as it neared the red line. The Hughes craft was rocking in place like a row boat in heavy surf, vibrating the air thick with moisture.

Suddenly, Meg cut loose the brake, and the sleek transport sprang from its haunches, pulling away from the starting line like a daredevil shot out of a cannon. Within seconds, the dull illumination coming from airport lights were but a blur in her peripheral.

Meg started singing nervously, and out of tune, as usual.

K-K-K-Katy, beautiful Ka-ty,
You're the on-ly g-g-g-girl that I a-dore...

The crowd gasped as Meg entered the dense, menacing cloud. She kept a studious eye on her air speed as she blindly rocketed toward the end of the runway, now marked by the headlights of a truck temporarily positioned on either side of the tarmac.

When the m-m-m-moon shines o-ver the cow-shed,
I'll be wait-ing at the k-k-k-kitchen door...

Meg strained to see the barely visible center line. When she was a breath from the vehicle lights, Meg pulled back on the wheel with all her strength.

K-K-K-door!

As the nose lifted, Meg retracted the landing gear. The fuselage skimmed a thick fence post, shearing off the belly antenna. She wrestled with the wheel to keep the nose from dipping then managed to right it skyward.

Forced to just listen, I noticed the sound of the Hughes craft in the air, banking for the Pacific. A huge applause broke the early morning silence, drowning the announcer's words. I suddenly realized I had been holding my breath for some time. I leaned backward, took a whiff of air, and sighed with relief. I checked my wristwatch. It was half past three in the morning.

Meg checked in with the Cleveland Municipal Airport tower when she was 30 minutes out, requesting a weather report and landing instructions. The airport was flooded with spectators who had been attending the weekend air show.

She positioned the Hughes prototype for the final approach. Behind her was the beginning of a beautiful red sunset.

The wheels of the Hughes craft touched down on the runway like it was a bed of fresh eggs to the applause of thousands.

"Ladies and gentlemen," the announcer's voice bellowed, "Megan Reilly, daughter of the Great War ace, Rye Reilly, has just landed in second place. Let's hear it for Miss Reilly!"

A moderate encore from the crowd went unnoticed as Meg taxied to the grandstand area. Grinning, Rye hobbled on his crutches to greet her. Meg immediately recognized the rugged smile as she greeted her father at the door.

Flash bulbs went off like a fireworks display, blinding Meg as she stepped down to hounding news writers, busily scratching notes as they blurted out questions. A hand went up to protect her eyes.

Rye moved in close. "That was a great job. You made your father proud."

Meg hugged him and gave him an unexpected kiss on the cheek. More flash bulbs went off, blinding them both.

"Well, how'd the others do?" she inquired in an apprehensive tone.

"So far, you're in second place," sounded an unfamiliar voice.

Meg turned. It was Howard Hughes, grinning widely. With him were Shotgun Thomas and Major Beatty.

"Hi, Mr. Hughes, General Thomas. Who's in first?" Meg asked with an anxious tone.

"So far, Hub Martin," answered Hughes.

"That jerk?" she blurted.

"Don't feel badly," offered Hughes. "No one could have

gotten off the ground in that fog and made the time you did. Not even me." Hughes grinned.

"That was a terrific performance, Meg," Thomas said. He turned to his old friend. "Rye, great job designing this transport."

Rye cracked a smile. "Thank you, Bob." He winked at Meg. "You would've finished first with a high-performance prototype."

She caught what he meant and quickly changed the subject. "What about Jackie Cochran? Did she take off after us?"

"From reports, Jackie is ahead of schedule," Howard answered. "She may just do it."

"I suppose you heard about Bob Hyselmann?" Meg offered.

"Yes, Bob will be missed," Howard said mournfully. "He was a great aviator."

The press corps was quick to jot down Howard's every word. Bulbs continued to flash. By now, the crowd was ten-deep, pressing for details.

"Howard, can we have a picture of the four of you?" shouted one of the photographers.

Howard knew the power of the press. He immediately stood next to Meg and put his arm around her, sandwiching her against Rye. A bevy of flashes filled their eyes. Meg's smile was less than genuine.

Her eyes scanned the faces for Hub Martin. She spotted him some 20 yards away, surrounded by a horde of young girls propped about him, one under each arm while answering a shower of reporter questions. Much of the attention shifted from him when Howard Hughes arrived to greet Meg. Hub had one eye on the Reilly proceedings. Then he spotted Meg and fired off a smirking, arrogant grin.

Meg pivoted to face Howard. "This one was for you, Mr. Hughes. The next one is for us Reillys."

Rye smiled, studying her expression. It was the same determined look he had seen so many times on her mother's face. Meg was her spitting image. A shiver raced through his entire body.

Meg excused herself and strode over to Martin. He spotted her approach and hugged one of the girls, kissing her behind the ear, drawing a giggle. She couldn't have been more than eighteen.

"Congratulations, Martin."

He turned his head briefly then pompously resumed answering reporter questions.

Angered, Meg spun around. "Jerk." She flashed him the bird behind her back as she stomped toward her father.

Rye placed a comforting arm around her shoulder.

"That arrogant sonofabitch!" she growled. "I'm gonna beat that smart-mouth next year, just you see."

The announcer's voice bellowed again, causing everyone to orient his or her ears in the same direction. "Ladies and Gentlemen, your attention to the south. Jackie Cochran is on the final approach."

Meg jumped up and applauded, joining the crowd in cheers and whistles. She bobbed her head, trying to spot Hub's reaction. She wasn't disappointed. The press scurried off toward Jackie suddenly abandoning him. He frowned, his lip raised at one corner. Glancing toward Meg to get her reaction, he saw a huge taunting grin. Hub took a cigarette from his mouth and slammed it to the ground. Meg laughed.

Rye gave his daughter a look. "What was that all about?"

Meg smirked. "Sweet revenge."

* * * * *

The acrid smell of burning steel stung my nose as I opened the door, causing me to turn away, fighting the urge to sneeze. The Reillys were feverishly back to work on their own prototype, trying to perfect it before the next Transcontinental race and eventually the Bendix.

The pursuit prototype was even sleeker than the version Shotgun Thomas had previewed. I marveled at its elegance. It reminded me of the British Spitfire, slim and powerful. It promised to be the fighter of all fighters.

One of the Reilly sons was busily welding a bracket to the belly of the fuselage. Sparks were shooting in all directions, falling on several pairs of highly polished shoes just feet away. Rye was pointing out specific items on a blueprint to General Thomas, his aide, and two other staff officers who I had never seen before, a full-bird colonel and a major. Beatty was now wearing the silver maple leafs of a lieutenant colonel. The success of the small Hughes transport had earned Rye another Top Brass audience. There were much head-nodding and sucking-up on the part of the staff officers. It was amazing what a third-place finish at the Bendix Transcontinental had done for futures.

Captain Reilly was more animated than I had ever seen him. He smiled politely at me as I approached. Meg was nowhere in sight.

Thomas nodded at me but kept his focus on what Rye was saying.

"General, this baby is more sleek than the one Seversky built for Frank Fuller, and faster," Rye pronounced. "The top end should exceed what I told you a few months ago." He cleared his throat as he pointed at the massive Packard engine hanging from a chain hoist attached to the center I-beam."

"How many horses?" inquired Beatty.

"1695 big ones, right out of the chute."

"Jesus H. Christ, Rye," Thomas exclaimed. "You sure the wings can take the stress?"

"Yes, Sir," Rye answered, unblinking.

"What about gas consumption?"

"A gallon a minute at 395 miles per hour at 25,000 feet," Rye noted confidently.

Shotgun surveyed the expressions on his subordinates' faces. They were flabbergasted.

Rye held up a hand to stop him. "There are three 85-gallon tanks, one in each wing and one in the fuselage, giving it a range somewhat in the neighborhood of 1000 miles."

Thomas and his staff nodded at one another in amazement.

"As you stand here, Sean is installing brackets for auxiliary drop tanks that will extend it to 2100 miles," Rye added.

"If the Captain's right about this," the colonel interjected, "we'd be able to provide bomber escort all the way to the target."

"It'll be able to out-maneuver anything the Germans have got," Rye continued. "Imagine how many more of our bombers could make it back from the target.....the number of bomber crews it'll save. If the pilots are able to nail them on the ground before--"

"Hold it right there, everyone, especially you, Rye," Thomas said. "You know the Army's position on pursuit escort."

"All too well," Rye grumbled.

"Our bombers are heavily fortified and armed to fend for themselves," Thomas continued. "Just having a long-range fighter in our inventory would suggest that we're intending to break our neutrality." Shotgun leaned close to Rye and spoke quietly. "General Bolden won't budge, Rye, and you know it. It could cost me my stars to even suggest such a change to policy. We've got three pursuits in the inventory that fulfill the current policy."

"Don't you think that Tojo and Hitler know that? For Christ's sake, Bob, why do you think the bastards are shovin' people around? There ain't nobody with guts enough to stop 'em. The Japs are chasing the Chinese into the sea. Peking, Shanghai, and Nanking fell to those riceballs almost two years ago. The limies and the French are afraid of the Nazis, too. Last year, they caved in and let Hitler have Sudetenland. Earlier this year, they gave the krauts Czechoslovakia and renounced the non-aggression pact with Poland. Mark my words, they're next on his list."

Thomas took a deep breath as he put a hand on Rye's shoulder. "Ole buddy, Congress will never add a long-range fighter to the arsenal, and that's all there is to it."

"Scum-sucking doves!" Rye snapped, stomping his crutch against the concrete.

The general's staff buzzed.

Rye's temples were throbbing. "How long do you think we'll be able to stay neutral--a year, two years? Every time the Japs and the Nazis grab a little bit of territory here and there, they're snatching up valuable natural resources, not to mention building morale. Once the bastards have enough planes, tanks, and subs, they'll be testing our neutrality."

Thomas took his hand away from Rye's shoulder. "Rye, come on. You're only hurting your case. My hands are tied, and you know it. The only way I'll be able to get you in the door is with a short-range pursuit, understand?" He winked at his friend.

Rye took a deep breath and relaxed on his crutch, nodding up and down. He had gotten the general's message. "I need a contract.

I've hocked everything."

"Getting a military appropriation out of those doves in Congress these days is like tryin' to shoe a high-kickin' jackass," Thomas howled.

Rye snickered.

"Hell, Rye, I literally have trouble requisitioning goddam paper clips," Thomas dryly added.

Cackling, Rye nodded, patting his old comrade on the shoulder.

Thomas looked at Rye's eldest son. He assumed Sean would be the pilot. "So, Rye, who's your pilot this time around?"

Rye noticed the presumption and paused with the slightest of smiles. "We'll make the announcement later."

Beatty leaned toward his boss and whispered.

Thomas turned to Rye. "We must be going. Good luck, Rye. I hope you can pull it off. A victory could strengthen your cause."

Thomas then looked my way. "Masters, Aviation Life magazine, right?"

I smiled. "Yes, how have you been, General?"

"Very fine. I read that piece you did on last year's Bendix." Thomas offered his hand. "Terrific job. Very perceptive. It's good to see you again."

"Thank you," I responded.

Thomas then shook hands with Sean. "Take care, young man. Very impressive work here. Good luck in the race."

"Thank you, General," responded Sean with a sly grin. "Have a safe trip back to Washington."

"Thank you for coming, General," Rye said in a serious tone, visibly upset that he had not gotten a commitment.

"Rye, tell the twins that I said hello," Thomas added as he turned to leave.

Rye eased up with a friendly smile. "I will."

"Speak of the devil," Sean drawled.

I turned to see Meg and Garrett stepping smartly through the large hangar doors. Garrett was carrying a heavy-looking, wooden box. They stopped briefly to exchange greetings with Shotgun then continued their entrance. Both were wearing their seasoned flight jackets. Meg's long hair was youthfully jousting with her shoulder blades.

"Hey, Dad!" Garrett shouted. "We got the parts."

A giant grin filled Meg's face as she spotted me. "Brooks Brothers! You made it," she blurted, lunging forward to kiss me.

I suddenly realized my palms were sweating. "Ah, er.....Hi, Megan."

Her family was chuckling at my awkward, blushing reaction.

She glanced back in forth between her father and older brother. "All right, what's going on, you two?"

"I wanted to surprise you." Rye's eyes dropped to the ground.

"What do you mean, surprise me?" she asked with a half-puzzled, half-expecting gaze.

Sean had a smirk on his face.

"Go on," Rye directed him. "Tell her. It was your suggestion."

"Tell me what?" Her eyes kept racing between them.

"You should be the one to pilot our future," Sean announced.

Meg looked at Garrett, her mouth open.

"I'm all for it, Sis," uttered Garrett reassuringly. "You proved yourself to the world at the last race, and if it ain't broken, don't fix it, if you know what I mean, Sis?"

"I know I've been pretty vocal about wanting a rematch with that jerk Martin," she stammered, somewhat embarrassed. "But I eventually realized that I was being a little selfish. Sean built it. It should be his turn."

"It's simple. You're the better pilot," Sean countered. "You proved it at the last Bendix."

Garrett turned to me. "When everything's at stake, you go with the best."

Meg looked at me and took a deep breath. "I lost the Bendix."

"But you didn't have a high-performance pursuit like the others," Garrett noted.

"This was a business decision," responded Rye. "It was unanimous."

Meg folded her arms over her chest. "I thought to be unanimous, that all of us had to vote."

I looked about their faces. The words were genuine. This was a proud moment for her father. I got the feeling that this had something to do with something else.

Rye put his arm around her strong shoulder. "You've grown up without a mother. Most of the time, I ain't been much of a father. After your mother left us, I thought my heart had been ripped from my chest. I felt responsible. But it would be wrong to hold you back." He paused, looking down. "She was so...." his voice cracked. He managed to regroup his poise. "This is your chance to be somebody with the only thing I could ever give you."

Meg's eyes filled with tears. "I don't need your sympathy when the family's at stake. We're all in this together."

"It's not sympathy, young lady," Rye insisted. "You're the best pilot for the job, and that's all there is to it."

I suddenly felt uneasy, like an intruder. Then I realized that it was meant to be.

A young, pretty brunette in a bright flowered dress suddenly appeared at the open doorway.

"Hey, Sara, I'm in here," Sean shouted.

She bounced youthfully our way, smiling with her hands folded politely in front. Sean offered his arm for her to take then introduced her to the rest of us.

Suddenly, Meg left my side, spreading her arms as she lurched at her father, hugging him. He seemed a little embarrassed; his arms still at his sides. He gently kissed her forehead. Her two long, feminine but strong arms coaxed in her brothers. The hug was tight and long. It was a sensitive moment.

Sara looked at me with an awkward expression.

I smiled. "It's a family thing."

"Easy, young lady," Rye reminded his daughter. "We still got a lot of work to do over the next few months. We've got something to prove to those skeptics."

"I'm gonna beat the pants off that jerk Hubcap Martin," she blurted. "We're gonna win that government contract."

The final summer months leading up to the Bendix Transcontinental was filled with anticipation and excitement. First,

Hub Martin then Jackie Cochran set a slew of speed, distance, and altitude records at an unbelievable pace. Megan Reilly was becoming impatient with her father's gag policy but honored his strategy, knowing that she had far exceeded either Hub or Jackie's accomplishments.

    Keeping it a secret was as hard on me as it was on Megan Reilly, but I had given my word.

CHAPTER 6

September, 1939:

Again, the Los Angeles Airport was bursting at the seams with air show spectators, military purchasers, and civilian contractors displaying their wares, instruments, and prototype aircraft. The roads and streets leading to the airport were just beginning to clog. Because of faster air speeds, contestant take-offs would begin at 7:00 in the morning with both Hub and Meg scheduled for take-offs around 8 a.m. To their disappointment, the reigning champ, Jackie Cochran, would not be competing. This time, Garrett, Rye, and I decided to position ourselves at the finish line. We all had a strong feeling about the outcome of the race.

Two dozen crews and pilots were busily prepping their planes. Meg and Sean were standing next to "Quest," as Megan had fondly painted on the nose of the plane. They were being interviewed by a quartet of sleepy-eyed reporters. Several Army Air Corps officers and aero-engineers were circling about the Mustang, talking and pointing.

"Gentlemen, thank you very much," announced Sean. "But we must get ready for take-off." He immediately herded them away.

Sean unrolled one of the charts. "Remember, Sis, you must cruise at 330 miles an hour to conserve fuel. With the wind currents at 20,000 feet, three drop tanks should get you there, but it'll be close. I estimate that actual flying time to be in the neighborhood of seven and a half hours, no more than eight and a half. That should get you in New York around six or seven, Eastern Standard Time."

"Gotcha." She glanced up to see Hub Martin surrounded as usual with a bevy of stunning young women, hanging on to him as he talked to a crowd of press, Top Brass, and autograph hounds.

"Hotshot jerk!" she snapped.

Sean looked up from the chart to see who she was looking at. "Hey, Sis, keep your mind on the race."

"He's such a sap."

"Those records of his are real, Meg. That's one hell of a plane he's got there. He's packing two 1325-horsepower Allison engines. He took it last month to 38,000 feet and 400 miles per hour."

"What's his range and speed?" she asked.

"With those two added drop tanks, he should get 1600 miles out of it at 330 miles per hour at 10,000 feet. That means one fuel stop, probably in Kansas City. That's at least 30 minutes on the ground, but remember, he's been used to making pit stops. Probably using his former Indy pit crew so refueling should go faster than normal."

Meg faced Sean. "So what's your analysis? Think he'll try to go faster than 300?"

"He may open it up, considering the tail winds at higher attitudes and more fuel," Sean guessed. "Don't go speed crazy on me up there, okay? You've got just enough fuel to get you there. If he's going slower, back off a bit."

"Check."

"You're up after Fuller and Martin," Sean advised her. "Better get in."

Hub looked up, making eye contact with Meg. He then fired off one of his cocky grins. Meg flashed him the bird.

Hub broke away from his entourage and strutted directly at Meg, flipping his leather flying jacket over his shoulder, staring a seductive hole through her.

He gave the Mustang the once-over, snickering. "So your old man is really gonna let you fly this here.....pregnant cigar, huh?" he sneered, looking at the drop tanks.

"That's right," Meg answered soberly. "It'll beat the hell out of that.....that tinker toy of yours."

A smartass grin crossed Hub's lips. "Tinker toy, is that the best you can do?"

"Don't you have something to do like shine your wings or something?" she sneered.

"Hope you don't mind suckin' my vapor trail all the way to New York." Hub spun on his heels and strutted back to his plane.

"Horse's ass jerk!" Meg growled. "Who in the hell does he think he is, God?"

Sean turned. "Ignore him, Sis. He's just trying to get your goat....take you out of your concentration."

"You're probably right." Meg hopped on the wing and slid into the cockpit to begin her preflight.

Sean followed her to assist. "Remember, land in K.C. if you run into trouble," he shouted. "Now, make your father proud."

As Sean hopped down, Meg reached inside her jacket and pulled out the white scarf Amelia had given her. She looked at it fondly then draped it around her neck, clutching its tails. A tear slid down her cheek, stopping on her chin. She reached up and dabbed it with her fingers.

Hub taxied his prototype from its parking spot, drowning all sound. He leaned forward in his cockpit like he was challenging her to a drag race. He fired off a brilliant, cocky smile. Meg put a hand on her other biceps and gave him an up-yours.

Sean signaled with his hands. "Okay, Meg, go ahead. Fire her up."

Meg pushed on the starter button. The giant engine spitted fire from its manifold pipes as it caught. Sean quickly disconnected the power booster cables and backed away, shouting. "You owe me one....Good luck!"

Meg nodded and smiled, saluting with two fingers.

As she taxied, the photographers unleashed a barrage of pictures.

The air show audience stood in awe as the sleek Reilly prototype taxied up behind Martin who was on the ramp, going to full power for the take-off. He turned to face Meg who stopped dead on his tail. He gave her a dirty look then blasted down the tarmac, barely clearing the end of the runway.

Five minutes later, Meg shoved the throttle forward. The nose of the Mustang bolted upward as she took off the brake and screamed down the runway, clearing the take-off point, this time with inches to spare.

Meg banked eastward and climbed to 20,000 feet. The race was on.

Meg was cruising at 330 miles per hour when she picked up on a strong east-bound wind. Before she realized it, she had raced past her first reference point by 20 miles. She adjusted her course and glanced at the drop tank fuel gauge. She smiled at her progress and began singing "I've Got a Gal in Kalamazoo," out of tune.

In less than 90 minutes, she was bearing down on the beauty of the Grand Canyon. Her singing picked up new vibrancy.

After passing over the Rockies, Meg pulled the D-handle to the belly drop tank. The aluminum, cigar-shaped tank tumbled end-over-end into the clouds below. A leg stretch was impossible so she settled for the isometrics that Sean had taught her. Afterwards, she rewarded herself with a Coke, removing her oxygen mask periodically to take a swallow. Suddenly, the thought of a juicy, charbroiled T-bone, medium-rare, entered her mind. She shook off the mirage and began singing again.

Meg rotated her wrist to check the time. It was almost 3 p.m., Central Time. She radioed ahead. "Kansas City Control, this is Amelia's Quest."

"This is KC Control, go ahead."

"I'm one of the Bendix contestants. Heard from any of the others yet?"

"Roger.....Hub Martin's refueling," answered the air controller. "Will you be landing?"

"Negative, KC Control. How long has Martin been on the ground, over?"

"This is Kansas City Control.....about 15 minutes, over."

"Roger, thank you, out." She checked her watch again, talking to herself. "At this pace, I should be at the finish line by 6:15, New York time."

As she neared the Mississippi River, the radio chatter increased. Meg listened intently for more word about Hub Martin.

An air controller contacted her from St. Louis. "We have you on radar, seven-five miles to the north on a heading of zero-seven-zero, over."

"Roger, St. Louis," she answered.

Another male voice entered the conversation. It was a race representative. "Amelia's Quest, how are you fairing up there?"

"Like a five-pound tuna in a two-pound can."

"Understand, a little cramped, over."

"Roger, St. Louis. Any word on the others?"

"Negative."

Meg frowned and began talking to herself. "I wonder where that jerk is refueling.....I'm gonna beat that hotshot....I'll be w-w-waiting at the k-k-k-kitchen door."

The afternoon sun reflected off her instrument panel, forcing her to shield it with her hand. Ahead, the sky was deep blue, void of any clouds. She searched the radio channels for music. Finally, she found a station playing "Begin the Begine" by Benny Goodman. She whistled along, clicking her fingers.

Meg barreled past Indianapolis about 35 minutes later. She leaned both ways, trying to see the ground below. At this altitude, even something as large as the Indy 500 Race Track was too tiny to see. The radio channel came alive with the smooth trumpet of Harry James. When the music ended, Meg flipped the channel selector switch, landing on a frequency alive with race chatter.

Glancing at her gauges, she checked her fuel. "It's gonna be a tight fit. . . . In-flight refueling would be a novel idea," she murmured to herself.

She squeezed the push-to-talk switch located in the neck of her oxygen mask.

"Pittsburgh Air Control, this is Amelia Quest. I'm one of the Bendix contestants. Request weather update, over."

The air controller dressed in a white shirt and a boring striped tie looked at his fellow workers in shock. "This is Pittsburgh control. Where are you?"

"I'm northeast of Indianapolis in a pursuit prototype, over."

The air controller shook his head as he commented to a fat co-worker. "Some kid must be trying to pull a prank on us." He walked to the tower door leading to an outside deck. "This is Pittsburgh Control. Identify yourself, over."

"This is Meg Reilly, over."

"This is Pittsburgh Control. Sorry, we thought maybe you

were some prankster. We have clear skies with winds out of the north at eight knots, gusting to 12, over."

"Roger, Pittsburgh Control. Heard anything about Hub Martin, over?"

"This is Pittsburgh Control. Affirmative.....Martin's just a few miles ahead of you," he paused. "Good luck."

"Thanks," Meg ended. "Damn, Hotshot must have upped his speed." She reached out and eased up the throttle, settling for 400 miles per hour.

Just twenty minutes away, Meg again contacted the controller at the finish line. "New York Control, this is Amelia's Quest, over."

"Amelia's Quest, this is New York Control, over."

"This is Amelia's Quest. Request approach and landing instructions, over."

"This is New York Control. We have you on radar. How's it going, over?

"This is Meg Reilly. I'm low on fuel. What's the traffic like?"

"This is New York Control. Pretty heavy with the air show. Descend to 5000 feet and approach from the south. We'll get you in, don't worry."

Rye suddenly entered the control tower.

"Hold on," the controller added. "There's somebody here that wants to talk to you."

"Looks like you might do it, young lady."

Meg's eyes brightened. She squeezed her throat mike. "Good afternoon, Dad. I understand hotshot is slightly ahead of me."

"Roger that. How are you doing on fuel, over."

On the light side, over."

Rye's face depicted his concern. "How much is light, over?"

"I'm down to about 20 gallons, over."

"Damn," he swore as he looked at the radar scanner. "I've got you about five-zero miles out. Martin is about three miles ahead of you, over."

Suddenly, she spotted the sun's reflection off Hub's prototype below. She eased the throttle forward. "I'm taking it up a notch, over."

"Be careful, young lady. Your life is a lot more important

than some damn contract."

"I will. I know what I'm doing." Meg glanced at her air speed.

The needle was at 435 with some to spare. She would play it cool until it was necessary to go full-throttle.

By the time Meg passed over the Delaware River, Hub's aircraft was less than 2000 yards away, two-, maybe three-hundred feet below. Pointing the nose down, she accelerated until she was at his port side wingtip. Hub looked left and did a double-take. Suddenly looking worried, he jammed the throttle forward and began creeping ahead.

Meg held her breath and accelerated. She wanted to do more than to beat him time-wise. She wanted to land before him. It would be a dead-heat race to the finish line. Both Meg and Hub jockeyed for the lead. Meg checked her fuel. The needle was teetering on empty.

"Amelia's Quest, this is New York Control, standby."

Rye took the mike. "Megan, what's your fuel situation, over?"

"Pretty slim, Dad, but I'll make it," she said in a confident tone.

Overhearing Meg's words, the air controller turned on the airport siren. Within seconds, an ambulance and two fire trucks sped toward the main runway while the eyes and ears of thousands strained toward the southwest. Soon, Meg and Hub appeared as two shining dots, wingtip-to-wingtip, sparkling in the early-evening sunlight as they dropped altitude for the final approach, disappearing behind a tall windbreak.

"Ladies and gentlemen, your attention please," the air show announcer bellowed. "Approaching from the south are the first race arrivals, neck-'n-neck."

The crowd shifted to its tiptoes as the high-powered grind of their engines thundered louder and louder. The air show spectators that had started to depart, brought their cars and trucks to an abrupt halt and stood on their running boards, shielding their eyes against the intense sunlight.

A nearby spectator leaped in the air, pointing. "There!"

Heads were bobbing about, trying to grab a glimpse of the

silver birds as they screamed over the trees, their invisible props swiping at the top branches, disarming their leaves.

Both pursuits swooped down, blazing just a few feet above the tall grass near the end of the runway. It was a thrilling, incredible site. The crowd erupted with cheers and shrill whistles. Car and truck horns soon joined in the chorus with a variety of beeps and blasts.

With falcon-like intensity, Meg bored down on her prey. "When the m-m-m-moon shines o-ver the cow-shed....."

With her fuel gauge needle bouncing on Empty, Meg estimated her remaining fuel and shoved the throttle wide open, blasting ahead of Hub. "He'll be wait-ing at the k-k-k-kitchen door....."

Hub sank back in his seat, helpless against the superior Reilly pursuit, thinking about the humiliation of being beat by a girl. He pounded his fist against the instrument panel.

Meg shrieked, "K-k-k door.....Sucker!" She reached down and grasped the landing gear lever, manipulating it at the last possible second. As her wheels made contact with runway, her engine coughed, caught then coughed again. Hub touched down just two seconds behind her.

As Meg reached the end of the runway, she turned and taxied toward the grandstand. Her Mustang coughed to a stop. She sighed with relief.

The energized crowd celebrated the arrival of the first contestants, cheering and running past airport security like a tidal wave toward these young celebrities.

Rye was perched on the tower railing, cheering.

Suddenly, I found myself being picked up and carried backward by the crowd, eventually being spun around like a revolving door. Caught up in the emotion of the moment, I began running at full-stride, notebook in hand, nearly dropping my recorded thoughts as I got knocked from side to side by a gauntlet of shoulders and feet. I pushed and shoved my way to the front, hoping that the *Aviation Life* photographer had made it before me.

Megan Reilly had done it. The entire nation deserved to see the emotion in this young heroine's face as she shoved back the canopy and emerged. A number of photo flashes assured me that some determined photographers had made it to the front, waiting for her to stand in her cockpit.

I had to laugh as I looked back at the tower. Rye was waving a single crutch, singing without voice, shocking many of the snobbish, well-dressed dignitaries about him. Garrett quickly prompted him down the steps to a waiting sedan. Soon, they were speeding toward Meg.

A stubby Army Air Corps major standing near the sleek, Reilly prototype, nudged my arm. "I'd give my left nut to have that pilot flying for me."

I chuckled as I glanced at his name tag. His name was Pine. He must have missed the announcement that it was a female pilot. Boy, was he in for the surprise of his life.

I motioned for my photographer to reposition himself in order to capture Pine's expression as Meg emerged from the cockpit.

Garrett hopped on the wing and clasped her wrist, helping Meg to her feet. She leaned backward to stretch her cramped muscles as she righted herself. He gave her a hug, shocking the spectators unaware of her gender.

Meg then waved at the excited crowd while speaking to Garrett out of the corner of her smiling mouth. "Get me to a bathroom, fast."

Garrett chuckled. "What's wrong, Sis. Couldn't bring yourself to use the funnel, huh?"

"Ha! Very funny, smartass."

Then came the moment I had been waiting for. Meg removed her leather flying cap and shook loose her matted hair, primping it with her fingers. I turned to catch the look on Pine's face.

"I'll be dammed. It's a girl!" Pine blurted, mouth hanging open. "I can't believe it," he continued to stammer. "This must be some kind of a prank."

I spotted my photographer snickering, giving me a thumbs-up. He had captured the moment on film. I couldn't wait to see the major's shocked expression in print. It would look great in the two-page spread that would be published soon, right next to the one with Meg unveiling her long auburn locks. It's really true that a picture is worth a thousand words. In the case of these two shots, a million words.

"Ready to sign her up, Major?" I asked.

Pine gave me a dirty look. "She must have cheated. Switched pilots en route or something."

I turned to watch Meg wobble cautiously down the wing, balancing herself against the fuselage with one hand. "No, Major.....She's for real," I said, keeping my eyes on Meg as Rye arrived.

Rye's voice sounded from behind, "You made your father proud."

Meg spun around. "Dad!" She leaped for a hug.

Rye returned it but with his usual embarrassment.

Suddenly, a flock of teenage girls pushed in close to touch Meg as they had so many times with Amelia, hooting and applauding with increased potency. Her beautiful eyes were racing with excitement.

More reporters of all shapes and sizes bull-dozed through the pushing crowd, snapping pictures and taking notes. A bevy of teenagers, so much like Megan when I first met her, thrust everything from air show programs to social security cards in front of her, pleading for autographs. Meg quickly scribbled out the first thoughts that came to mind, working feverishly to oblige her fans. Those within reach grabbed at her, trying to touch Meg's magic. She was finally getting some respect. She had not only become the new First Lady of the Air but also the premiere pilot in the world, male or female.

Looking around, I spotted Martin refueling, ignoring the questions of pushy reporters and a flock of teenage boys. A tall beautiful blonde standing near him appeared to be getting an earful of Hub's impugned ego. Her arms were folded, electing to admire Megan Reilly. I pondered what Hub could be up to as I walked over to congratulate Meg personally.

A few dozen officials in boring Robert Hall suits were roaming about, keeping a watchful eye on the happenings. Some were taking notes. I presumed them to be engineers, pointing and measuring dimensions. Rye and Sean's design had stole the spotlight.

Meg finished autographing a brown lunch sack belonging to a perky, teenage redhead when I walked up. "Brooks Brothers! It's about time." She thrust the sack at her fan and opened her arms to me.

I could feel my blood pressure soar. "Congratulations, young lady. You did it in seven hours. Wow!"

Sliding her slender arms around my neck, she pulled herself up and kissed me gingerly. I felt as though I had been struck by a thunderbolt. Yet, I found myself still holding back. To me, she was still a teenage tomboy with a crush.

Over her shoulder, I could see Rye smirking at us. My face turned red as a photographer's flashbulb blinded us.

Meg turned and pulled on Garrett's sleeve. "I've gotta pee like a two-headed race horse," she whispered desperately.

Garrett grinned. "Hang on, Sis. Relief is near."

Meg turned to me. "C'mon, Brooks Brothers." She latched onto my arm.

We excused ourselves and hustled for the sedan. Meg and I climbed into the back as Garrett moved out smartly, parting the disappointed crowd reaching out to touch their new heroine.

"I hope they don't think I'm stuck up, but I've gotta go real bad," she announced.

"They'll get over it," I said.

Garrett looked into his side mirror. "Look back, Sis."

Meg rotated in her seat. A throng of teenage well-wishers and reporters were chasing the sedan.

"Meg, something tells me you don't have to worry about fans," I added proudly.

Looking upward, she spotted Hub's prototype taking off. "What the?"

CHAPTER 7

The elegant ballroom with its 50-foot sculptured ceiling and majestic crystal chandeliers was brimming with energy. Hundreds of attendees dressed in beautiful gowns, black tuxes, Army dress blues, and Navy whites, milled about in small groups, smoking cigars, discussing the topic of the day, Japanese and Nazi aggression. It was a reporter's banquet.

I arrived refreshed with a good night's sleep and a relaxing day at the air show, looking about for familiar faces. Meg and most of the other contestants had yet to arrive. Howard Hughes was rubbing shoulders with generals Bolden and Thomas. I licked my pencil, hoping for a good story. After exchanging pleasantries, I got an earful.

"Hitler has got everybody second-guessing," Thomas scowled. "Even the Japs are pee-ohed. Hell, he's gone ahead and signed a non-aggression pact with Stalin."

"According to my sources," Howard injected, "Japanese and Russian troops have been mixing it up pretty good in Mongolia. No love lost there."

"You're really amazing, Howard," Bolden noted. "I just got the report hours ago. Have you got agents on my payroll, or somethin'?"

Howard winked at me. "I pride myself on staying up on such matters."

"Remind me to call you next time I need some timely INTEL," Bolden said facetiously, looking at his aide.

Beatty spoke up quickly. "Er, ah....I'll get a hold of G-2 tomorrow." He then turned to Howard, wisely changing the subject.

"You must know that the British and French signed a mutual assistance treaty."

Howard cackled. "So much that'll do for them. They're both paper tigers. Hitler and Stalin are dividing up Europe like it's a game of chess."

"And the rest of Europe are the pawns," Beatty drawled.

"We haven't learned a damn thing from the Great War," Rye added. "All those boys that died in those trenches. The war to end all wars. Ha! The French think that a line of concrete bunkers and tank obstacles facing the German border will stop the krauts. Hell, all the Gerries have to do is take a detour through Belgium and sting 'em in the ass."

"The French have always been one war behind," Thomas sneered.

"Remember, General, how that French brigade of lancers charged into the teeth of those kraut machine guns back in '17?" Rye reminded. "Mowed 'em down like blades of grass. Horses, too."

"I remember," Thomas drawled. "More bullets were fired in that battle than all the rounds fired in the entire Civil War. Just plain stupid, it was."

"Personally, I think Hitler is setting up Stalin with that bullshit non-aggression pact, lulling him to sleep while his Nazi storm troopers ready for a major attack," Beatty added. "Stalin trusts no one. Shot thousands of officers during his purge of the military a few years back. Paranoid bastard thought everyone was out to overthrow him. He's in no position to take on the krauts."

Rye nodded in agreement. "China, too. We were given the warning signs in China two goddam years ago when the Japs attacked the Panay on the Yangtze River. Not only did the bastards sink a ship flying our colors, they machine gunned the survivors."

"Know what was really disturbing about that whole affair," said Beatty, "was that the U.S. Embassy had informed the Japs about the Panay's presence. Tojo deliberately provoked us to see how much spine we've got. Since we did nothing, he looks upon it as a sign of weakness."

"Claire Chennault has been cleverly moving his squadrons around to prevent the Japs from taking out his entire group in one bombing run," Beatty continued. "He's really been giving them hell."

I stopped scratching on my note pad long enough to snatch a glass of champagne from a passing waiter. Suddenly, the Reilly clan entered, grabbing everyone's attention near the foyer.

Gracing a white lace formal, Meg had piled her dark-red hair high on her head. Two French curls tickled her cheeks. Her youthful gait was wholesome.

Sean and Garrett wore matching black tuxes while Captain Reilly looked very dashing in his Army dress blues. Sean was a younger duplicate of his father; Garrett and Meg on the other hand favored their mother.

Meg firmed her grip on Garrett's arm, trying not to twist an ankle as she hinted at a wobble. I snickered without cracking a smile.

The loose clusters of attendees near the entrance turned and applauded formally, nodding with smiles. Meg blushed, obviously uncomfortable with all the attention. Several young teenage girls flocked closer for a glimpse. Others leaned against their escorts, whispering and nodding.

A black waiter in a white uniform and black bow tie appeared with a tray of champagne glasses and a small white serving towel draped over his tray arm. His manners were very proper as he moved from guest to guest, offering the bubbly refreshment.

Meg took a glass of champagne and put it to her lips. The bubbles went up her nose, forcing her to sneeze. "Yuck! This stuff's awful. Do you have a Bud?" Meg sputtered, wiping her chin with the back of her hand.

"Bud?" he questioned.

"Budweiser!" she blurted. "Beer."

The waiter was somewhat taken back. "A beer?" he scoffed.

"Yes, a beer. I don't like that bubbly stuff."

"Stuff?" He had an arrogant expression on his face. "Bud?. . . Beer?. . . Stuff?"

"Yeah," Meg reiterated. "Beer."

"I shall try to find you a . . . beer, Miss," he uttered arrogantly as he faced her father. "And you, old chap?"

"Jack Daniel's Black," Rye responded, somewhat disgruntled over the reference to old. "On the rocks," he snapped, drawing snickers from Meg and her brothers.

"Yes, Sir." The waiter hesitated then addressed Garrett and Sean. "And you . . . gentlemen?"

"A Bud for me," responded Garrett.

"Yes, of course," the waiter snapped arrogantly. "A beer."

"A Bud and two fingers of Jack Black," Sean ordered, gesturing with his fingers.

"I shall see to it shortly, Sir." The waiter pivoted on his left heel and sauntered off toward a new group of arrivals with his nose in the air.

Sean turned to Garrett. "That colored waiter sounds like he's from England, doesn't he?"

"Yes, he certainly does, doesn't he, old chap," Garrett imitated.

Meg slugged Garrett in the arm. "You guys."

Everyone cackled.

Meg suddenly began inspecting her herself. Beginning with the long white suede gloves, her eyes move up her arm and slowly down her torso on to her white high heels. "I'd just die if any of the guys back home saw me in this . . . this dress," Meg moaned in a distressed voice.

"I doubt that flight suit of yours would have cut the mustard, young lady," Rye pointed out. "You're making your father proud. Your mother was very beautiful in a gown," his voice trailed off.

Meg looked at her father, matching his sudden change of morale.

Garrett became instantly aware of the negative tone and jumped in to save the evening. "Hang in there, Sis. You look swell." He nodded in two directions in which young military pilots were trying to catch her eye. "From the looks of it, I'm not the only one who thinks so."

Rearing back, Meg slugged her twin's arm.

Trying to avoid the next stinging jab, Sean flinched backward, ramming into the black waiter, butting him into the group behind him. The drinks from his tray took a dive, splashing alcohol on the legs of those around.

The waiter straightened himself and glared at Garrett. "I

should have known—so typical of commoners," he grumbled arrogantly.

"Sorry," Garrett quickly apologized. His face turned beet red as he bent over to help retrieve the broken glass.

Meg hid her face with a massaging hand. "C'mon, quit it, you guys."

Rye rapped Garrett on the thigh with a crutch. "Knock it off, you two."

I excused myself from the group of reporters and strolled over to join the Reillys who were beginning to move away from the entrance, casually shaking hands and waving at well-wishers.

"Meg," I addressed her from behind.

She spun around, almost falling backwards. Sean thrust an open palm to catch his sister.

She blushed as she regrouped. "Brooks Brothers!" Her eyes billowed with excitement as she stepped forward to hug me.

Rye smiled as he reached around her to shake my hand. "Aaron."

"Captain." I smiled, half-staring at the gold medal hanging from a blue ribbon with white stars, draped around his neck. "This is the first time I've seen a Medal of Honor. It's beautiful."

Meg looked fondly at her father. "Very handsome and dashing, don't you think, Brooks Brothers?"

"The epitome of a war hero," I acknowledged.

Embarrassed, Rye turned his head to pan the room for familiar faces. "Anyone seen Bolden or Thomas?"

"Yes," I answered. "They're on the other side of that big group of military types."

I turned to Sean and Garrett who had their eyes glued to a gorgeous ash blonde in a stunning red gown with a string of pearls. Her soft hair was expertly styled, as were most of the other female guests. It was a fashion show.

Meg poked her brothers in the kidneys, startling both.

Garrett placed a hand over his heart. "I think I'm in love."

Sean looked at me with excited eyes. "Did you see that babe in the red?

"That's more action than two wildcats in a gunny sack,"

Garrett cooed.

"You guys are disgusting," Meg scowled.

I peered around Meg to get a better view, drawing a slap to the forearm. "God, you're as bad as they are. I swear," Meg uttered with a hint of jealousy.

Sean and Garrett cackled loudly and slapped at each other's shoulders, drawing admonishing stares from nearby sophisticates.

The waiter returned with their drink order, visibly perturbed that they had moved to the other side of the ballroom, forcing him to chase them down.

Sean grabbed a Budweiser and the shot of Jack Daniel's, raising the latter in a toast to his sister. "To the best pilot in the world."

I took a glass of champagne from the waiter to join in the toast. "Here, here," I responded.

"I'll second that," added Garrett, admiring his twin sister. "You sure showed Hub Martin a thing or two about flying."

"Here, here!" Sean chimed.

Meg looked into my eyes.

My heart was pounding. "Some pretty fantastic flying," I uttered.

"Definitely," Sean agreed, still eyeballing the girl in red. "Nice drop tanks."

"C'mon," Rye prompted us, beginning to move toward the cluster of Top Brass.

I rushed to deposit my empty glass on the waiter's tray while frantically trying to take a note pad from my inside tux pocket on the run. Meg was gesturing for me to hurry, giggling at my fumbling awkwardness.

"Get a grip on it, Brooks Brothers," Meg scoffed. "You'll be late for your own wedding."

The champagne was going straight to my brain. I was feeling pretty cocky, confident, and uncontrollably turned on by her. I wondered if my increased attraction to her was due to the attention she was suddenly paying toward Hub Martin, no matter how negative it seemed. I was sure that my green gills were showing.

She clutched my arm, squeezing it as she pulled me along.

A commotion near the entrance grabbed everyone's attention. Meg and I turned, peeking between heads to see who it could be. Jackie Cochran, the previous champion, was standing next to her husband Floyd, smiling pleasantly. Everyone applauded. It was a grand reception, befitting the out-going Queen of the Air, dressed elegantly in a blue-sequin, V-neck gown with a long string of pearls draped about her neck. Floyd was sporting a well-tailored black tux. Jackie and Floyd exchanged handshakes and greetings with those near the entrance.

Meg looked at her own, more simple dress. "She looks so.....so beautiful in that gown."

I stared into Meg's beautiful face. "As do you," I uttered reassuring.

Meg looked into my eyes then gave me a warm kiss. I sensed a heartbeat in my fingertips as my arms floated around her back in a warm embrace. I was under her spell. But I wondered how long her crush would last.

I caught something in my peripheral and glanced up. Jackie and Floyd were standing behind Meg.

"Congratulations, Meg," sounded Jackie. "Mr. Masters."

I nodded as Meg spun around on a heel, balancing herself with a hand in mine. A smile as big as a lion's den swallowed Meg's face.

"That was an incredible race," Jackie continued. "You have represented our gender with great distinction."

"You women are really showing us men a thing or two about flying," Odlum complimented.

"Thanks, Miss Cochran.....Mr. Odlum. That means a lot coming from you two."

"Maybe now the men will give us the respect we've earned," Jackie said, looking to me.

Meg beamed with pride. "We haven't even begun, Jackie."

Flash bulbs began blinding us. My fellow writers bombarded the two queens of the air to the point of being ridiculous.

I thrust up my free hand. "Gentlemen, please. One question at a time."

"Miss Cochran, do you think you could have won had you

entered the race?"

"The woman of the hour next to me deserves your attention, gentlemen." Jackie smiled at Meg. "This is your night, Meg. I'll talk to you more later." She shook Meg's hand, leaning in close. "I'd like to fly that gorgeous plane of yours."

"Dad would like that," Meg responded.

Floyd leaned toward Meg. "Please tell your father to contact me on Wednesday." He handed his business card to her.

Jackie and Floyd smiled as they excused themselves, sliding off into the crowd to continue their tour.

"Wow!" Meg howled as she turned to me. "You do know that Floyd is chairman of the largest airplane company in the world."

"I know. This could be your father's big break."

Again, the tall doors opened, causing everyone to turn. The crowd parted slightly, enough to see Hub Martin in a snow-white tux with a white-and-black lace shirt, white bow tie, and white bucks. A gorgeous, honey blonde in a black velvet, strapless gown was attached to his forearm. It was the same girl that had greeted him after the race.

The reporters and photographers picked up and moved through the crowd like a flock of geese, pushing and weaving through the crowd toward Hub.

Hub soaked up the attention like a sponge. With the blonde in tow, he began to stroll into the crowd like a high-pockets lawyer, exchanging handshakes, flirting with other women, rubbing up to military officials.

Meg was seething. "Hotshot looks like a sap in that ice cream suit."

Although her words were less than complimentary, I noticed that Meg was unable to take her eyes off Hub.

"Martin really bothers you, doesn't he?" I murmured, testing her.

She turned her head to face me. "Not in the least. Not at all," she uttered nonchalantly but unconvincingly.

Over Meg's shoulder, Hub spotted me and changed his course of direction.

"Good evening." Hub turned to his escort. "This is Aaron

Master's of *Aviation Life* magazine."

"Hi." She offered her long beautiful hand. "I'm Liz Hunter." I shook it. "It's a pleasure."

Hub addressed Meg who had yet to fully turn around. "I'm afraid we've never met," half-flirting.

Meg remained at a profile. "I'm afraid we have."

"Oh?" He had a puzzled look.

"I'm the pilot that whipped the pants off you today.....in that pregnant cigar." She turned to face him.

Hub lost his flirting grin as though someone had killed his puppy. Liz began talking to me, but all I could hear was Meg and Hub's words. I nodded at the right times but kept a close, protective vigil on her actions.

Flabbergasted, Hub looked Meg up and down with awe. This couldn't be the tomboy that had flown against him.

"I guess congratulations are in order," Hub sputtered.

"Thanks. . . . Hotshot."

"Hotshot?" he growled.

Craning her head back, Meg gave his all-white attire a smug look. "Very, very yachtish."

Liz turned her head to snicker.

Hub glanced down at himself then up, pointing at his own chest. "What in the hell is that supposed to mean?"

Meg rolled her eyes.

A photographer bounced up with his camera ready to shoot. "How about a shot, you two?"

Hub put his arm around Meg's shoulder and flashed a Hollywood smile. I noticed Meg resisting, forcing a smile just as the bulb flashed.

"Thanks." The photographer scampered off toward Jackie Cochran, his camera bag swinging back and forth to the point of knocking people over.

Hub kept a grip on Meg's shoulder as she addressed his escort, extending a hand. "Hi, I'm–"

"I know, Meg Reilly. I've been dying to meet you. I'm Liz. . . . Liz Hunter."

The handshake was warm and genuine.

"What a fantastic finish," Liz complimented her. "I don't suppose you'd give me your autograph, would you?"

Hub stopped flirting with a young brunette standing a few feet away and gave Liz a dirty look. "Some loyalty." He was seething.

Liz ignored him.

"Me?" Meg asked humbly.

"Of course," Liz responded. "I can't tell you how delighted I am to discover you are the pilot that won the race."

"Thanks. . . . Are you a pilot?" asked Meg.

"No." Liz took an event program setting on a nearby table and handed it to Meg She took it and began writing then gave back it to Liz.

Liz read it aloud. "There is no greater sensation than flying. You honor me beyond that. Best wishes flying, Meg Reilly."

The blond beauty looked at Meg dumbfounded. "But I'm not a pilot."

"You will be," Meg responded confidently. A slow smile grew, extending ear to ear.

Hub became impatient. "I broke your altitude record," he said matter-of-factly.

Liz winked at Meg. "It about killed him to lose the race so he went back upstairs."

"I heard," Meg noted. "So I went up this morning and topped you by 2000 feet."

Hub bit his tongue, refusing to look depressed. "That's all right. My sponsor agreed to a military contract offer just four hours ago."

"So what," Meg countered. "Floyd Odlum wants to do business with my dad."

Hub's veins in his temples were throbbing.

I figured I better change the subject. "Considering Frank Fuller came in third, you two are in good company."

"Thanks," Hub said. He grabbed Liz's hand and began to drag her away.

Liz rolled her eyes. "Nice to meet you, Aaron.....Meg. Thanks for the autograph."

"Bye, Liz," Meg responded, smiling.

Meg and I looked around for her father and brothers. Rye was pitching the prototype to the general's staff while Sean and Garrett were homing in on the redhead.

Rye rested his weight on one crutch. "General, you know goddam well that the Gerries are hackin' up Europe with their Messerschmidts," he barked.

"Poland's the crossroads to Moscow," Thomas professed. "They've been massing their troops along the border. I think it's only a matter of time, maybe days."

"Does that mean I get a contract?" Rye blurted.

Bolden raised his brow. "Captain, your pursuit is a marvelous piece of engineering." He took a deep breath. "If it were up to--"

Rye looked at Thomas who was gazing out the veranda doors. "What in the hell am I supposed to do for money in the meantime, Bob?"

Suddenly, Glenn Miller and his band took the stage and began playing "In the Mood."

Meg spotted Hub and his escort heading for the dance floor and grabbed my hand. "Let's dance, Brooks Brothers."

"You know, you're starting to give me a complex, calling me that," I joked then paused. "Hey, wait a minute. I thought you didn't like to dance."

"Maybe it's the booze," Meg cracked. "Lighten up, handsome." She clutched my hand and dragged me to the dance floor.

I couldn't help but notice that she was keeping a close watch on Hub who was doing the boogie-woogie.

"Show-off," Meg sneered, pulling me closer.

Suddenly, an Army colonel walked up briskly to Glenn Miller and spoke something in the band leader's ear. Glenn brought his baton around and down, signaling the band to stop immediately.

The colonel sidestepped to the microphone and spoke into it, causing it to shrill, forcing most guests to wince in their tracks.

His expression was granite. "Ladies and gentlemen, distinguished guests. I am sorry to cut the evening short. All military personnel have been ordered to report to their respective duty stations."

The shocked crowd buzzed with expressions of concern.

"I repeat, all military personnel are to report immediately to their respective bases."

The roomful of grace and dignity transformed into one of grave concern. As military officers began escorting their partners toward the main entrance, the civilian attendees tugged at them, pressing for more information.

My reporter nose went into action. "C'mon." I grabbed Meg's arm and hustled toward General Bolden. "General, Aaron Masters, *Aviation Life* magazine. What's going on?"

Without losing a step, he turned his head enough to answer. "The Nazis just invaded Poland."

CHAPTER 8

The parking lot and driveway were jammed with automobiles, limousines, and cabs trying to exit the party. Perspiring, frantic valets were busily trying to clear a path to expedite VIP vehicles while impatient civilians stood about, demanding immediate service.

Garrett and the redhead joined us on the front steps. "Where's Dad and Sean?" His head was swiveling back and forth, panning the crowd.

Standing on her toes, Meg strained to see over the now impolite crowd. "I lost sight of them."

Enlistment would soar in the morning. I studied Garrett. I knew from the look in his eyes that he planned to enlist. Sean, too. It was time for me to return to Europe where aviation was changing warfare.

Hub and Liz walked up behind us.

Garrett turned to Hub. "Joining up?"

"Of course," Hub responded. "As soon as the recruiting office opens."

Meg glanced at me. "Well, Brooks Brothers? What about you?"

"I'll be off to Europe, I suspect."

She gazed at me in shock. "Europe?"

"That's where the story is."

I spun around as Rye crutched up behind us. How I wished I could be a brain cell in that head of his about now. He was still the best combat pilot in the world, one leg or two. I looked back at Meg for a reaction. There was talk about the formation of a ferrying force in the event America entered the war. Someone would have to fly war planes from the factories to the ports of embarkation.

Jackie was standing with Floyd, waiting for their car. She was fidgeting as I walked up from their flank.

I addressed her. "Well, Miss Cochran?"

She glanced over her shoulder. "Mr. Masters," she said nondescriptly.

"I understand you've been talking to General Bolden about a female fer--"

She cut me short. "I've already been in touch with the British."

I was puzzled. "The British?"

"They offered me a consulting contract," Jackie explained. "Bo turned down my idea of training a female ferrying force if we go to war."

I looked at Floyd who shrugged his shoulders. "Jackie makes her own career decisions."

"Is that a yes?"

"Yes, Mr. Masters."

I excused myself and returned to Meg on the steps.

"So what did Jackie have to say, Aaron?" Meg asked impatiently.

"She's been offered a contract with the British to train pilots."

"Well, is she going?"

"Yep."

"That's typical," Rye murmured. "I reckon most of our experienced pilots will be in China or England soon. Bolden told me earlier that the Brits had already started recruiting volunteers for a special aviation unit called the Eagle Squadron."

I looked at Sean. "And what about you?"

A slow smile grew on his face. "Ah, heck, I suppose I'll check into it. I heard that General Chennault is looking for pilots in China."

"Not on your life, young man," Rye growled. "They'll be needin' our pursuit now, and I'll need all the help I can muster."

Sean took offense. "What about Garrett and Meg? They'll be around to help."

Garrett stuck his head into the action. "Speak for yourself, Sean. I'm joining up in the morning."

"Bullshit!" Rye snapped. "You're stayin' put."

Garrett flinched backward. "Jesus, Dad. I'm older than you were when you joined up."

Meg bunched her long hair in back. "Think I could pass for a man?" she uttered, lowering her raspy voice a full octave.

Sean glanced at her breasts. "Your hair–it's a dead giveaway."

Looking at Liz's well-endowed chest, Meg crossed her arms to conceal her modest bosom. Looking up, she noticed Hub was snickering. "Thanks a lot, guys."

* * * * *

The crowded train station was jammed with soldiers and sailors, clamoring for transportation back to their bases. Rye was hunched over his crutches, sad but reluctantly supportive of his son Sean. Unwilling to wait for neutral America to enter the war, his oldest son had volunteered to fly pursuits against the Japanese. He would be leaving on the next train for Great Falls, Montana. From there, he and other volunteer pilots would fly refurbished P-40 Warhawks to Alaska then on to Kumming, China, to join the Flying Tigers under the command of General Claire Chennault. Although drastically low on planes, pilots, parts, and supplies, the Flying Tigers were waging a courageous battle in India, Burma, and China against the invading Japanese with just four squadrons of volunteer pilots in P-40s decorated with the open jaws of a hungry shark. Now Sean's showman abilities would be tested in combat against the faster, more maneuverable Japanese Zero.

I was headed to Europe where there were strong intelligence indicators that Hitler was planning to invade England. But to be successful, he would have to soften up the British defenses and destroy the Royal Air Force. And that would have to be accomplished by air attacks.

Seats on civilian flights to Europe were booked solid so I found myself on a grungy, beat-up tin can of a supply transport ship to England. The seas were rough with storm, churning my stomach. I spent more time hanging over the rail than in my cramped, musty quarters. It was the longest, most agonizing trip ever. I vowed never again to travel by sea. When I arrived, I had lost 15 pounds.

Sean eventually reached China and had already bagged three Jap Zeros. I often marveled how the Flying Tigers could do it with aging P-40s, battered and bruised from overuse, a lack of spare parts and good tires, and low-octane fuel. Every pilot there feared being grounded at the slightest damage to his plane. Sean and his fellow pilots were exposed to constant bombing, strafing, and artillery attacks. Most of the pilots lived in bunkers just a few yards from their planes. Some, including Sean, slept in their cockpits to minimize reaction time.

In England, the pilots of the Eagle Squadron were learning to fly the British Spitfire. The squadron was comprised of Canadian and American volunteer pilots, readying themselves for the combat-tested German Luftwaffe.

The first Canadian troops arrived in England three days later, the same day that an air training agreement was signed with the rest of the British Empire. The day after Christmas, the first Australian pilots arrived, joining the American volunteer pilots, including Garrett Reilly.

It was early in the morning when I got a call at my hotel room in London. I fumbled with the lamp next to my lumpy bed, knocking over a stale drink of bourbon and water.

"Hel.....hello," I muttered.

"Aaron, did you hear?" It was my editor. "The Japs just bombed Pearl Harbor."

I cleared my parched throat. "Was there a land assault?" I reached out for a pack of Lucky Strikes and lighted one.

"So far, no," he responded. "Three waves of Zeros sank or disabled every damn ship in the harbor. Most of our Pacific Fleet was in port for the holidays. The Arizona went down with most hands aboard."

I sat speechless on the edge of the bed, trying to develop enough saliva to speak. "What about the Philippines?"

"Nothing yet. I want you to get over to Berlin and see what you can find out. The President will certainly ask Congress to declare war. Be careful, Aaron. The Nazis will be rounding up anyone they suspect is a spy."

"Don't worry. I have no desire to spend the war in some Gestapo torture chamber." I set the phone down, missing the hook. I let it dangle, too groggy to pick it up. I could hear rain striking the window as I stumbled into the bathroom and splashed water in my face. I gazed into the mirror. We had a war on our hands whether we wanted one or not. I pondered joining one of the Armed Forces. I knew that I could never hack it at sea, nor in the sky as an aviator. That left only the Army or the Marines. And I could never get drunk enough to join the latter.

Picking up the toothpaste tube, I squeezed. The metal seam separated, squirting gooey white paste all over my chest. "Shit," I uttered. I could see that it was going to be one hell of a day.

* * * * *

Meg boisterously charged into the cluttered hangar office. "Heard anything from Sean?"

Rye's ear was glued to the ham radio receiver. "Negative, I tried to get through to Kumming. The airwaves are busier than a one-armed paper-hanger. It's total chaos in China. I could hear gun shots just before the radio went dead."

"Jesus!" Meg hustled around the counter and sat on the edge of his desk, anxiously waiting for more information. "Have the Japs landed in Hawaii?"

"Not according to the radio chatter I picked up. The military is on full alert. Most of the entire Pacific Fleet was either sunk or disabled."

"It ain't fair," Meg uttered.

"What's that?"

"I've gotta hang out here while Garrett and Sean have all the fun."

"War ain't fun, believe me," Rye spouted, tapping his wooden leg with a free knuckle. Yet, the look on his face was one of disappointment.

Meg hopped off the desk and entered the hangar. There it sat, the most phenomenal fighter the world had ever seen. Meg sauntered over and climbed aboard. She settled in the cockpit seat and caressed the instruments, wondering why Floyd Oldum had temporarily reneged on his offer to manufacture the Mustang.

Rye soon appeared on his crutches in front of the left wing. He knew what she was going through. "You okay?"

"I want to take it up."

"We can't spare the fuel," Rye howled. "We need it for dust-croppin'."

"Oh, I know," Meg said solemnly. "Maybe the Army will wake up and give this baby a chance."

"I tried to place a call to General Thomas. Couldn't get through. The long-distance lines are all tied up."

"That figures," Meg sneered.

Rye turned on a single crutch and slowly limped back toward the office.

Meg climbed down and hurried to catch him. "Do you think Jackie might have a spot for me in England?"

Rye didn't turn or answer her. "Not on your life, young lady," he snapped. "Besides, I need you here."

"What, dustin' crops at five dollars a pop?"

"That's what is keepin' us in operation," he growled, high browing her. "If and when our prototype gets the nod, I'll need you here."

Meg took a deep breath and sighed. Her morale was at an all-time low. Her eyes peered upward, gazing at the sky. Her father noticed. Rye knew it would be only a matter of hours before America would declare war.

"It's going to be okay, Dad." She walked over to her father and hugged him. "I wish Aaron was here," she mumbled.

Rye broke the hug. "Have you heard from him lately?"

Meg shook her head. "Nope, the last time I heard from him, he was on a special assignment in Berlin."

And the bombs did rain. Europe and Asia fell even deeper into the Dark Ages. I couldn't help but think about the teachings of Richard Higgins, my former history professor at Yale. The Europeans had always had a penchant for war, torture, and massive defensive positions. The only difference was that massive underground bunkers constructed of concrete and steel, relatively immune to heavy bombing and artillery had replaced the large-stone castles. The catapult for attacking castles had been replaced by long-range, four-engine bombers. This was the beginning of the air wars such as the world had never seen.

In the days that followed, the Army Air Corps was renamed the Army Air Force. It was on that day, September 1, 1942, that Meg Reilly was to leave for ferrying duty.

****

The scene was all too familiar at Grand Central Station. Hundreds of recruits in civilian attire and soldiers in uniform were milling about, shaking hands with close friends and proud fathers, and hugging fearful mothers and sweethearts decked out in colorful summer frocks. The country had mobilized in a matter of months, thanks to the vast oceans that isolated America.

Rye had dropped everything at Reilly Flying Service to accompany Meg to the train station. The prototype that had been subsidized by Floyd Oldum was now perfected, and a huge contract was awaiting Congressional approval. It was to be called the P-51 Mustang. There was nothing more that Meg could do for her father. Now, it was her turn to take an active part in the war effort.

Meg was carrying a duffel bag over her shoulder and clutching her leather Gladstone bag, sifting through the crowd, running interference for her father as he crutched along behind her. The deck was lined with teary-eyed lovers saying good-by to their soldiers.

"Stubborn, that's what you are, Megan Reilly," Rye snapped. "You're just like your mother. I never kept your feet on the ground in the past, but--"

"Don't bring her into this," Meg retorted. "We've been over this a million times."

Meg stopped. "This is it. This is my car."

They squared off on one another. Suddenly, Rye couldn't stop talking. "You take care of yourself, you hear? Don't do anything foolish. Things can get pretty damn dangerous up there, even in the States."

"I know that, Dad. You act as though I've never flown before."

"But this is different. Other pilots will make errors. Manufacturers and mechanics will make mistakes."

Meg bit her lip, trying to avoid an argument. "I know."

"Make your father proud, Megan."

She wrapped her arms around his like a python then stood on her toes to kiss his cheek. "I love you, Dad."

His hands danced across her shoulders.

"Dammit, Dad. You just can't bring yourself to say it, can you?" Meg stammered.

"You know I do."

"All aboard!" shouted the conductor.

"I guess this is it," Meg announced, almost afraid to break his best hug ever. She gave him a peck on the cheek.

Surprisingly, he returned the kiss.

Wiping the tears with a first finger, Meg broke the hug. "Well, I guess it's time. Thanks for the use of your service duffel."

She half-squatted and shouldered the large, olive drab bag he had carried throughout World War I. She caressed it with her hand. This was a meaningful gift with all the patches and pins acquired from extensive military travel.

As Meg moved toward the car, the conductor standing next to the steps rotated his large hips so she could squeeze by his giant belly and climb the steps.

"Joining the WACS, huh, miss?"

"No, the WAFS!" Meg answered proudly.

A puzzled look crossed the conductor's chubby, milky face. "WAFS? What in daylights will this crazy government think up next?"

Within a minute, Meg's lonely but enthusiastic face appeared in a window, waving vigorously.

Rye forced a smile and nodded with his head. He rendered a casual salute then turned and crutched away before she could see his tears.

Meg sat back in her seat, pressing the side of her face against the cool window as the world whizzed by her excited eyes, hypnotized by the clanging of the wheels against the tracks. On her lap was the tattered diary, open to the last recorded page.

Queen of Aces 91

Behind his eyes I could see fear, fear that airplanes, which had given him everything in his life, could now take it all away. He will face it the only way he knows how--guns blazing and head on. And I was off to make him proud.

    The hot train car was crowded with a steady flow of hyper soldiers and recruits keeping on the move, introducing themselves to one another, boasting how they were going to show the Japs and Gerries a thing or two about fighting. A sizeable congregation of young studs remained near Meg, each vying for her attention.
    New Castle Army Air Base freckled with huge tin hangars and neat rows of wooden administration buildings, Post Exchange, and two-story barracks, many in the frame stage of construction, was nestled on a flat, sprawling Delaware plain. A heavy coat of dust blanketed everything in sight.
    Countless civilian workers and soldiers under the close supervision of Corps of Engineers personnel, were sawing and pounding nails to accommodate the demand for more troop housing, training, and operations facilities.
    A mix of prop planes cluttered the busy flight line and taxi area, including cargo and utility planes, pursuits, and trainers. Men and women in both civilian and military attire were hustling about, performing a multitude of duties. They would stop only to execute crisp salutes to passing officers. Squads and platoons of airmen and soldiers were riding to-and-fro in trucks or marching toward training and duty assignments with a variety of construction and military equipment.
    A beautiful blonde stepped out of a yellow cab, wearing an expensive-looking tweed blazer and tan slacks. Parted at one side, her long shiny hair draped her slender shoulders, falling to the small of her strong, youthful back.
    A stout M.P. in his mid-twenties, stepped out of a small guard shack, chest puffed to the point of bursting his shirt buttons. He gawked at the ravenous beauty who stood and stretched, pausing momentarily to gaze about with excited eyes.
    The chubby cab driver slowly emerged and waddled slowly

as he circled around to the trunk, breathing asthmatically. His short, fat fingers fumbled as he grasped the suitcase handle and flight bag strap. He grunted as he lifted them from the trunk and plopped them on the ground in front of the blonde. She handed him a five-dollar bill, motioning for him to keep the change.

The blonde shouldered her purse, picked up her bags, and plodded toward the statue-like M.P. who was staring through her.

"Good afternoon, Miss," he said with authority. "Your name and business, please."

"Elizabeth Hunter. I've come to join the WAFS." She smiled as she dropped her bags on the ground, nipping his right spit-shined boot.

The M.P. glanced down to check for damage then deliberately panned up slowly, checking out her shapely, long legs. "You got a letter or some orders?"

She held up a folded newspaper, pointing to an article circled in red. "The newspaper didn't say anything about needing any letter," Liz responded.

The M.P. executed an about-face and entered the guard shack, shaking his head. One of his bulky hands grasped a black phone.

"Ma'am, a fancy one just showed up.....no orders."

After a couple of nods, he set down the phone then approached Liz who, by now, had inched her way just outside the door. "Miss, they're sendin' a vehicle to pick you up." He stepped back into the shack and sat on a tall stool, stealing occasional glances at the blonde.

Within ten minutes, a jeep came to an abrupt halt just a few inches from Liz, causing her to hop backward. A thick cloud of dust from the skidding wheels forced her to turn her head. She fanned the air in front of her face as the skinny driver in duty fatigues slid out of his seat. The bill of his cap was turned up, and his neck was a straight line from his chin to the middle of his hairless, bony chest. He was a mass of freckles.

He awed her Helen-of-Troy face. "Y'all waitin' on a ride?"

Liz nodded, too excited to get upset with his obnoxious behavior.

The daffy soldier fetched her bags and lobbed them carelessly into the back. As Liz slid into the passenger seat, the driver took off the emergency brake and bolted into a U-turn. Liz grabbed the inside edge of the seat with her left hand to avoid being hurled out of the passenger side.

The jeep bounced along the gravel road, cluttered with sharp stones and potholes, leaving behind a violent tornado of churning dust. He swerved back and forth to avoid the large chuck holes, jabbering the entire distance, pointing out landmarks and points of interest. The ends of her long blond hair whipped her face as she struggled to clutch the edge of the seat with one hand and the top of the windshield with the other. What had started out as a simple taxi ride had become an adventure.

The route was a gauntlet of construction crews who whistled and hooted at Liz as the jeep whizzed by them. They passed a platoon of soldiers marching along to the cadence of their growling sergeant who got in their faces as they stole glances of the striking blonde.

Turning a sharp corner, Liz could see a large two-story wooden building with a large sign above the door reading: BASE HEADQUARTERS. A variety of colorful unit crests were neatly tacked to either side of the main doors along with battle slogans, instilling a sense of esprit de corps.

The driver slammed on the brakes, and the jeep skidded to a halt in front of the entrance, nearly throwing Liz into the windshield.

"Nice landing!" Liz snapped facetiously, stepping out.

The dust swirled about her as the smirking driver leaped off the seat and snatched her bags. "Here ya go!"

Liz straightened her blazer and combed her disheveled hair with her fingers as she hustled to catch up with the driver. Clutched in one hand were a weathered, black logbook and the folded newspaper. She stepped inside the entrance, closing the screen door behind her.

The boring gray and white walls of what appeared to be an outer office were simply decorated with a standard-issue bulletin board and a line of straight-laced chain-of-command photos in black frames perfectly spaced apart. Two marred, wooden desks, one with an ancient typewriter, and a gray metal filing cabinet were the only furnishings in this otherwise impersonal administrative area. Behind the typewriter was a nerdish-looking corporal who stopped pecking at the keys and executed a double-take. Behind the other desk was an attractive blonde of medium height in a baggy, khaki flying suit.

She stood to greet Liz. "I'm Nancy Love, Director of the Women's Auxiliary Ferrying Squadron. And you are?"

"Liz Hunter. I'm here to fly for the WAFS," she said pleasantly, looking at Nancy's less-than-attractive outfit.

The director smiled politely. "Do y'all have a letter of acceptance? Did you contact anyone about coming?"

Liz held up the newspaper, pointing to the relevant article. "It says here that a WAF unit is being created, so here I am," she bubbly announced, bouncing on her toes.

In her late-twenties, Nancy raised a brow as Liz leaned toward her with the open pilot's logbook. Nancy studied it as she walked around from behind the desk with a noncommittal expression. "Have a seat. I'll be right back."

She disappeared behind a nearby door. The sign on the entrance read:
COL ARTHUR STUDEBAKER
Base Commander

Liz began to fidget after several minutes, irritated at the cool welcome. She sat on a folding chair and stared at the commander's door. It finally opened and Nancy emerged with a serious look on her face. Liz suddenly realized her heart was thumping like an artillery barrage.

CHAPTER 9

Liz bolted to her feet. "Look, I got my commercial license in the spring, flew to Nashville to join the Air Transport Command, only to be told that women cannot fly for it. So, I went home, earned an instructor's rating, and got turned down as an instructor. One week later, the jerks hired two young guys as instructors. I--"

"Hold it," Nancy stopped her. "Your flight test is at 0800 hours tomorrow morning."

"It is?" Liz stammered with disbelief. "I've made it?" A large grin began to grow on her face.

"Providing you pass," Nancy noted.

"Oh, yes. Of course," responded Liz. She flashed a giant smile.

Nancy prompted her with an outstretched hand, heading for the front entrance. "Y'all can stay in the B.O.Q."

Liz looked puzzled.

"B.O.Q., Bachelor Officers Quarters," Nancy explained. The male officers loaned one to us.....Well, not really. We kinda hoodwinked it from them, if y'all know what I mean."

Nancy picked up Liz's flight bag. "C'mon, I'll take you over and introduce you to the other girls."

Liz leaned down, grasped the handle of her suitcase, and followed Nancy toward the door. Suddenly, a slender young black woman appeared on the step on the other side of the screen, wearing a worn, brown leather flight jacket and a new pair of gray slacks. A long, bright-red scarf hung loosely around her neck.

Nancy stopped abruptly. "Can I help y'all with something?" She found herself staring at the tall figure.

It did not take a genius to figure out why the black woman was there.

"I'm Thelma Washington. I have a letter from y'all," the black pilot stammered nervously. Perspiration beads began to form on her forehead.

An official looking document appeared in Thelma's free hand. "I'm here to join up."

Nancy opened the door, forcing Thelma to step backward. "Would y'all mind stepping over here to the side, Miss Washington?"

Smiling nervously, Thelma shuffled sideways a few short steps and stopped.

Nancy joined her. "Look, I can tell from your outfit that you're a solid pilot...."

Thelma quickly revealed her pilot's logbook, fumbling nervously to open it to the last recorded page.

"....But I can't consider you," Nancy finished.

"Because I'm a Negro?"

"They're are no provisions on this base for coloreds," Nancy explained. "Us white females are lucky enough to be flyin'. I'm sorry, Miss Washington." Nancy smiled sympathetically. "I truly am."

Emptiness swept Thelma's face. Managing to keep her head high with pride, she turned on a heel and walked away before they could see her weeping.

Liz turned to Nancy who shrugged with her hands. "There's nothing I can do. My hands are tied, and as you'll soon discover, I have enough battles to wage just to get us white girls into the air. Believe me, it would hit me the same way."

Thelma climbed into an old Ford coupe and executed a heady U-turn.

Liz watched until the black coupe was out of sight. "It isn't fair."

Nancy sighed with remorse. "We're both very lucky to be here."

A perky brunette in a pixy hairstyle and freckles walked up to

Nancy. Her 5'2" frame was drowned in men's khaki flying overalls, the cuffs of which had been rolled up several times. Mary was cute with a crank between her eyes.

"Nancy, what was that all about?" inquired Mary.

"Oh, hi, Mary. That colored girl was here to join up. She had a letter," Nancy answered. "Somebody overlooked something.....I've had a belly full of this political stuff. I only took the director's position so I could fly."

Mary smiled pleasantly at Liz. "Got another one, huh?"

"Mary, this is Liz....Hunter." Nancy looked at Liz for approval. "Right?"

"Yes.....Hi, Mary," said Liz, offering her hand. "Glad to meet you."

Mary shook her hand. "Mutual, I'm sure."

Suddenly, a white limousine with gold trim pulled to a stop. A square-jawed chauffeur in his mid-thirties in all-white attire, including the cap, gloves, and a satin bow tie, hustled around the car and opened the door.

Watching intently, Mary crossed her arms. "Now I've seen everything."

A mid-twenties, carrot-bright redhead swung her body around and took his hand. Her shapely pair of legs was the gate between two French poodles and freedom.

"Is this where the female pilots report in?" the redhead asked.

"Affirmative," answered Nancy. "What's your name?"

"Stacy Pitman from Beverly Hills, California," she answered bubbly, adjusting her mink stole with the other.

"I'm Nancy Love, Director of the Women's Auxiliary Fer--"

Both poodles, one white, one black, jumped over Stacy's bent knee and took off.

"Oh, you naughty boys!" Stacy sputtered. "Richard, please catch them before they get all nasty."

The driver let go her hand and began chasing the two romping K-9s headed for a nearby stream. Liz and Mary began to cackle, covering their mouths.

"Hurry, Richard!" Stacy turned to Nancy, shoving the stole at her. "Would you be a dear and hold this?"

Nancy looked down, surprised at the pile of fur in her arms. She turned to the others, meeting astonished expressions.

"Mary, would y'all take Liz over to the B.O.Q. and introduce her around?"

"Sure." Mary grinned. "C'mon, Liz. One nickel tour coming up."

Before Mary and Liz rounded the corner of the building, Stacy was standing at the top of the bank, barking out instructions. Soon, the glazed-eyed chauffeur appeared, walking up from the creek, carrying a wiggling, muddy poodle under each arm. Richard's white uniform was covered with thick, brown mud to his waist. His shoes sloshed with each step.

Stacy commenced scolding the poodles as the irritated, stone-faced chauffeur stomped back toward the limo, drawing laughter from a gallery of soldiers and WAFs congregating outside the Headquarters Building. Nancy looked at the gawking crowd and rolled her eyes. Just a few days into the program, and the WAFs were already the laughing stock of the base. This was not the beginning Nancy had envisioned.

"Oh, boy," Mary shuddered. "This squadron is getting to be a very interesting bunch."

The Bachelor Officers' Quarters was nothing more than a two-story wooden structure painted battleship gray. Every window was open. A giant floor fan blasted air down the corridor, trying to keep the stuffy air moving. A mixture of perfume and cigarette smoke filtered past them as they entered through the screen door.

Most of the doors to the two-person rooms were open, providing good light in the long narrow hallway. Passing by the first room, Liz spotted a group of early arrivals talking loudly about their flight tests, filling the building with boisterous laughter.

Mary poked her head in the door. "Girls, this is Liz."

A chorus of "Hi, Liz," echoed down the hallway.

Many were very attractive and dressed in expensive casual civilian shorts and dresses. Four rested a tennis racket on their lap.

Liz smiled. "Hi, everybody."

"Where ya from?" yelled one.

"Philadelphia," Liz answered.

"We're neighbors," responded another. "Trenton, New Jersey!"

"Manhattan, Kansas," spouted a slender one in a straw cowboy hat.

"Asheville, North Carolina," announced a long-haired brunette with a soft, Southern drawl.

"Fort Myers, Florida," blurted another. "Drop your bags. We were just about to invade the O' Club."

"We'll be right along," Mary responded, "after I get Liz situated."

Liz and Mary peeked briefly in each room, looking for a vacancy. One girl was sleeping, another lying on an unmade mattress, writing a letter, her bare heels bobbing up and down.

When they reached the end of the hallway, Mary turned. "It looks as though you've got three to choose from, including this one."

"Great, right next to the bathroom," Liz exclaimed.

"You won't think so about four in the morning," Mary cracked. These hens make a lot of noise."

Liz snickered as they entered a two-person room half-way down the hall. Liz found matching steel-framed beds, wooden foot lockers, and two steel wall lockers. Stacked at he head of each bunk were two folded sheets, a pillowcase, pillow, and a rolled mattress.

Liz lobbed her bags on one of the beds, but as she started to leave, Mary stood in her way.

"Do you have a lock?" inquired Mary.

Liz shook her head. "Uh, uh."

"You best put your stuff in the foot locker and take your valuables with you."

"You mean we have a thief among us?" Liz uttered naively.

"It's regulations," Mary specified. "Besides, this building is open, if you know what I mean. Valuables have a tendency to grow legs."

"Gotcha. My money's in my purse." Liz crammed both pieces of luggage in the foot locker, rolled out the mattress to lay claim to a bunk, and joined Mary who was standing in the hallway.

Mary shut the door and stuck a note in the crack, reading: "Do not disturb."

"Clever idea," Liz complimented her.

"Thanks. I have my moments," said Mary proudly, shining her nails on her uniform. "C'mon. There's some real dishes hangin' at the O-Club, just ripe for the pickin'."

Liz and Mary quickly climbed the steps of the Officers' Club Annex, a single-story building that looked like all the others except for a few battle slogans and military crests neatly painted on signs tacked to the siding. They could hear everybody singing along to "Blue Skies" by Frank Sinatra.

"More testosterone here than a western rodeo," Mary commented.

"Yuck!" Liz coughed as they entered. "Cigar smoke. Whew!"

"Smells like burning hemp," Mary continued. "Helps these boys feel like real men. Hell, most of them don't shave yet," Mary chuckled, "much less grow hair on their chest."

Two large fans on tall pedestals were positioned behind the tables, straining to keep the stale smell of alcohol and smoke moving.

The conversation picked up as Liz moved away from the intense sunlight. Her eyes adjusted to the darker light as she panned the tables for the other WAFs. Suddenly, she realized that every man in the club was staring at her.

"Looks like a grazing area to me," Liz remarked facetiously.

Mary chuckled. "Move 'em or lose 'em, fellas."

The duo navigated the sea of crisscrossed legs and misarranged chairs, ignoring the clicking fingers and suggestive lines as they sauntered toward the other WAFs who were sitting at two square tables that had been moved together. Four macho pilots swooped down for the kill, hustling with wing guns blazing.

A lone pilot scarred from a bad case of teenage acne, stood at the bar near the massive jukebox. He continued to gawk at Liz, snapping his fingers, singing loudly to the Sinatra tune.

A chorus of greetings and applause erupted from the WAFs as Mary and Liz reached the their tables.

A baby-faced, chunky brunette with short hair and an enormous chest, stood and smiled. "I'm Judy Jasinski, Hamtramck, Michigan. My friends call me Ski." She offered a handshake.

"Liz Hunter, Philadelphia." Liz smiled. "It's a pleasure to meet you, Ski."

Ski reached around and picked up an empty chair with one hand as though it was made of balsa wood. She lifted it over the head of a male pilot sitting next to her and set it on the floor. "Here, plop your bod. We're swappin' B.S. with the guys."

"Yeah, watch where you step," added Mary. "It can get pretty deep."

Liz smirked. "I see what you mean."

Ski took a drag off a cigarette. "Want a brewski or something?"

"Yeah, a vodka martini up," Liz answered. "So when did you check in, Ski?"

"Three days ago." Ski signaled a waitress for service.

"Had a flight check, yet?" asked Liz.

"Oh, God, I gotta tell you," Ski burst with excited eyes. "The check pilot, Lieutenant Livingston, used to be one of my flight students a couple of years ago. He's really cute. Anyway, I executed some spins and snap rolls and was leveling off when we spotted a flock of birds. Suddenly, this kid grabbed the stick and chased them at full-throttle."

"You're kiddin'!" Liz sat wide-eyed. "What did you do?"

"I was so dammed shocked that I forgot he wasn't my student any longer and chewed his ass out," Ski cackled. "When we got on the ground, he stalked off with a stone face."

"Well?" Liz prompted her. "Did you pass?"

"Yeah," Ski said with a growing smile.

"We'll be flying in good company." Ski turned in her seat and pointed at a tall, stout, somewhat attractive woman with pouty lips at the far end of the table. "The one with boxy shoulders, Edith Dreisbach, is the wife of a pursuit pilot in England. They used to operate their own airport before the war. Flo, the one with the black hair pulled back, sitting kitty-corner from you, is the daughter of a well-connected Italian family."

Mary stuck her head between them. "Word has it, her daddy is Mafia. She's already pushing her big hips around."

"I think she's nice," Ski countered.

"Oh yeah," Mary challenged. "Yesterday, I was dancing with this guy, and she horned in. Flo is a piranha."

Liz leaned on the table and scanned the other faces. "Who are the others?"

"Mildred, across from you in the Shirley Temple curls, is the daughter of a Chicago commodities broker. Lots of bucks. Joann, two over from you, is the heiress of a grocery chain in the Carolinas." Ski leaned close to Liz, shielding her words with a cupped hand. "Mary's folks own half of downtown Reno."

Edith chimed in, "We figured up our average hours. Eleven-hundred each."

"One of the girls was a Bendix winner back two or three years ago," Ski added.

Liz's eyes brightened. "Meg Reilly?"

"Yeah, you know her?"

"I got her autograph after the Bendix race," Liz answered. "I used to date the jerk she trounced in the race. Where is she?" Liz pushed up on the arms of her chair and looked around the club.

"Where she's been since she arrived." Mary pointed upward. "Flying."

Liz stood and walked toward the entrance, ignoring the rude comments and flirtations. Before she reached the screen door, a shapely figure in khaki flying overalls appeared. The glaring afternoon sun blinded Liz. The rays beamed around the figure's legs onto the floor. Everyone quieted and turned in their seats as the screen door swung open with crispness.

"Got an ice-cold Bud in here?" sounded a husky female voice.

Liz stopped walking and grinned. "Meg, remember me?"

Meg proceeded with confidence, trying to focus her eyes in the darker surroundings. "Who is it?"

"Liz....Liz Hunter."

A big smile crossed Meg's tanned face. "How could I forget my first autograph. How in the hell are ya?"

They hugged briefly.

"This calls for a drink. C'mon," Liz prompted her toward the bar. "Finally, someone I recognize."

"I know what you mean," Meg responded bubbly. "God, it's

great to see you."

As they proceeded arm-in-arm toward the bar, the male pilots stared at the two best-looking women that ever set foot in the club.

One had a nasty scar on his chin. "Things are looking up," he flirted.

Meg and Liz ignored the rude comments and undressing eyes of the two pilots at the bar as they pulled up to an open spot.

"A Bud and a vodka martini up," Liz ordered. "With a breath of Vermouth."

The hefty bartender flipped a white bar towel over his shoulder and went to work.

"God, you'd think these guys never seen a woman before," Liz sneered.

"They haven't till now," Meg jested as she reached into a pocket, took out a nickel, and flipped it in the air, smartly catching it. "What we need is some real music in here."

Meg and Liz walked past the acne-faced pilot on their way to the jukebox, ignoring his lustful stare. They studied the play list then selected "I'll Be Seeing You" by the Tommy Dorsey Orchestra with Frank Sinatra singing the vocals.

Shirley, Flo, and two other WAFs began dancing with the male pilots sitting at their table.

"Good choice," Liz agreed, turning back toward the bar.

The acne-faced pilot stuck his legs out to block their path. "Hey, baby, want to club a rug?"

"No thanks, baby," Meg sneered.

The pilot reached out and grabbed Meg's hand as she stepped over his feet. "Hey, don't make me look like a fool in front of the guys. Dance with me, or I'll break your damn arm."

Meg tried to pull away, but his grip tightened. "Remove the paw, or lose it!"

"C'mon, you know you came over here just to meet me," he persisted.

Meg glared at his hand. "I don't dance out of my species."

His grip tightened. "A tough broad, huh?"

"Watch it, Buster," Meg snarled. "I can go to bitch in 4.5 seconds."

Liz nervously chuckled.

The bartender was keeping a close watch over the disturbance. He reached for a ball bat setting upright against the back bar.

"I guess I'm all yours, Lieutenant," she smiled slyly.

As a smug smile grew on his face, Meg looped his hand in a Judo move and flipped him, slamming his body hard onto the floor.

"What was that you said about arms?" She grinned slightly.

Embarrassed by the cackling, heckling crowd, the acne-faced pilot slowly got to his feet and dusted off his uniform. "Goddam bitch! I'll get you for this."

Meg ignored him as she grabbed the longneck off the bar and paid the bartender for the drinks.

"Pretty slick move, Miss," the bartender smiled. "Whereja learn that stuff?"

"My older brother." Meg smiled as she turned to Liz. "Let's join the others."

CHAPTER 10

The jukebox changed songs. A half-dozen WAFs and male officers began cutting it up with a variety of jitterbug steps on the dance floor to "Stompin' at the Savoy." as Meg and Liz joined Ski, Edith, and Mary at the table.

Hi, gang," Meg sounded.

"What in the hell was that all about?" asked Edith with a startled look.

"A drunk punk who can't hold his liquor," Liz answered.

Ski's eyes were wild. "Boy, Meg, did you ever teach him a thing or two." She sat down for a breather. "That was some fancy move."

Meg and Liz plopped down next to Ski and Mary. Edith moved a few seats closer to talk.

Meg took a drink of beer. "So when did you start flying, Liz?"

"At Vassar." Liz sipped her martini. "With a Ford tri-motor, no less."

"Then you shouldn't have any trouble flyin' the planes here." Meg peered around the table. "Have you met everyone?"

"Yeah, they all seem nice." Liz looked at Meg. "I'm especially looking forward to flying with you."

Meg's eyes panned the faces. "Looking around, you'd think that we enjoy being guinea pigs."

"The chauvinists are standing in the wings," Edith chimed in, "just waitin' for us to lose our struts."

"Like that nitwit I used to be married to," Ski sneered. "I'd get home after teaching for ten friggin' hours, and he'd start in about dinner not being on the table. Hell, he only worked six-hour shifts at the cannery. Then he'd go down to Eddie's Pool Hall and slam down longnecks till dark."

"I used to go steady with a ditz like that." Meg's eyes stole looks around the club. "So, what happened, Ski?"

"I flipped him a box of macaroni and cheese and walked out," Ski cracked, drawing snickers from the others.

Meg looked back at Liz. "Whatever happened to Hotshot Martin? I thought you two were an item."

"Hubert?" Liz mocked. "You're asking about good ole Hubert Martin?"

Meg laughed at her tone. "Hubert, huh?.....Is he still in love with himself?"

"You hit that one on the head," Liz howled. "He's a legend in his own mind."

"Aren't they all," Ski sneered.

"Except for my brothers," Meg boasted. "They're the--"

"So ole Hubert got to you, huh?" Liz interrupted. She studied Meg's face for the reaction.

Meg looked away, blushing. "That egomaniac? You must be kidding. I've got other plans for my life."

Liz smirked. "So, how are those two good-looking brothers of yours?"

The grin on Meg's face grew wider. "Sean was in China flyin' P-40s with the Flying Tigers." She sat back with a proud look on her face. "He bagged five Jap Zeros before his transfer."

"Wow! An ace," Liz exclaimed. "You and your dad must be really proud."

"Yeah, now, he's with 23rd Fighter Group. Some of the Flying Tigers, including Sean, were absorbed into the Army Air Force once we officially entered the war. He's a First Lieutenant now," Meg bubbled. "Garrett enlisted in the Army Air Force. He's with the 8th Air Force, flying B-17s."

"Wow!" Liz hummed, pausing. "Heard from Aaron Masters?"

"Brooks Brothers?" Meg purred. "Yeah, a couple of centuries ago. Na, he's all wrapped up in his news job."

Liz's mouth dropped open. "Look who's calling the kettle

black." She paused. "He's sweet on you, you know."

Meg nodded, shaking her head. "I had a crush on him a million years ago."

"You were jail bait then," Liz noted. "Hey, girl, I want him if you don't." Liz flicked her brows. "What a dish."

Meg blushed, grinning.

"Ever make love to him?" Liz asked devilishly.

"Cool your engines, Liz." Meg turned and rested her elbows on the table. "Did you hear the latest about Jackie Cochran?"

Liz set down her martini. "In reference to what?"

"Dad said that she approached Bolden about a women's ferrying force better than a year ago, claiming that it would release a great number of male pilots for combat duty. Word has it, he shot it down cold."

Edith stopped drinking and pointed her beer bottle at Liz. "Doesn't surprise me a bit."

Liz scrunched her forehead. "So what happened to change his mind?"

"About ten days ago, Jackie finished up her contract with the British and flew back to New York." Meg took a swig of beer. "When she arrived, she picked up a newspaper. Damn near had a stroke when she read about a squadron being formed up without her. Thought Bolden double-crossed her."

Ski snickered. "Really pissed, huh?"

"Steamin' is a better word for it." Meg shook her head. "I hear she kicked the shit out of the newspaper racks. The old fart that runs the news stand was so scared, he took refuge behind his shack."

Laughing hard, Liz moved closer. "So tell me all the juicy stuff that happened."

"Put it this way. The newspapers couldn't print what she said," Meg chuckled. "Ole Jackie barged into Bolden's office with that article rolled up in her fist and pounced on him, demanding an explanation. He swore that he had nothing to do with it. True or not, he convinced her that the Secretary of War instigated the whole thing during his absence from Washington."

"Oh to have been a fly on the wall," Edith cooed.

"Meg, do you think Jackie believed him?" Liz's eyes sparkled with anticipation.

Meg shrugged. "Hell no. Jackie's long-range plan is to train female pilots, but while she was in England, Nancy's brother who works for General Nelson, was putting a bug up his boss's ass so Nancy got a shot at the title. Chickenshit Bo left town unexpectedly the morning of the announcement. He had to know. It's not like he had been gone a week or two and couldn't get back. By the time Jackie found out about it, the WAFS deal was signed, sealed, and delivered. Bo gave her the training school to shut her up." Meg took a swig of beer. "He swore up and down that he didn't know that Stimson was going to implement the plan. Supposedly, they were only to conduct a study."

"If something goes wrong," Edith inserted, "Stimson gets the blame."

"Very political, if you ask me," Liz murmured.

"Dad's dead sure that Bo was in on it from the beginning. Cochran's plan called for women to be permanent Army personnel. Nancy's plan is temporary. Not threatening to their male ego. When they're through with us, we're history.....out of their hair."

"Par for the course." Liz scoffed. "Just like I got treated by the A.T.C."

"Rumor has it that Bo's gonna give Jackie the training program," Meg noted. "She'll be instructing would-be female pilots."

"But I thought you said that he's against anything permanent?" Liz sipped her martini, puckering from too much Vermouth.

"Don't you see? The precedence has been set. Nothing will be long-term. They'll never get it out of Congress by the end of the war. By then, we'll be gone." Meg paused. "Look, I like Jackie, don't get me wrong, but when you're married to one of the biggest aircraft manufacturers in the world who's got half of Congress in his hip pocket, strings get pulled. Bo's a politician as well as a general."

"He'll make a great Presidential candidate someday," Liz sneered facetiously.

Meg laughed. "Covers his tracks well, doesn't he?"

"I've only been here a short time," Liz murmured, "and I already feel very used."

"Something tells me, we ain't seen nothing yet." Meg finished her beer.

Mary snickered. "Thank God Nancy isn't into the political stuff. She only accepted the Director's position so she could ferry aircraft."

"That political, huh?" Liz said it more like a statement.

Edith took a sip of beer. "Just watch. Don't be surprised if Jackie eventually gets the whole program under her wing. She has designs on being a general some day.....of her own branch of women pilots."

"That should prove to be interesting, if and when it happens," Liz added. She finished her martini then popped the olive in her waiting mouth.

"Now, do you want to hear the bad news?" Meg blurted, slugging down the last half of her beer. "Congress screwed up. The two-faced jerks made no provision for making us officers or paying us."

"That wasn't a screw-up," Liz growled. "It was a planned screw-job."

"Liz is right." Edith leaned forward in her chair. "Female pilots can't be legally commissioned in the WAFS until the legislation is amended."

"If you ask me," Ski surmised, "Congress did it on purpose, clear and simple."

Liz was sitting, open-mouthed.

"It's like a man with a full bladder and no pecker," Ski continued. "Just ask Mary. She knows."

Mary stopped dancing when she heard her name. "What's that, Ski?"

"Mary, tell this babe in the woods about the pay."

Holding onto her partner's hand, Mary stepped closer. "Dad said that we cut our own throats by not waiting until those slippery politicians pass an amendment."

"Hold it!" Meg snarled, clearing her throat. "Don't you guys get it? They don't want our help. This was Eleanor Roosevelt's idea, not theirs. They'd rather be short aircraft in the combat zone than let us women get a foot in the door."

Edith reached for her drink. "We've already got a foot in the door just by showing up here."

"That may be true." Meg took a sip of beer. "But take a page from my past. A number of skeptics had the gall to suggest that my brother Garrett piloted my Dad's prototype in the Bendix, and that we pulled a switcharoo just before the finish line."

Liz shook her head. "You must be kidding. Even Hubert didn't come up with a lame excuse like that. Talk about male insecurity."

Edith suddenly looked pale. "I wish Dick and I hadn't sold the airport now," she moaned. "Eventually, we'll win this war, and when we do, one hell of a lot of male pilots will be coming back, looking for civilian pilot jobs. If we thought it was tough finding a flying job before the war, it'll be worse after it's over."

"Some progress, huh?" Ski uttered facetiously. "Seems like us women are headed in the wrong direction."

Liz took a fresh martini from the waitress and paid her. A bewildered look overcame her half-drunken eyes.

Meg cocked her head. "Liz, what in the hell is wrong with you. You look like someone just shot your puppy."

"I've been shut out at three organizations, and now that I've found one, I'm not going to get paid. What a bunch of horse pooh." she stammered.

"Horse pooh?" Ski mocked. "The word is *horseshit*."

"Yeah, horseshit!" Liz snapped.

The others cackled at her tone.

"Bo cut a deal with the devil, if you ask me," Edith piped up. "He sacrificed our future security by hiring us as provisional civil service employees."

"That means that if we get paid, we'll get just $250 a month," slurred Mary. She downed the better part of a fresh beer. "The men get $380. That's 50 percent more."

"Pure bullshit," bellowed Ski. "It's damn unfair."

Meg grabbed a fresh longneck off the table. "Then we'll just have to be twice as good." She guzzled a third of her Budweiser.

"Get this," Mary continued. "Nancy told me just yesterday that we'll be limited to a 200-horse power rating, and that we'll have to go through a 40-day training orientation. Male ferrying pilots don't have to do either, and most don't have half the hours we do."

"Your dad's prototype had a 1600-horse power rating in the Bendix, didn't it?" Edith noted.

"Yeah." Meg nodded. "It's kinda like goin' from an Indianapolis racer to a Ford sedan."

Mary snickered. "The men can be 19 to 45 years of age; us girls, 21 to 35. Everybody knows that women mature faster than men."

"That's stinkin' discrimination," added Ski. "So much for women's suffrage."

"Twenty-one, 19, 35, 45. What does it matter?" Meg snapped. "There's nobody even close to 35, much less 45, in this here group. The war will be over before we have to worry about it." She tipped her longneck and took several swallows. "We're all forgetting something, girls. We're gettin' the opportunity to fly. That sure beats the hell out of working in some hot, smelly jeep factory for two-bits an hour."

"But it's the sonofabitchin' principle!" Ski barked. "That's what!"

"Meg's right," Liz agreed. "We'll just have to be twice as good as the men."

"Even so, get ready for complete humiliation," Edith warned them.

"They'll be dumpin' on us every time we get behind a friggin' joystick," Ski howled. "Mark my words. I betcha they'll ground us when we're on the rag."

"Your language," Edith scowled.

The other WAFS joined her in laughter.

"I heard that," sounded a rich, deep voice from behind.

Turning in her seat, Ski found herself confronted by a bulging crotch. Her mouth dropped open, and her eyes panned upward several feet. He had a homely but rugged face.

"I'm in love," Ski stammered, staring into his eyes.

"Hi, I'm Bob.....Bob Reynolds." His eyes seemed glued to her well-endowed blouse. "My friends call me California."

Behind him were three more Army Air Force pilots with cocky grins, surveying the WAFs, moving in for the kill. None looked old enough to shave. "Blue Skies" by Frank Sinatra began to boom from the jukebox. Everyone in the bar stood as they began to sing along. Beer mugs and mixed drink glasses swung wildly back and forth in sync with the lyrics.

"Well, cop a chair, California. I'm Ski." She stared at his behind. "Well, pinch my titties."

The other three male pilots raced to grab empty chairs from nearby tables and squeeze in between Liz and Meg.

Flo spotted the action from the far end of the table and wasted little time joining them, easing herself between Ski and California. "Hi, I'm Florence," she said, bubbling in her seat.

Ski's mouth dropped open. "Such gall," she murmured at Meg.

Mary leaned toward Meg. "I trust you brought along your shovel. The BS is about to get deeper."

Meg snickered. "Yeah. Looks like a full-court press to me."

Flo pouted as she stood and moved back to her end of the table. Mary winked at Ski. "What a bitch," she lipped.

Ski snickered.

The blond pilot with a strong, square jaw introduced himself to Liz. "I'm Billy Ray Johnson from Mobile, Alabama," he drawled.

"I'm Liz." She smiled kindly at him.

Billy Ray grinned. "You're as pretty as a new-born filly."

Liz winked at Meg. "How nice of you to say so, Billy Ray."

Billy Ray glanced at his freckled-faced buddy with a handsome, boyish face who had seated himself on the other side of Meg. "That's Hondo."

Meg turned to him, her brow wrinkled with humorous sarcasm. "Hondo?"

"That's what my friends call me. My real name is Mike Halloran." He noticed her freckles. "I know this sounds like a line, but you look awfully familiar. Where you from?"

Liz leaned toward Hondo. "That's Meg Reilly."

Hondo pondered briefly. "That sounds awfully familiar.....Meg Reilly, Meg Reilly, he uttered to himself.

"She just happens to be the reigning Queen of the Air," boasted Liz.

"Of course. You won the '39 Bendix. I was there. Wow, what a finish." Hondo turned to his buddies. "Hey, guys, this here's the gal that trounced ole Hub in the Bendix."

"You know Hub?" Meg inquired.

Hondo nodded. "Yep. Trained together at Pursuit School."

"Is he here?" Meg asked, bobbing her head to look around their shoulders.

"Nope," Hondo answered. "Stayed on to train pilots."

Meg noticed that Liz was grinning. "What?"

Liz smirked. "So, Hubert didn't get to you, huh?"

"Hardly," Meg retorted defensively. "He's too in love with himself."

"You've got that right," Liz attested, rolling her eyes. "We didn't last long. Hubert likes his women barefoot and pregnant."

"Don't they all?" Meg cracked.

Glancing at the bar, Meg noticed the acne-scarred pilot glaring at her, and stopped laughing. "Hondo, do you now that pilot standing at the bar? The one smoking a cigarette."

Hondo hiked himself up in his chair enough to see. "No. Why?"

"I had a run-in with Crater-face there before you guys rolled in."

Hondo shook his head. "Must be new."

"I think his name is LaRocca," answered California. "Reported in a couple of days ago. Keeps to himself."

"You should have been here to see Meg in action," Liz pointed out. "Put him on his ass."

Meg turned her attention to Hondo who had been watching her every move. "So what are you guys flying?"

"Pursuits. So do the others. But for now, Billy Ray and I will be instructing you on the trainers," he announced.

"Drinking with the enemy," Mary sneered.

"Hey, we're nice guys," Billy Ray protested. "When we get done with you, y'all be able to take apart and reassemble an engine."

Liz looked at her fingernails. "Does that mean we have to handle nasty ole grease?"

The others broke out in laughter.

"Of course," Hondo snickered.

"Just put hot wax under your nails," Ski spoke up. "It'll keep the grime from staining your nails."

"Boy, now I've heard everything," Hondo chuckled, looking at his own fingernails. "Hot wax, huh?"

"Yeah, hot wax," Ski confirmed. "Think you could handle the pain?"

California took a pack of Pall Mall cigarettes from his flight jacket and lighted one. "If you can, I certainly can," California blurted.

Ski rolled her eyes. "Get off it."

Liz noticed LaRocca headed for the door, glaring at Meg as he opened the screen door. "Meg! Craterface is leaving."

As Meg looked up, LaRocca pretended to shoot her with a forefinger.

Liz shivered. "Uh! That guy gives me the willies."

CHAPTER 11

It was very difficult to maintain a personal relationship considering my vocation. And once the war was on, one-night stands seemed to be the order of the night, but my thoughts never left Megan Reilly. She had a grip on my heart like a vice.

I never knew from one day to the next where my editor was going to send me. Once Roosevelt and Congress had declared war on the Axis powers, I got the hell out of Germany. I immediately flew to France and worked out of the Paris Bureau, reporting on the air war which was becoming more intense as the days passed.

It was there that I met Nicole, a pretty model that I had met at a New Year's Eve party held at the American Embassy. We had been seeing a lot of each other, but my thoughts constantly drifted toward the First Lady of the Air. Then the Germans moved into Paris, and I was evacuated to London. I tried to coax Nicole out of harm's way, but to no avail. She was an important member of the French Underground, a contact that would become very useful as the war progressed. As we walked toward the transport, arm-in-arm, I wondered if she had any idea of the danger that lie ahead. We held an embrace until the portable stairs were about to be pulled away. As the plane taxied, I sensed it would be the last time that I would ever see her.

I took a beat-up passenger plane to London and immediately visited the Aviation Life Bureau Office. The long hours Bureau Chief Mike McCartney had been spending on the job showed in his face. His eyes were sunken and red. Most of the young male reporters had already returned to the States to enter military service. I spent the next four hours briefing Mike on the evacuation of Paris and filing my riveting story about the German conquest of the French capital.

Although short-handed, Mike's assistant, Bea, took the time to help me arrange for a room, modest as it was at a nearby boarding house. Later that evening, I joined her and Mike for roast beef and Yorkshire pudding at a pub, rebuilt in 1667, called the Cheshire Cheese, located in an alley off Fleet Street. The only females were employees, not a single one attractive. Needless to say, Bea, dressed in a stunning black evening dress, was the center of everyone's attention. She was always upbeat and vivacious. We enjoyed the piano music and later played darts. I couldn't help but think about Meg's dart release. It was like everything else in her life - unique.

*****

The quiet flight line sparkled in the early morning sun as Liz reported to the flight line with an enthusiastic, youthful bounce. A slender male pilot in his mid-twenties, stood waiting, clipboard in hand, tapping his right foot impatiently. A single gold bar on his shirt collar sparkled in the brilliant sunlight. His name tag read: LT. LIVINGSTON.

Liz brought herself to an abrupt halt. "Hi, I'm Liz Hunter. I'm here for--"

"Get in!" Livingston barked, pointing at a nearby trainer. "I've got five more like you."

Taken back by the lieutenant's abrupt tone, Liz comically imitated his manner as she quick-stepped toward the trainer, climbed up the fuselage, and slid into the front cockpit. "Five more like you," she lipped to herself.

Livingston spotted her lips moving. "Did you say something?"

Liz shook her head as she reached forward to start the engine.

Soon the single-winged trainer was on the move, taxiing toward the runway.

"Take it up to 5000 feet, Hunter," Livingston ordered.

The wheels lifted off smoothly. Liz then pulled back hard on the stick and directed the trainer into a steep climb before leveling out at 5000 feet.

Livingston dropped his eyes briefly to record his evaluation of her performance thus far. Without looking up from the clipboard, he snapped his next instructions. "Show me a stall then some spins."

Liz cut back on the throttle and brought the nose up to a point where both wings stopped flying. The air flow over the wings began to break up, enough to reduce the plane's lift. Suddenly, the nose dropped and the trainer began plunging downward. Liz built up enough air speed then shoved the stick to the right. The trainer began to rotate on the tip of the right wing, spinning around and around for nearly 20 seconds like a carnival ride. Liz brought the stick back and left then increased the throttle. She leveled the trainer and awaited her next instructions. "So far, so good," Liz whispered to herself.

Livingston wrote down a single word on the clipboard. "Okay, now a chandelle and lazy-8s."

Liz directed the trainer into a half-bank, half loop to the starboard side. She completed the routine with two expertly executed lazy-8s before leveling out.

"Take it down, Hunter," the check pilot ordered without emotion.

Liz guided the trainer smoothly onto the runway like it was a mother eagle landing on her eggs.

Glowing with confidence as she climbed from the cockpit, Liz straightened her slacks, looking about for her friends. Meg, Ski, Mary, and Stacy flashed a chorus of thumbs-up from the nearby Operations Building entrance.

Livingston walked up behind Liz and rudely snatched the logbook out of her hand. He then lumbered off toward Operations with a sour expression. Meg and the others parted enough for him to pass through their gaggle.

Ski imitated his nerdish gait. "Good morning, Oscar," she chided him.

He entered the building without so much as a murmur.

Liz giggled as she bled into the group of upbeat friends. "Oscar?"

Mary patted her on the back. "I see you drew Lieutenant Smiles."

"Lieutenant Asshole is more like it," Liz corrected her. "Think I did okay?"

"Couldn't have done better myself." Meg grinned widely.

"I should have flunked the little brat when I had the chance," Ski snarled. "You can tell Oscar's parents spoiled him rotten."

Oscar returned. "Pitman, you're up," he snapped.

Meg, Liz, Stacy, Mary, and Ski were standing anxiously near the bulletin board in front of the Headquarters Building when the main door swung open, and Nancy Love exited with a clipboard and several logbooks in hand.

With a somber expression, Nancy strutted up and stopped in front of Liz. "We had a meeting of the Ferrying Division Civilian Pilots' Selection Board. For the WAFS, I am permitted to sit on the Board as an unofficial member."

An anxious look swept across Liz's face.

"Don't worry, Liz," Nancy quickly noted. "You're in. You and Stacy have been accepted."

Liz and Stacy clasped each other's forearms and jumped up and down with excited squeals.

Nancy smiled. "Welcome aboard, girls." She turned to Meg and Mary. "Would you be so kind to take Liz and Stacy over to the Quartermaster?"

"Be glad to," Mary agreed, turning to Meg. "Let's go see our favorite sergeant."

Meg glanced at Mary with a disbelieving wince. "Favorite?"

"You'll love him," Ski announced. "He's such a cutie."

Stacy's eyes brightened. "Cute, huh?"

Mary winked at Meg. "Yeah, cute....like a bulldog "

"Great!" Stacy ignited. "Let's go."

Mary turned to Meg, shaking her head. "It's really true. Popeye had a daughter, and she flies for the WAFS."

Mary's sarcasm sailed over Stacy's head.

Meg shook her head. "Unbelievable."

The Quartermaster Building consisted of two long, single-story wooden structures connected by a covered boardwalk. Several young men in duty fatigues were busily unloading large boxes of clothing from a semi-truck backed up to the loading dock.

Meg, Mary, Liz, and Stacy, buzzing with excited talk, walked up the steps in stride and entered through the double doors. A long line of new arrivals, some in civilian attire, moved slowly along a service counter, announcing their sizes to a dozen clerks standing at equal intervals behind the counter, dispatching a variety of fatigue uniforms and equipment from the floor-to-ceiling bins along the back wall. A graying sergeant with a butch cut, his shirt straining at the buttons from being overweight, moved back and forth along the counter, snapping orders. A spit-soaked stub of a cigar was clenched tight in the corner of his growling mouth. His stomach bulged as though he had swallowed a medicine ball. The name tag above his right shirt pocket read: FLOWERS. Three stripes with three rockers on each of his shirt sleeves signified the rank of master sergeant.

With a wave of double-takes, every soldier and airman in the building turned and gawked at the four WAFs as they entered, stopping at the entrance where they briefly studied their surroundings. Flowers, his back toward the entrance, spun around to see what the distraction could be.

Like a charging bull, Flowers bolted for the entrance to stop the WAF advance, his arms spread. "Whoa, right there, girls. I thought we were done with y'all."

"We need outfits, Sergeant," Liz blurted.

"Outfits? Outfits?" Flowers stammered, flabbergasted. "The Army don't stock outfits." He gestured toward the neatly stocked bins behind the long issue counter. "Those are military-issue u-nee-forms. Get it, girls? U-nee-forms!"

"Then issue us some u-nee-forms," Stacy howled facetiously.

Meg grinned. "Liz and Stacy here need a full issue, including flight overalls, goggles, flying scarves, the works."

Flowers slowly panned Liz then Stacy from foot to head. His eyes were glowing with a certain lust. "Scheesh! What in the hell is this here man's Army coming to?" He reached up and snatched the cigar from his mouth. "You got a req. this time?"

Meg snapped her fingers. "Damn!" She turned to Ski.

Ski shrugged. "Don't look at me. I haven't got it." She turned to Mary. "Have you got it, Mary?"

Mary shook her head. "Nope, not me."

"Well, you need a Requisition Form, first," he enunciated

facetiously.

"Ah, come on, Sergeant," Meg pleaded. "Don't you have an extra one layin' 'round here?" She glanced over at his desk. "Can't you issue them what they need? We'll bring one back later."

Flowers wrinkled his prune-like face, visibly thin on patience. "Enough!" He turned to his clerks who were struggling to hide their laughter. "Get 'em what they need," he shouted, stomping off toward the counter, vigorously grinding his teeth on the stub of his cigar, grumbling, "Damn bossy girls. I shoulda joined the Marines." His brushy eyebrows stood out like porcupine needles. "Jesus H. Christ. How do they expect me to conduct proper business?" he mumbled. "Damn, you girls are a pain in the ass. Come on, follow me," he growled, turning toward the crowd of gawking, open-mouthed soldiers.

Stacy wrinkled her turned-up nose. "The girls were right, Sergeant. You're such a cutie."

The soldier nearest Flowers, smirked. "Yeah, a real cutie, Sergeant."

The men behind him cackled.

Flowers glared at the chiding young men. "As you was! Git your sorry asses moving. You've seen girls before."

The soldiers immediately dropped their grins and spun around, drawing snickers from the WAFs.

The supply sergeant sauntered up to the counter and tossed two sets of khaki overalls, goggles, parachutes, and scarves on the counter. He took the cigar from his mouth and flipped a large ash on the floor.

Neither Liz nor Stacy moved.

"Well?" Flowers snapped. "What in the hell you girls waitin' on, for Hell to freeze over?"

The WAFs bubbly bolted toward the counter.

Looking around, Stacy picked up one of the overalls. "Sergeant, where would I find the change room?"

The supply sergeant's eyes almost left their sockets. "A what?"

"The bathroom," Mary clarified.

"She wants to try them on, Sergeant," Meg added. "You

know. See if they fit."

"Won't matter, no how," Flowers growled. "I ain't got nothin' here that'll fit you girls." He pointed at the overalls. "That's as small as they come."

"Still, I would like to use your bathroom," Stacy said politely.

"It's called a latrine, girls," Flowers corrected her.

"We're female pilots, Sergeant," Meg pointed out. "Not girls."

Flowers pointed over his shoulder with a thumb. "In the back near the loading dock. Damn! Give you hemlines the right to vote, and you want to run everything. Just like my ex-, demanding this, demanding that. I should've stayed in Alaska."

The WAFs chuckled at the sergeant's grumbling as he turned toward the grinning soldiers behind him. "What in the hell you slimeballs looking at? Get back to work."

Leaving Mary behind to guard their new issue, Meg, Liz, and Stacy proceeded toward the back of the building, side-stepping uncooperative soldiers who stood in their way, giving them a disclothing stare. As they turned the last corner, the doorless latrine set dead ahead. They walked past a young soldier buttoning up his fly as he exited. He blushed with embarrassment when he spotted them, lowering his head as they walked up to the open doorway, stopping briefly to check it out before entering.

In the middle of the room, two urinals sandwiched one lonely toilet stool.

"Typical male domain," Liz roared sarcastically. She eyed the raised toilet seat. "No stalls either."

"First night I got here, some asshole put Vaseline on the toilet seats at the B.O.Q.," Mary sneered.

"I'll stand guard for you," Meg volunteered. "I get the feeling we'll be doing a lot of this in the days ahead."

Liz steered her blue eyes from left to right before entering. Stacy followed, bubbling with small talk.

Stacy winced and pinched her nose. "Whew! What are they feedin' these guys?"

Liz humorously fanned the air in front of her face. "Smells like rotten eggs."

Meg laughed from the doorway. "Ole Sarge should've issued

us gas masks."

Holding their breath, Liz and Stacy quickly stripped, hung their street clothes on a line of hooks then slipped on the khaki overalls. Meg peered out and spotted several soldiers straining to look past her. She took up an authoritative stance and gave them a look to kill. They quickly snapped their heads around.

Both Liz and Stacy looked like little girls in their daddy's clothing as they quickly rolled the cuffs and sleeves several times then primped in front of a small mirror before gathering their civilian clothes and exiting. Meg chuckled as Liz and Stacy, eyes bulging, took a long-awaited breath of air.

Liz looked down at the baggy overalls. "God, this looks like Omar the tent-maker designed these.....these whatever they are."

"Zoot suits," Stacy quipped.

They exited the Quartermaster Building to a chorus of whistles and heckling.

"Little brats," Liz snapped as the door slammed behind them.

Meg, Liz, and the other WAFs huddled closely in front of the unit bulletin board, their breath swirling in the crisp morning breeze. Liz reached out with a pencil and crossed out the 40th day on a countdown calendar, drawing a rousing cheer from her fellow WAFs.

"We're official, ladies," Edith sounded in a high-pitched voice.

The WAFs bubbled with small talk, waiting for their assignments to be posted. Soon, a homely, frail unit clerk, wearing the rank of corporal, sauntered out of the Administration Building, carrying a sheet of paper. He apprehensively approached the WAFs who quietly parted, forming a lane for him to pass. As he did so, they crowded his backside. He nervously posted the announcement with thumbtacks. Ski and Stacy began to pick on the clerk, blowing on his neck. Pinned against the bulletin board, he raised his arms high over his head and began to wade out of the horde of hyper female pilots, all jockeying for a closer look at their orders. Unable to move, the clerk slumped down to his knees and began to crawl out on all fours through the sea of shapely legs to escape. One of the WAFs goosed him, sending him sprawling on the ground. Without looking back at the cackling taunters, he quickened his four-point pace and scrambled toward the sanity of the Administration Building.

Liz strained to see the assignment sheet over Meg's shoulder. "Where are they sending us?"

"Hagerstown," Meg answered without turning. "We are to pick up PT-19s from Fairchild and deliver them to Chattanooga."

"Hate to tell you this, girls, but PT-19s have got open cockpits." Ski shivered. "It's November, remember? We'll freeze our big tits off."

Meg looked down at her own meager breasts then glanced at Ski's massive chest. "Surely, you jest."

Mary, Edith, and Liz broke into uncontrolled, gut-wrenching laughter. Ski looked dumbfounded. "What? Why?"

"It says here to report to the Quartermaster for a cold-weather issue," Meg added.

"That ought to make Sergeant Smiles' day," Mary uttered dryly. "Think we should get a Requisition Form first?"

"Na!" the others chorused humorously.

The military transport landed in Hagerstown, Maryland, amidst the backdrop of a dark cloudy sky and heavy drizzle. Meg and the other nine WAFs assigned to this particular ferrying mission looked like Eskimos as they stiffly climbed down the cargo ladder and herded themselves toward the Operations Building to coordinate their flight plan.

Meg and Liz pressed their noses against the only window, impatiently waiting for the weather to clear enough to take off. The adverse conditions were nothing new to them. Most had logged dozens of hours in stormy conditions, but their presence as quasi-government pilots was obviously under a microscope. Plus, they had not been trained to fly in a military formation, a concern Meg had noted in her diary.

Behind them, four of the WAFs were sitting on folding chairs, sleeping. Edith and Stacy were having a snoring contest while four others played cards, trying to fight the boredom.

Ski got up from her chair and peered outside over Meg's shoulder. "We've been sittin' on our cans for almost three hours."

"If we don't get rollin' pretty soon, it'll be too late to make the entire trip during daylight."

Liz reached inside her overalls to scratch. "Damn, I still itch all over."

"From what?" Ski asked. "I thought you took off the woolies, Liz."

"I did, Ski. Once exposed, you're exposed."

Mary entered the room from an adjoining office. "Listen up, girls. The clouds are lifting. We have a go."

Needing no other prompting, the WAFs quickly donned their fleece-lined flight jackets as they exited the building and humorously wobbled toward the flight line, their enthusiasm renewing with each step. Each carried their own set of flight charts and a small equipment bag containing items for their overnight stay.

Meg quickly climbed into the open cockpit of her assigned PT-19 and immediately tied her charts to her left leg to keep them from blowing out during flight.

She then surveyed the instrument panel. "No radio!" she loudly exclaimed to herself. She threw her hands up in frustration. "This should be fun. No canopy, no radio in this kind of weather, flying through the mountains. Sheeesh!"

Meg made eye contact with the other WAFs. With shocked, concerned expressions, everyone signaled about the lack of radios. There was nothing they could do about it now, and none of them were about to complain, giving the men a reason to criticize female pilots. The WAFs started their planes.

The collective roar of their engines filled the dense air as the WAFs throttled up to taxi. Meg led the entourage to the tarmac where she shoved the throttle forward. The PT-19 blasted down the runway and lifted away. Liz, Mary, and Stacy followed her as they climbed to 5000 feet before leveling out. Within a minute, their planes disappeared from sight as they plunged into the darkness of the swirling clouds.

Liz checked the temperature. It was ten degrees. She shivered as she read the speedometer. The needle was quivering at 100. Looking out, she could see the aviation lights of the other PT-19s blinking in the sky about her. She reached up and adjusted her flying scarf, repeating, "It's going to be okay."

It was time to start looking for the pit stop. Although cold, the clouds had spread themselves thin. Meg panned the terrain below. There it was, a small airfield nestled in a narrow valley. She signaled the others with her hand then shoved the control stick forward. The other WAFs within eyeshot followed suit, landing smoothly on the blacktop runway. A gasoline truck rolled to a stop as they cut their engines.

Stiff from the long, cold flight, they climbed out of their cockpits and waddled toward the tiny terminal with a mission. Clutching hot cups with both hands, they gulped hot coffee, warming their frigid hands and faces while taking turns using the single-stool bathroom. Some exercised their stiff legs to help stimulate circulation.

Meg turned to Liz standing beside her in the toilet line. "How are you fairing without your long undies?"

Liz tilted her head. "Oh, other than my kneecaps, fingers, toes, and nose freezing off, I was having a blast," she sneered sarcastically.

"Got anything in that bag of yours to wrap around your legs?" Meg took another drink of coffee.

Liz shook her head. "A towel."

"Good. Use it. Use anything, your charts if you need to," Meg suggested. "We have a long way to go before we reach Chattanooga."

Soon, they were in the air again, blazing through the swirling winds.

Her face nearly frost-bitten, Meg wrapped the scarf Amelia had given her around her face like a mummy. She then reached down and tucked a towel under her thighs to keep the ends from working themselves loose. She sang to help take her mind off the cold and boredom.

It was late in the day when they climbed to avoid striking the higher peaks of the Appalachians. Meg noted in her diary that the clouds were becoming denser. It began to snow, making visibility almost impossible. She now feared colliding with the other planes. Without radios, it was impossible to coordinate in the air. She kept a close watch on Liz who was off her starboard wing.

It was early in the evening by the time they spotted Chattanooga Airport through a break in the clouds. Meg signaled the others then pointed the nose of her trainer downward, cork-screwing to a near-perfect landing. Again, Meg and four others bailed out of their cockpits and stumbled toward the terminal, their legs pinched together, fighting the urge to pee in their suits. Again, they gulped down hot coffee and sandwiches while taking turns at the only bathroom, stomping their feet to get some feeling back in their toes and limbs, anxiously awaiting the arrival of the other ferriers who had become separated by the sometimes dense cloud cover. It was a tense situation with the eyes of the military establishment all focused on the female ferrying experiment. A single accident could end the project.

CHAPTER 12

It was 9 p.m. when they loaded onto a waiting bus that would transport them to a hotel. Ski and Mary had difficulty, being short-legged, negotiating the steps in their fleece-lined suits. They looked more like little boys in winter snow suits, drawing snickers from the redneck bus driver. Drained of energy, they ignored him. Several of the women feel asleep within seconds as the bus pulled out of the airport and headed for town.

Looking out from the rocking bus, every eating place was already closed. The driver took them to an older, medium-sized, red-brick hotel in the downtown district. Half asleep and numb from the flight, Meg and the others stepped off the bus with their parachutes and baggage and stumbled into the hotel lobby, decorated in dark maple, worn and scarred since its better days. Tarnished brass electric lanterns barely lighted the modest lobby. Cigar smoke permeated the damp, musty smell of a nearby in-house laundry.

An elderly, obese man in a wrinkled white shirt, sitting on a tall stool, stopped talking to an aging black man in a red bellhop uniform too large for his frail frame. Both simultaneously executed astonished double-takes when they spotted the woman pilots. Liz sneezed as she and Meg scuffled slowly up to the registration desk.

An old man in a plaid housecoat and slippers slouched on a worn Victorian couch, reading a newspaper. He emitted a hefty belch as he looked over the top of his reading glasses to inspect the new arrivals.

"What the?" the clerk sounded in an astonished tone.

Meg set her parachute and canvas bag on the wooden floor. "We need six doubles for the night."

The clerk raised up enough to look over the counter at their fleece-lined outfits and boots. "Luggage?"

Liz motioned at her parachute and equipment bag. "Just what you see."

The clerk continued to pan their faces. "Y'all with a carnival or somethin'?"

Meg laughed. "We're WAFs.....ferrying pilots. We just flew in. How much for your rooms?"

Mary stepped forward and stuck her head between Meg and Liz. "Have you got a restaurant here?"

"And a hot bath," added Meg.

"That'll be three dollars a room and ten cents for Uncle Sam. A hot bath will cost ya an extra two bits," the clerk answered dryly.

Meg turned to the others. Half-asleep, they all nodded their approval.

"A place to eat?" Mary restated.

"I reckon y'all ain't from these parts," the clerk observed. "Ain't no eatin' places open past eight."

"Looks like we'll hit the sack early tonight, girls," Meg responded. She reached out and signed the register. "We'll need a wake-up at 0600 hours."

The clerk looked at her questioningly.

"Oh, I mean 6 a.m.," she reacted.

The bell walked from behind the desk and picked up their loose bags.

After a tiring trudge up three flights of stairs, Meg and Liz dragged into their room. Liz immediately sat on the end of one bed while Meg tested the firmness of the other. She shrugged, as she looked over at Liz who was shivering, too tired to undress.

"I can't do this," Liz whimpered.

"What?" Meg turned in amazement.

"I can't do this."

Staring forward, Meg forced a grin. Reaching up with a hand, she ran her fingers across her dry, wind-burned face. She touched her forehead with the palm of a hand. It felt hot. "It doesn't get easier, but you'll get used to it." Meg glanced back at her friend. Liz was fast asleep, propped up by her bulky winter clothing.

Meg stood and began taking off her fleece-lined boots, jacket, and leggings then undressed Liz and tucked her into bed before climbing into a soothing tub of hot water. Meg lay back, placed a wet wash cloth over her forehead, and closed her eyes.

It was late in the afternoon when Meg, Liz, Stacy, and Ski arrived at the Headquarters Building in a cab. They collected their satchels, parachutes, and fleece-lined suits then climbed out of the cab, shielding their eyes from a bright autumn sun. They strolled into the Orderly Room, exhausted from the long bus ride.

"I don't see why we couldn't have hitched a military hop," Liz griped.

"It's against regulations," Mary noted. "Military personnel must take commercial transportation when available. Something to do with government competition."

"But we're flying for the military," Liz protested. "Look how many more sorties we could fly if we could get back faster. I thought the President called on everyone to put their personal and corporate profit-making goals to the side till this war is over?"

Standing at an open filing cabinet, the company clerk turned as the WAFs entered. "So, how'd it go, girls?"

"Don't ask," Liz snarled.

Ski dropped her satchel and parachute on the floor next to the filing cabinet, causing the clerk to jump. "If you don't mind freezin' your ass off, it was a blast."

The clerk winced as he turned back to his filing.

"Aside from having to listen to a rash of crap about these Zoot suits at the terminal," Stacy growled, "then the bus ride back here with a bunch of homely, smartass rednecks with bad breath and smelly pits, we had--"

"A great friggin' time," Ski howled.

The clerk pulled out a single manila folder, pushed the drawer shut then squeezed through the group of anguished women to get to his desk. Ski goosed him as he passed by, causing him to jump and squeal, showering the contents of the folder about the room. The WAFs burst with cackling hoots as he retreated to the safety of his chair.

Suddenly, Nancy appeared at the threshold of her adjoining office. "Congratulations, ladies. Not one of our WAFs failed on the first assignment. According to reports, some of the men ferriers turned back because of the weather. Washington is very pleased with us."

Meg and the other WAFs looked at one another with triumphant expressions.

Nancy glanced at the black clock on the wall. "Take the rest of the day off, and be here in the morning at 8:30 sharp. Now get some well-deserved rest."

Meg, Ski, Liz, and Stacy traded questioning looks before turning, picking up their gear, and shuffling to the door.

"It would be nice if Nancy let us in on what it is we'll be doin'," Liz griped. "I don't know whether to wear my long johns or not."

"Screw the long johns," Ski quipped. "Let's get cleaned up and raid the O-club. I could use a shot of California's cute butt about now."

Stacy snickered as she reached for the door knob. "You horny bitch."

"You should talk," Ski countered. "You, the queen of the Mile-High Club."

Just as they opened the door, Mary, Edith, and Flo pulled up in a cab.

"Pass the word on to the other girls," Nancy called out.

The clerk leaned back in his chair and checked out the WAFs' behinds.

"Y'all better suck in those eyeballs, Corporal," Nancy scowled, "before somebody stomps on 'em."

The clerk sat up quickly, spun his head around, and immediately began typing.

Nancy chuckled. There was no paper in his typewriter.

"And request a bus. I want it here at 0800 sharp!" she ordered.

"Ah, er, a yes, Sir....I mean, Ma'am," the corporal stammered in a flustered tone.

Dear Diary,

Queen of Aces 131

> *Nancy surprised us with a visit to a tailor shop in Wilmington to get new uniforms. Then she told us the bad news - we had to pay for our own, but they're really neat. The slacks and jackets are gray-green and the open-collared shirts are light-gray. Everybody sang "Bugle Boy" as we made a mess of the shop. Ski told me that I sound just like Tallulah Bankhead....I don't think my voice sounds that deep. Anyway, me and Liz sneaked off to get our pictures taken. When we walked in, Mary and Edith were already there. Everyone broke into hysterical laughter. When we got back to base headquarters, the colonel informed Nancy that we would have to march in the review on Saturday. A bunch of VIPs will be here. That should be interesting! None of us got any drill training, including Nancy. Anyway, she requested a drill instructor. Thank God, nobody I know will be here to see this fiasco.*

The next morning, the WAF Squadron formed up in two lines of 12 on the parade field. They were the center of attraction in their new tailored uniforms, trying to march to the cadence of a nail-chewing drill instructor by the name of Sergeant Harvey Jones. It was a complete calamity.

Jones' leather-like face was a road map of his career, animated with each WAF screw-up. His already thin patience was growing paper-thin. He had taken Studebaker's order harder than the WAFs had. Jones threatened early retirement "rather than be saddled with a bunch of giggly broads," as he put it.

Nancy was busy coordinating her squadron's next ferrying mission when the WAFs formed up for their first two-hour block of instruction. Half the WAFs were constantly out of step while the other half looked down at their feet, causing them to be a half-step behind. Liz kept walking into Ski to her front. Embarrassed, both giggled, drawing a raised brow by the DI.

"Column, right!" Jones shouted.

Stacy, Flo, and Ski turned left instead.

With clenched fists, he caught up to them and yelled in Stacy's ear. "I said, your military right!"

Startled, she jumped, turning into Jones, knocking the DI hat from his head. All three hustled back into formation while he comically chased his hat in the wind.

Jones caught up to Stacy as she marched with the others and began brow-beating her. "You have got to be the worst marcher I've seen in my 18 years of military service. You are sorry. You hear me, girly? Sorry! How in the world you fly planes is beyond me. I hope I'm in another state the next time you go upstairs."

The other WAFs giggled.

"Knock it off!" he bellowed.

After drill training, Jones made a beeline for Studebaker's office to protest having to work with the WAFs. The door open, the clerk eavesdropped from his desk in the outer room.

"This is not what I volunteered for, Sir."

Studebaker's lips formed a slight smile. "That's just the way it is, Sergeant. We all have to do things somewhat distasteful from time to time when there's a war on."

"But, Sir--"

"Carry on, Sergeant."

Aggravated, Jones saluted the colonel and exited the office, gritting his teeth. The clerk swiveled his head around and began typing as Jones, nostrils flaring, stormed toward the main door.

"Say anything, Corporal, and I'll crush you like a bug."

The clerk's head dropped on his typewriter with anguished relief.

The rest of the day was consumed with flight formation training, capped by a rousing happy hour at the officers' club where Meg, Liz, Ski, Stacy, and Flo bitched about their DI, drawing belly laughter from California, Billy Ray, and Hondo. Flo spent most of the time trying to move on Billy Ray, Liz's new flame.

Flo reached over and touched his forearm. "Gee, Billy Ray, you're really a swell guy."

Ski noticed. "Jesus, Flo, you just gotta have them all."

Flo gave Ski a dirty look.

Billy Ray looked down at Flo's hand then ignored her, turning his attention back to Liz who seemed less bothered by Flo's encroachment than was Ski.

Tuesday began with an early parade drill. Again, the WAFs struggled to follow the DI's commands, stepping frequently on one another and missing turns.

"Halt!" Jones bellowed as he began stalking the files, browbeating them. "You girls are a disgrace to the Army Air Force."

"I hate to be the one to tell you this, Sergeant," Ski spoke up, "but we're not military. We're civilian ferriers."

"That's close enough, Sister, for government work," Jones snarled. "Now get with the program!" He turned and stalked back to his usual position.

Liz lost her cap as the WAFs stepped forward with their left foot. As she bent over to pick it up, Meg accidentally bumped into her, sending her sprawling on the grass. Ski, Flo, Mary, and Stacy burst with laughter. Meg leaned over and helped Liz to her feet.

Jones threw his arms up. "Get back in formation," he growled. "She can get herself up."

"Spoken like a true gentleman, Sergeant," Meg barked back facetiously.

"Jesus Christ, I've had it with you damn girls."

Jones whirled around and stomped toward Studebaker's office, exploding past the clerk who was typing a report. The corporal started to stop Jones but wisely reconsidered when he saw the sergeant's protruding, wild eyes. The DI knocked firmly on the colonel's door, startling him.

"Come in!" Studebaker snapped.

Jones burst through the door and stopped in front of the colonel's desk at the position of attention, eyes forward. He saluted. "Sir, may I speak frankly?"

Studebaker finally glanced up from his paperwork. "What is it now, Sergeant?"

"Sir, I respectfully request a transfer."

"Sergeant Jones, are you in the habit of barging in unannounced?"

"No, Sir, but those damn giggly broads are not catchin' on to the basics. I'll gladly take combat over this.....this ball of wax.....Sir!"

"First of all, Sergeant, those are not broads," Studebaker hummed. "They're woman ferriers. Secondly, you will get them in shape for Saturday's parade. The Top Brass will be here. This is your *life's* assignment. Am I making myself crystal clear, Sergeant?"

"But, Sir--"

"But nothing, Sergeant," Studebaker growled. "Get your tail back out there and finish the drill. That's a direct order, something you should be able to understand after 18 years."

"Yes, Sir."

"Dismissed."

Jones saluted then spun on a heel and exited, nostrils flaring. He stomped past the clerk who was staring at the door from the filing cabinet.

The DI snarled at the clerk, "Who you eyeballin', you little weasel?"

The clerk snapped his head around and pretended to be filing.

Jones returned to the two-dozen WAFs stilled formed up on the Parade Field. "Ladies, we are going to try something different."

Meg and the others looked at him quizzically.

"Over the next three and a half blocks of instruction," Jones continued, "each of you will have the distinct pleasure of calling cadence."

"Ooh, that sounds like fun, Sergeant," Stacy commented.

"Step forward, young lady."

Stacy didn't move.

Jones walked over to Stacy. "Well, what are you waiting for? You're burnin' daylight." He pointed to the spot where he had just been standing.

Stacy looked at Meg then tiptoed to the proper position, midway along the formation. She stood there for a minute, thinking.

"Well?" Jones prompted her.

"Squadron, forward, march," she shouted.

The WAFs stepped off in unison. Jones checked their alignment. They were straight, and everyone was in step.

He blinked twice and refocused. "Well, I'll be."

"Column, right," she blurted.

The WAFs executed almost perfectly then marched about 20 yards. Stacy suddenly realized the squadron was headed for a drainage ditch, and panicked. She began shouting a number of unintelligible commands, all of which were incorrect. Before the DI could stop them, the WAFs in back of the formation collided with those to their front, forcing them over the side. Several, including Meg, Stacy, and Ski found themselves hurdling down the muddy bank into the grungy water.

As the DI attempted to restore order, Meg and the others tried in vain to climb up the bank, slipping and sliding, falling back on one another. Meg quickly organized the muddy band of WAFs. Soon, they began to appear at the top of the bank, looking much like Stacy's limousine driver after retrieving her poodles. The other WAFs doubled over from belly laughter. Jones, the veins in his neck bulging, fell into a bellowing frenzy.

I arrived at Wilmington that Friday evening after an exhaustive flight from London. I had twisted my editor's wrist to come back to the States to write a story on the WAFs. He had accused me of returning just to see Meg, which I flatly denied. I could tell from his voice that he didn't swallow my reasoning.

I called Meg from my hotel room, finally locating her at the B.O.Q.

Meg picked up the phone. "Hello?"

"Meg. It's me, Aaron."

"Brooks Brothers!" she shouted in my ear. "Where are you?"

I winced, pulling the phone away from my ear. "I'm in Wilmington," I answered.

"What brings you here?"

"I convinced my editor to do a story on the WAF Squadron."

"God, it's great to hear from you, Aaron. How have you been?"

"Better now," I answered. "Can you join me for dinner?"

"Of course," she responded excitedly.

"I need some time to clean up from my trip. How's 7:30?"

"Why don't I pick you up instead," she suggested. "I've got a car."

"I'm at the Grand Hotel. I'll meet you out front at seven."
"It'll be great to see you, Aaron. I've really missed you."
"Ditto," I stammered.

Meg arrived in a white '39 Chevrolet convertible, wearing her new WAF uniform.
"You look terrific in that uniform. Is it new?"
Her hand went to a lapel. "Yeah, do you like it?"
"Yes, nice material, too," I joked.
"Smarty.....nice suit, yourself, Brooks Brothers." Meg patted the passenger seat. "Hop in."
Before I could seat myself, Meg lurched at me, nearly knocking me backward out of the car. She planted a terrific kiss on my lips. I eyeballed the valet and the hotel guests over her shoulder. Some were gawking, some smiling. I must have been blushing.
Meg downed a porterhouse steak, charbroiled rare. I gobbled down a lobster while catching up on mutual friends and events.
"Liz is here," Meg offered.
I looked at her puzzled. "Liz?"
"You know, the blonde that was with Hub Martin at the Bendix Ball."
"She's a pilot?" I asked in a surprised tone.
Meg took a swallow of beer. "Yeah, and a damn good one."
"Is she still dating Hub Martin?"
"Nope. One of the guys who trained with him at Pursuit School said that he stayed on to train other pilots."
"Oh," I responded. "I would've figured him to be overseas by now, flying pursuits against the Germans."
"That surprised me, too," she added. "All show and no go."
I reacted defensively to that comment. "How about me, Meg? Do you think that about me?"
Meg tilted her head. "Heavens no, Aaron. Going to Berlin then Paris is hardly child's work."
"Thanks, but lately, I've had to sit back, reporting government-massaged news. I feel out of it. One way or another, I am determined to become a player."
"Doing what?"

"I tried to join up, but like an idiot, I put down that I had rheumatic fever when I was a kid."

"I'm sorry," Meg reacted.

"So, how's it going so far?"

"I'm bored," she griped. "The only thing the Top Brass will let us fly are these stupid trainers. All they want us around for is to be their lap pilots.....you know, show pieces."

That has to be tough after flying high-performance prototypes."

"You've got that right." She looked out the window at the stars. "There are Russian women flying in combat, you know. Both Sean and Garrett are flying in combat right now."

"Yes, I know...and I know that you want to prove that you could fly in combat, but the politics are pretty thick here in the U.S. Things might be different if the battles were being waged on American soil."

Meg's eyes brightened. "So tell me more about Europe."

"After America entered the war, I was ordered back to London where I got stuck reporting censored, cultivated news so I talked my editor into letting me do a story on the air war in North Africa."

"How'd that go?" Meg asked.

"I met General Patton who seemed very forthright and honest. To say that he is a character is putting it mildly. Carries two ivory-handle six-guns. Anyway, he told me that the Brits air support had failed miserably. He had to embarrass them into doing their job. Do you realize that it was the first real test of American troops in the European Theater? Anyway, he pulled some strings for me and asked his surgeon to re-evaluate my medical condition. I should know the results soon."

The look on Meg's face was one of great surprise. "I thought you were told that you have a heart problem?"

"Maybe, maybe not."

Meg's eyes dropped to the ground once again.

"Hey, I thought you would be happy for me."

She lifted her eyes slowly and squared off on me, holding both of my hands in hers. "Don't take this wrong, Aaron, I'm happy for you, but I'm tired of flying bullshit missions at home while everybody else is overseas, including WACs and nurses."

"I understand, Meg."

The waiter returned. "Dessert?"

"Not for me." She patted her stomach. "Couldn't eat another bite, thank you..... Come on, Brooks Brothers. Let's drive out to the base. I want to talk to you more about joinin' up."

It was a perfect evening. The sky was crystal clear and the moon bright. I could see for miles. The natural light reflected off the rows of silver birds parked along the flight line. It was so peaceful, a million miles from the terrible destruction in Europe.

I turned in my seat and looked at Meg. She had really matured. If there had been any doubts before, they were erased that evening. It all seemed so comfortable as I leaned over and kissed her.

It was midnight by the time she drove me back to the hotel.

Dear Diary,

I went galaxy-hopping last night. I felt like every cell in my body was exploding into space. It was even better than the first time dad let me solo in the Spad. I wish I could wake up every morning in Aaron's arms. It was wonderful! And to think that he actually thought that I had the hots for that jerk Hub. I really love Aaron, and now I know he loves me, too. My heart is pumping fast just thinking about last night.

I've been thinking a lot about Mom today, too. Aaron asked me about her. At first I didn't want to tell him, but he finally got it out of me. I miss her terribly. I know why Dad has trouble showing affection. It's because I look so much like Mom. He says we're two peas in a pod. I know. I can see the pain in his eyes. Aaron and I finally got together, and now he's leaving. Why does everybody I love leave me?

CHAPTER 13

The WAFs were already dashing about, busily dressing, shining shoes, and putting on make-up. Some were experiencing great difficulty positioning their hat to look attractive. Nervous excitement rippled from mirror to mirror as they sang to the Glenn Miller tune, "I've Got a Gal in Kalamazoo," blasting from a nearby Philco radio.

Mary stuck her head in the door of the latrine and shouted, "It's time, girls."

Meg and the other WAFs began filing out the B.O.Q. onto the street, still adjusting their uniforms and hats, jabbering demonstratively. They formed up in two rows but remained at ease, waiting for their director to arrive.

Soon, Nancy Love and Sergeant Jones sped up in a jeep and stopped abruptly.

She climbed out and addressed her squadron. "Good morning, ladies. I will be marching at the head of the formation."

Liz turned to Meg. "This ought to be interesting. She's missed every *enjoyable* practice," she said facetiously.

"So, girls, do you know how to march?" Nancy asked.

Meg and the others nodded enthusiastically, murmuring affirmatives.

Nancy smiled sheepishly. "I must confess. I'll have to wing it."

All 24 WAFs did a double-take.

"Whatever I fail to say, do it anyway," Nancy added seriously.

"Don't worry," Mary responded, "we've had a lot of practice doing that."

Everyone but Nancy broke out laughing. Nancy then caught

on and joined the chorus of giggles and chuckles.

I was talking to the other news hounds at the reviewing stand when the various military units began marching onto the field. Each carried its usual colors that fluttered in the brisk, mid-morning breeze. Some marched in quietly to the commands of their leaders. A few arrived, singing cadences, smartly executing their turns as they took their usual positions, facing the reviewing stand.

Soon, the WAFS appeared at the edge of the field in two files. Nancy made a beeline for her squadron's assigned position between two squadrons of male pilots, avoiding any unnecessary turns. I looked for Meg as the WAFS neared the reviewing stand. There she was, head up high, the lead guide behind Nancy, marching with surprising precision. I beamed with pride.

New voices behind me diverted my attention. I turned. It was Colonel Studebaker and the rest of the command group along with a dozen visiting dignitaries, mostly military. General Shotgun Thomas was busily talking to two Senators, pointing and nodding. I smiled and shook their hands as I was introduced.

"Look, it's the WAFs," Studebaker interrupted, pointing.

All eyes turned, shoulder-to-shoulder, the WAFs took their last few steps and halted.

Nancy turned to Meg. "What now?"

Meg leaned slightly forward so only Nancy could hear her whisper, "Left face."

Nancy shouted authoritatively, "Squadron, left face!"

The WAFs executed the command, pivoting on their left heel, forming two rows. Looking out from the reviewing stand, I could see that the second row was on the heels of the first. They had failed to create some space between the two files before coming to a halt. Afraid of drawing more unwanted attention, they remained frozen.

Studebaker certainly noted it. I could hear him whispering to himself, "C'mon, Nancy, Second Row, one step backward." He took a deep breath and turned toward Sergeant Jones, giving him a raised brow.

Looking left at the adjacent unit commander, Nancy realized that she needed to be centered in front of the first row. She calmly marched to her left, stopped, and executed a right-face.

Queen of Aces

Thomas turned to Studebaker. "I've just got to get a closer look. Come on," he prompted.

They were joined by Beatty and Studebaker's sergeant major as they stepped down from the reviewing stand and marched in unison toward the WAF Squadron.

Liz, standing directly behind Meg, whispered to her friend, "Of all the units here, they just had to pick ours to review."

Meg and the other WAFs in the front row locked their nervous eyes straight forward, anxiously awaiting the arrival of the reviewing party.

Thomas and the others stopped in front of Nancy.

"Good morning, Mrs. Love," Thomas said pleasantly.

"Good morning, General."

"Come with us while we review your girls," he prompted, nodding for her to take the lead.

One problem--Nancy had no idea where to start. She clumsily turned around and paused. Studebaker immediately read the situation and stepped ahead of the others to guide her. All in all, it was hardly noticeable. Without stopping, the reviewing party walked along the first row. Thomas occasionally complimented a WAF about her spit-shined shoes or new uniform. They beamed with pride, keeping their eyes forward.

When Thomas reached the end of the first row, he stopped and faced Meg. "Good morning, Megan," he sounded. "I hear you've been doing a great job here."

"Thank you, Sir. It's good to see you again," she responded without blinking.

"Your father's design is in its final stage of production," Thomas continued. "The first Mustangs are rollin' off the lines as we speak."

Meg beamed. "I'm looking forward to ferrying them."

"That's not in the plans, young lady," Thomas noted. "The WAFs will be ferrying trainers, a very important mission."

Meg dropped her smile. "I've got over 400 hours on the Mustang. I was my dad's test pilot as you well know."

Studebaker and Nancy winced at her outspokenness.

Thomas ignored her comment. "You're an exceptional pilot,

Megan," Thomas responded as he quickly stepped around her. "Keep up the good work."

As he began reviewing the second row of WAFs, he was forced to shuffle sideways due to the close proximity of the rows. Three of the WAFs with endowed chests tucked in their chins and exhaled to give Thomas enough room to squeeze past them. He then came to Ski who thrust her chest out, pinning Thomas against the WAF in the first row. Suddenly, a button on her blouse snagged the ribbons above his left breast pocket. Flushed red with embarrassment, Thomas tried unsuccessfully to unhook them. Looking around, he noticed at that everyone was gawking at the spectacle.

Taking control, Thomas reached down to grasp her button, making unintentional contact with her left breast, causing her to jump and squeal. The general jerked back, keeping both hands up for everyone to see. Several male pilots in the adjacent unit fought to control their laughter. A few faltered. Soon, every man present was snickering.

He glanced left then right to take note of those laughing at him. "Young lady, I suggest you unhook us."

Ski smirked as she reached down and slowly unhooked her button from the general's ribbons, glancing up to see if he was staring at her breasts. She wasn't disappointed. His eyes were locked on the target.

Nancy rolled her eyes. This is all her WAFs needed–another embarrassment.

Thomas quickly stepped backward to join the rest of the reviewing party. With a smug, conquering grin, Ski took a step forward to rejoin the second row.

The VIPs that had remained behind at the reviewing stand had turned, trying to conceal their uncontrollable laughter as Thomas and his contingent returned to the reviewing stand. With composure, he turned and addressed the units. After a brief speech in which he praised the WAF Squadron, he backed up, turning the podium over to Colonel Studebaker.

"Thank you, General, for your inspiring comments," Studebaker's eyes panned the formation. "Pass in review," he ordered.

One by one, the units began to march past the reviewing stand, executing a snappy eyes-right, signifying a salute to the command group. Soon, it was the WAF's turn.

"Eyes, right!" Nancy snapped. She turned her head and saluted the brass. Everyone in the right file faced right in unison. Liz snapped her head so crisply that her cap stayed pointing ahead. Contagious snickering erupted from the reviewing stand.

As each unit cleared the parade area, the unit commander dismissed the men. Most remained behind to watch her squadron. After Nancy finally halted her WAFs, the men began to converge on them.

"With the exception of Meg Reilly, First Row, dismissed," Nancy barked. "Second Row, stand at ease."

Mary and the other WAFs in the first row dispersed quickly to mingle with the pilots and airmen that had encircled them. Mary kept an eye on those that had remained in formation to see what was happening.

Meg turned to Liz. "What now?"

"Follow me," Nancy ordered those remaining behind.

Meg, Liz, and the others complied.

Liz leaned toward Meg as they followed Nancy toward the reviewing stand. "Everybody that doesn't have big tits or a pretty face got dismissed. What's up?"

"Two guesses," Meg responded. "Top Brass and VIPs."

Nancy heard her and turned. "We've been invited to join them for lunch at the Officers Mess."

"Well, it certainly didn't take them long to turn us into lap pilots," Mary sneered.

"Considering the size of the glands on Ski and some of the others," Stacy added, "I'd say that the generals' minds are on more than just chow."

"That's enough," Nancy snapped. "Step it up."

Once inside, Meg and I sat together at the VIP table. She seemed particularly upbeat throughout a meal consisting of charbroiled steak, baked potatoes, buttered Lima beans, and hot buttermilk biscuits. Afterwards, Meg and I walked with our arms wrapped around one another down by the flight line. We stopped next to one of the trainers.

"What about me, Brooks Brothers? Just about the time I get you corralled, you leave me." Tears trickled from her watery eyes.

I leaned forward and found the curvature of her lips. I reached around with a hand and found her bra clasp. The softness of her modest breasts drove my heart into third gear. We clamored for each other's waist buttons. Soon our trousers were cast aside. To the roar of a P-47 Thunderbolt taking off, I found myself between her soft but very firm thighs wrapped around my waist.

CHAPTER 14

I began to pick up more and more reports about Meg and the other WAFs. Word about the Mile High Club was traveling faster to England than the combat reports from North Africa. Although we were short-handed at the London Bureau, I finessed a military hop through General Thomas to report on the air war. Maybe the military didn't want me, but I wasn't to be denied.

General Patton welcomed me with a bottle of his best wine, a hand-rolled Havana cigar, and an exclusive interview. I marveled his ivory-handle six guns as he ranted about the German air superiority, blaming Field Marshall Montgomery for a lack of air support. He savored each puff from his cigar as he filled me in on his plan to finish off Rommel's forces. Afterwards, he took me on a tour of the mansion where he had set up shop. That evening, I accompanied Patton and his aide to a boring piano recital at some palace. He was quite charming and very patient considering the quality of the entertainment.

Later over a glass of cognac at his headquarters, we launched into a discussion about his experiences in France during The Great War. He was quite fond of one pilot in particular, a gutsy fighter pilot who had shot down three of the German fighters that had been bombing and strafing his brigade for several hours. The name of the pilot was none other than Rye Reilly. He glowed when I told him about Rye's two sons and his daughter who were contributing so greatly to this war.

He finally got around to why I wasn't in uniform. When I told him about the heart murmur, he seemed quite compassionate, especially when I asked him if he could write a letter of endorsement.

By the time I awoke in the morning, his aide presented it to me. He had arranged for his personal surgeon to conduct a comprehensive physical examination. It also recommended that I be sent to Officer Candidate School. I thanked General Patton personally for the endorsement, asking that I remain with him for the balance of the African campaign to report on the tough fight ahead.

I started to write Meg then elected to wait until after the medical re-evaluation.

*****

Seven days later, a half-dozen WAFs, including Meg and Liz, huddled around the bulletin board, drinking hot coffee in the frigid winter air, reading the latest memo.

"I knew it!" Ski bellowed.

"What is it now?" Meg groaned, glancing her way.

"Every day, we gather here like one big happy litter of puppies only to discover another demeaning edict, telling us how the Top Brass plan to stick it to us."

"Touché," chimed Liz.

"Read it, Ski," Stacy prompted.

"Women entering the military, I guess they mean us, too, must meet the same age and weight criteria as the men."

Liz rolled her eyes at Meg. "That's utterly ridiculous. You'd think the medical officers could exercise a little mind-flex. They know better than anyone that female tissue is lighter. Christ! I'd look like a pregnant rhino at 139 pounds."

"What do you mean, would?" Meg jested.

"Screw you!" Liz snapped humorously.

The other WAFs cackled.

"My, my, Liz," Meg continued, "you're developing quite a salty tongue."

"Yeah," chimed Ski, "two months ago, you would have said baloney or go to H."

Liz put her hands up to stop them. "All right, all right, you guys. Give me a break," she pleaded, joining the laughter. She looked down, inspecting her own figure. "I'd have to wear lead panties, stuff my bra with cantaloupes, and eat two dozen bananas to weigh that much."

"Sounds like a plan to me," Meg snickered.

"Well, anyway, girls," Liz continued, "we have a date at the dispensary to get a physical."

"Ah, that's just the Army's way of finding out when we're on the rag," Ski sneered.

"Ski! You're gross," Mary uttered.

Ski spun around to face her. "Well, pinch my titties."

The brakes on the Army bus squealed abrasively as it came to a stop in front of the base hospital. Standing in front of the bus, Nancy winced as she turned to address her WAFs. "Okay, girls, we're here. Don't forget your shot records."

"Meg, Liz, Stacy, and Ski stayed in the back of the bus while the others stood and filed out of the front door. The foursome was stuffing their faces with bananas and sandwiches thick with peanut butter. They passed a bottle of milk back and forth to help wash down the sticky substance.

"I can't eat another bite," Meg groaned.

Liz set down the milk and dabbed her mouth with a napkin. "Me neither. I feel like a swallowed a bowling ball."

Ski burped as she stood. "Oops! I think I'm gonna barf."

Liz bolted for the open door with her hand over her mouth.

Meg frowned at Ski as she followed Liz out of the bus. Liz was hunched over the grass. Ready to vomit herself, Meg took a deep breath as she hustled to her friend's side.

"Whatever you do, don't throw up," Meg ordered. " You'll need the extra weight. Now, sit down and put your head between your knees."

Liz moaned but complied.

Ski exited the bus and jogged into the hospital. Minutes later, she returned with an ammonia inhaler. She broke it and waved it under Liz's nose. Her head reared backward, shaking.

Soon, Liz was able to stand. Teeth clenched, all four entered the hospital, ready to undergo their flight physicals.

Dressed in hospital gowns, Nancy led her squadron along in trail formation to the weight scales. A muscular medic in hospital whites stood next to the scales, adjusting the weights as each WAF stepped onto the scales.

Liz turned to Meg who flashed crossed-fingers in support. All four had skin diving weight belts around their waist.

Suddenly, a handsome doctor in an Army uniform appeared with a clipboard, drawing a significant amount of whispers from the WAFs.

Liz spoke over her shoulder at Meg. "Oh, my god, he looks just like Cary Grant, don't you think?"

Meg bobbed her head back and forth, inspecting his facial features. "A little."

"I'm in love," Liz beamed.

Ski stuck her head between them. "Liz, you certainly recovered fast."

Liz pushed her head away. "Excuse me, but you're in my sight ring," she said, staring. "God, he's got beautiful blue eyes." She tilted her head to read his name tag: "John Mathews, M.D."

"Next," Mathews said very business-like.

He looked up to see Liz stepping onto the scales. He was in awe of her beauty. She was still four pounds under her height-weight requirement of 139.

Meg thought quickly. "I thought I told you to cool it with that diet. I know Billy Ray likes you on the skinny side, but--"

"Okay, okay, already," Liz interrupted. "I got the point." She stepped down as the doctor recorded her weight on the clipboard.

Meg peered around his shoulder to see what he had recorded. He had recorded 139 pounds.

Eyeing Meg in his peripheral, he spoke. "Miss Hunter, get your weight up before your next physical," he said quietly, followed by a wink.

"Yes, Sir," Liz responded with a relieved tone. She took her first breath in more than a minute and licked her lips. Her hormones were racing.

He watched Liz blend into the crowd as Meg took her place on the scales.

With a female nurse accompanying them, the WAFs continued with their exams, including a mammogram and a pap smear by Dr. Mathews. Ski purred when Mathews examined her, causing him to turn scarlet red with embarrassment. Liz was next to climb onto the exam table. By then, he had been reduced to putty.

As suspected, each WAF was interviewed regarding their menstrual cycle.

A line of airmen, WACs, and military dependents wearing a variety of casual, winter attire, stood outside the base theater, waiting to buy tickets to see the Howard Hughes western, "The Outlaw," starring the very buxom Jane Russell.

Meg, Liz, Stacy, Ski, and Mary piled out of a military bus, paired with California, Hondo, Dr. John Mathews, and two other pilots. Flo was last to exit, hanging onto Billy Ray, Liz's former boyfriend.

Ski turned to the others as they quickly got in line. "I heard that Howard Hughes made this movie two years ago but got censored because of the controversial bra he had specially designed for Jane Russell.

"I read in Variety that this bra thing was nothing more than a publicity stunt to sell more tickets," Liz noted.

"Howard shelved the film for the last couple of years to build up controversy and demand," Ski added, shuffling sideways to keep up with the ticket line. "I'm gonna buy one of those bras when they arrive at the stores." She thrust her chest out more.

Liz bobbed her head from side to side, humorously inspecting Ski's chest. "Yep."

"What?" Ski glanced down self-consciously.

"You better get one of 'em before your end up bruising your knees."

"Screw you, Miss Vassar," Ski snarled humorously, "and the horse you rode in on."

Everyone broke out laughing.

Ski kept a straight face as she mimicked Liz's actions. "Liz, where were you when they handed out the tits?"

"In line ahead of you, Ski."

Their laughter grew.

Finally, they arrived at the ticket window and shuffled into the lobby wreaking of fresh popcorn. Meg, Hondo, Liz, and Dr. John joined the long line at the snack counter.

Meg turned to Ski. "Hey, you guys, grab us a seat. We'll get the pogey bait."

"I'll take a Coke," Mary shouted over her shoulder, "and some Jewels."

"Gotcha," Liz responded. "What about Stacy?"

"I want a large 7-up and some M & Ms."

After a ten-minute wait, Meg and the others entered the theater just as the "Universal Newsreel" began to roll. Footage of the North African campaign filled the screen. German troops were advancing on foot behind a line of Panzer tanks firing their cannon. The American tanks returned the fire in an awesome display of firepower and determination as they attacked from three sides.

The United States Second Corps and the British Eighth Army slug it out with Germany's elite Afrikan Corps under the command of Field Marshal Rommel at Kasserine Pass.

General George Patton was standing atop a ridge, observing the progress of a smoke-filled battlefield through his binoculars. Several younger Army officers and radio operators, antenna bobbing in the air, were milling around him, shouting orders and pointing. Two were looking at a map spread over a jeep hood. One was talking into the jeep's radio handset. Artillery shells began exploding about them, sending all but the general diving for cover. Patton was a pillar of strength in the face of certain danger. Through a break in the smoke, American tanks were firing at will, destroying German tanks and advancing infantry.

The theater audience applauded vigorously when the footage changed to Patton standing in a jeep, leading his victorious troops into a North African town, the streets of which were lined with Arabs waving American flags.

General George S. Patton, Jr., rides victoriously, following the defeat of Germany's famed Desert Fox, reversing the tide of Allied misfortunes in North Africa.

The film report then cut to aerial footage of an American bomber formation being attacked by German fighters. From an over-the-shoulder camera view, a tail gunner blazed away with a 50-caliber machine gun at a German fighter zeroing on his prey. American fighters took on the German intercepts in a vicious aerial dogfight. A wing camera recorded tracers slamming into a German fighter. It broke up and exploded. The American pilot broke right to avoid the debris.

In Western Europe, Allied powers wage a costly air war against Germany to destroy the heart of Nazi transportation and manufacturing.

The news cut to a wintry scene with Russian troops fighting a fierce battle in the blowing snow against stalled Nazi forces.

On the Eastern Front, the siege of Stalingrad has come to a bloody conclusion. Its back against the wall, the Red Army mounted a last-ditch counterattack against their German invaders, pushing Hitler's elite panzers back to Kursk, cutting off their line of supplies.

Her eyes glued to the screen, Meg feverishly ate buttered popcorn. The news report shifted to heavy naval and aerial combat scenes. American fighters and Japanese zeros battled each other over the Pacific. A bomb dropped from an American fighter tumbled onto a Japanese warship and exploded. Jap seamen began jumping into the water as the ship broke in two and immediately sank. American seamen assisting enemy survivors from wreckage-strewn waters followed the last flutter of a Japanese flag.

While in the Pacific, U.S. Naval and Air forces fight a desperate sea and air battle, inflicting heavy losses upon a Japanese convoy during the

> *Battle of Bismarck Sea near New Guinea, helping to reverse the tide of Japanese successes since the vicious surprise attack on Pearl Harbor.*

The footage cut to a young Army Air Force pilot kneeling on the wing of a P-47, painting a seventh Japanese flag on the fuselage, just below his canopy.

> *Congratulations to Army Air Force fighter pilot Sean Reilly, eldest son of World War I ace Patrick "Rye" Reilly, as he registers two more kills in the skies over Bismarck Sea.*

He rotated his body to face the camera then smiled.

> *A real chip off the old block.*

Meg jumped in her seat, spilling her popcorn as she reached over Hondo to poke Liz. "Jesus!"
"That's your brother!" Liz shrieked, bouncing in her seat.
Mary, Ski, Stacy, and everyone around them bobbed their heads to look at Meg, buzzing and pointing.
"What a hunk!" Stacy cooed.
Liz turned to Stacy. "You ought to see her twin brother Garrett."
Stacy leaned forward to see around the others to study Meg. "Yeah, cut your hair, you could pass for a male pilot."
Meg sat back in her seat with solemn expression.
Hondo looked at her oddly. "What's wrong?"
"That's as close as I'll ever get to flyin' in combat. It ain't fair, that's what."
"You're a girl," Hondo said dumbly. "Combat's for men."
Meg fired off a look to kill.
Liz quickly changed the subject. "Garrett's flying B-17s, isn't he?"
Meg softened. "Yeah, with the Eighth Air Force in England."
"B-17s?" Hondo sneered. "With your pappy being a WWI

ace, I would've figured him to be in a peashooter."

"The bums changed his orders before he got to England. They had a shortage of pilots in the Eighth."

"That's gotta be gnawin' at his crawl," Hondo continued.

Meg nodded. "It is, especially with Sean makin' ace."

CHAPTER 15

Hondo and California saw Meg, Ski, and Mary to the door of the B.O.Q. then left on foot, walking back to their quarters. Liz and Dr. John had ventured off toward the flight line, hand-in-hand, to gaze at the stars.

As Meg, Mary, and Ski walked past Flo's room, they could hear a bed squeaking, followed by moaning and squealing.

Mary grabbed Ski's arm to stop her from peeking into Flo's room. Ski pulled her arm away and quietly opened the door. The moaning immediately stopped as the light from the hallway flashed across the room, settling on the head of the bed where Flo was sitting on top of Billy Ray. Both startled faces turned toward the door.

Ski was enraged. "Well, that conniving slut!"

Meg reached in front of her and pulled the door shut. "Ski, it's none of our business. Liz has a new boyfriend now."

"Meg," Ski protested, "screwin' someone's old boyfriend is taboo."

"That don't give us any right to stick our nose where it doesn't belong."

"But Flo is a snake," Ski argued, "and she'll do it to you, too, just like she did me. Tried to hustle California behind my back."

"If Hondo is tempted by Flo, which he isn't, but if he was, then they deserve each other." Meg paused. "Anyway, Hondo's just a friend."

Ski asked, "So who ya waitin' on, Hub Martin?"

Meg laughed. "Not on your life, Ski. . . . Aaron Masters."

A light drizzle rolled off the unit bulletin board roof. Meg, Liz, and the other WAFs huddled underneath, shielding themselves from the damp, cool early morning air. Several were cradling cups of hot coffee while reading the latest posting.

"Well, those bastards!" Ski screeched. "They went and did it."

Stacy shuffled over to read over Ski's shoulder. "The Air Transport Command has officially ordered us females grounded while we're on the rag."

Mary choked on her coffee and instinctively lurched backward, spurting and coughing. "Stacy! Such language. You're startin' to sound like Ski."

Liz patted Mary on the back. "Are you okay?"

"I betcha the Brass are bitching right this minute about delivery schedules," Meg sounded. "And all they care about is our monthly curse.....Dumb asses can't make up their minds what they want."

Ski quoted the memo at yet another octave, "A history should be obtained of any menstrual abnormalities--"

"Abnormalities?" Stacy interrupted, shrieking. "Abnormalities, they call it? I wonder if that term covers needle dicks?"

Meg and Liz grabbed their stomach where contagious, uncontrollable belly laughter overwhelmed their bodies.

Ski managed to clear her throat. "Abnormalities, pregnancies, and miscarriages. All women should be cautioned that it is dangerous for them to fly within a period of three days prior and three days after the menstrual period."

"Let's see the dummies try to enforce this directive," Meg scowled. "We haven't had one incident since this squadron got organized. The Top Brass sure forgot that Great Falls snafu. Six out of six of us girls made it, but only six out of 17 guys completed that trip."

"Here, here," Liz crowed.

"And we're proving that more and more everyday," Nancy's voice sounded from behind.

Meg and the others spun their heads around to face their

Queen of Aces

director.

"And I'm not letting the Brass forget it," Nancy continued, walking to the middle of the group. "I know it's only a week before Easter, but I've got a big job for five of you. Five lend-lease PT-26s are destined for Russia. They're to be picked up in Hagerstown and ferried to Calgary in Alberta."

"Canada?" Ski whined. "That's 2500-plus miles."

Flo poked her head in. "How fast are they?"

"About 100 miles an hour," Nancy answered. "They're like a T-19, except they got a canopy.....and radios."

"Thank God," Liz said with a relieved tone.

Meg was quick to volunteer. "When do we leave?"

Nancy smiled at her best pilot. "As soon as you pack and get over to the flight line."

> *Dear Dad,*
>
> *I really miss you. I trust you are feeling okay.*
>
> *Well, the Brass have relegated us to primary trainers, but I wouldn't give this up for anything in the world. Oh, well.*
>
> *Remember the gorgeous blonde that Hub Martin brought to the Bendix Ball? You won't believe it. She took up flying after that and is now a WAF. She's a damn good pilot. So are the other girls.*
>
> *Anyway, five of us ferried PT-26 Primary Trainers to Calgary. which proved to be a very interesting trip. After landing in Joliet, we took a ride to Chicago in a sardine-packed taxi, and after hunting for two hours, we finally ended up staying in this rathole boarding house run by a frizzy-haired, elderly lady in an old housecoat that looked like Aunt Mame. Later, we went to eat at a fancy supper club where all the celebrities go when they're in town. Actually, it looked more like a museum with a bunch of stuffed wild animals. Speaking of stuffed shirts, the maitre d' kicked us out for wearing slacks, a part of our uniforms! Anyway, this AAF major saw the whole*

thing and told that fatso maitre d' that we were wearing Army dress uniforms and promised to get the place blacklisted for being unpatriotic. That really put the fear of God in the maitre d' who caught up to us and apologized. You'll never guess what happened then. Fatso invited us back in and announced us to the entire dining room. Everyone stood and applauded. Man, it was great! For the rest of the evening, they treated us like heroes with the house picking up the tab. Making the experience even sweeter, several of the women walked up to our table and asked for our autographs.

The view above the Rocky Mountains was spectacular with its snow-capped peaks. When we got to Calgary, we found out the Russian pilots hadn't arrived yet to pick up the planes. So, we had to wait on them. When they finally got there, one looked just like Boris Karloff. I mean it. They weren't shocked in the least to see that we were girls. The interpreter said that a number of the Russian combat pilots are women!

With their backs against the wall, they gave their women the chance we should get in America--to fight for our country.

Better get some sleep. I hope everything is all right at home. I really miss you.

All my love,
Meg

Almost seven days later, Meg and her comrades stepped off a bus in front of Headquarters Building with their parachutes and flight bags, worn out from the long bus ride.

Nancy greeted them at the door with a big smile. "Terrific job, girls. I can't tell you enough about the phone calls I received. You really impressed the Brass with this performance."

Colonel Studebaker appeared behind Nancy. "I second that. Exemplary job. All of you can expect an official commendation."

Meg grinned. "Thank you, Colonel."

"Yes, thank you," Liz added. "I don't mean to be rude, but I have something I must do."

"Like a hot date with a certain pill-pusher," Ski blurted.

"That handsome doc, huh?" Nancy chuckled. "You're all excused.....except for Meg."

"I'd like to see you in my office," Studebaker added.

Meg entered the building, set down her gear then followed Nancy into Studebaker's office. Nancy shut the door behind them.

"Go ahead," Studebaker instructed Nancy. "Tell her."

Nancy took the far seat then pointed at the other chair for Meg to sit. "Meg, what I am about to tell you is classified information."

Nodding that she understood, Meg eased herself down on the leather chair.

Nancy continued, "The first P-51 was recently delivered to Long Beach. Because of your experience flying the prototype, I would like you to join my advance party in California as my Assistant Director and to be one of the first pilots, certainly the first woman, to officially fly the Mustang."

Meg's eyes were bursting with pride and excitement. "Why yes, of course, Nancy. When are we leaving?"

"In five days."

"May I ask who is going with us?"

Nancy smiled. "Please submit a list of recommended personnel by noon tomorrow. Three others will join us as an advance team to prepare the facilities for the entire squadron. The rest will join us later."

"Yes, I will. Thank you." Meg smiled as she stood. "Is that all, Colonel?"

Studebaker smiled warmly. "Reilly, you're one hell of a pilot. Now, get the hell out of here and get some rest."

"Yes, Sir!"

Meg selected Liz, Ski, and Stacy. Edith was left in charge of the WAFs remaining behind, and Mary was named as her assistant.

Their noses pressed against the windows of the C-47, the WAFs gazed down at the white caps atop the brisk waves rolling onto the beautiful sandy beaches of Long Beach, peppered with dozens of sun worshipers. To the northwest, there was sprawling Los Angeles.

Stacy strained particularly hard to spot Hollywood.

"Stacy, can you see it?" asked Meg.

"Yeah," Stacy responded, "Cary Grant's walking his dog by our house right now."

Liz snickered. "You're real funny, Stacy."

The C-47 settled into its final approach and landed. Weary from the long trip, the advance team climbed down the steps and onto the concrete, stretching in the bright sunlight.

Stacy breathed in deeply. "Ahhh, I love the smell of the sea."

Liz immediately spotted the lone P-51 sitting along the flight line. Beautiful and elegant, it was like a rose among weeds.

"Meg, your father did a great job designing that baby," Nancy complimented, her mouth open with awe.

"Here, here!" chimed the others.

Everyone took a detour to circle the silver-winged powerhouse.

Stacy caressed the cool, smooth surface. "How many horses?"

"Fifteen-hundred and ninety-five," answered Meg proudly.

Stacy's eyes bugged out. "Jesus!"

"I would have stayed behind at New Castle, Meg, had it not been for your prototype," Liz admitted. "Anyway, Doc promised to fly out here to visit me."

"I can hardly wait to see my boys," Stacy added.

Ski looked at her oddly then laughed. "Oh, your dogs."

"C'mon, girls," prompted Nancy. "We've got unpackin' to do. Let's get with it then celebrate with a drink."

The sun broke over the trees as a determined pair of boots stomped along the flight line, stopping as they reached the cigar-shaped Mustang. There was a brief pause before the boots climbed aboard and stepped into the open cockpit. A pair of tight leather gloves began flipping switches. Soon, the massive Packard engine began to roar, humming about the pilot's body like a giant vibrating glove. A pair of excited eyes admired the instrument panel with a hand. It contained twice as many instruments and gadgets as the prototype. It was the Rolls Royce of pursuits.

"It's time to show them what you can do, sweetheart," sounded Meg's voice.

As the P-51 began to taxi, Nancy and the others flashed a thumbs-up. Glowing, Meg returned the gesture. The slim, low-winged pursuit of clean conventional design began to thunder down the runway.

Liz spoke to Nancy without looking at her. "That's one gorgeous hunk of metal."

"What about that gorgeous hunk of a doctor back at New Castle?"

"Doctor who?" Liz joked. She paused reverently. "I really miss him, Nancy, but I wouldn't have missed this for the world."

"Good, because you're taking it up next."

Stacy leaned in close to Liz. "You better hope that Flo doesn't get her hooks into your hunk. I saw her eyes light up when your name was read off."

"Flo ain't got a chance with Doc," Ski said in support.

The expression on Liz's face was appreciative. Still, a hint of insecurity showed.

All eyes turned to Meg as she guided the roaring P-51 down the runway and lifted off, pointing the nose upward in a steep angle. Her head was pinned against the back of the seat from the G-force until she leveled off at 5,000 feet.

She rolled right and gave it full-throttle. The needle on the speedometer jumped to 410.

"Megan, it's a crime you're not a man," she said to herself. "What I could do with this baby in combat."

Meg took the P-51 through a series of dives, climbs, loops, and rolls. The sun reflected off its silver skin. As Meg finished with an impressive fly-over, several small throngs of soldiers and civilian workers craned their necks as the Mustang rolled over on its back. The spectators burst with loud cheers at America's new hope to gain air superiority in the desperate war overseas.

Nancy wasted little time getting things organized. She began by locating the Officers Club and the Post Exchange. Within four days, it was business as usual, flight-testing an array of recently repaired red-lined aircraft.

Three PT-19s took off from a hot, simmering runway and climbed to 3000 feet before leveling out above the white sandy beach. Wingtip-to-wingtip, Meg, Liz, and Ski waved at one another as they proceeded along the coastline. Ski soon positioned the stick between her knees to steady the trainer then slipped off her blouse and bra and leaned back to bask in the sun.

Meg radioed her. "Better watch it, Ski. You've got two bandits comin' in fast."

"Yeah, right," Ski said unbelievingly, but she still glanced to the left, expecting to catch a reaction from Liz.

Two Dauntlesses piloted by two wide-eyed young men were ready to leap on her wing.

"Holy palominos," blurted one over the radio.

Making no attempt to cover herself, she swiveled her head, trying to spot her comrades. Both Liz and Meg were rolling with tear-filled laughter.

"Hang onto your jockstraps, boys," Liz snapped, cackling.

Just feet away, both male pilots elevated their planes, jockeying for a better view of her enormous chest. Their eyes were wild.

Ski teased them, smiling and waving.

Still laughing, Meg radioed Ski. "Okay, put your tarp back on those cannons of yours before those boys have an accident."

Smirking, Ski scrunched her shoulders at the gawking male pilots then reached for her blouse. "You heard the boss, boys. Show's over."

The wind turbulence suddenly caught hold of her blouse and snatched it from the open cockpit. Meg and Liz rolled their eyes as Ski reached down for her bra loosely looped around the control stick. Fumbling to put an arm through one of the loops, her plane began to weave, causing her to grab at the control stick. Suddenly, the wind sucked her bra from her grasp. As she thrust an arm to catch it, her plane veered toward the nearest Dauntless. Both male pilots instantly lost their grins and jerked hard on their control sticks to avoid a mid-air collision.

Ski laughed. "Just checking your reaction-time, boys."

Within seconds, however, both maneuvered back alongside Ski's trainer.

"How about a date tonight?" asked the nearest male pilot.

"That's enough, Ski," Meg warned her. "We better get you back to base before those guys have a heart stroke. And try to find something to cover up those rockets of yours."

Finding nothing in the cockpit, Ski resorted to covering her nipples with her free forearm and hand.

As they turned their planes around, the WAFs spotted a variety of military and civilian planes converging on their formation. The radio came alive with male chatter.

Approaching the Long Beach runway, the aerial armada buzzed about the WAF formation, maneuvering for a look at Ski's bare chest. Meg and Liz were finally able to position their trainers on either side of Ski's wingtips, trying to avoid any further mishaps.

Finally, Ski landed, followed by Meg then Liz. Waiting for them was a crowd of airfield personnel, all trying to catch a glimpse of the topless WAF as their planes came to a halt in front of the operations building.

Liz quickly unfastened her seat belt, stood in her cockpit, and shouted at Meg. "I'll try to find a blanket or something while you hold off those sex maniacs."

Meg nodded as she climbed down and hustled over to Ski's trainer, cutting off a charging herd of wild-eyed airmen.

"Hold it!" she bellowed, using her outstretched hands. "Hold it there, gents!"

Liz returned with a wool blanket and climbed aboard Ski's plane, positioning it over her shoulders. Ski stood to a cheering crowd of horny males. She smiled and waved at the pushing throng of fans while several of the planes still airborne swooped down for one last look.

As Meg looked around, she spotted Nancy stomping out of the Operations Building with a concerned look. Next to her was a no-nonsense colonel with a white sidewalls haircut.

"Oh, oh," Liz stammered. "Don't look now."

Meg spun her head around and spotted Nancy and the base commander. "Oh shit! We're in for it now."

The airmen spotted the colonel and immediately scattered in all directions, leaving the WAFs to face the music.

"Meg, what in the hell's going on?" Nancy demanded.

Ski lost the smirk on her face. "It was my fault, Nancy. I thought I would catch up on my suntan, but my shirt blew out. I didn't know those guys were on my tail."

"Ski, this is intolerable," Nancy snapped. "We're under a microscope as it is. I've been killing myself trying to get us bigger and better planes to fly."

"Somebody could have gotten killed up there, young lady," the colonel added.

"I'm sorry, Colonel. It won't happen again."

"It better not. Not on my base."

Nancy glared at Ski. "Get a shirt, Ski, then report to my office." She turned to Meg. "I want to see you, too."

Her face was rigid, unsmiling.

"Yes, Ma'am," Meg responded.

CHAPTER 16

Dear Brooks Brothers,

It has been over 10 months since I became a WAF. We have flown everything from small single-engine trainers to large cargo planes, bombers, and every pursuit made, including Dad's Mustang in a variety of weather conditions to just about every out-of-the way place in the States, flying missions the chickenshit males are afraid to. I suppose we should feel used, but we're just happy to be flying. It's an opportunity to prove ourselves to some of the base commanders who are still reluctant to let us fly bigger and faster planes.

It seems like we just got settled in here, and now the Air Transport Command is moving us to the Ferrying Division Headquarters in Cincinnati. I'm going to miss the weather here in Long Beach.

I knew it wouldn't last forever. General Arnold finally gave Cochran what she wanted--all the female pilots under her wing. She's now Director of Women Pilots in the AAF and Assistant to the Air Staff for Commitments and Recruitment. I guess that shouldn't really surprise anyone. She's been politicking ever since Nancy Love got the WAFS. Nancy, now the Director of the WASPs, reports to Jackie Cochran, and all of us WAFs are now called

WASPs. That's short for Women's Airforce Service Pilots. I already miss our WAF designation. We were the first. Nancy would rather be flying anyway and leave the pen-pushing and political stuff to Jackie. It's just the way it was handled that ticked us off. WAFs, WASPs, WACs.....what's a name anyway?

As for me, I was given my own WASP squadron. All but two of the old WAFs will be staying with me. Several WASP squadrons have been formed at bases scattered throughout the country.

I'm packing up for Camp Ford which is smack dab in the middle of a North Carolina swamp where our squadron will join up with 25 WASP grads to tow targets for antiaircraft gunnery practice. According to rumor control, the male pilots have been balking at such duty and want a shot at combat, but then, who doesn't?

Camp Ford is one of the largest and oldest antiaircraft artillery training bases in the world. It's located all too close to Blue Swamp near the Atlantic Coast. Word has it that the large mosquitoes are sometimes confused with our aircraft and that they get refueled when they come in for a landing (ha).

Anyway, I never have figured out which is worse, Camp Ford or Erwin. It's kinda like comparing the armpits of two grisly wrestlers. They both stink.

The male ferriers are behind schedule, delivering P-39 pursuits destined for Europe and Russia. I don't know why the Army is still fooling around with that damn Airacobra pursuit. They ought to call it the flying coffin. Bell mounted the 1200 horses behind the cockpit and the fuel tanks under the seat. Several male pilots got killed when they got their nose up too high and spun out.

I'm sure you've heard that your hero, General Patton, rolled into Messina after defeating the krauts.

I would love to be flying air support for him.
Enough shop talk. I miss you, Brooks Brothers. When are you going to be back? Have you joined up, yet?

Love,
Meg

P.S. You're a writer, so write!

    Meg's letter was eventually routed to me while I was training at the Office of Strategic Services, better known as the O.S.S., forefather of the CIA. The O.S.S. was less concerned about the heart murmur I had when I was an infant than were the regular military services. I was to remain on the payroll of *Aviation Life* magazine but work as an undercover agent against the Axis powers, specifically the Nazis. Upon graduation, I will receive a commission as a second lieutenant in the Army, and my branch would be MI; that is, military intelligence.

    One of the enticing factors that led to my acceptance in the O.S.S. was my German heritage on my mother's side. Her mother had come from Munich. As such, I grew up speaking both English and German. I also spoke French quite fluently, thanks to my schooling and years of reporting in Paris. Still, two foreign language instructors were assigned to tutor me on the various border dialects. The balance of my training included radio communications, encryption, photography, map reading, agent drops, demolitions, and how to eat meals, European-style. At the Army INTEL School, I learned to pick locks and open safes, followed by counter-intelligence, survival, and interrogation training.

    Here's the real grabber for someone with a phobia of flying--airborne school. I had to cope with my fear of heights and tight leg straps on either side of my groin. One particular class was something called "Suspended Agony." For an hour at a time, we would hang in a parachute harness and practice slips until I thought my testicles were going to pop. During our "cherry jump," I sat inside the C-47, thinking about the insanity of jumping out of a perfectly good airplane. Something that didn't help my confidence was the constant bombardment of passed gas. By the time we got to the drop zone, a steel chain couldn't have kept me from jumping.

The worse part was not being able to tell Meg about my new role in the war. She would have to think that I was turned down by the military a second time. I wrote two letters, one to Meg and one to General Patton. I had hoped to tell him someday after this terrible war was over that I had served a vital role, and to thank him for his help. The letter to Meg--well, that will have to wait till later.

* * * * *

Decked out in their new WASP uniforms, Meg and her excited contingent of former WAFs departed by C-47 transport for Camp Ford in the Carolinas, to prepare for the arrival of Jackie Cochran's hand-picked graduates from Sweetwater, Texas.

"We'll also be joining 600 male pilots, girls," Meg announced matter-of-factly.

Ski jumped in her seat. "That's twelve-to-one odds." She then gave Flo a look. "Maybe now one of us can leave the other girls' boyfriends alone."

Flo stuck her nose up in the air and turned her head. "Maybe if you had more class, Ski, you could keep a guy for more than a single date."

"Stuff it, Flo," Ski snarled.

"Okay, girls, at ease," Meg snapped. "Just think about the change of pace. No more ferrying trainers to podunk towns."

"Clay pigeons, that's what we'll be," Stacy blurted. "My younger brother Bill is stationed there. He said that we'll be towing 20-foot muslin targets so a bunch of cross-eyed, trigger-happy trainees can get some realistic target experience with pilots trained to fly like the krauts and the Japs. They also practice at night, using searchlights. From what he says, they have enough trouble hitting their assigned targets in broad daylight."

"Terrific," Liz moaned. "All the guts and none of the glory."

"Right down our alley," Meg said facetiously as she looked out a window. "Clay pigeons at a skeet shoot."

The sun was disappearing over the horizon. She could see the military camp and airfield below.

The crew chief approached Meg. "We're almost there, Miss Reilly. Would you prepare your girls for the landing? We're about to start on the final approach."

"Yes, Sergeant. Thank you."

"Good, I'm starved," Ski announced.

"You're always starved," Flo mumbled. "Definitely a case of hoof-to-mouth disease."

Ski sat up in her seat and glared at her rival. "Flo, get bent!"

From the moment they set foot on concrete, the intimidating stares began. Standing near the open doors of a maintenance hangar, a pouchy tech sergeant with a white-sidewalls military haircut, stopped working on a Dauntless engine. He reached for his back pocket and extracted a green handkerchief that he used to wipe the grimy sweat from his brow. The late-thirties sergeant spoke to a younger mechanic. "Must be those new feline pilots we've been hearin' so much about."

The rangy corporal with a gravy of sweat and grease coating his arms and face raised up quickly, bumping his head on the engine cowling. He rubbed his head as he peered outside the hangar. He spotted Liz and Meg walking by.

"Golllleeeee!" he whooped with a high-pitch, southern drawl. "Look at the girth on them two cuties."

"Looks like a double-breasted mattress-thrasher to me," the sergeant sneered. "I ain't servicin' no damn plane for no dumb broads." He glared at the WAFs. "Ain't nobody else on this here base gonna, either."

The tired, but bubbly WASPs were led to the mess hall where they chased down ham sandwiches and left-over potato soup with stale coffee, heavily laden with grounds. The mess steward grumbled through most of the meal, forced to stay on duty to prepare their food and wash their dishes. From there, they were escorted to their new home, the nurses barracks where they sat up talking until the early-morning hours.

High on the moment, they had just gotten to sleep when the roar of powerful engines shook them out of their beds. Propping herself on both elbows, Liz blinked her eyes and looked out one of the windows. "Shit! They stuck us on top of one of the runways. Welcome to Blue Swamp."

"Up and at 'em, girls," Meg shouted down the hallway. "Time for breakfast. We've got a long eventful day ahead of us."

Ski swung her legs around and stood. "I hope breakfast is better than that sorry excuse for a supper."

Stacy covered her head with a pillow. "I'll pass. Wake me when it's over."

Ski prompted her with a flying pillow on the buttocks. "C'mon, get up! We've got a real mission, flying real airplanes this time."

"Better not hold your breath," Stacy cracked.

* * * * *

Breakfast consisted of rubber eggs laden with broken shucks, half-fried bacon, burnt toast with a splash of butter, watered-down orange juice, and scalded, strong coffee.

Meg panned the walls. They were drenched with military crests representing the various units on post and dozens of framed, enlarged photos of the men and their flying machines. It was all very macho.

The officers gawked and pointed at the WAFs as they filed past the food line. Some flirted back and forth, but for the most part, it was a cool reception.

"I hope the food's warmer than the hospitality," Mary said sarcastically.

Stacy coughed when she tried the coffee. "Jesus, you could paint the walls with this stuff."

"It's got chicory in it," Mary noted.

"Whatever it is, it's awful," groaned Liz. "Yuck!"

"Damn, I knew I should've stay in the sack," Stacy chimed.

"Better step on it," Meg snapped. "We've got a date at the flight line."

* * * * *

The anxious WASPs were greeted at the flight line by a

chubby, expressionless captain in his early-40s. He motioned for them to follow him, parading them past the dive bombers then the transports, finally stopping in front of the Cubs.

"You are to check out these L4s and L5s," he announced.

Meg approached him, holding back her anger. "Captain, can we speak in private?"

"Spit it out, young lady. I've got a lot to do and little time to do it."

"We were sent here with a promise to fly meaningful missions in B-26s and B-24s."

"Look, Miss, I just follow orders. This is the Army. If you've gotta beef, take it to the colonel."

"I plan to." She turned to Liz and the others. "You guys get started. I'll be back in a little while."

Suddenly, the captain rendered a snappy salute. Meg turned to see a colonel come to a stop a few feet from her.

"Good morning, girls. I'm sorry that I was detained from greeting y'all myself," he spoke in with a deep Southern drawl. "I'm Colonel Pine."

"Colonel, may I speak freely?" Meg asked.

"Is there a problem, young lady?" he asked, looking at her name tag. "Reilly. Um, that name sounds familiar."

"She's the Reilly that won the '39 Bendix Race," Liz crowed.

Pine looked at Meg skeptically. "I was at the finish line in New York. I thought you were a man. I was a major then......So here you are."

Meg was not about to be compromised by clever public relations. "Yes, Sir," she answered coolly. "Now, we were told by our director that we were coming here for target-towing duty. We've worked hard to prove ourselves over the last year. We've been ferrying pursuits and bombers only to be told that we have to again prove ourselves by testing out on Cubs?"

Suddenly encircled by the angry WASPs, the colonel backed up a step. "Look, you girls, while you were chowing down, I was assailed, first by my enlisted men then my pilots. They're demanding transfers, but I talked them into waiting a spell until we see if you girls work out."

Her face noticeably filled with anger, Meg folded her arms over her chest and tapped her fingers on her forearms. "But why these Cubs, Colonel?"

"Like I said, my pilots feel their non-combat role will be diminished if I let you fly the same missions in the same birds they do." Pine took a long breath. "I simply cannot afford to humiliate them more than they already have been."

"What about us, Colonel?" Meg demanded. "What about our humiliation?"

"The majority of those boys got sent here against their will. For the sake of good morale, please humor me for a few days."

It was quite clear that Pine's mind was set. To argue further would only alienate him.

"How many days, Colonel?" Meg continued.

Sweat beads began to roll off his brow. "Ah, er, a three?" he answered nervously.

Without looking for support from her fellow pilots, Meg responded, "Okay, three days."

A certain relief showed in Pine's eyes. He sighed ever so slightly.

Dear Garrett,

Greetings, Brother, from Camp Ford, the armpit of the world! Hot, wet, hot, wet, hot!

You and Sean are really something. Dad must be bursting at the seams with pride. Me, too. There isn't a day that goes by that I don't think of you two.

Guess what? I got my own WASP squadron. I love the challenge of leadership, but the bullshit the Top Brass has been dumping on us girls is the pits.

You'll never guess the crap they put us through here at Blue Swamp. Then again, I guess you can. Anyway, they made us check out on Cubs. All of us girls were really pissed. Most of those dumb L4s got heel brakes right near the rudder pedals so when we step on the pedals, our heels tend to hit the brake. Several girls almost nosed over, and when one did, the jerks on the flight line laughed at us. We looked like complete fools.

To make matters worse, Ski almost kissed the end of the runway when the flap handle didn't work. The mechanics don't consider them any big deal. That goes for the instruments and the radios, too. Most of them don't work. The mechanics don't seem to give a shit most of the time. I almost pasted one upside the head when he made a crack about us not earning our pay. We're the ones taking all the risky missions.

In short, the condition of the aircraft around here can be summed up in two words--a joke. Few of the mechanics have been properly trained. Me and Edith know more about engine repair than any of those dummies. The two or three who do seem to know something, seem to care very little about doing their job. I suspect it's due to the shortage of parts, especially spark plugs and good tires - most of which are threadbare. Blow-outs during landings are common, and the octane of the fuel is worse than the stuff Dad said they used in the Spads during the last war. I drained off a cup of water from a carburetor the other day. The lazy bastards need to fill the tanks at the end of the day, and not use fuel from the bottom of the barrels. In fact, the fuel problems are so bad that we suspect sabotage. Even the worse ground crewmen should not be so consistently negligent. At first, we kept our mouths shut, but the bullshit keeps piling higher.

Want a good laugh? One of Jackie Cochran's 90-day wonders was sitting in the cockpit of a redlined Dauntless this morning. She seemed a little puzzled by a bag she found stored in the side pocket. When she held it up for me to see, I laughed. It was a urinal-relief bag.

Well, little brother, I have to get this in the mail before the plane leaves. We have a special briefing at 1500 hours. It all sounded so serious.

Oh, don't tell Dad any of this. He'd have a coronary. Take good care of yourself. I wish we were still flying together.

Love,
Meg

CHAPTER 17

It had rained throughout the night and most of the morning, followed by a blazing sun. Meg could see steaming heat rising off the runway as she and the other WASPs anxiously stood in formation for Colonel Woodrow "Woody" Pine to show his face.

Stacy turned to face Liz. "I haven't had this much fun since I rearranged my sock drawer," she snapped facetiously.

"It isn't as though we're military personnel," Liz added. "At least the Old Man could have the courtesy of showing up on time for his own formation." She looked at her watch. "The little creep is eight minutes late."

Colonel Pine exited the headquarters building almost ten minutes later and wobbled up to the irritated females. Meg saluted him then turned and joined the rest of her squadron.

Within five minutes, Pine was breathing heavy. His summer uniform looked like a drenched wash cloth.

After the usual bullshit announcements, he got to the real purpose of the formation. "Because of your exemplary performance to date, the WASPs are authorized to fly search-and-rescue missions, beginning today."

Ski leaned toward Meg. "That's a crock. Woody certainly changed his tune overnight."

"Woody?" Meg snickered. It was the best laugh she had had in days. "First, they stick us with red-lined crates then bullshit us why we get stuck with search-and-rescue."

"As if morale doesn't already suck," Mary injected from the other side. "Just color us Jackie's guinea pigs."

Stacy leaned backward so she could whisper at Meg. "Speaking of Jackie, you're a friend of hers, aren't you? Why don't you clue her in about the sorry state of affairs?"

"She used to be an acquaintance and a competitor. That's all," Meg countered in an irritated tone. "I'll take the matter up with Nancy. Now, pay attention."

Colonel Pine continued, "As y'all know, we've had a rash of incidents lately involving some of our pilots that crash landed in the swamp. The S.O.P. for ditching in the muck is to remain visible from the air. The pilot is to remain with the plane, spread out his parachute, and continue to radio for help, giving accurate coordinates and reference points."

Liz whispered out of the corner of her mouth at Meg. "He's presuming the pilot is a male, and that he is still alive after all this. I love it."

He looked their way. "At ease, young lady. What I'm telling you may save your life."

Liz straightened up and lost her smirk. "Yes, Sir."

The colonel finished outlining the procedures then turned the formation over to the base medical officer, a stout opposite of the colonel.

He seemed quite pleasant as he stepped forward. "Good day, ladies. I'm Colonel Schmidt. Beginning next Monday, all of you will be required to undergo complete physical examinations on a monthly basis."

The WASPs stood with their mouths open, flabbergasted.

Meg spoke for her entire squadron. "The male pilots aren't required to get a physical every month."

"I'm sorry, girls," Pine drawled. "That's just the way it is until further notice."

Meg dismissed her squadron then headed for the Operations Building with Liz, Ski, Mary, and Stacy were at her side, griping all the way.

"If these damn planes were kept in better shape," Liz roared, "they wouldn't have to worry about search and rescue."

Meg turned to the others as she reached the door. "I know, I know!" Meg reacted. "You're preachin' to the preacher."

Inside, Meg searched out Major Brenner who was standing at the operations board with a grease pencil in hand. "Major, may I have a word with you?"

"Brenner dropped his hands as he turned around. "Yes, Reilly. What is it?"

"It's about the Cubs. They are *not* what we are about. My WAFs have been flying jugs, mustangs, and flying fortresses."

Brenner seemed unmoved by her words. He had an annoying little habit of clicking his jaw while listening to others. "You and your girls will continue to fly Cubs."

"But, Sir--"

"In addition," he cut her short, "you will be allowed to conduct search-and-rescue flights up to 50 miles beyond the coast."

"Well, thank you, Major," Liz snapped facetiously. "Should we ignore any pilot that ditches 51 miles out?"

Brenner glared at Liz momentarily before looking back at Meg. "What were you doing before the President gave your girls the green light to fly expensive military aircraft?"

"Teaching half of your male pilots at this camp how to fly," Ski answered matter-of-factly.

Mary nodded in agreement. "If these damn planes were kept in better shape, you wouldn't have to worry about search and rescue."

"Meg's father developed the P-51, Major," Ski noted.

"And Meg was the pilot who flight tested the prototype each time it went up," Liz added. "In fact, she won the '39 Bendix with it."

Ski leaned around Liz. "So what we're trying to say here, Major, is that none of us who started as WAFs ever flew a Cub. As Meg here tried to tell you, we've been ferryin' pursuits and bombers to out of the way places."

"As well as the missions your men think are beneath them.....like target-towing," Liz interjected.

Meg got in his face. "You didn't suspect for even the slightest of moments that Jackie's target-towin' experiment didn't have Bo's blessing, did you?"

Brenner's right hand went to his jaw as he held his ground. "So you're the gal who won the Bendix, huh?"

Early the next morning, Meg was the first to take a mission. The A-24 engine started rough, back-firing five times in rapid succession, startling everyone within earshot. Visually inspecting the wings, she noticed rivets popping up and down in their holes, trying to escape the vibration. Determined not to complain, at least not yet, Meg waved at the young corporal standing by to climb aboard. It was his job to operate the cables that controlled the target sleeve.

When they reached the beach, the corporal uncranked the winch, letting out the target to flap and flutter in the strong coastal winds. Once they had made two passes, Meg was to fly low over the gun emplacement and release the target so the trainees could be graded for accuracy.

The gauntlet began at high altitude for three-inch gun crews. The pilots would then drop altitude to give the 40-mm and 35-mm gun crews practice on moving targets. Finally, they would drop to a lower altitude, mimicking Japanese and German air tactics, to give the infantry riflemen one last shot at targets.

The large-caliber gun crews had been motivated by their feisty instructors to lead their targets more. But this was training, not combat. Precise communications was a must, and that was far from happening. As Meg began her first pass, she could hear the battery commanders over the radio, shouting, "More lead!"

Suddenly, Meg's plane was rocked with storm-like turbulence and a series of explosions. Her first instinct was to look upward for storm clouds. But the sky was clear. She panned downward where black puffs of smoke loomed in her peripheral.

"Jesus Christ! That's flak!" she shrieked.

The panicked assistant began banging on the fuselage with his fist. "Hey! Hey! Those bastards are shootin' at us. I just got back from Europe with 25 missions in B-17s. Who needs this shit?"

"Notch number 26 in that gun butt of yours, Corporal."

More explosions rocked the battered Dauntless. Meg grabbed the joystick with both hands, trying to keep the Navy dive-bomber from straying off course.

She radioed the range commander on the ground. "Cease fire! Cease fire!" she screamed. "We're taking flak." She had barely uttered the words when more flak slammed into the stabilizer.

"Cease fire, dammit!" she shrieked.

Meg could hear the radio chatter taking place on the ground. A number of training cadre was repeating her cease-fire pleas.

Without making a second pass, Meg shoved the stick right and forward. The Dauntless dove at the guilty gun emplacements below. The stressed corporal grasped the release lever near his seat and unhooked the target sleeve as the A-24 swooped low over the heads of the gunners like a mad hawk, causing them to drop on the ground.

Meg radioed the range officer as she eye-balled the damage to her aircraft. "This ain't Germany, boys. Five holes in the fuselage. That's a bit close."

She jerked back on the stick, and the Dauntless sputtered into a steep climb. The boyish-faced lieutenant glanced upward with an astonished expression. He could see the damage to the A-24. It looked like a colander with fist-size holes in both wings, the rudder, and the rear fuselage.

She flew back to Camp Ford, and without so much as a word, hooked up a fresh muslin sleeve and headed back toward the target range.

Four hours later, Meg stomped through the door of the Operations Building and marched up to the counter. A square-jawed sergeant in his mid-twenties was adjusting the day's flight schedule on a blackboard with a piece of squeaking, white chalk. A crew-cut topped off his impeccable appearance. Although awed by Meg's face, the sergeant maintained his poise.

"Excuse me, Sergeant," Meg said authoritatively.

"What can I help you with, Ma'am?"

"Your phone." Meg pointed at the black phone setting at the end of the counter. "I need to use it."

"Official business?" he inquired politely.

Meg nodded as she picked up the handset and dialed. "Person-to-person to Nancy Love."

The sergeant's eyes protruded like a frog's. "Person-to-person," he yelped.

Meg began speaking. "Nancy, the camp commander is dickin' with us. They've got us flying Cubs."

"What?" Nancy bellowed, loud enough for the sergeant to hear. "That's certainly not what Jackie had in mind when she sent y'all there."

"I tried to tell them that."

"Is the camp commander there?" inquired Nancy.

"Negative. I think we will need some help on this one before everyone goes AWOL. The attitude toward us girls stinks."

"Y'all partying too much?" Nancy asked.

"Negative," Meg answered, somewhat perturbed. "The girls mutually agreed to put our best foot forward. No drinkin'. No mile-high antics."

The sergeant stopped writing on the blackboard and looked wide-eyed at Meg.

"That must be killin' Ski," Nancy sneered jokingly.

Meg giggled. "Affirmative. She's been bouncin' off the walls."

"Meg, tell the girls I'm behind 'em 100 percent. I'll give Jackie a ring as soon as we hang up. If she won't take action, I will."

* * * * *

A small, sleek transport touched down at Blue Swamp less than 24 hours later on a rain-puddle runway. Nancy was the first to appear in the doorway, panning the faces before her. Although exhausted from the long trip, her eyes were like sharp cavalry sabers, ready to joust with the Top Brass. With a flight bag and brief case in hand, she smiled wearily.

Meg was the first to greet her. "Where's Jackie?"

"She's tied up in Washington, right now," Nancy explained. "Where's the camp commander?"

"Colonel Pine and that little weasel of an OPS officer are playing hard-to-get," Meg responded. "I guess they expect you to come to them."

"Then let's not disappoint them," Nancy snarled. "Fill me in on the way."

When Nancy and Meg emerged from behind closed doors, Nancy winked at Liz and Ski who had been patiently waiting outside, leaning against the building.

Liz grinned. "So?"

Meg answered for Nancy. "We start flyin' A-24s tomorrow. And the monthly physicals are hereby cancelled."

Ski whooped and hollered. "Nancy, how in the hell did you get ole Iron Pants to change his mind, anyway?"

"I asked him one question. Did he actually think that Jackie Cochran had initiated such an experiment without General Bolden's blessing?"

It was near dusk two weeks later when Mary reported to the flight line where a young mechanic was tightening a screw.

"There!" he declared, giving the wing a slap of the hand. "She's ready, Miss."

Mary looked quizzically at the wing. "What was wrong with it, Corporal?"

"Beats the hell outta me, Ma'am. The sarge just told me to close it up. You'll have to talk to him. He's the one that made the repairs."

Mary stepped around an organized sea of parts as she made her way to the adjacent Dauntless. The sergeant's head was lodged under the cowling, adjusting the engine with a long torque wrench. He was chewing a large chaw of tobacco.

"Sergeant, what was wrong with the other Dauntless?" Mary asked, pointing.

The sergeant bumped his head as he pulled it out, causing him to almost swallow his tobacco. He rubbed the spot vigorously as he answered Mary. "Check the Form One, Sweetheart," he spouted coldly. "Got three more like this one to get ready." He spit tobacco on the floor, just missing her toes.

Mary held her tongue as she checked the mechanics clipboard leaning upright against the nearest wheel strut. She sorted through the stack of Form Ones, looking for the respective tail number. It said, "Sticky throttle." Mary set down the clipboard and returned to the other plane.

"Takin' her up, Miss?" the young mechanic asked.

Mary began climbing aboard. "Affirmative."

"Make sure you let the engine warm up before taking off," he cautioned her, "or it might quit on ya."

"Gotcha," Mary settled into the cockpit.

She lost no time conducting a preflight check, including the wing flap controls. "Feels a bit sloppy," she said anxiously.

Not looking up, the sergeant shouted, "Take it or leave it."

Meg was already towing a muslin sleeve over the target range when Mary took off on a dark runway. The camp was under a coastal blackout because of its proximity to the Atlantic.

Without moonlight, she strained to see the outline of the treetops through the scratched-up canopy of the lumbering A-24 that sputtered as it climbed. She could almost smell the fragrance of the towering pines as the Dauntless flirted with their peaks, coughing like a chain smoker. Her stomach tightened like dried-up cowhide.

Because of the blackout, Mary was forced to fly low, struggling to spot the firing range start-point. Suddenly, she realized that she had over-flown it. Mary shoved the stick to the left. As the Dauntless went into a tight turn, it began to stall.

Mary manipulated the throttle, but the A-24 sputtered. Suddenly, the Dauntless lurched forward then flipped on its back. Grimacing, she braced herself for the pending crash. "Mayday! Mayday! I'm going down."

Two trees stripped the hapless bird of its wings before the fuselage made contact with the ground. The belly skidded in the shallow water, breaking into a dozen, flaming pieces that projected long shadows behind the backdrop of the billowy pines.

Flying past, Meg swooped down for a closer look. She pushed back the canopy, hearing only the roar of the burning, screeching metal.

Meg strained to look for a place to land. Terrible flashbacks of Robert Hyselmann burning to death rocketed across her mind. "No!" she shrieked. "Dear God, Mary! Get out.....Get out!"

With no place to land, Meg continued to circle above until relief aircraft could reach the scene. Another day would come before a ground rescue team arrived at the crash site. Meg, her thoughts numb from shock, quietly wept for her comrade.

* * * * *

Denied permission to visit crash site, Meg went to a friend in Intelligence and got a map sheet of the area then commandeered a jeep. Liz joined her in conducting an accident investigation of their own.

"I can't believe that toad-faced major had the gall to blame that accident on Mary," Liz bitched.

Meg's face was drawn and tired. Her eyes were red from the lack of sleep. "Next to you, Liz, she was the best pilot at this stinkin' hole." Meg reached into a shirt pocket and took out a folded piece of paper. She handed it to Liz. "Here, read this."

Liz reverently opened it. Her eyes bulged at what she saw. "Shit! How'd you get this?"

"Ski got it from that little twirp in Operations," Meg answered. "She went over there as soon as we heard about the accident."

"Meg, this could cost a couple of jokers their stripes."

"I want to match it up with what we may find at the crash site," Meg continued.

Liz leaned forward in her seat. "So you suspect sabotage?"

Meg shrugged. "All I know is, the major sure went into a tizzy when I told him we were comin' out here to look around."

Meg and Liz arrived at the crash site just as Major Brenner and Colonel Pine were departing. Reacting instinctively as they had so many times in the air, both women ducked off the side of the path and hid in the brush. She and Liz waited until the colonel and his investigation party passed by before continuing.

"Be careful," Meg warned her friend. "Be careful. I heard there's tons of snakes out here."

Liz swiveled her head, looking about their feet. "Snakes?"

"Water moccasins," Meg explained. "Snakes!"

Liz kept glancing down for the slithering pests as they proceeded.

"Liz, the major said something about the canopy collapsing under the weight of the fuselage. The cockpit filled up with swamp muck."

"Thank God they didn't burn to death," Liz uttered. "That's the one thing that scares the hell out of me about towing targets."

Meg grabbed Liz by the upper arm. "C'mon, Liz. We've got a lot to do and little time to do it."

Fifty meters down the foot path, Meg and Liz came across the spot where the wings were sheared off by the trees. Meg moved in for a closer look. One wing lay scattered about like pieces of twisted foil, opened by some giant can-opener.

Meg and Liz continued searching, finally coming upon the fuselage that lay in several chunks, some of which had burned into molten blobs. Meg noted the shattered canopy strewn about them.

"Liz, wouldja mind checkin' the cockpit?" Meg suggested. "I'm gonna look around for one of the gas tanks."

"Sure."

Liz came upon a gas tank that was setting in three feet of swamp water. "Now we know why that one didn't explode."

Meg immediately began wading through the muck toward the fuel tank.

"Better keep a sharp eye for those snakes you were talking about," Liz warned.

Meg unscrewed the refueling cap then reached into her jacket pocket and took out a small fruit jar. She took a sample of fuel then replaced the cap.

CHAPTER 18

Tuesday, August 24, 1943:

Piloting an AT-17, Jackie Cochran landed at Blue Swamp just before noon, accompanied by a female assistant. This was not the upbeat pilot that Meg had competed against in the 1938 Bendix Race. Jackie's eyes were sunken deeper than the Titanic. The stress of command had taken its toll.

Standing rigid, Meg coolly greeted her director as she reached the bottom step. "Jackie, it's been awhile."

Looking about, Jackie extended her right hand. "I wish this visit were under better circumstances."

"I thought maybe Nancy would be with you," Meg said, accepting the handshake.

Jackie shook her head. "I sent her to Chattanooga to coordinate a massive ferrying job."

Disappointed, Meg began to walk away slowly. "The girls are waiting to meet with you."

"Where's the camp commander?" Jackie asked.

"Not much on manners 'round here," Meg blurted. "The respect for women is the worst I've seen. They have fought us at every turn.."

"Um," Jackie conceded. "I had planned to meet with the camp commander first."

"Just as well," Meg continued. "This way we can clue you in on what's been going on 'round here."

"After lunch," Jackie held. "I haven't eaten since noon yesterday. Please lead the way."

Although visibly upset about the delay, Meg kept her cool.

"Yes, Ma'am. After mess."

Only two of the WASPs ate lunch. The rest were pacing the floor of the Operations Building.

Leaning against the wall, Liz stared at her hands. "These girls are walking powder kegs."

Meg panned the faces. "You'd have trouble cuttin' the air in here with a machete."

Ski strolled by slowly. "Where in the hell is she, any--?"

Suddenly, the door swung open, and Jackie stepped inside, remaining noticeably apart from her fellow WASP pilots.

Without fanfare, Jackie got right to the point. "Okay, girls, let me hear you, one at a time."

Liz was the first to step forward. "Two engines quit mid-air two days ago. One was the newest A-24."

"Yeah," sounded Ski. "Twelve forced landings since we got here. We've logged hundreds of hours trying to spot downed pilots in the swamp and the Atlantic."

"With the coastal blackout and all, we're flying blind," added Liz. "It's damn dangerous work. I nearly crashed when one of those idiot mechanics accidentally closed up the wing with a tool box inside it."

Stacy motioned to speak with the wave of a hand. "I grew up around the film-making business in Hollywood, and I can recognize a bad set when I see one."

"I concur," Liz chimed. "A Boy Scout camp is better run than this place."

Jackie was visibly upset with Liz's words. "Do you think we can keep this meeting constructive, girls?"

Meg's anger surfaced. "Okay, let's examine the facts. One in five radios works, and we average three blowouts a day because of thread-bare tires."

Ski nodded. "Meg's right. The mechanics openly admit that only three of the planes are fit to fly."

"Form Ones are a joke," Meg continued, "because the mechanics can't get the parts. They don't even bother to look at 'em."

"Adding insult to injury," Liz growled, "not only did Colonel

Pine stick us in Cubs, he had a bunch of male rejects checking us out."

"Wash-outs from a training course or pilots that had an air accident," added Ski. "Who are they to judge us? And another thing, Jackie, we don't even have a flight schedule board."

"Ski, that wouldn't matter anyway," Liz injected. "They wouldn't pay any attention to it even if they did have one. Assignments are based on favors 'round here."

"Half of the planes here got twice as many hours since their last overhaul as they should," Meg continued.

Jackie held up her hands. "All right, all right, girls. I'll check out the logs myself." She looked at her wrist watch. "Let's meet back here after the memorial service."

"You better be careful when you go to the bathroom, Mrs. Cochran." The voice from behind sounded familiar.

Jackie turned to see one of her own recruits. "Why's that, Beatrice?"

"The men sneaked into the nurses quarters to put Vaseline on the john seats."

Jackie put up a hand. "Okay, girls, we'll continue this after the memorial service."

Still wet in the eyes from Mary's tear-jerking memorial service, the WASPs quietly filed into the operations building to wait for Jackie Cochran. A large fan on a pedestal kept the stale, humid air moving. Several lighted cigarettes and began pacing the room, nervously puffing.

Suddenly, Jackie appeared in the doorway, letting in the intense sunlight, silhouetting several figures that marched inside. Behind her were Colonel Pine, Major Brenner, and a lieutenant who was introduced as the camp's information officer.

Ski leaned toward Meg and whispered. "I smell a rat."

"You mean a nest of brass rats," Liz sneered.

Stacy stuck her head in. "Complete with the mother rat."

Ski chuckled. "At least we have all the liars present in one room."

Meg nodded her head in agreement. "I'd like to wipe the

smug expression off the colonel's ugly face with a scouring pad."

Jackie nervously cleared her throat. "I asked Colonel Pine and his staff to join us so he could hear what you have to say, first-hand."

Meg scanned her comrades' faces. Cochran's recent flight school graduates were listening intently to what Jackie was saying. On the other hand, the former WAFs reserved their judgment until they heard what their director had discovered during her research.

Meg and Liz's chuckles drew unpleasant looks from Jackie and the colonel.

"I've studied the flight and maintenance logs, and while there are some planes that need repair, I did not find enough discrepancies to collaborate your claims."

"What about Mary?" Stacy blurted.

Jackie stood mute for a long moment. "Pilot error."

"That's bullshit, Jackie, and you know it!" Ski bellowed. What about the sticky throttle?"

Liz jumped in, "What about sugar in the gas?"

Meg thrust a hand like a bolt of lightning in front of her friend's face. "No!"

Jackie raised her head instantly. "Let me see you two in private."

Meg and Liz followed Jackie to the corner of the room where Colonel Pine and Major Brenner joined them.

Liz was the first to speak. "Jackie, somebody 'round here is using sabotage to make us look bad."

"The fuel from her plane. I had it tested," Meg explained. "Somebody put sugar in her gas tank."

"And that was directly responsible for her death," Liz decreed.

The colonel was staring at Meg. "That's a restricted area. You violated my directive."

"How do you know all this?" Jackie demanded.

Pine leaned toward Major Brenner and whispered before quietly addressing the small group. "Ladies, we understand your sorrow and frustration at this moment. We've all been under a ton of strain lately. May I suggest that we put a lid on this matter? I shall assign an investigator to look into your allegations."

Liz shook her head. "This is a smoke screen, clear and

simple."

"We lost a good friend and a great pilot to negligent maintenance conditions and certain sabotage, and you're swallowing this.....this smooth-talker's attempt to cover it up. How many of our fellow WASPs have to die before we do something about it?"

Jackie was cringing, and the male officers were grinding their teeth.

Liz fired back a look to kill at Cochran. "And you, Jackie, of all people, knuckling under to this obvious attempt to discredit us."

Jackie snapped at Liz. "That's enough!"

Meg studied her cohorts' expressions. Jackie's grads stood speechless, unbelieving, while the original WAFs beamed with pride over Liz's moral courage.

Having regrouped his composure, Colonel Pine stepped forward. "I would like to tell you girls how happy we are to have you assigned at Camp Ford."

Liz turned her head toward Meg and whispered. "He is totally ignoring my comments."

"Whaja expect, to take a cold shower with him?" Meg retorted facetiously.

The camp commander glanced only momentarily at Meg as he continued, "I will do everything possible to make your stay here a pleasant one."

"That's a crock!" Ski whispered with wild eyes. "Just wait. As soon as Cochran leaves, they'll start dumpin' on us like a garbage truck."

Meg had plenty of time to think and reflect in her diary as she sat next to a window on a slow train.

> *Funny, I can't remember a train ride lasting so long. Me and Liz are escorting Mary's casket back to her home in Cincinnati to be buried. Since us woman ferriers are not military, her family will have to bury her as a civilian. Of course, we had to pay for our own tickets to get there and back.*
>
> *I dread the thought of meeting her family. I'm*

not quite sure what I should say. I know they will want to know what happened. How can I tell them that their only child died at the hands of an American saboteur or a foreign agent? I must think of a good story to tell them. They must think she died for a purpose.

Jackie Cochran visited us at Blue Swamp after Mary's murder. She has gone over to the enemy. It seems like only yesterday that she was a woman alone in a man's world, afraid of nothing, making us all very proud to be women pilots. Now, she seems more intent on pleasing the Top Brass than charging into the future with both guns blazing.

Prior to our departure, Nancy ordered me to report to her office in Ohio after the funeral. It all sounded so hush-hush. Wondering what good (or bad) news is waiting for me is just adding to my anguish. I wonder what will come of it all?

Where is Aaron when I need him? Why doesn't he write me? We live in such different worlds. I fear we'll never be together. God, I miss him.

* * * * *

I returned to England after my training with the O.S.S., where I continued to write about the air war. I was also put on the trail of a German agent whose identity had eluded British military intelligence. Once I had determined who he or she was, I was to make contact.

* * * * *

General Armstrong called Nancy into his office. "You and your WASPs have all been checked out on B-17s, correct?"

She knew that he knew. "Yes, Sir. Why?"

"As you may or may not know, many of my pilots are reluctant to ferry bombers across the Atlantic. They perceive such flights to be a bit Lindbergish. Morale is at an all-time low. Simply put--I need your help to get these bombers over to the Eighth Air

Force."

Nancy lurched forward in her chair, bug-eyed. The star-bursts on either side of her nose said it all. "You've got it, General."

"I want you and your best pilot to ferry a B-17 to Scotland. Once these prima donnas see that a couple of women have done it, they'll step forward."

Nancy snickered. "What about a crew, General?"

Armstrong stood and walked over to a wall map and picked up a pointer. "I'm loaning you my personal crew," he answered. "You'll fly to New Castle to pick up a new B-17. Get comfortable with it before you start the mission. My navigator, Captain Bell, will fill you in on the flight plan. We've added two extra stops to shorten the distance over water."

"That isn't necessary, General. We've been on hops longer than this."

"Why take unnecessary chances," he responded. "The B-17 is a proven bomber with a great track record, but the manufacturers are pushing their shifts around the clock to meet an ever-growing shortage. You of all people should know, mechanical defects are going to surface, especially on extended missions."

"Yes, of course," Nancy acknowledged. "We've worked hard to get this far."

"Exactly." Armstrong set down the pointer and strolled back to his desk. "You seem puzzled about something."

"I guess I'm somewhat surprised that General Bolden changed his mind about women ferrying anything overseas, especially to a combat zone. As you well know, I've had to beg, borrow, and steal to get us missions flying pursuits and bombers, and that's only because the men didn't want to go on those unpleasant, often risky missions, especially to places where they might be forgotten, shelved for the duration of the war. We either get stuck in nurses quarters or sharing a B.O.Q. with a bunch of sex-starved zoo gorillas only a partition away. Yet these same boys use trumped-up excuses to deny us the chance to ferry pursuits to Alaska, not because of flying over treacherous terrain, but because the men stationed there, and I quote, haven't seen an American broad in several months. Except for you, General, the men feel that we are neither fit nor competent to fly every route to every destination. Everywhere we go, we sense their resentment and suffer because of their anger."

"Look, I know it's been a hassle for you and your girls, but I ran this mission past Bo's deputy. It's a lock.....Official."

Nancy tightened her grip on the arms of the chair. "What about Bo?"

"He's in England."

Nancy stood. "In that case, we better get our tails in gear before Bo or Jackie catch wind of it."

Three days of damaging thunderstorms along the Northeastern Seaboard slowed the first leg of the trip to Maine. Although the weather remained intense, Meg and Nancy managed to get airborne with layovers in Greenland and Iceland before taking the big leap to Scotland.

Nancy and Meg were in the cockpit conducting a preflight check when a dark figure in a rain coat exited the Operations Building. He ran toward their B-17, waving a piece of paper, limp from the heavy drizzle. It wasn't until he reached the nose of the bomber that Nancy recognized him. It was the base commander with a smug look on his face. He gave the signal for Nancy to open her side window.

Nancy took a deep breath as she stuck her head out of the cockpit window. "What is it, Colonel?"

"Your mission has been scrubbed, Mrs. Love." He held up the TWIX for her to see, pointing at it with his other hand. "Straight from General Bolden."

Nancy sighed as she slumped in her seat. Her face looked longer than the runway. "Shut it down, Meg."

"What's wrong?" Meg asked apprehensively.

The WASP Director began to unhook her safety belt as she faced Meg. "Just what I was afraid of. Bo scrubbed the mission."

Nancy climbed out of the pilot's seat and exited the bomber, lowering herself out of the belly hatch. Meg followed her lead. Without speaking, the colonel handed the message to Nancy. With a look of horror, Nancy read it silently then thrust it at Meg. General Bolden was replacing them with male ferrying pilots to complete the final leg to Scotland. She and Meg were to return to ATC Headquarters.

Meg's long face dropped to her chest, filled with disappointment. "That damn bastard. My dad warned me about him. Said that he was a two-faced politician."

"C'mon, Meg." Nancy started walking. "I betcha I know who's behind this royal screwing."

"Who, Jackie?"

"Affirmative," Nancy confirmed. "She ferried a Lockheed Hudson Bomber to England two years ago. I reckon she wants to be the only woman to have done it."

Meg stopped walking. "She did? When? I never heard anything about it."

"It was all kept very hush-hush." Nancy paused. "Somehow, some way, I'm going to fly missions in combat areas."

Meg's face brightened. "If anyone can pull it off, Nancy, you can."

I caught wind of what happened when I interviewed Bo's aide. The general had been eating dinner when the message arrived at ATC headquarters in Scotland.

Bo rocketed out of his seat, sending his chair flying into a nearby table. He bolted for a telephone to send a wire message to his deputy commander. "No women to fly transoceanic planes until I have time to study and approve."

Bo's aide continued, "General Bolden feels that women flying overseas is a preposterous, dangerous concept because of what it could do to the morale of our fighting men."

Having to turn over planes to male pilots at the Canadian border and the Atlantic Coast was a pure waste of manpower, citing that it would be a crime to send females on missions over vast stretches of frozen, deserted land or oceans. However, Bolden contradicted himself by permitting the WASPs to fly red-lined aircraft on target-towing missions with trainee gunners belting flak at them, often riveting their planes with dozens of holes.

Meg knew that it would only be a matter of time before the pilots returning from overseas duty would be replacing them as ferriers. Although sensing the beginning of the end, the WASPs held their heads up high as they did their part.

And right she was. Bolden was already plotting the demise of woman ferriers.

For several days after Jackie Cochran's return to Washington, D.C., the WASPs at Blue Swamp were grounded, and when they were finally given flying assignments, they were relegated to tracking targets in L4s and L5s.

CHAPTER 19

Meg arrived at Blue Swamp several days after her meeting with Nancy Love and was immediately confronted with the flying conditions that had not improved. She could see the fear in each of their faces. When would the next act of sabotage come?
Her own morale at an all-time low, Meg had to draw from every calorie to motivate herself to deal with Major Brenner and Colonel Pine, even if for a few days. She was to collect her squadron and take it back to where it had all started--New Castle Army Air Force Base. They would soon be ferrying pursuits and bombers. Ski and Stacy beamed at the thought of being reunited with the Mile High Club.
Taking their place at Camp Ford were 25 new WASP graduates, unaware of the state of affairs at Blue Swamp. Their arrival date had been purposely been set for a week succeeding Meg and her squadron's departure. Jackie Cochran did not want the new arrivals to know anything about the adverse maintenance conditions or the sabotage incident.

Shortly after Meg's return to New Castle, she was assigned the job of picking up a P-47 Thunderbolt from Long Island, destined for Evansville, Indiana, where it would be modified with the latest combat technology before overseas delivery. She was then to return to New Castle in a modified P-47.
No sooner had she touched down in Evansville, a warrant officer soft-talked her into flying a much-needed P-51 to Long Beach, some 1800 miles away. After grabbing some lunch and two hours of sleep, she took off, landing only twice briefly to refuel and eat. However, before she had a chance to climb out of the cockpit, a Long

Beach operations officer rushed up to her plane and yelled that she was a lifesaver–another P-51 was due in Newark immediately. So with only four hours of sleep, Meg took off for New Jersey.

She ran into an unseasonable blizzard high over the Rockies and tried to radio the airfield tower at Colorado Springs, but failed to contact anyone. Soon, the wind velocity picked up intensity. She glanced at the wings. Slush was beginning to build on the moving parts. Normally, she would have dropped altitude to let the snow melt, but she feared that she might hit one of the high mountain peaks. Suddenly, she spotted what appeared to be dim airfield lights. Meg began circling, frantically trying to make radio contact.

Finally, she heard a man's voice. "I'm orderin' the smartass kid who has been hogging this push to get off it pronto. I've got an emergency situation here."

Meg radioed back, trying to tell him that she was flying a military fighter and was requesting emergency landing instructions.

The impatient air controller roared at her. "For the last time, will the youngster interfering with official airport business kindly shut his mouth and get off this frequency. I'm trying to contact the pilot of a military pursuit in trouble."

Thin on patience herself, Meg shouted back slowly. "I'm not a kid. I am a WASP pilot in the P-51 you have been trying to contact so listen up. I am circling around to make a final approach. This is an emergency landing, over."

Finally, he got it. "You're cleared for landing. Just keep your current heading."

After grabbing something to eat, Meg checked into a hotel where she watched three additional feet of snow accumulate on the ground.

Meg washed her shirt, bra, panties, and stockings and hung them up to dry. Barely able to afford sandwiches and coffee to keep her going, Meg could ill afford to buy a shirt or any new underwear. She was destined to do laundry every night during this marathon ferrying mission.

Tired and butt-sore, Meg finally delivered the Mustang to the port of embarkation on the New Jersey coast, only to be soft-talked into delivering a P-47 to Oakland, California. Her endurance was being tested every turn. Although stressed and tired, she took the papers from the operations officer with a smile. "What the hell, it sure beats a long bus ride back to New Castle."

Twenty cups of coffee and 2500 miles later, Meg took an aerial sight-seeing tour of the Golden Gate Bridge before setting the Thunderbolt on an Oakland runway. The sun shined brightly on this otherwise mildly cool afternoon. For the past thousand miles, she had been licking her lips, just thinking about a fresh boiled lobster. Clean shirt or not, she was prepared to use her last five dollars to eat a good meal.

After parking the Thunderbolt, Meg happily bounced into the operations building. Before she was able to utter a word, a young lieutenant, who looked barely old enough to shave, waved a fistful of papers in his hand.

"Are you the pilot who just landed in the Tunderbolt?" he asked, noticeably staring at her badly wrinkled slacks and shirt.

"Oh, shit," she murmured, taking off her flying cap. "Where ya sendin' me now?"

Before he could answer, the long soft hair now flirting with her modest hips distracted him.

"I'd like to wrap my hand 'round some Jack Black 'bout now," Meg announced.

The lieutenant looked at her with a blank expression. "Black what?"

"Whiskey," Meg chuckled. "A shot of Jack Daniel's, the stuff with the black label."

"Oh." He glanced at a coffee pot setting on a small stand. "I don't have any whiskey, but I just made some fresh coffee," he said dumbly.

Meg primped her hair with her long fingers. "That would do just fine. Thank you, Lieutenant."

He walked over to get her a cup. "Cream? Sugar?"

"No thanks," she answered. "I'll take mine straight up."

"Where are you from, Miss?"

"Bendix Field, New Jersey. How 'bout you?"

He walked back with a cup in his hand. "Dubuque, Iowa."

"Pretty town," she complimented, taking the cup of coffee

from him. "Thanks." She blew on it before taking a careful sip. "Good cup of Java."

"Thanks, Miss." He eyeballed the unopened orders. "Aren't you the least bit curious?"

Meg grinned apprehensively as she raised the cup to her lips. "Okay, give me the bad news."

"That tired, huh?" he inquired. The youthful officer thumbed through the stack of orders. "You gotta help me, Miss. I've got planes stackin' up faster than a Paul Bunyon pancake-eatin' contest."

Meg groaned. "I'm sure you do, Lieutenant."

"I've got one each P-47 that needs to be ferried to New Castle."

"New Castle?"

"Yes, Ma'am," he answered. "It's in Delaware."

"Yes, I know," Meg sighed. "That's where I started this 10,000-mile gig. It'll be good to get back."

> Dear Sean,
>
> I returned to New Castle in a uniform that could stand up in the corner of my room, really gross. I wore the same shirt, bra, and panties for 20+ days.
>
> After I visited Finance and got my pay and travel, I charged off to Wilmington to catch a few longnecks and a big, thick, juicy steak. You know, the kind they just cut off the horns and run a match under it.
>
> Another one of Jackie's schooled pilots died in another target-towing accident over Blue Swamp. Thank God I got my squadron out of that God-forsaken place.
>
> It's now been almost two years since us girls first reported for ferrying duty. A lot of Budweiser down the hatch, if you know what I mean.
>
> I can only imagine what our boys on the ground are going through. What a hell it must be in those frozen foxholes. As for you and Garrett and the rest of the combat pilots, I am green-eyed with envy.
>
> Lt. Colonel Tibbets is just a cutie. And only 25

years old. He's the hotshot B-29 C.O. at the Very-heavy Bomber School in Birmingham. Anyway, he was having trouble getting enough male pilots to train because of frequent engine fires. More faulty engineering at Boeing. They should have consulted with you, big brother. Idiots designed the engine cowling too tight. About every 50 hours of engine time, fires break out. Tibbets found out about me being related to his hero, Rye Reilly. He proposed that me and one of the girls go down to Alabama to embarrass the boys into flying B-29s. Well, the Top Brass caught wind of his little project and gave it a karate chop, but not before we got a mission in. Me and Liz left Alabama the next day as the only two women to ever fly a Superfortress. Finally, I got one leg up on Jackie. I wish I could have been a fly on the wall when she found out. Then again, she probably had something to do with killing the project.

By the way, big brother, I haven't gotten a letter from you in almost nine months. You're as bad as Aaron. But I still love you.

Meg

I later caught wind of Colonel Tibbett's controversial project. A year later, he would pilot the Enola Gay, the Superfortress that dropped the world's first atomic bomb on Hiroshima, ending World War II.

In the meantime, the WASPs had become the exclusive source of test pilots for P-47 deliveries off America's assembly lines. In effect, they were the test pilots for the heaviest fighter in existence. In fact, half of the pilots ferrying fighters were females, and three out of four deliveries within the continental U.S. were ferried by woman.

In the spring, Jackie Cochran had briefed General Bolden on the state of WASP affairs. I got word that he would soon appear in front of Congress to ask that female ferriers become members of the military. Other than the shaky start at Blue Swamp, the WASP program had been an overwhelming success. They had lower accident and fatality rates than the men and were now towing targets in a variety of military aircraft and ferrying every type of plane except the B-29 Superfortress.

Once the WASPs had become a full-fledged military arm protected by medical benefits, Jackie planned to propose that women pilots would serve in all theaters of war except forward combat areas.

Armed with these facts and figures, General Bolden ventured to Capitol Hill to testify to the Military Affairs Committee on behalf of the WASPs. Accompanying him were Jackie Cochran, Nancy Love, and Meg Reilly. Meg was there not only because she was Nancy's Assistant Director, she was the star attraction, a living aviation hero who had out-performed any of the male ferrying pilots. I had arrived early to cover the story for *Aviation Life*.

Meg and I met for dinner the evening before. She was unusually uptight. I studied her as she brought me up to date on everything, particularly the bizarre events that had occurred at Blue Swamp.

Dissatisfied civilian male pilots who had avoided combat duty, distasteful ferrying missions, and often dangerous target-towing duty were now the very pilots complaining to their Congressman that the WASPs were stealing their jobs from them. Bolden nearly coughed himself silly when a number of Congressmen verbally attacked his recommendations.

A veteran of Capitol Hill politics, Bolden kept his cool. "A.A.F. policy states that any man who has had any flying whatsoever will be given a chance to qualify either as a pilot, bombardier, or navigator. If he cannot qualify, he will be given the opportunity to serve the Army Air Force in some capacity. We will not lower our standards just because a man has logged a few hours in the air." Bo turned toward his female escorts sitting in the back. "These women have demonstrated great courage and a willingness to take any mission, regardless of its danger. They have volunteered time and again for missions the male pilots have felt beneath them. We're talking about a total commitment toward the Big Picture. These women, gentlemen, have put their country ahead of any personal agenda."

Meg herself beamed with pride. Could this be the same Bo

that had killed her mission to ferry a bomber to England? Had he suffered brain damage? He was certainly taking a strong stance against the male pilots who were bellyaching. Meg panned the faces of the Congressmen who were studying her, Jackie, and Nancy as thought they were lab rats. Some seemed to be nodding thank you. Others appeared to be fearful or just plain bored with the proceedings.

If approved, the WASPs would be a full-fledged branch of the military; hence, they would receive medical treatment and life benefits.
In short, Bo had drawn a line in the sand for a Congressional decision as to the fate of females ferriers. Had he done so in September of 1942 when the demand for qualified pilots was at its highest, the women would have had better leverage. I still believe to this day that Bo may have waited until they proved themselves to protect his career, leaving it to Congress to be the bad guy.

Regardless of his underlying motive, Jackie sat pleased in her seat. Bo had phrased her position very succinctly. Her frustration threshold with Bo had apparently diminished with this trip to Capitol Hill.

He had been there before to speak to this committee and had always gotten what he wanted, even a Negro combat squadron. No small feat considering the large number of Dixie legislators who still perceived blacks as ignorant livestock incapable of learning or performing even the simplest administrative tasks. The Tuskegee Airmen went on to fly Rye Reilly's Mustang, attaining remarkable success against Germany's super aces, some with 200-plus Allied kills. Although the women had not been afforded the opportunity to ferry aircraft overseas or fly in combat, the WASPs had proven themselves capable of flying America's largest and fastest aircraft anywhere under the worse conditions.

"Unlike the young men you have eluded to," Bolden added, "these WASPs and hundreds of young women like them have met the AAF's highest standards, just like our best male combat pilots. Unlike some male recruits whining about their roles, the WASPs have been performing superbly without questioning orders. Two years ago, I was very skeptical about women flying military aircraft. Today, gentlemen, I am a believer."

Meg swiveled her head toward Nancy. "Wow! I sure wish Dad was here to hear Bo."

"Why's that?" asked Nancy.

"Bo questioned Dad's logic in letting me fly his military prototype in the Bendix Race."

Nancy grinned. "And you won." She turned her head to look at Bolden. "Too bad it took another four years for it to sink into that Neanderthal skull of his."

Meg giggled quietly.

"I need combat pilots overseas, gentlemen," Bolden continued. "And each WASP releases one male pilot to fulfill that need. Your approval of H.R. Bill 4219 will show our gratitude to these brave young women for a job well-done."

After a brief closing comment, Bolden, Meg, Nancy, and Jackie exited the committee room.

"So what happens now?" Meg asked.

Jackie answered without turning. "We await the Committee's recommendation. I think we look pretty good. Congress is not bound to go with the committee's decision, but it normally does, right General?"

Bolden looked down at his feet. "Normally, but I sensed a lot of hostility in there today," Bolden responded. "More than I've ever experienced. Although small in number, the civilian flight instructors and their trainees are squawking louder than a wounded duck, and getting the desired response. Most male thinking on the Hill favors the men. You're a serious threat to what has been a male domain. I think it will take more than a Constitutional amendment to guarantee you women's rights. It's going to take a complete change in attitude."

"I hate to admit it, Meg, but our timing is probably shitty," Nancy conceded.

Bolden noticed, wide-eyed. "I think it's going to take several generations to change perceptions. It's only been 20-some years since women's suffrage. You've got to convince as many women as you do men that you should be allowed to leave the kitchen. You girls are the darndest bunch of female Daniel Boones, I swear."

Meg and the others forced a chuckle. Their stress showed. She could tell that both Bolden and Cochran were nervous about their chosen course of action. Bo was obnoxiously tapping his nails on his brief. She wanted to reach out and smack his chubby phalanges.

Nancy seized upon the pause. "I trust your non-policy of keeping this program under wraps doesn't come back to haunt our future."

Cochran sighed, looking to Bo for help. "Maybe we should step up our efforts to build public support."

"Based on today's events," Bolden countered, "it appears you have a ways to go to catch up to the male pilot lobbying efforts."

CHAPTER 20

H.R. 4219 debuted in Congress mid-February, 1944. The War Department brought the poorly planned public relations project to a screeching halt. The WASPs' efforts to change public opinion had backfired. They were perceived in the worse possible light--as self-serving, ambitious "eager beavers."

Cochran immediately dispatched a communiqué, ordering all WASPs to stay clear of the airfields in and around Washington. They were to avoid any unnecessary contact with Congressmen and the press. Jackie was fearful of dissident opinion about her and the WASP program being leaked to reporters.

In the weeks ahead, the animosity shown toward WASP pilots became more and more intense, especially at the Army Air Base in Long Beach where a great number of government contracted flying schools had been recently closed. Hundreds of demoralized, laid-off male civilian instructors reported to the base to take ATC physicals and flight tests. The WASP presence only intensified their anger.

The showdown came in March 1944 when the Military Affairs Committee commenced hearings regarding the militarization of the WASPs. Jackie Cochran and General Bolden were present to state their case. And although Bolden had been getting his way, America was winning the war on all fronts, and thousands of pilots with combat experience were returning from overseas assignments. They were fearful of their future in aviation and were present to protest against female ferriers who were threatening their domain. If Bolden was successful in getting the committee's approval, the battle promised to extend beyond the committee hearing with a likely debate on the House floor. The defeat of H.R. 4219 would lead to the immediate inactivation of the WASP program. Jackie and Bolden sensed that it had to be now or never.

Bolden testified, "The WASP opponents on the Hill prefer to ignore the superb, unselfish female pilot performance. It's all come down to women taking men's jobs. I assure you that the WASPs will not be replacing qualified pilots. To the contrary, they will be releasing the men for combat duty. We are still very short of qualified pilots in both theaters. New pilot recruits stand a better chance of combat assignments if we retain the WASPs."

Jackie Cochran's position was that of an ultimatum. "Unless my girls get the same rank, pay, and recognition as the male pilots do for performing the same duty, and are afforded the same medical and veteran benefits as the men, my WASPs should not be exposed to the dangers of flying in combat zones. I am not suggesting that women fly combat sorties," Jackie explained. "My strategic plan all along has been to get my women commissioned as officers and ferry aircraft to and from combat zones."

Several hours later, an emotionally drained but confident Bolden emerged from the obvious grilling he received during the closed session. "It was the most negative situation I've ever experience behind that door, but I've been assured that the committee will recommend the passage of H.R. 4219."

* * * * *

Two months later, Jackie and Bolden removed the gag on WASP-disseminated information.

In the meantime, Meg and her squadron resumed ferrying factory-fresh P-51s and bombers. On June 21st, just two weeks after the D-Day invasion, the future of the WASPs was dealt a deathblow in Congress.

December 20, 1944:

Around the country, the WASPs stood in line at supply buildings to turn in their parachutes, flight suits, and their Santiago blue uniforms. They were headed home for Christmas. Meg, Liz,

Ski, and Stacy had traveled from their last duty stations to New Castle to turn in their equipment. Sergeant Flowers' sadly greeted them as they entered his supply building with their heads high and shoulders straight. Maybe he had mellowed over the past two and a half years; maybe he held a soft spot for the spunky young female pilots. He reverently and respectfully accepted their gear. Upon their departure, he hugged them all.

Meg turned in the doorway to look back one last time at the neat stack of WASP uniforms setting lifelessly on top of the counter. Standing next to it was their grouchy supply sergeant, fighting back the tears. He removed the soggy cigar stub from his mouth and saluted her.

After Meg shut the door, Flowers turned to his gawking staff, bellowing, "Who in the hell you boys eye-ballin'? Get your sorry asses movin'!"

* * * * *

I arrived early that morning to cover the inactivation activities. On my way from the airport, Robert St. John of NBC radio spouted a commentary on the state of WASP affairs. "Today, all over the country, these girl fliers will be bidding each other and their male colleagues.....tearful good-byes. They'll be turning in their parachutes and giving some last affectionate pats to warplanes they've been flying around the country. And they'll have lumps in their throats as they take off their uniforms and slip into their civilian clothes. They'll be.....home for Christmas."

"But ask any one of them," he continued, "and you'll learn that they don't want to sit out the war. I've met some of the WASPs. They are intelligent girls, sincere and capable. They were doing an important work, efficiently well. And dangerous work it was, too. But today, they go back to civilian life. I called Washington this morning. I was told there isn't going to be an official ceremony.....just some tearful farewells. A thousand-plus WASPs go back to civilian clothes because a narrowly-focused Congress doesn't think they're needed any longer."

Their civilian flying future looked dismal at best on their last government service day.

I escorted Meg to a dinner at the New Castle Officers' Club, honoring the downtrodden WASPs. Colonel Studebaker personally presented a rose to each of the WASPs then delivered a tear-jerking oratory on their successful exploits. As we stood to dance, a waiter streaked through the tight rows of tables, screaming "Fire! Fire!"

I was impressed with the manner in which everyone calmly flocked outside just as the fire trucks came to a screeching halt. Outside the fire perimeter, the look on everyone's face was one of mixed emotions. The officers and their wives stood like mutants staring at the fire, tearfully saddened about the destruction of their club. I turned to Liz. She was staring coldly at the flames, grinding her teeth.

"Good, that's good," she droned. "I hope it burns to the ground."

An ironic ending to the WASP saga, I thought.

Painfully collecting their civilian clothes, memorabilia of past missions, and posters of Frank Sinatra and Clark Gable, they forlornly packed and funereally exited the base. Nearly all paused briefly to glance back one last time at the long flight line. Dozens of warplanes desperately needed in combat areas sat quietly with no one to ferry them. Still others stole envious glimpses over their shoulder at planes landing or taking off in the late-morning sun. The roar of the powerful engines swelled their already dispirited emotions. And a sudden vacuum in their hearts.

Some of these women had hocked everything and quit their civilian flying jobs to serve their country. Many of Jackie Cochran's female pilot candidates assigned to Class 1-45 were informed of the inactivation upon their arrival at Avenger Field and instructed to return home at their own expense. Some were forced to hitchhike hundreds of miles, and in some cases, thousands of miles to return home. Lockheed, North American, and Northrop who had financially thrived with female ferriers in the cockpit of their planes turned them away for civilian jobs in favor of male pilots. The WAFs and WASPs had logged over 60 million miles in 77 types of military aircraft from small utility cubs and redlined antiquated fighter-bombers to streaking, high-performance pursuits and massive, powerful bombers.

The largest recruiter of the ex-WASPs was the Civil Aeronautics Administration, but they were non-flying positions, including control tower operators and ground-to-air communicators at navigational aid stations. Even Jackie Cochran, considered by most aviators to be one of the most versatile pilots, male or female, was forced to settle for a job at Northeast Airlines, not to fly but to motivate women to buy tickets on commercial flights. Ski had already accepted a position as a stewardess with American Airlines while Stacy returned to Hollywood as a stunt actress. Unwilling to accept anything less than a flying slot, Meg planned to return to her father's aircraft design company as a test pilot. She had gone a full circle. And Liz? There was talk of her marrying Doctor John.

I arrived at the nurses quarters to see Meg before she departed for Bendix Field. The roar of a pursuit taking off from the adjacent runway interrupted the reverent silence. Meg finished packing and was closing her father's duffel bag when I knocked on the open door.

"Good morning, gorgeous."

Meg looked up and managed a smile. "Good morning, yourself, Aaron. Come in."

Her eyes were tired from the lack of sleep. I could tell she had been crying. I walked up to her and gave her a hug and a kiss.

"Can you come with me?" she asked.

"I wish I could," I answered. "I've been ordered back to Europe."

She turned to the weathered Gladstone bag setting on her bunk. Setting next to it was the white scarf Amelia had given her. She picked it up and stared at it silently then buried her sullen face in it. Suddenly, her eyes gushed like a flash flood, and her composure sagged. "Oh, Mom, were are you when I need you most?"

* * * * *

A fancy yellow convertible whizzed along a dusty gravel road lined with tall, strong oaks. The car suddenly braked in front of the Reilly home and pulled into the driveway, stopping next to the front steps leading to the long wooden porch. The driver honked the horn. From a nearby field, Meg and Garrett looked at one another then broke into a running stride, their lunch buckets swinging wildly as they scampered toward their home. Marilyn Reilly opened the door and emerged with two suitcases. A distinguished looking man in a business suit climbed out of the car and helped her with the luggage.

Their lungs burning, six-year-old Meg and Garrett raced to the driveway as their mother climbed into the passenger seat. The convertible wheeled around in the yard and headed for the road. The driver brought his car to a halt as it reached the bewildered twins. Marilyn Reilly climbed out and approached them.

"Where are you going, Mom?" Meg looked perplexed.

Marilyn stooped to hug them both. "I'm going away."

Dazed and frightened, Garrett cried, "When will you be back, Mom?"

She ignored his question. "Your dad will be home soon," she responded. "Go in to the house and have a snack."

She kissed them both and climbed back into the convertible. Meg and Garrett waved at the car as it rounded the corner and sped away, leaving a trail of swirling dust.

* * * * *

"Are you all right?" I asked.

Meg nodded. "Yeah," she said unconvincingly.

"Would you like to talk about it?"

Without answering, Meg packed the scarf in her Gladstone bag.

I sensed there was a hidden agenda. "What about your mother. Why won't you talk to me about it?"

"This is not the time. Trust me."

I walked over and hugged her. "So, what are your plans? Are you going back to Bendix Field?"

"Liz and me are going to visit Mary's grave. Then, I guess so...I need to sort a lot of things out. Nancy said that she wants to talk to me before I leave."

"Any idea about what?"

Meg shook her head.

I wanted to close the door and make love to her, but it was the wrong moment. I pulled her in close for a hug that seemed to last an eternity. I was afraid I was losing her. Maybe I had waited too long. Maybe I should have had the courage to ask her to marry me.

With her head high, Meg walked into Nancy's office as she was packing a footlocker with memorabilia. "Hi, Nancy."

She looked up. "Oh, hi, Meg. Did y'all get your stuff packed?"

"Affirmative. Aaron is going to give us a lift to the train station."

Nancy walked over to the doorway and looked both ways before shutting the door.

"So why all the cloak-and-dagger?" asked Meg.

Nancy sat down on the edge of the desk. "How would you like to keep on flying?"

"Is this a trick question?"

"No, but what I'm going to tell you is classified. A certain general who is particularly fond of us has asked me to conduct transition training on your dad's P-51 to free up his combat pilots."

"If I rejoin my dad, at least I'll be flying," Meg responded.

Nancy kept a sober face. "I know. That's what is beautiful about all this. We'd be getting better pay as government contractors. We've got more experience than anyone has in his command. He lost two of his best pilots last week trying to wing it on their own. They're used to flying Thunderbolts."

Nancy reached around for a pack of Lucky Strike cigarettes on the desk and offered one to Meg. She struck a match for Meg's cigarette before lighting her own. "You don't want some inexperienced pilot flying wing for your brother, do you?"

Meg took a deep drag. "That's a low-blow, Nancy."

"I didn't mean it that way. I need your help and so does your country whether the dummies realize it or not."

Meg took a puff and exhaled. "I'm doing this for you and Garrett. No one else."

Nancy walked over to the window and looked out. "We need one more pilot."

Without hesitation, Meg responded, "Liz Hunter. Besides, everyone else has already departed."

"What about her doctor friend?"

"That may be a problem, all right." Meg took a last drag from her cigarette then squashed it in an ashtray. "What should I tell my dad? He's expecting me for Christmas."

"You'll all have to come up with an excuse. No one is to know about this, understand?"

"When do we leave?"

"We have to be in New York in four days."

"Jesus!" Meg exclaimed. "That's Christmas Eve."

Nancy spun around. "Yes, I know. I'm sorry."

"Anything else?"

"That's it for now, Meg. I want you and Liz to meet me at the Black Angus at 1800 hours. I'll brief y'all then."

Meg called me at the hotel. It all sounded so mysterious. Had she found someone else? She said that she would write to me, but I got this empty feeling. I walked down to the hotel lounge, ordered a drink, and finished my article about the WASP inactivation. I then left for Washington to report to the O.S.S. for my next mission. I was to return to France behind enemy lines and make contact with the French Underground to help effect the escape of downed pilots.

CHAPTER 21

Four days later, a C-47 transport touched down on a lush green English airfield freckled at one end with large Quonset huts and concrete block buildings. A light mist gave off a dull shine on the grass as Meg and her comrades off-loaded with their gear, gazing about with excitement. It had happened. They were really in a combat zone.

As they began walking away from the whining engines of the transport, they could hear church music blurting from one of the buildings. The rain picked up intensity as the duo, ignited with renewed enthusiasm, neared a military Quonset hut. Above the door, a white sign with black letters, read: HEADQUARTERS.

An OD sedan passed by and made a sharp turn, heading away from the Operations Quonset hut. The driver gawked at Meg and Liz who were standing under the eaves, sporting khaki slacks, leather flying jackets, and long flying scarves draped down the front of their jackets.

A young, muscular clerk in a well-tailored duty uniform looked up from a small desk. His name tag read: Ramirez. "Yes, can I help you with something?" he stammered.

"We're reporting in, Sergeant," responded Nancy in a deep drawl. "We're your new P-51 instructors."

Sergeant Ramirez got up from his desk, walked over to a closed door, and knocked on it.

The WAFs could hear two boots plop down on the wooden floor, followed by heavy footsteps toward the door. Meg and Liz smirked as a sleepy-eyed colonel stuck his head out of his office. "Yes?"

"The instructors you have been expecting are here, Colonel," Ramirez announced.

Nancy took a step forward. "Hello, Colonel. May we have a word with you?"

His eyes instantly brightened. "Certainly! Come in. Come in." He turned sideways to let them enter then addressed his clerk. "I don't want to be disturbed, Sergeant."

"Yes, Sir."

Although short, the colonel carried himself with the confidence of a tall man. He shut the door and walked to his desk. He picked up a half-smoked cigar and lighted it with a Zippo.

Nancy, Liz, and Meg sat on folding chairs.

"I see you made it safe and sound." He blew a cloud of choking smoke as he glanced at Meg then Liz. "Welcome to England," he said. He was visibly engrossed with their beauty.

Nancy introduced her comrades. "Colonel, this is Liz Hunter and Meg Reilly. Girls, this is Colonel Trevor Douglass."

Douglass glanced down at the *Aviation Life* cover as he deposited an ash in a nearby tray. It was a picture of Meg sitting in the open cockpit of a P-51, smiling. The cut line read: 'WASP Stung by Congress." He studied Meg for a long moment. "You're Rye Reilly's kid," he uttered, matter-of-factly.

Meg nodded bashfully. That was one of the many great things about her--modesty.

"Rye was a hell of a pilot." He gave her the once over. "I met him near the end of the last war."

"Thank you. I'LL tell him you said so, Colonel."

"Now, ladies, I want you to know that the general and I are darn glad to have you here. I'm short on pilots, and I'm even shorter on serviceable fighters. I've got three P-51s with a dozen more en route and no qualified pilots. We lost two of our best pilots recently when they tried to take 'em up without a proper orientation. The Germans have downed a lot of our aircraft during this counteroffensive. They pushed us back into France. It was a pretty desperate situation until Patton diverted his Third Army to relieve the 101st at Bastogne. Now, we're striking back, and I need pilots qualified to fly the Mustang. No press or fanfare, understand?"

"When do we get started?" inquired Nancy.

"This afternoon, if you aren't too tired from your trip."

Nancy stood. "We've been sittin' on our butts for two days. We're ready to get started. The sooner we get our boys trained, the sooner this war will end."

"Thank you, Nancy, for your positive attitude."

Meg cleared her throat. "Not to change the subject, but I'm anxious to see my brother Garrett. He's been flying bombers over here. I was ho--"

"This classified project is on a need-to-know basis," Douglass interrupted. "I"m sorry, Miss Reilly."

"Excuse me, Colonel," said Nancy, "If we're to get started this afternoon, can we get settled in."

"Yes, of course. You girls can use my quarters. I'll move in with my X.O. for the time being. Have you eaten?"

"We haven't had a good meal since yesterday," Nancy answered.

Douglass walked over to the door and opened it. "Follow me, ladies."

* * * * *

Over the next seven days, Meg, Liz, and Nancy watched four squadrons of Thunderbolts and bombers take off every morning to attack targets in Western France and Belgium. Each afternoon, they saw fewer P-47s and bombers return. German aces, some now flying the new jet-powered Messerschmidts, hacked apart American bomber formations, easily outmaneuvering the lumbering Thunderbolts. Nancy stepped up the effort to get more pilots trained and into the air. With under-wing fuel tanks, the new D-model Mustang could now escort their big friends deep into Germany and back. Overnight, the percentage of Super Fortresses returning from bombing missions increased.

After two weeks, the German winter offensive had been stopped, and it was time to move the balance of the fighter group to France. Pilot replacements would continue to report to England for in-processing before being transported to France or Italy.

* * * * *

It was just after Sunday breakfast that Sergeant Ramirez knocked on the door. "Mrs. Love?"

"She's not here," Meg answered. She walked to the door and opened it. "What is it, Sergeant?"

"The Colonel needs her, ASAP!"

"She went to church services," Meg informed him.

"Thank you, Ma'am." Ramirez turned on a heel and left.

Meg turned to Liz who was lying on her cot, reading a magazine. "I wonder what that was all about."

Without looking up, Liz said, "It's starting."

"Oh, don't be such a skeptic," Meg countered. "The only flying we've done is around here. Meg walked to her cot and flopped. She then opened her diary.

Ramirez jogged up to the briefing hut where church services were being held. He opened the door and peered inside before entering, removing his overseas cap. It was a full house. He bobbed his head, trying to spot Nancy. He finally saw her near the far aisle, and quietly walked around, stooping as he reached her chair. Ramirez put a hand on her forearm.

Nancy turned. A puzzled look grew on her face.

"The Colonel needs to see you right away, Ma'am"

Nancy half-stood and began following Ramirez, slipping on her leather flight jacket as they reached the door.

When they got to the colonel's office, his boss was pacing the floor.

She halted at the doorway. "Yes, Colonel?"

He stopped and looked out the window. "We've got a problem," he said in a serious tone.

Anxiety set in. Nancy took a deep breath, almost afraid to say anything. "What's that, Colonel?"

"Four of our squadrons in France took heavy losses yesterday, and three others are stressed out from a lack of rest. "I've got to get that new shipload of Mustangs over to France. Problem is, I haven't got any capable pilots available." He turned to face her. "I'll come to the point. I called the general and briefed him on the situation. I told him that I don't have anyone here capable of flying them except the contracted pilots. And you know what his response was?"

Nancy's eyes became more intense. She reached up and scratched her cheek.

As she stumbled for a response, the colonel continued, "He said that he didn't care if they were contracted labor or not–if they can fly a Mustang, use them."

Nancy's mouth fell open.

"What do you say, Nancy? Can you help us?"

She was flabbergasted, almost waiting for the punch line. "You mean, you want us to ferry P-51s to France?"

"You'd have to keep a low profile. . . . and don't take off your flying caps, no matter what," the colonel added. He picked up a cigar and lighted it. "Of course, unless you cut your hair."

"You aren't joking, are you Colonel?"

"These will be quick hops, in and out." He exhaled a billowing smoke that suddenly filled his office.

She could tell he was being serious. "I'm game. Of course, I will have to talk to the other girls. That decision will be up to them. You know how those two are about their long hair."

* * * * *

With a renewed confidence in their step, Meg, Liz, and Nancy reported to the flight line, dressed in military-issue fleeced-lined flying suits and jackets. With the opportunity of a lifetime, they had cut their long hair, and wore no make-up. Because of their height, they moved about unnoticed. The colonel had been very exact in his planning. Their I.D. cards reflected just their initials and last name. The colonel had already walked the orders through operations so no one else would know that three women were about to make history. Of course, no one could ever know about it. He had also posted just their last names to the Assignments Board, and supplied them with return orders.

They were to deliver the P-51's then return in older pursuits in need of maintenance. He had it all arranged at the other end with one of the general's trusted operations officers. This was now a top-secret mission on a need-to-know basis. And if everything went well, there would be plenty more missions. They were excited but nervous. After all, they had performed brilliantly before, only to be kicked in the stomach, time and again.

"If Jackie or Bolden ever get word of this, they'll have a coronary," Meg quipped.

Nancy whirled around. "Bolden would probably relieve the general and everyone else involved. That's why this must be done smoothly without a hitch, understood? And remember to drop your voices--think before you speak on the radio or to anyone on the ground."

Both Meg and Liz nodded that they understood.

Nancy greeted the colonel who handed them their orders and charts. He quickly went over the flight plan and call signs then stood back as they conducted their pre-flight inspection. Soon, all three climbed aboard and started their engines. One by one, they began to taxi and take off.

Meg cheered as she gave everyone a thumbs-up. It was really happening--flying in a combat zone.

Within 10 minutes, the formation reached the English Channel. The sky was clear of any clouds or planes except for a small cub searching for German U-boats. They climbed to 15,000 feet and cruised into France, passing over the coastal city of Calais. They saw patches of snow as they traveled farther east. Within 40 minutes, they landed on a former French airfield in the middle of a vast plain of farmland. At one end was a concrete tower, partially destroyed from bombing. Nearby were several rows of GP tents and Quonset huts. Smoke poured from their chimneys. A number of anti-aircraft gun emplacements and bunkers were positioned around the base of the perimeter. A mix of destroyed Allied and German aircraft lay strewn both inside and outside the perimeter, testimony to the desperate battles waged to this point. A young colonel in his flight jacket greeted them as they pulled up to the flight line and parked. He quickly pointed out the pursuits they were to ferry back to England, and within 20 minutes, they were airborne. It had been a well-coordinated round trip.

Colonel Douglass greeted them as they landed. "Great job, girls. The general is very pleased. And I'm impressed that you were professional enough to cut your hair. Hell, if I didn't know you, I'd assume that you three are fresh young faces. No offense. Now, get some rest. You'll have a full day ahead tomorrow."

"We're looking forward to it, Colonel," responded Nancy.

"Thank you, Colonel," said Meg.

"You're welcome, young lady." He watched them walk away in unison. He shook his head. "Wish I had a hundred more like 'em," he uttered to himself.

Meg and the others found themselves making at least three round trips a day, delivering the equivalent of five squadrons of P-51Ds

Liz bounced into the room with a copy of *Stars and Stripes* and two cups of coffee. She set the cups on a small table then handed the newspaper to Meg who was writing in her diary.

Meg looked up. "Thanks." She reached out for one of the cups and took a sip of coffee. "That really hits the spot." Looking over, she spotted Liz opening a letter. "Sugar reports came in, huh?" Meg hid her disappointment.

"Yep." Liz sat on the edge of her cot.

"So, how's Doc?" Meg inquired. She took a pack of Lucky Strikes off the table, took one out and lighted it.

"He said to say *hello*. Hey, he's been promoted to lieutenant colonel!" Suddenly, Liz lurched forward. "That bitch!"

Meg lowered the newspaper to see. "What's wrong now?"

"Doc ran into Flo at the O-club. Says that Flo took a job as an air controller at Wilmington Airport."

Meg blew a smoke ring and watched it flutter away. "Well?"

Liz suddenly wadded up the letter and threw a strike at Doc's picture setting on the dresser.

"You never talked much about your relationship with Hub," Meg noted, "What really happened?"

Liz thought for a moment. "My father didn't like him much so he hired a private detective to check him out. It seems Hub's father was a mobster. His mother was a beautiful flapper who liked hanging around guys with fancy clothes, expensive cars, and big wads of bills in their pocket. Anyway, she got pregnant with Hub, so his dad married her. Here's the clincher--his real name is Roth."

Meg shook her head. "Roth?"

"Joey Roth was a big time bootlegger. After Prohibition, he got involved in extortion and gambling. He was very tight with some hit man by the name of Bugsy Siegel. Anyway, that's how Hub got the money for his Indy racing team and planes to fly in the Bendix."

Meg sat upright on the side of her cot. "And that government contract--mob payoffs?"

"It gets better," Liz continued. "Hub hurt his neck and knee during a race a few years ago. His race car slammed into a barricade. From that point on, his dad forbade him from racing cars. That's how he got into flying.

"So how did Hub get through the Army physical with a bad neck?"

"Simple, he lied."

"That's what Aaron should've done,' Meg observed, "but why did Hub change his name to Martin?"

"His father didn't want his son to be involved in the family business."

"Maybe he just wanted Hub to have a better life than he did," Meg guessed.

Liz bobbed her head left and right. "Maybe, but they still have relatives living in Germany. The name Martin draws less attention than Stein or Fredenberg. Besides, the military would have never allowed him to get a security clearance with the name Roth, and you must have one to attend Flight School."

"I agree," Meg uttered. "So why are you telling me all this now, Liz?"

"Because I was too embarrassed to tell you before. And because I had to promise my folks not to see Hub anymore or talk about him if I wanted to finish college or take up flying. Besides, he was a jerk to me. The choice wasn't hard, especially after he lied to me about his past. How could I trust him? He hustles every good-looking chick he sees."

Meg stood and walked over to Liz. "No wonder you ditched him."

"And what about you, Meg? Did you ever level with Aaron abo5ut your mother?"

Meg was taken back--she had been less than open with me, but I hoped it had something to do with me being a reporter. She was afraid I might publish it. The next entry in Meg's diary that day said that she was planning to tell me everything about her mother the next time she saw me.

* * * * *

Meg and Liz leaned over the side of the jeep and grabbed their gear. Meg clutched her Gladstone bag with a free hand and hustled to the flight line where the P-51s were parked, looking for their assigned tail numbers.

"Where's Nancy?" asked Liz. "She usually meets us here."

Colonel Douglass strolled up to them. "Good morning, ladies. Here are your charts. You'll be flying into a different airfield today. It's farther west, a bit closer to the front. We took that airfield once, but the Gerries recaptured it during the Battle of the Bulge. This is a must mission. We've mounted a new offensive and have dozens of new pilots that need these planes--ASAP."

Meg glanced around his shoulders, looking for Nancy. "Have you seen our illustrious leader?"

Douglass began unrolling the first chart. "The general flew in a few minutes ago and wanted to meet with us. She said for you to handle this one."

Meg shrugged with a glowing expression, "Fine."

Wingtip-to-wingtip, Meg and Hub flew their Mustangs in low for the final approach. Meg glanced down. Blanketed with snow, the former French airfield set in the piedmont of a hilly forest near the Belgium border. On one side were several rows of GP tents, Quonset huts, and two concrete blockhouses. A nearby concrete tower set adjacent to the frozen runway. A number of anti-aircraft gun emplacements and bunkers were positioned around the base near the perimeter.

The femme duo roared onto the runway and taxied to the flight line, joining the long line of P-47s. A refueling truck arrived as they climbed down. Two grounds crewman hustled to hook up the hoses to Meg's wing tanks. She looked around for an operations officer that should have been standing by to greet them, but there were only enlisted men moving about, working on the planes.

Meg turned to Liz. "Somebody screwed up the coordination on this one."

"No shit!" Liz shivered. "Damn, it's cold here. Maybe we should ask one of these guys."

Meg shook her head. "Let's give 'em five minutes."

Finally, Meg and Liz walked up to one and asked directions to Operations. He pointed toward a large tent with a sign above it, reading, OPERATIONS.

As Meg and Liz approached the door, a tough-looking tech sergeant exited and saluted. He held the salute, waiting for Meg and Liz to return it.

"Good morning, Sirs!" the noncom obnoxiously blurted. The sides of his head were white from a recent military haircut.

It finally dawned on Meg and Liz that they should return the salute.

The sergeant finally brought down his arm, shaking his head as he marched away. "Wet-nosed pilots," he muttered to himself.

Meg opened the door and peeked inside. A young lieutenant was talking on a field telephone and a sergeant was glued to a copy of *Stars and Stripes*.

She turned to Liz. "Better wait here. I'll try to find out what's going on."

Liz snapped, "Hurry up, I'm freezing."

Meg entered and approached the sergeant who looked up from his newspaper. "Sergeant, where is everybody?"

"At the mess hall or the officers' lounge. The rest are flying escort or air support".

"Where's the officers' lounge?"

"Next to the messhall, behind this building," he said, pointing.

"Thank you, Sergeant." Meg turned and exited.

"Well?" demanded Liz, still shivering.

"Everyone's at chow. C'mon." Meg started walking.

Liz hustled to catch up. "Where are we going?"

"To get a beer."

"What?"

"I was just kidding." Meg kept walking. "I'm hungry. Let's catch some lunch."

Liz ran to catch up with Meg. "I'm game."

Benny Goodman's "Flat Foot Floogee" belched from the officers' lounge as Meg and Liz strolled up to the door and entered. The crowd of mostly young male pilots and a few Red Cross girls and nurses sat about several round tables, dancing in their seats, clicking their fingers to the music. Stale cigarette and cigar smoke hung in the still air like a heavy fog, forcing Liz to rub her eyes. Several model planes hung by string from the ceiling, and pictures of aerial combat graced the plywood walls.

The balding bartender, a lanky man in his early-forties, was busy mixing drinks behind a rustic-looking bar along the back wall. He wiped his hands with a white towel then slung it over a shoulder, eyeing the new pilots in their flight suits and leather flying jackets as they sauntered over to the bar and sat on stools. "Name your poison."

Meg signaled him with two fingers. "A Bud and two fingers of Jack Black for me," she said in a low voice.

"Vodka martini," Liz hummed, "with two olives."

The bartender made small talk as he flipped a bottle of Jack Daniel's, catching it directly over a shot glass, not losing a drop as he expertly poured the shot. He then set a frosty bottle of Budweiser on the bar in front of Meg. He grabbed a clean glass off the back bar and shoveled up chipped ice. Looking at Liz, he poured a hefty jigger of vodka. The ice crackled and snapped from the warm liquor. "Hey, newbie, do you know what an olive is?"

Liz looked at him with skeptical eyes. Dropping her voice, she said, "Is this a joke?"

"It's an old maid's cherry turned green with envy," he said with a poker face.

Meg howled.

Liz rolled her eyes at Meg. "I really needed that."

Suddenly, the music ended.

Liz reached into a pocket and pulled out a coin. She flipped it in the air, catching it as she slid off her stool. "So, what's your pleasure?"

"Something peppy."

Liz headed for the jukebox.

Suddenly, a young male pilot emerged from the darkness of the bathroom area and headed toward his table, passing by Liz who was looking down, avoiding eye contact with everyone. He glanced backward with a puzzled look then took his seat next to his companion. "That guy sure looks familiar . . . the one over there at the jukebox."

His comrade craned his neck to see whom his friend was talking about, but he could only see the back of Liz's head.

Soon, "Straighten Up and Fly Right" filled the lounge. Liz turned and rejoined Meg at the bar.

The male pilot stood. "I'm sure I know that guy." He slowly sauntered toward the bar and tapped Liz on the shoulder.

Liz stared at her martini, ignoring him.

The pilot tapped her again. "Don't I know you?"

Liz turned her eyes ever so slightly to see who it was. "Shit," she uttered quietly to herself.

The pilot leaned closer and raised his voice. I said, "Don't I know you?"

Meg turned her head enough to see his face then turned away with anxious eyes.

CHAPTER 22

Meg swore to herself, "Of all the friggin' luck."
Without looking up at him, Liz answered, "I don't think so."
"How can you tell, you haven't looked at me," the pilot countered.
Meg took the lead and stood.
It was though he had seen a ghost. He glanced back at his companion who was still sitting. He motioned for him to join them. He turned back to Meg. "Good God! I don't believe it."
Meg quickly panned the faces to see if anyone was eavesdropping. The other pilots were busy singing and talking to the nurses and donut dollies. She looked back at the pilot who was sporting a thin mustache, and put her finger over her lips. "Hub, don't say another word," Meg ordered.
The other male pilot navigated the throng of pilots to arrive at his companion's side. His eyes burst from their sockets. "Jesus Christ!" He glanced at Liz. "What on earth?"
Meg quickly motioned for him to quiet. "Garrett, don't say a word. Come outside with me now, both of you."
She pulled Garrett and Hub closer and whispered aloud. We're here on a classified mission. No one is to know that we're women, understand?"
Hub stepped backward in shock, his eye sockets exploding at Liz. "Well, if it isn't my ex-favorite blonde."
An equally shocked Garrett turned to Meg and said, "Okay, Sis, what's up?"
"Follow us outside, and I'll fill you in." She turned to Liz. "Finish your drink, we're leaving."

Liz gulped her martini as she stood. The four left together.

Once outside, Meg turned to Garrett. "What's Hubert doing with you?"

"I didn't know he was going to be here. Hub arrived by transport about four hours ago. I arrived in a Jug just an hour before you...from my old bomber base. Everyone was too busy to process me in so I took off for the officers' lounge. I haven't even been assigned a plane, yet."

Liz turned to Hub. "How about you, Hotshot?"

"Yeah, a big lumbering Jug."

"Now, Sis, what on earth are you doing here?" demanded Garrett.

Meg took the lead with Garrett by her side. Liz walked with Hub behind them.

Hub noted Liz's flying jacket and flight wings. "When in daylights did you take to flyin'?"

"How ya hanging, Hubert."

"Don't call me that. My name is Hub, remember?"

Meg overheard them and laughed. "I recognized you, Hubert, even with that odor-holder." She grinned over her shoulder at Hub who was wincing.

"It's the little Reilly girl," Hub scoffed. "Still tryin' to act like a man, I see."

"And I see you're still a jerk in man's clothing," Meg retorted. "Will there ever be any justice?"

Liz glanced back and forth at Meg and her twin brother. "I can hardly tell you two apart."

"So, Sis, what's all this cloak-and-dagger stuff?" asked Garrett.

Meg glanced about before responding, "Supposedly, we're here to train pilots on the Mustang, but due to a shortage of pilots, the general ordered us to start ferrying Mustangs. It's all very hush-hush."

Garrett turned to Meg. "Does Dad know you're here?"

"We were instructed not to tell anyone," Liz injected.

Garrett shook his head. "I hope you know what you're doing, Sis."

"I do."

"I talked to Dad on the short-wave just awhile ago," Garrett said. "He's very worried about you. He was expecting you on Christmas."

Meg dropped her eyes. "That's because we were in the air. Don't worry. I'll write him tomorrow."

"So, what have you been flying?" Meg asked.

"B-17's," he answered. "I just finished up with my 25th mission. I could've gone home, but I wanted a shot at the krauts in a peashooter"

"Well, maybe they'll let you have one of the new P-51s we just ferried in here," she said, pointing.

Both Garrett and Hub gazed at the sleek silver pursuits. They could see someone holding the refueling hose.

"Which one did you fly in here, Sis?"

She strained to read the tail numbers. "The second one."

"Well, let's check 'em out," suggested Garrett.

He began walking toward the Mustangs. Liz joined him while Meg and Hub pulled up the rear.

Meg turned to Hub. "So, are you anxious to try one of one of these pregnant cigars?"

Hub cleared his throat. "You don't forget easily, do you?"

"Why should I?" she came back.

"I'm gonna be an ace," Hub announced.

Meg pulled her head back slightly. "I see you've lost none of your cockiness," she sneered. "Recorded any kills yet?"

"Not yet," he answered. "I just got here from the States. I've been training pilots at Pursuit School."

"I thought that's what the returning pilots were supposed to do."

"That's true, so I was finally able to get my request approved for combat duty."

Suddenly, they could hear "Blue Skies" blurting from the officers' lounge.

"Great song," Hub murmured, "don't you think, Baby-face?"

Meg stopped walking, squared her shoulders, and looked Hub square in the eye. "Don't call me Baby-face!"

"Ah, don't get your panties in a bunch," Hub drawled as he resumed walking.

Meg bolted to catch up. "I see you're still a jerk, Hubert."

"Don't call me that," Hub snarled. "My name is Hub."

Meg looked upward, thinking. "Now I remember. That's short for Hubcap."

"And what about you, little girl?" Hub countered. "I suppose you've still got a crush on that *sweet* writer."

Garrett turned to Liz. "I'm surprised that Meg is still interested in Aaron after all this time. I was starting to think that maybe he was a little light in the loafers."

"She didn't tell you?"

"Tell me what?"

"Meg spent the night with him at his hotel room."

Garrett seemed surprised. "Has he seen her since?"

"Yes, a couple of times," answered Liz, "but he has been spending a lot of time in Europe. Before that, she went out on a couple of dates with a pilot called Hondo, but she was never serious about him. She's saving herself for Aaron, all right, but he better start writing more."

Everyone came to a stop in front of the first Mustang. Meg rejoined her twin brother.

Garrett marveled at his father"s plane. "It's a beaut, Sis. I like the modifications."

Hub stepped between Garrett and Meg. "By the way, Baby-face. I heard that you skirts had it made. Lots of leave time and powder-puff missions."

Meg's nostrils flared. "That's a crock.....*Hubert*!"

Liz joined the others. "After you and I broke up, *Hubert*, I earned my pilot's license. Then, *Hubert*, I went on to become a damn good flight instructor. Most of us *skirts* were flight instructors before we joined the WAFs. Half of the male pilots that fought in the early days of the war got their licenses through one of us *skirts*. We had a better safety record than the male ferrying pilots did. We took all the shit jobs while you hotshots got all the glory."

"Well, well, I don't believe it. Miss Vassar College here has developed a sailor's tongue," Hub said facetiously.

"If we ever got the chance, Hubert," added Meg, "us *skirts* would show you guys a thing or two about shootin' down krauts."

Hub held up a hand to stop her. "I just remembered something--how much I dislike pushy skirts."

Garrett faced Hub. "Cool your engines, Hub. That's my sis you're talkin' to."

"Pushy?" Liz snarled. "We've been shoved around since the day we signed up." Her lips were tight.

Garrett slid between them like a referee at a boxing match. "What do you say we bury the hatchet and have some lunch?"

Meg gave Hub a distasteful glance. "This should be interesting," she uttered facetiously.

Garrett looked at Meg with scolding eyes. "Truce, you guys. I mean it!"

Suddenly, an air raid siren disrupted the relative silence, followed by distressed shouting. The foursome spun around to witness a dozen pilots scrambling for the flight line.

Garrett grabbed Hub by the jacket sleeve. "C'mon, move it!"

As Garrett and Hub bolted for two nearby P-47s, a hefty voice from behind them grabbed Meg and Liz's attention. They turned to face a barrel-chested major in his late-twenties.

He said, "Are you the pilots who just landed in those Mustangs?"

"A, er, yes, Sir," Meg responded.

"Then get them up top before they die a quick death. Half the kraut air force is chasin' our bombers back from the target. Another dozen bogeys are heading this way to divert our attention. Now, get the lead out!" he snapped then took off at a run to warn the others.

Meg and Liz immediately hopped aboard their Mustangs.

"They certainly don't waste much time gettin' to the point round here," Meg sputtered over the radio.

"I just hope they checked the ammo in our planes," Liz radioed back.

"I guess we'll find out pretty soon," Meg said apprehensively.

"What about call signs?" asked Liz.

"To hell with call signs. Just wing it!"

Within a minute, both pursuit engines were roaring, waiting

to build enough RPMs to taxi.

Meg looked to the east. "Oh shit!"

A dozen Messerschmidts and Focke-Wulfs flying at tree top level, swooped in, their wing guns blazing. As Meg, Liz, and the others thundered down the runway, the base aircraft guns opened fire on the Germans. Red tracers streamed at the attacking enemy aircraft.

Hub's voice bellowed over the radio. "Bogeys at three o'clock, over."

"Get those birds into the air, now!" screamed the air controller.

Meg bolted into the lead, followed by Liz. Their Mustangs picked up speed as they raced toward the northern end of the field. The German formation spread out and took them head-on.

"It's now or never," Meg said aloud to herself, pulling back hard on her control stick. Just as her wheels left the ground, the Germans opened fire, strafing the field. A taxiing P-47 nosed forward and burst into flames.

"We're sitting ducks!" Liz cried anxiously.

"Get some altitude then bank right," Meg said coolly. "Stay on my wing."

"Gotcha," Liz responded.

Just then, enemy rounds ripped into the fuselage and starboard wing of Liz's Mustang.

"I'm hit!" Liz cried out. "I'm goin' down."

"No!" Meg cried out. "Get out of there!"

Suddenly, the wounded Mustang winged over and exploded, filling the air with flying debris. Hub in the P-47 behind her was forced to instinctively bank right.

"Kraut bastards!" Meg shrieked. Briefly glancing backward, a distraught, shocked Meg directed her Mustang into a steep climb. Her flying instincts had taken over.

Both Hub and Garrett were in shock. A woman pilot had just been shot down in a combat zone.

Garrett shook it off and radioed Meg, "When you get enough altitude, circle around. I'll be there in a sec."

Meg spotted four FW-190s heading at them from the side,

"Bogeys at two o'clock!"

She broke off then tested her guns. "Thank God, they work!"

Suddenly, the fuselage of Garrett's P-47 was raked with enemy bullets. He slumped in his seat, bleeding from the mouth. Another burst of enemy fire tore off his rear stabilizer. As his pursuit began to tumble out of control, Garrett gurgled, "Hub, take care of my sis."

Meg screamed. "God, no! Jesus....not Gar. Bail out! Bail out!" She instinctively broke to follow her brother's Jug.

Seconds later, her twin's P-47 crashed into a group of trees and exploded. Her head slumped against the seat. She was numb, unable to think. Grief filled her face.

Suddenly, she could hear her father's voice. "Sometimes you lose friends in combat. All you can do for them is win the battle. Now, make your father proud."

Hub broke with her. "Snap out of it, Baby-face." He shoved his throttle forward. "Get back here. There's nothing you can do for him now. I'm takin' the lead. Stay behind me."

Meg sat up in her seat and increased her airspeed. "I'm with you. I'm with you."

Hub jockeyed for the lead as Meg steered toward two Me-109s busy strafing the field, her eyes wild and calculating. As the enemy fighters circled around to make another run, Meg fixed herself on the tail of a Me-109 and manipulated the control stick until the trailing enemy fighter was in the middle of her sight ring. She opened fire with her wing guns. Pieces of cowling separated from the Me-109. The propeller slowed, and the nose pointed down. Meg fired again. This time, her prey's right wing ripped apart. The Messerschmidt spun around like a boomerang then careened into the trees below.

"That's for Garrett!" she snarled, her eyes wild. She was now experiencing the scent of the hunt. She now knew what her father Rye had experienced.

Hub was astonished. "That's the way, Baby-face!" he cheered. Forgetting for the moment that his new partner was a woman, he growled, "Let's get the bastards!" He twisted his neck to clear his tail. "Oh, oh. I've got big trouble."

Two Me-109s had climbed onto Hub's tail. He broke right and cut his throttle. Now, he had one in front, almost in his sight ring, but the other was still riding his tail. "I need some help here. Get that kraut off my tail."

"I'm on my way," Meg sounded. She pulled a hard right, accelerated, and circled around.

Suddenly, the antiaircraft gunners below started blasting at everything in the sky, including friendly planes.

Hub took three hits in the tail. "Sonofabitch! Those dummies are firin' at us!"

"Get used to it," Meg howled. "Those dummies got lots of practice shootin' at us over Blue Swamp."

"Real comforting," Hub said facetiously. "When I get back on the ground, I'm gonna teach those idiots the difference between us and the bad guys.....after I pound some faces." He opened fire on the Messerschmidts in his sight ring.

Hub watched as the rounds plowed into the tail section and fuselage of the Me-109. Smoke trailed the enemy fighter as its nose tipped downward and went into an uncontrolled dive. Seconds later, it skidded onto the grassy field, bounced up, flipped over on its back, and burst into flames.

Meg leaped in her cockpit seat like a cheerleader. "Great shootin', Hotshot!"

"Applaud me later, Baby-face," Hub said anxiously. "Get that bogey off my tail."

"Hang in there, Hotshot," Meg purred with new self-control. "I've almost got him in my sight ring. Pull up when I give you the signal."

Hub began weaving left and right. The German pilot fired but missed. Tracers streaked past Hub's canopy, narrowly missing his propeller.

"Pull up!" Meg shouted.

Hub pulled back hard on his control stick and went into a steep climb.

Meg fired short bursts with her wing guns. Without warning, a Thunderbolt came in from the side and fired at the Me-109. The German fighter burst into flames and disintegrated, forcing Meg to pull up hard to avoid flaming, mushrooming wreckage.

"What in the hell?" Meg swore. "Where in the hell did he come from?"

Hub activated his throat mike. "Forget him. We've got company at six o'clock."

A swarm of Messerschmidts and Focke-Wulfs came at the trio like a swarm of beady-eyed vultures from the opposite end of the airfield. Following them was a barrage of ground fire that was still indiscriminately shooting at everything in the air. Meg and Hub split off into a tight turn to rid themselves of the attacking enemy fighters.

"Check fire! Check fire!" Hub bellowed at the antiaircraft gunners.

The lead Me-109 slipped behind a distracted Hub and fired his wing guns. Bullets walked laterally along his fuselage. Hub broke hard to the right. "Sonofabitch!"

"Hey, Hotshot, just remember what they taught you at Advanced Tactics."

"I know what I'm doing, Baby-face."

She pulled a hard left and went into a tight turn. Accelerating out of her turn, Meg came at the Me-109 on Hub's tail, guns blazing. "Come on, tough guy," she murmured. "Show me whatcha got."

Her tracers peppered the side of his Messerschmidt where dozens of swastikas decorated the fuselage under his canopy. The German pilot's eyes exploded when he spotted the nose of Meg's Mustang coming at him like a rocketing shell. He pulled a hard right. Now, they were headed at each other like a deadly game of chicken. Working their rudder pedals like expert craftsmen, the opponents adjusted their aim and fired. It was a head-on duel between a masterful ace and the daring newcomer.

Unflinching, her challenger blasted away, his rounds narrowly missing Meg's high-pitched propeller. Again, she unleashed a devastating barrage of fire, forcing the German pilot to peel off. As she had so many times with her father, Meg plunged into a gut-wrenching, heart-stopping roller-coaster dive, mimicking her opponent's every loop, spin, and roll-out as she coolly zeroed in. Meg's eyes burned with revenge.

He rolled left then right, but she stayed with him. Finally, he was in her sight ring. Eyes like knives, she pressed her firing button. Her wings came alive with muzzle flashes. "I'll be wait-ing at the k-k-k-kitchen door..."

The red tracers filled the damp sky, slamming into his tail section. Smoke began to trail the wounded enemy fighter.

Every cell oozing with adrenaline, Meg unleashed another burst of fire that sailed into the kraut's canopy. "K-K-K-door!"

Red splotches filled the glass. The German ace clawed at the canopy as he went into an uncontrolled spin, end over end, sputtering as it crashed into a tall tree line at the edge of the airfield, followed by a fiery explosion that rocked the base. Meg's Mustang zoomed through the billowing smoke then climbed.

"That was for Liz!"

Hub was afraid she would slip and say something wrong. "Radio procedure, Baby-face."

"Roger, Hotshot." Meg's head swiveled on her shoulders, looking for Hub. "Where in the hell are you, Hotshot?"

Hub was behind her. "To your six o'clock, coverin' your behind."

"What happened to the other Gerry?"

"Running like a scared rabbit," Hub whooped.

"Where?" She snapped.

"Nine o'clock."

She turned to look in that direction. Several miles away, in the cloudy, dark horizon, three dozen American Super Fortresses lumbered westward, distinguished by their vapor trails. Around the B-17s, a hoard of Messerschmidts and Focke-Wulfs buzzed about the sky like a hive of killer bees, diving and weaving with their guns blazing. The handful of American P-47s was fighting valiantly to help their big friends. Meg broke left and rocketed in a 30-degree climb toward the bomber formation.

"Dammit," Hub swore to himself. He opened his throat mike. "Jesus, give me a little warning, will ya?" Hub shoved his control stick left and accelerated.

As Meg neared the battered bomber formation consisting of three combat boxes, one of the B-17s burst into flames and fell back of the formation. Hyper, desperate chatter among the bomber crew filled the radio frequency as two German Me-109s closed in for the kill, riveting the wounded bird until it disintegrated in mid-air.

A dozen other German fighters were spitting tracers at the bombers. Another B-17 was hit and broke in two. Over the radio, the sound of machines could be heard then screams. She could see both waist gunners fall from a truck-size hole in the fuselage. The Germans circled around and came at the remaining bombers, diving and firing their guns like pesky mosquitoes.

Meg flanked one of the 109s then fired. The shells pierced the skin of the Focke-Wulf. The German pilot spotted her Mustang converging on him and peeled away. His mission was to shoot down American bombers, not get into dogfights. Dozens of American flags were displayed on his fuselage, testimony to his heroism and combat skill. He had nothing to prove. Unlike the American pilots who were taken out of the fight after a certain number of missions, German pilots would continue to fly combat sorties until there were either killed or the war ended. He was flying on borrowed time. And now an American rookie was challenging him. He noticed that her Mustang displayed no swastikas, and chuckled. Little did he know whom he was dealing with--a young woman with combat savvy, two kills to her credit, and a lust for revenge.

Meg crammed the stick to the left and pursued the German ace that was trying to shake her off his tail. Suddenly, he chopped his throttle, hoping that Meg's airspeed would reverse their positions. To his surprise, she cut her throttle in the nick of time. The frustrated German pilot accelerated and began scissoring. It was shaping up to be a classic dogfight.

Suddenly, the FW broke right and plunged into a steep dive. Meg followed it down and adjusted her aim to position the FW in her site ring. "Come on, Gerry, you can do better than that."

Meg fired a short burst as the German ace cut right, accelerating into a tight turn, trying to circle behind her. Kicking rudder, Meg laughed as she coolly banked right, remaining behind him. She fired another burst. The rounds hacked up her opponent's stabilizer then penetrated his cockpit. A bony hand struggled to push back the canopy, smearing the glass with blood. Out of strength, he slumped in his seat. The nose of the Focke-Wulf pointed downward and plunged toward earth in a fiery blaze, exploding on contact.

Meg's eyes were colder than the frigid air outside her canopy. "That was for my father's leg."

Hub was in awe. This scrappy gal was showing him a thing or two about combat. He opened his mike and muttered, "Looks like kindergarten is over."

"Jesus.....Some kindergarten," she hummed.

"Had enough, Baby-face?"

"Enough? I'm just warmin' up, Hotshot."

"I'm runnin' low on ammo. Let's return to base."

Frantic pleas for help from the beleaguered bomber pilots grabbed their attention.

CHAPTER 23

Meg opened her mike. "Go if you need to, but I'm goin' to help our big friends." She shoved the joystick left and streaked toward a Me-109 hammering at the lead B-17 whose gunners were desperately fighting back. Grudgingly, Hub followed her lead. Meg grabbed the trigger to fire then stopped when a single Thunderbolt slid between the bomber and the Messerschmidts, heroically using his pursuit as a shield. The German fired a burst. The rounds slammed into the engine cowling of the Jug, tearing a chunk of it away. Smoke and fire began to pour from the engine. The P-47 slowed and began to wing down. The American pilot frantically struggled with the canopy.

"Bail out, little friend!" screamed the bomber pilot. "Bail out!"

Suddenly, the Thunderbolt exploded.

Streaking past the action, Hub glanced out the side of his canopy. He could see the American pilot falling lifelessly toward the ground. "Come on! Pull the handle," he prompted. "Pull it!"

Finally, a white parachute appeared below. Hub breathed a sigh of relief.

Kicking rudder, Meg turned to see the Messerschmidts bearing down on the bomber. Tracer rounds struck the bomber's fuselage. Excited chatter filled the radio frequency. The German pilot jerked the Me-109 into a tight turn and kept pulling. Slats began to pop out, and buffeting began. Still, he out-maneuvered the Mustang, knowing that the P-51 tended to stall in a tight turn. Meg climbed, circling to make another run, again latching onto his tail, shadowing his moves. The German chopped his throttle, hoping to swap positions with his foe.

Hub noted the action. "Baby-face! Chop your throttle!"

Meg instantly cut her airspeed, keeping the Messerschmidts to her front. The German pilot accelerated then banked hard. The maneuver failed to rid him of the persistent American. The German again went into a tight turn. Risking a tuck, Meg briefly climbed, stalled her engine then dove, trying to position him in her sight ring. He shoved his stick forward and went into a deep dive. Meg instinctively followed, not losing a foot. Her face distorted from the gut-wrenching G-force, but she managed to unleash several bursts of fire, scoring hits on his wing. Gas and black smoke began to trail the Messerschmidt. Then, it caught fire and tumbled downward out of control.

Not waiting to see the results, Meg pulled up hard and climbed toward the tattered bomber formation with Hub now just off her wing.

She was stunned, white as a ghost, still shaking from the adrenaline rush. "Take the lead, Hotshot."

"Roger," he answered in a surprised tone.

Suddenly, the balance of the German squadron broke off, retreating to the east.

The bomber formation commander radioed Meg. "Good shooting, little friends."

"You guys okay?" Meg inquired.

"Thanks to you and your wingman.....You've got a huge set on ya."

Hub almost choked. If their big friends only knew that it was a woman pilot they were talking to.

The formation commander contacted the rest of his bombers. "Let's head home, gentlemen."

As Meg and Hub streaked past the bomber formation, they received a chorus of appreciation over the radio. She shuttered again from the adrenaline rush as the bomber formation headed for the

English Channel.

"Thanks again for the support, little friends," the formation commander repeated.

"The pleasure was all ours," she answered.

Meg and Hub teetered their wings in an aerial salute before breaking off.

"Now, Baby-face, can we head back?" Hub stammered.

Meg suddenly slumped in her seat, her face stone-like. It had just hit her--Garrett and Liz had just died a very painful death in front of her very eyes. Meg's stomach was tight with emotional pain. She was unaware that she was but one kill away from becoming a surrogate ace.

With visibility now reduced to a half-mile, Meg and Hub circled the airfield, waiting for the damaged pursuits to land. Several first-aid vehicles, fire trucks, and jeeps loaded with rescue personnel raced to position themselves on either side of the runway to assist in the event of a crash-landing. Then it happened. A P-47 came in hot with just one wheel down. The badly wounded pilot dumped the bulk of his petrol before he masterfully touched down on the rain-slick runway, balancing his crippled plane on one wheel. Unable to use his brakes and dangerously running out of concrete, the smart-thinking pilot steered the massive Thunderbolt toward the grass where there would be less chance of an explosion. When the lone wheel whizzed into the softer turf, the seven-ton fighter began to plow, spinning it like a top. Standing on the concrete deck of the control tower, several sober-faced officers watched intently as the rescue force, sirens screaming, rushed to the scene. They arrived before the lumbering Jug had come to rest. The rescuers struggled to pull the limp pilot from the wingless, twisted wreckage before it might explode.

Meg and Hub were the last to land and taxi to the flight line.

A young, scrawny corporal hopped on her wing and assisted Meg out of the cockpit. "Sir, I'm Corporal Ray. We heard it all....over the radio," he drawled. "Whew, doggies.....Y'all really put it to the krauts up there."

Still in shock, Meg looked at him blankly. She silently stepped out of the cockpit and climbed down. Not waiting for Hub, Meg began to stumble toward the Operations hut.

Hub ran to catch her. "Wait up, Baby-face."

Meg kept walking like a zombie.

He grabbed her arm to stop her. "Whoa, there. Where in the hell you think you're goin'?"

Meg stared at him a long moment then began sniffling, holding her stomach.

"You sick?" he asked, somewhat surprised.

"Yeah, and I gotta take a whiz." Her face was filled with anguish.

"You did a fantastic job up there today.....Four bogeys, right?"

"If you say so." Meg continued walking. "Swallow," she ordered.

"Swallow?......Why?" he asked.

"My dad said that with the first one, you can taste the fear."

He ran his tongue along the roof of his mouth. He suddenly realized that his mouth was dry. "Did you?"

Meg answered with a nod.

"Bullshit!" he snapped. "You were like ice up there."

"Courage is doing what you're afraid to do, Hotshot. There can be no courage unless you're scared."

"Oh, and where did you hear that one?"

"Eddie Rickenbacker."

Hub turned to watch an overdue P-47 land, but he was really trying to change the subject.

Meg turned and watched as well. Tears began to flow down her cheeks.

Hub turned. "No one's gonna believe it when they find out you're a girl."

Staring at the cloud ceiling, Meg thought for a long moment. "We're not telling anyone, understand? The score ain't even close to bein' even."

"You lose a screw up there?"

"Not at all. The bastards killed Garrett and Liz. I've got a big score to settle."

"This is the most preposterous idea I've ever heard. I'm going to the colonel right now."

"Then I'll tell them that you lied about your background and medical condition. You'll never fly again."

"You don't know shit!" he sputtered.

"Liz spilled all the beans. Her dad had you investigated."

Hub stood speechless. She had him, and he knew it. "You'll never get away with it. How long do you think it'll be before they discover that you're a girl?"

"What's wrong, Hubert? Afraid a girl might show you up....again?"

"Hell, no," he barked.

"Look, I've been flying in and out of this combat zone for more than a week, and no one caught on." Meg grasped both of his biceps and looked him square in the eyes. "I'm going to do this. I owe it to Liz and Garrett. One more kill, and he will be an ace. I'm doing it for him."

Hub pulled away from her and put up his hands for her to stop talking. He reached up and massaged the bridge of his nose. "You're doing it for yourself."

"Okay, I'm doin' this for me and Garrett and Liz. Besides, the major ordered us to take 'em up. There wasn't time to debate the order."

"I know, but he didn't know that you're a woman." He began to pace back and forth. "This is crazy. . . . You're crazy. They'll figure it out."

Corporal Ray double-timed up to them. "Y'all better git to Debriefing. The major don't like to be kept waitin'."

"I've gotta take a leak," she announced.

Still running backward, the corporal pointed toward a small, block building. "Sir, the officers" latrine over yonder, next to the mess, but y'all better shake a leg."

Both wobbled up to the archaic French latrine. They could hear voices as they opened the door.

"Check to see if there's stalls," Meg ordered politely.

Hub nodded as he dashed in and took an open spot between two pilots standing over a rickety tin trough. As he relieved himself, he surveyed the surroundings. Along the same wall, there were two stalls without doors near the back of the latrine. He turned his head toward Meg who was anxiously peeking in, and nodded toward the back of the latrine. Meg took a deep breath and hustled past the stinky trough. She slid into the back stall, unzipped her fleece-lined flying jacket, and lowered her bulky trousers. In her haste, she had forgotten to check the seat before sitting--someone had left the seat in the upright position. The frigid porcelain drew a brief squeal. The other two pilots snapped their heads in the direction of the stalls then glanced at one another with a questioning look. Meg quickly stood, lowered the equally cold seat, and sat again, this time clamping a hand over her mouth.

Hub reacted quickly to rectify the situation. "Hey, Rye, everything comin" out all right?"

"Yeah, yeah," she responded with a deep voice. "Man, this is one cold seat."

"C'mon, Garrett," Hub prompted. "Let's go. The major doesn't like to be kept waiting."

Meg finished urinating then reached up and pulled on the long chain hanging from the wall-mounted flusher. She then stood to button up. She peered around the partition. The other pilots had departed. Meg quickly washed then joined Hub who was waiting for her outside the latrine.

"I'll take that as a yes."

Hub took a deep breath and sighed. *Oh, what the hell. They'll figure it out, sooner or later.* "Just remember, I don't know anything about it."

"You've got a deal, Hotshot."

"Call me that one more time, and I'll blow the whistle on ya."

Black smoke spiraled from two cylindrical stacks, poking through the roof of the large canvas tent. Meg and Hub entered through a wooden door labeled: BRIEFING ROOM. Three dozen exhausted pilots were sitting and standing among the rows of folding chairs, divided by a four-foot isle leading to a full-width, wooden platform with a giant map on the back wall. A small podium and a blackboard easel set to one side.

Most of the pilots were too young to shave. Several quietly stared at their feet. Others talked to their comrades with excited eyes. And there were those who were too spoiled not to gripe and moan. Due to the bulkiness of their winter flight suits, some of the shorter pilots looked like little boys dressed in bulky snow suits with their sleds in hand. Meg felt more comfortable with her disguise as she and Hub shuffled past the rows of seats, looking for two empty seats together. While Hub nodded greetings at strangers, Meg surveyed the pilots for anyone that might recognize her from years past. So far, so good.

There was the tall, square-jawed, blond major in his late-twenties, who had confronted them earlier in the day. He was dressed in tan trousers and a brown dress jacket and tie. His hair was Clark Gable groomed. He sat at the end of a table setting on the wooden platform, asking questions from a group of weary pilots, writing down what he heard on a legal-sized note pad. Colorful unit patches were sewn on both upper arms.

"Next," he instructed.

The group he had been debriefing stood and shuffled out the door. Another group moved in to take their seats. A homely captain with a bony, hawk-like nose and thin lips ignored the signal to sit. He was visibly shaken.

"What happened up there, Captain?" asked Hamilton.

"A wave of Messerschmidts and FWs hit us just before we got to the target....Stayed on us till the flak started." The captain was faint but angry, enough to stutter. "The cloud cover over the target forced our bombers to circle around for a second pass. The flak was thicker than flies on fish."

A short, nervous lieutenant jumped out of his seat, frantically yelling. "It was a bloody nightmare, Sir. Krupa's B-17 took a hit and disintegrated. I knew all those guys."

The captain reared his head up and grabbed the baby-faced lieutenant, jerking him back in his seat. "Get a handle on it, Mike." Leaning forward in his seat, he turned to the major. "The krauts hit us again at the German border. I'm tellin' ya, Major. We were sittin' ducks at 15,000 feet. Sixteen big friends and seven peashooters went down before we knew it. If it wasn't for that pilot in the P-51, we would've bought the farm."

The major scanned the room for unfamiliar faces. "Anybody seen the Mustang pilot that flew in here earlier today?"

Two pilots pointed at Meg and Hub. "They're the only

newbies I've seen around here," one answered.

Hamilton motioned with a hand at Meg and Hub. "Front and center, gentlemen. Have a seat."

Hub and a reluctant Meg stood and shuffled sideways past the other pilots then marched down the aisle to the table where they took a seat.

"Your names," he instructed, "besides Baby-face and Hotshot."

The other pilots began laughing.

"Captain, I'm Hub Martin. Sorry about the radio procedure. We had to wing it."

"Lieutenant, Garrett Reilly," she responded in a dry military drone.

"Either of you got combat experience before now?" asked Hamilton.

"I do now, Sir," answered Hub. "Ole Rye here already had 25 bomber missions under his belt. Now, he's got four bogeys"

Again, the other pilots reacted in their seats, nodding at those sitting or standing next to Meg. Some seemed impressed--the others envious. Most had been flying pursuits in combat for months without as many kills, if any at all.

Meg perked up with the unexpected compliment from Hub. "Hub got one, too."

The other pilots applauded.

The major held up a hand for quiet. "At ease!" He faced Meg and Hub. "We at the base here owe y'all a debt of gratitude, but let's get somethin' straight. You stay alive in this hell hole by usin' the gray stuff upstairs and one hell of a lot of teamwork. Breakin' formation and improper radio procedure ain't gonna cut it."

Meg stirred uneasily in her seat. "Yes, Sir."

The major leaned back in his chair. "Grab some chow then get settled in at the B.O.Q. Be here at 0530 hours for a briefing." Hamilton focused on those sitting in the back of the briefing room. "Chamberlain, Hastings, how 'bout squaring these two away?"

Captain Bob Chamberlain and First Lieutenant John Hastings slid off their seats and strutted over to the table. They were the top guns of the Air Force group, aerial gunslingers--every inch aces--both of them. They were rugged and handsome--tough as nails. Chamberlain was Errol Flynn smooth; Hastings--John Wayne cool.

The foursome introduced themselves and shook hands.

Meg emphasized a firm handshake. "I'll catch up to you later. I need to talk to the major."

"We'll be in the messhall," Hastings informed her.

Meg turned to Major Hamilton. "Sir, I need to speak to you in private."

"Is this about the mission or something private?"

"Very private, Sir."

Meg glanced at Hub who was instantly anxious. "I'll handle it," she said.

She followed Hamilton out the back door. He turned to talk, but Meg kept walking in a zombie state-of-mind, gazing straight ahead.

Hamilton had to run to catch up to her. "Hold it right there, Lieutenant. I'm not in the habit of chasing down junior officers."

Meg stopped as though she had just been awoken. "Oh, I'm sorry, Sir. I was preoccupied."

"Lieutenant, what's going on here?"

Meg was fighting back the tears. "Sir, my sister and her best friend got killed earlier today when the Germans attacked the airfield."

The major's mouth dropped open. "Your sister, you say, and another woman. I'm sorry, Lieutenant. You certainly have my sympathy."

Meg hid her face in her hands as she nodded.

"Was she a WAC?"

"No, Sir," she mumbled. "Meg and Liz were ferrying Mustangs for the general. It was a classified project."

Hamilton's eyes grew large. "I would have certainly known about it."

Meg took a deep breath to regroup her emotions. "Apparently not. Meg mentioned that someone had dropped the ball on this one."

"What did she mean by that?" the major asked.

"She was supposed to be met on the ground by one of the general's hand-picked men who would immediately put her and the other women into planes in need of an overhaul for the return trip."

"You can bet I'm going to get to the bottom of this. Until then, do not mentioned this to anyone." The major put a hand on her shoulder. "Are you going to be okay, Lieutenant? I'll arrange for compassionate leave."

"Thank you, Sir, but no. I need to keep busy. It'll help keep me from going berserk."

"I'll talk to the colonel, and let you know."

"Thank you, Major."

"Now, if you're up to it, you better try to eat something," suggested Hamilton.

Meg nodded.

"C'mon, Lieutenant. Follow me." Hamilton began walking toward the messhall. "We better shake a leg before there's noting left but Salisbury steak and peas."

"It's that bad, huh?"

"And then some."

"This is of little consequence considering what you've been through today, but four kills on your first day is extraordinary. I just wanted you to know that."

"Thanks, I had a big score to settle."

"Lieutenant, I don't want anybody going upstairs with anything less than a cool head."

"Yes, Sir."

On one side of the mess hall, full complements of officers were eating dinner at several long tables draped with white tablecloths. On the opposite side sat the enlisted men. Perfectly aligned along the walls were aerial combat photos and a unit crest. At the far end was the kitchen where a pot-bellied, balding steward was busily organizing the young enlisted men assigned to KP duty. Two sat with doleful expressions on stools, hunched over a giant tin pot of water, peeling potatoes. Three others stood unenthusiastically behind the food service line, spooning out portions to their fellow enlisted men.

Hub, Chamberlain, and Hastings had already taken seats near the entrance and were awaiting their food. Meg took a seat next to Hub.

Hamilton spoke to Chamberlain, "I need to talk to the colonel. Order me the broiled salmon and rice, okay?"

"Yes, Sir," Chamberlain responded.

After Hamilton departed, Meg whispered in Hub's ear. "The major wants to keep everything quiet about Gar and Liz, at least until he's had a chance to talk to the colonel."

Hub nodded.

A muscular, six-foot enlisted man in duty fatigues walked up to the table.

Hastings looked up. "Alabama, meet Lieutenant Reilly who just arrived today."

Alabama flashed a big smile. "Welcome aboard, Lieutenant."

Meg cracked a smile to be polite. "I'll have the salmon as well."

"Salmon, it is," Alabama repeated. "An excellent selection."

"Alabama here is the best damn scrounger in these here parts," Chamberlain inserted. "If you ever need anything, anything at all, he'll find it for you."

Hub lifted his water glass and began drinking.

Hastings leaned forward on his elbows. "You never know when you might need a pair of silk stockings to get a little crotch."

Hub lurched backward in his seat, coughing and splattering water on the table.

Meg slapped Hub on the back. "I'll certainly keep that in mind, John."

Alabama soon returned with two fresh trays of food.

Chamberlain winked at Alabama. "Go ahead and serve the newbies."

Alabama served Meg and Hub. It was Salisbury steak and peas.

"I guess I'll have the Salisbury steak and peas," Hub said dryly.

Chamberlain snickered.

Meg inspected the chow.

"Those peas look like sweaty road apples, don't you think, Baby-face?" Hastings quipped.

Meg moaned, "I should've just gone to bed."

Hub quickly changed the subject. "So, have you two seen much action?"

"Is there a Jap in Tokyo?" Chamberlain quipped.

Hub grabbed his face with both hands. "All right, all right. Dumb question. How many kills have you two got?"

"Hastings has six," Chamberlain answered. "I've got nine."

"Both aces!" Hub complimented.

"So they say," Chamberlain droned.

"Where's home?" asked Hub.

"Cleveland," Chamberlain responded.

"Seven Valleys, Pennsylvania," said Hastings. "How 'bout you two?"

"I'm from Indianapolis," Hub answered proudly.

"Bendix Field, New Jersey," said Meg.

"John, how long have you two been here?" inquired Hub.

"Since Christmas Eve," answered Hastings. "Can you believe it? They shipped us out on Christmas Eve?"

"It's pretty hard to shoot down krauts when they ain't flyin'," Hub responded. "We just happened to be in the right place at the right time."

Hastings grinned. "I like these two. They've a pair on them."

Hub eyeballed Meg, looking for a reaction. If Hastings and Chamberlain only knew that Meg was a woman. He changed the subject. "What kind of missions have you been flying?"

"Until last week, tactical missions," Hastings answered. "You know, shootin' up trains, attacking fuel dumps, supportin' ground attacks--not exactly the kind of missions that give us the opportunity to chalk up kills; however, for the past week, we've been escorting our big friends. That means daily opportunities for aerial action."

Hastings looked at Meg who looked a bit pale. "Having a difficult time dealing with your first kills, huh?"

"You might say that," she responded. She was fighting the urge to cry.

"So, Hub, how long have you and Baby-face here known each other?" inquired Hastings.

"Ever since I raced against his sister in the '38 Bendix race."

Hastings stopped corralling the peas on his plate. "I thought your names sounded familiar," he responded. "So where did you learn your moves, Hotshot?"

"The Advanced Tactics School."

Chamberlain looked up. "And what about you, Baby-face?"

"My old man."

"So who's your pappy?"

"Pat Reilly."

"Reilly? Pat Reilly?" Hastings set down his fork. "Shit! I thought that name rang a bell. Everyone's heard of *Rye, the Mad Irishman*. He's a bloody god 'round here. They say he taught Rickenbacker everything he knew. Looks like he gave Baby-face a few pointers as well."

"And his older brother Sean, too," Hub explained. "He's got better than 30 kills in the Pacific."

"Jesus!" Chamberlain crowed. "Thirty, huh?"

"Affirmative." Hub stopped chewing. "Pat Reilly designed the Mustang, you know."

Hastings was impressed. "No wonder Baby-face knows how to jockey a Kite."

Hub looked at him oddly. "Kite?"

"That's what we call Mustangs here," Chamberlain explained.

Hastings finished with his food and took a sip of coffee. "So, what's happenin' in the States these days?"

"Women playing pro baseball. . . . broads ferryin' bombers and pursuits," offered an eavesdropping pilot sporting a thin mustache. "Before you know it, they'll be demanding to fly in combat."

Hastings stabbed the table with his knife. "Goddamn! Give them pelts an inch, and they'll take a mile."

Hub could see that Meg was about to explode and quickly changed the subject. "Tell me, John. How do you like flyin' Thunderbolts?"

"Jugs? . . . They oughta be able to dive. They certainly can't climb," he sneered. "Above 20,000 feet, the Jug is superior to anything the Germans got."

"It's kinda like doin' a 180 in a locomotive speeding downhill," Chamberlain injected. "They've got a bad habit of mushing during pullouts."

"So I noticed," Hub agreed.

"They're superior to the Me-109 at high altitudes," Hastings added, "but at lower altitudes, we can't compete with the Messerschmidts's rate of climb or maneuverability. Now that we're getting Mustangs, we oughta be able to kick Gerry's ass."

"It's supposed to be a lot like flyin' a Spitfire," noted Hub. "At least that's what is being taught at Pursuit School."

Hastings shoved his tray away and lighted a cigarette. "We'd be flyin' those Kites if Baby-face here hadn't had such a good day in the air. Bob and I were supposed to get the first two."

Chamberlain lighted a cigarette of his own. "And if, if-and-buts were candy and nuts, we all would've had a merry Christmas." He offered a cigarette to Hub and Meg.

Meg took one and lighted it. "Thanks."

Hub blew a smoke ring and watched it float upwards. "Got any tips?"

Chamberlain leaned back and crossed his legs. "Don't weave in the valleys of cumulus clouds. You'll have an kraut on your ass faster than you can say, Betty Grable."

"Yeah," Hastings agreed. "If a bogey is above you, don't climb. You'll lose too much speed."

Chamberlain nodded. "If the krauts attack on the same level, just remember, you can out-climb 'em. And stay away from thin cirrus clouds. Looking down, you can see through them, but the same isn't true looking up."

Hastings watched a smoke ring dissipate in the air. "When emerging from a cloud, always execute a quick turn and look back. You could have just maneuvered yourself in front of a kraut sight ring."

"Yeah, and when attacked by a herd, take 'em head on like Wyatt Earp," Chamberlain reinforced. "They usually break and dive. Take on those who don't."

Chamberlain chuckled. "If there's a large kraut gaggle below, dive at the one closest to your sight, blow him away, and pull up hard. While the rest of the krauts are still in shock, pick a specific target and focus on it."

"And if there's a large group high above you, stay down and to the rear," Hastings added. "They'll eventually lose their patience and come to you."

The pilot with the slim mustache said, "Learn to break at just the right time to make a head-on attack. The krauts hate it."

Chamberlain nodded in agreement. "Travis is right. Whatever you do, don't run. That's exactly what Gerry wants you to do."

Travis scooted his chair closer. "If caught off guard by a large kraut formation, fight like a sonofabitch until you can develop a hasty plan. Oh, and keep your air speed above 250 while engaging; otherwise, you won't have enough air speed for climbing when you need it."

Chamberlain held up a forefinger. "Speaking of formations, the krauts constantly change their attack pattern and habits. They like to use three in a unit, one to attack the bombers while the other two engage our fighters. Just last week they got above our Big Friends and tried knocking 'em out by dropping bombs. Of course, the bomber formation has to be tight for such a tactic to work. Since then, we've loosened up."

Looking around the intent faces of pilots sitting about them, it was vividly clear to Hub that the others worshiped this ace duo, yet were competing to wear their crown. "Anything else?" he asked.

Chamberlain nodded. "You and your sleepy-eyed buddy should do what we have been doing--trade off at the wing position."

"It's kept us alive," Hastings admitted. "That way, the wing man doesn't get impatient for success and put his partner in jeopardy by breaking away."

"There's been more than one wing man that's cried wolf," Chamberlain disclosed, "by shouting *break*. You know, the signal that a kraut's on your tail. So, when you take evasive action, the slime ball that yelled break, moves in and shoots down your target. Sooner or later, you might not break when there really is a bogie on your tail."

"By the way, is there anyone round here that we should be careful of?" asked Hub.

"Albert Devine," Hastings quickly responded. "That's how he

got two of his kills--stealing them."

Chamberlain lighted another cigarette, looking around for Devine. "Yeah, stealing kills and lying. He's one of the reasons that we confirm our kills via gun cameras."

The pilot with the mustache reached for his coffee then directed his next words at Hastings and Chamberlain. "Did you hear? Intelligence said that the der Fuhrer placed a bounty on your heads, 10,000 reichsmarks each, I believe. . . . Chicago and I are shootin' for 20 thou."

Hastings crushed his cigarette butt in the ashtray. "Hey, Hotshot, what about you and Baby-face? Lookin' for a shot at the crown, too?"

Hub played it dumb. "Crown?"

Hastings seemed surprised. "King of Aces. . . . Like Rye's pappy. . . . You know, the jock with the most kills."

"A little friendly competition never hurt anyone," Hub replied.

"Me? I've got a score to settle," announced Hastings.

Chamberlain leaned forward. "Johnny lost his brother early last year during Big Week--the raids against Berlin.....Blames himself for what happened."

Meg drifted into a more depressed state. Hub noticed.

Hastings was suddenly distant. "Bill and I came here together 14 months ago.....We were flying cover. Bill's dead because his wingman screwed up. He peeled off to chase the krauts instead of backing him up."

Chamberlain looked at Hub. "You need a grudge, but you won't live very long flyin' like you two did earlier today. Loners usually cash in their chips early."

Hub wanted to say something but held back. He gazed briefly at John. He reminded him of Meg's father.

"For me, my unit is my family," Chamberlain confided. "It's all I got."

Meg yawned. "Excuse me."

"You must be bushed," Chamberlain surmised.

With a meal in her, Meg was suddenly having trouble keeping her eyes open. "You have no idea."

Chamberlain chuckled. "I could use some, too. It's been a

very long day."

Meg yawned again. She began to think about Liz and Garrett. "About now, I could fall asleep on a high wire."

"Come on," Chamberlain prompted, "Let's blow this pop stand. It's time you meet Devine.

Hub gave Meg a look.

CHAPTER 24

The B.O.Q. was located in a pre-war, French-constructed concrete block building. It would take a direct hit to cause much damage. Inside were individual rooms constructed of wooden partitions, giving each officer his own room, small but nonetheless private. It was a definite step up from the other forward air bases that were primarily tent encampments.

Hastings stopped in front of a room with a nameplate reading: CPT DEVINE.

He pointed over his shoulder at the door and whispered, "This is the guy I mentioned. He's two pistons short of an engine."

"He's the jerk that likes to steal kills," added Chamberlain, rotating his index finger around his temple. "He's lost five wingmen over the last seven months. Knocks a screw loose in some guys."

"The colonel knows that Devine's ass should be shining a desk chair," Hastings continued. "But hell, we're at war, and we need bodies. When we got here, Devine was our flight leader, but after losing so many planes and so many complaints, the colonel replaced him with Bobby. Since then, he's been an even bigger prick."

Chamberlain took out a cigarette, tapped it on his Zippo, and lighted it. "He's been a dickhead, right from the get-go." Chamberlain paused. "He grounded one of the guys who had 13 kills to his credit. Ruined his career. They sent him back to the States for prangin' it."

"Prangin'?" Hub asked with a puzzled look.

"It's a hotdog move," Hastings explained. "Happened 'bout five months ago. Came in without his wheels down.....Nearly tore off the bottom of his Jug and bent his propeller like a sea gull clobbered with a baseball bat. Said it was better than gettin' a piece of ass."

Meg faked a laugh, but was having trouble focusing; she was very tired and stressed from losing her brother and Liz. She had been putting on an amazing front just to get this far.

Chamberlain flicked the cigarette ash on the floor in front of Devine's door. "Grove was showin' off for the press. The old man was so damn mad that he kicked the Press Corps off the base for a few days. Feels they're inciting us to misbehave."

Devine's door opened and a head popped out. He was a short, balding blond man in his late-twenties with bulging bloodshot eyes.

"Speak of the devil," Chamberlain stammered.

Devine put on his glasses. "Do y'all mind?" A vein at his temple pulsated as he spoke. "Some of us professionals are tryin' to sleep." He eyeballed Hub and Meg with a disconcerting stare. "Who are you two?"

"Garrett Reilly," responded Meg.

"A Mick," Devine sneered.

"Lieutenant Hub Martin....Jewish," he came back facetiously.

Devine stared momentarily at Hub. "I thought all you Hebes were doctors and lawyers." He slammed the door in Hub's face.

"I see what you mean about him," Hub exclaimed.

"What an asshole," Meg snarled.

Chamberlain chuckled, shaking his head. "That's a perfect example of what happens when you don't get enough oxygen at 30,000 feet."

Everyone chuckled.

"Anybody want to join me for a scotch before hitting the sack?" Hastings offered.

"I'll take a rain check," Chamberlain declined. "See you at breakfast." He disappeared into the next room.

"What time is chow?" inquired Hub.

"The mess starts serving at 0430 hours," Hastings answered. "Wake-up call comes 'bout 0400."

"In that case, I'll take a rain check, too," said Meg.

"Okay, Baby-face," responded Hastings. He looked at Hub. "You coppin' out, too?"

Hub glanced at Meg who appeared to be close to a nervous

breakdown. "Yeah, 0400 is going to arrive all too soon."

"C'mon, I'll point out the vacant rooms."

After getting Meg and Hub settled in, Hastings bid them a goodnight. "See you at chow."

Hub stepped inside his room but kept his door cracked. As soon as Hastings entered his own quarters, Hub quietly ventured into the hallway and tiptoed to Meg's room. He quietly knocked on the door.

After three attempts, she finally spoke through the door. "Yes, who is it?"

"It's me, Hub. Open the door."

Meg cracked the door then opened it wide enough for him to enter, quietly closing it behind him. She had slipped on her WASP dress shirt. Her face was a flood of tears.

"Are you all right?" he asked.

"Not at all. I just lost my twin brother and best friend," she sniffled. "Can we talk some other time?"

"Garrett was my friend, too. And so was Liz. I dated her for Christ sakes."

Meg studied his face. Hub seemed sincere enough.

"I'm sorry," she sobbed. Suddenly, she fell into his arms. "Oh, Hub." She began to cry. "I'd trade a thousand kills to get them back."

"Me, too," he responded. A tear trailed down his cheek. "They were . . . you know what I mean."

Meg cried all the more. They hugged for an eternity.

"Are you sure you don't want to talk?" he asked.

Meg gently pushed herself out of the hug. "I can't, not now. I feel like my heart was just jerked from my chest."

"That's what I was afraid of--you are not fit to fly in this state."

Meg's face reddened. "Look, you, I'm going to do this whether you like it or not, or I'll squeal on ya. Remember that! You'll never fly again, and you know it."

Hub's face had turned pale. He was genuinely scared. She had the goods on him, and he knew it. "You'd do that, wouldn't you?"

"You bet, Hubert. I'm going to settle the score. I've gotten a taste of blood and want more. I'm going to be the greatest ace ever."

"I knew you weren't doing this for Garrett and Liz. You're a self-centered little bitch who only cares about herself."

"I've earned this chance. I've been supporting this war and getting shit on at every turn. I'm going to prove that women can fight just as good as men. So you might as well get used to the idea and support it. If I go down, you go down, understand, Hotshot?"

Hub took a deep breath as he mentally regrouped. "I guess we better get some shut-eye. Like you said, we've both got a stake in this damn charade so we better come up with a plan."

Meg sighed. "I'll meet you at 0330 hours before the men hit the showers. I need to borrow a T-shirt and some boxer shorts until I get some from supply."

"Of course." Hub walked to the door and checked the hallway. "0330 hours, it is."

Meg shut the door after him and turned. It was a simple room with a metal-frame bed, an Army green footlocker, and a small table. She quickly made the bed then flopped on it. She reached into her Gladstone bag, took out her diary, and climbed under the covers. Trying to hold back the sudden tears, she opened her tattered diary.

I lost Garrett and Liz today. It all seems like a bad nightmare. I feel responsible. I sense a terrible emptiness like I did after Amelia died. Pretending to be Garrett isn't making it any easier. I could feel his pain in that crash. I'm not quite sure how I am going to explain all this to Dad. If I tell him, he'll have me shipped home faster than spit. I owe this to Garrett. I also owe it to Dad. He must think that his youngest son is an ace.

My other concern is Aaron. I had to lie to him about that ride to the train station. I hope he'll forgive me. I can only hope that he doesn't get married to someone else, thinking that I'm dead. Somehow, I must get word to him that I'm still alive.

So far, so good on pretending to be Garrett. I nearly slipped with my voice on a number of occasions. It's a good thing that so many of the guys sound young. My gruffy voice is now paying big dividends. I think the guys like me, so far. Time will tell.

I also killed people today, too. I wanted revenge but can't forget the bloodied face of that German pilot when he tried to claw his way out of that burning fighter. I almost tossed my cookies after I landed. I'm sure the events of this day will haunt me the rest of my life. Now I know why Dad was so humble and quiet about his war days. I wonder how Sean is doing. I pray for his safety.

I hope I can get to sleep. My heart is beating a million times a minute. Must get up before the men so I can shower. Oh, I wanted to name my Mustang "Amelia's Quest II," but that could draw too many questions. Wish me luck, tomorrow.

* * * * *

The slightest of knocks at the door brought Meg to her feet. She rubbed her tear-dried eyes, trying to focus on the hands of her wristwatch. She quietly cracked the door. Hub stood there in his trousers and T-shirt with a towel draped around his neck. He handed her a white T-shirt and boxer shorts. She told him to wait a moment while she slipped them on. A long moment later, she opened the door and joined him. Together, they tiptoed down the cold hall toward the latrine.

Six white wash basins were located in the front with a mirror above each for shaving. The back two-thirds was divided by a plywood partition with a row of closed toilets and a long, tin urinal. To the other side was a line of showerheads.

Hub checked the room then stood guard for Meg who walked into the shower room, stripped, and began showering.

She yelped, "Damn, it's cold."

"Let the water run a little longer," Hub suggested.

"Just keep your eyes on the door, Hubert."

"Hub!" he corrected her.

Soon, steam billowed as she quickly soaped down. Suddenly, someone exited a room with a towel wrapped around his waist.

Hub glanced at his wristwatch. It was 3:40 a.m.

"Hurry up!" he whispered loudly into the shower room. "Someone's coming." Hub stole another glance. "Oh, man. What a bod! This oughta turn you on."

Meg rushed to rinse off the soap and shut off the water. Hub tossed her a towel as she stepped into the wash area and began to dry her back, looking away. From the reflection in a distant mirror, Hub could see Meg's partially naked body. It was an innocent but sexy moment.

The door opened, and Devine entered the steamy bathroom. He looked like the Pillsbury dough boy in a hair shirt. He glanced at Meg and Hub, briefly studying Meg as she calmly draped the long towel over her soft but strong shoulders, being careful not to reveal her modest breasts. She rotated in the opposite direction as Devine walked past her to enter the shower area. He suspiciously glanced back twice as he hung his towel on a hook and turned on the shower.

"So that ought to turn me on, huh?" Meg whispered. "With all the good-looking studs on this base, I draw sparrow dick to take my first shower with."

Hub buried his face in his hands to muffle the laughter as he repositioned himself between the shower room and the wash area. Meg motioned for Hub to face away before she redressed.

Meg whispered over her shoulder. "I'll be breathing a whole lot better when the hair on my legs and armpits grow out."

"You better wait for me in your room," Hub suggested, "while I shower."

It was still dark as Meg and Hub sauntered into the group briefing room, wearing winter fleece-lined jackets, scarves, and leather flying caps. A sleepy-eyed pilot occupied nearly every chair. The duo discovered they were the center of attraction as they made their way down the aisle, stopping at the row where Chamberlain and Hastings were seated. As they shuffled sideways to the open seats, Hub spotted Devine a few rows away, sitting by himself, writing on a pad.

As they sat, the door behind them swung open. Colonel "Wild Bill" Middleton, the barrel-chested group commander, entered in his garrison uniform. Behind him and to his left was Major Hamilton.

"Ah-ten-shun!" shouted Hamilton.

Everyone quickly stood at the position of attention as Middleton and Hamilton walked up to the platform. The giant map had been mounted to the back wall.

Middleton stepped up and turned. "At ease....take your seats, gentlemen."

Everyone sat, including Hamilton who took an open seat in front.

"According to Intelligence," Middleton began, "the attack on our airfield yesterday was part of a massive air offensive by the Germans, dubbed Operation Bodenplatte. According to reports, the Luftwaffe struck airfields here in France, Belgium, and Holland. Over 150 German fighters were shot down. Unfortunately, they destroyed over 800 Allied aircraft, most of which were still on the ground. We lost the fewest, thanks to your readiness and the pilots who flew in here just minutes before the Luftwaffe hit us with a surprise attack."

The other pilots stirred, bobbing their heads to get a glimpse of the new arrivals. For some, this was their first view of Garrett Reilly and Hub Martin, the new kids on the block.

"At ease, gentlemen," Middleton continued. "One of those pilots is Lieutenant Garrett Reilly, the son of Rye Reilly, a former Medal of Honor recipient who shot down the infamous Red Baron. I know you will treat his son and Lieutenant Martin with the respect they have already earned. Glad to have you here, men. By the way, you two have been assigned to Captain Chamberlain's team."

Both nodded at Middleton. It was then that Meg spotted Devine staring at her.

She turned to Hub. "Needle dick is not very happy 'bout our assignment."

"Screw him."

Middleton signaled Hamilton in the first row. The major

stood, hopped on the platform, and grabbed a wooden pointer leaning against the map.

"Today, we're going to take advantage of our victory," Middleton continued. "We've got a date in Berlin to finish what we started."

The pilots sat up in their seats, buzzing. While the Allies had grabbed control of the air, losses over the German capital had always been heavy. Just about everyone in the room had a score to settle, especially Meg and Hastings.

"At ease!" Middleton quieted them. "I know that our mission has been tactical in nature. You've amassed a great record of ground support, cutting lines of communication, and blowing up fuel dumps, but as you know, our mission has changed to strategic bomber escort. We got a fresh supply of drop tanks in yesterday so we'll be escorting our Big Friends all the way to the target and back. Major Hamilton will fill you in on your targets. Have a good time on your date, gentlemen. I expect penetration and a climax."

The pilots whistled and laughed as Middleton hopped off the platform.

"Ah-ten-shun!" shouted Hamilton.

Everyone bolted out of their seat and stood rigid.

"As you were," Middleton called out. "I'll see you all this afternoon for happy hour."

The pilots took their seats as Middleton disappeared out the door.

"Listen up," Hamilton alerted. "We have a lot to cover. First, I would like to say something. Lieutenant Reilly has been credited with four confirmed kills. Lieutenant Martin has one confirmed kill."

Again, everyone glanced in his or her direction.

Hamilton continued, "Sergeant Rodman is handing out a packet containing everyone's code words, course settings, bomber markings, map sheets, call signs, etc. We'll be flyin' in low.....about 13,000 feet--"

Chamberlain turned to Hastings. "Jesus Christ, that's low."

Hamilton continued, "....Lieutenant Miller has the weather forecast, and Captain Hargrass the INTEL estimate." He turned to Miller. "Lieutenant."

Startled from the announcement about the bombing altitude, everyone hopped to the position of attention as the major began to leave.

"Break a leg, gentlemen," Hamilton uttered as he walked down the aisle.

Meg turned to Hub. "I know they say that for good luck, but Jesus, I wish they'd find another way to say it."

Hub lowered his head and massaged the bridge of his nose, nodding in agreement. "Yeah, I know what you mean."

After the briefing, the pilots stood, zipped their bulky winter flight jackets, and shuffled out the door, jabbering at one another. They emerged from the Briefing tent as the sun began to peek in the distant horizon. The four dozen pursuit pilots piled onto jeeps, 3/4-ton trucks, and bicycles. Meg and Hub rode in a jeep with Hastings and Chamberlain and raced for the flight line buzzing with support personnel that were readying their pursuits with drop tanks and .50-caliber ammunition.

As their jeep came to an abrupt halt in front of their pursuits, Meg noticed that her Mustang had been painted with the same markings as the other planes, a red nose and blue wings. All four hopped out and grabbed their parachutes and equipment bags. Devine arrived shortly thereafter in a 3/4-ton truck. He hopped off the back and joined them. His lips were as tight as a bowstring.

Chamberlain turned to Meg and Hub. "Newbies usually take the wing, but since John and I are used to working together, you two will team up. Devine, you'll fly off my other wing for the time being. Hotshot, you'll be Rye's wingman. Any questions?"

Devine's face turned scarlet. "One of the newbies should be my wing man," he angrily protested.

"I call the shots here now, Devine," Chamberlain snapped. "You got any beefs, I suggest you take 'em up with Wild Bill."

Devine glared. "You can bet on that, Captain."

Although jealous, Hub appeared congenial. Meg knew that this was a major concession on his part. After all, they had been mega-competitive since day-one, and she was a woman impersonating a male pilot.

"We'll switch off like you two," Meg conceded.

Hub nodded his appreciation. Devine was all the more irritated--and suspicious.

Chamberlain paused to light a cigarette. "Garrett, your call sign is Blue-three. Hub, you're Blue-four. Hastings is Blue-one, Devine Blue-two, and I'm Blue Leader.....If attacked, go into a finger-four formation. Now, if there's no more small talk, saddle up. We've got some big friends waiting on us."

Chamberlain and Hastings hustled to their assigned Thunderbolts.

Meg turned to Hub. "You do know what he means by finger-four, don't you?"

"Yes! It's like the tips of four fingers. The krauts were the first to use it. Each pilot can see to his side, and if need be, clear the tail of one or more of his buddies."

"If there are only four fingers, why do we have a fifth?" she asked.

"Is this a joke?" he groaned.

"No!" she responded.

"I guess it's like Chamberlain said, no one wants to fly with Devine.....See you upstairs."

Hastings hopped aboard the nearest P-47. Six Nazi swastikas were painted on the fuselage under his canopy, and near the nose, a caricature of Hitler, eyes bulging, giving the Devil a ferocious kiss on the ass. The words below it read: "Hell's Kiss."

She glanced over at Chamberlain's fuselage that sported nine swastikas. Painted on the nose of his Thunderbolt was a colorful caricature of Bob squashing a German plane under a boot. Above it were the words: "Kraut Kruncher."

Devine was again glaring at her from the wing of his Jug. On the nose of his Jug was a pair of dice with a single dot each and the words: "Snake Eyes." There were four swastikas painted on his fuselage, one short of an ace.

"Crapper or Craps would be more appropriate," Meg sneered facetiously.

Suddenly, Major Hamilton appeared in a jeep that came to a halt next to Meg. The look on her face became instantly anxious.

"Lieutenant, the colonel decided to let you continue to fly for

Queen of Aces 265

the time being while we figure out how to break the news to your father and the parents of the other girl."

"Liz Hunter," Meg reminded him. "Her name was Liz Hunter."

"We already know," the major said matter-of-factly. "Another thing--Your head better be on straight, or you'll be grounded. I don't want you to risk your life or the lives of your squadron because of some revenge thing. Understand, Lieutenant?"

"Yes, Sir," she responded in a respectful tone. "I won't let you down."

"Be careful up there, Lieutenant." The major let out the clutch, and the jeep darted away.

Corporal Ray was closing up the wing of Meg's Mustang when she walked up. Suddenly, she spotted four swastikas painted on the fuselage. On the nose were the words: "Rye's Revenge."

"How did you know, Corporal?" she asked.

"Your buddy," he answered. He nodded at Hub. "He said that Rye Reilly is your dad, and that he lost a leg to the German's in the last war."

What Hub had not said was that the name was created for Meg and Garrett as well.

Still in shock over her twin's death, only the slightest of grins grew on her face. "It's really swell, Corporal. Thanks." Meg glanced at Hub. She then noticed the single German swastika that had been painted under his canopy, and painted on the nose was the picture of an Indy racecar with a prop and wings. The name above it read: "Heaven's Chariot." Meg gave him a thumbs-up.

She ignored Devine's stare and looked up at her crew chief. "Well, Corporal, what do you think of my pappy's design?"

"It's a peach, Lieutenant." He closed up the wing panel and polished it with a rag. "It's the damnable lousy weather. Dampness seeps in these here parts and fouls 'em up. Watch it at high altitudes. It can freeze y'all's trim tabs and superchargers."

She was caught off guard by the change of subject. "What did you put on my guns, Corporal?"

"The same thang I put in your engine, Suh--some of that newfangled o'l with anti-freeze....on your guns' working parts."

"Thanks, Corporal," Meg said. "A pilot is only as good as his crew chief. I appreciate the attention."

He hopped down from the wing, beaming with pride. "Thank you, Suh."

Meg reached out and shook his hand. "I'm Garrett Reilly." She glanced at his name tag. "Thanks again, Corporal Ray. Where's home?"

"Memphis," he smiled widely. "How 'bout you, Suh?"

"New Jersey," Meg replied.

"Well, just let me know if ya ever need an'thang."

"I will." Meg climbed upon the wing. "Thanks again for the paint job."

"An' time.....Suh.....Git a couple fer us Legs."

Meg turned her head to face him. After a long beat, her head bobbed up and down, ever so slightly.

Their props spinning invisibly, three groups of roaring pursuits taxied toward the runway patched in places where the Germans had dropped some of their bombs. Two at a time, the pursuits took off and climbed, circling high above until the rest could join them. Meg's adrenaline raced at the sight.

She pulled back hard on her stick, and Rye's Revenge rocketed almost vertically. Her head pressed backward as though it was going to leave a permanent impression in the head support. Minutes later, she and Hub joined the circle of 16 red-nosed pursuits. Each flight had a different color on its wings to match its call sign. The group leader peeled off and headed north, followed by the balance of his squadron in V-formation, climbing gradually upward. They disappeared momentarily as they continued to climb through the gray clouds. A bright sunshine glimmered off the aircraft as they emerged. It was a magnificent sight.

Before long, the pursuits picked up tight formations of fortresses at various rendezvous points. To confuse the Germans, they headed north toward Bonn before turning east toward Berlin.

Middleton's voice sounded over the radio. ""Okay, gentlemen, let's spread 'em out. Keep your eyes peeled for Gerries."

The formation widened.

Meg flipped on her gun switches and checked the engine

gauges, jockeying the throttle to keep a constant 180 M.P.H. rate of climb and proper flying position. She looked over at Hub with an intense face. He smiled and gave her a thumbs-up. Devine noted the exchange.

As the vast formation of bombers and pursuits proceeded toward Berlin, the churning clouds became thicker and darker. Many of the fortresses and their pursuit escorts began to turn back for England. Chamberlain, Hastings, Devine, Hub, Meg and eight other pursuits continued on to escort the remaining bombers, keeping a tight perimeter around their big friends.

The altimeter on Meg's instrument panel read 13,000 feet. She leveled off and flipped the switch on her fuel tanks. Her speed was now a steady 200 m.p.h. She craned her neck to scan the sky for enemy fighters. She spotted them beyond the vapor trails of the friendly bombers.

Suddenly, a green flare signaled the beginning of a German fighter attack.

"Holy sh--!"

CHAPTER 25

"Brace yourselves," the squadron commander barked. "The krauts are early. Dump your tanks."

The auxiliary drop tanks tumbled downward as the outnumbered American pursuits took on two squadrons of Me-109s and FW-190s whose abilities were equivalent with both the P-47 and the P-51 at this lower altitude. The radio chatter cluttered the airwaves as the American pursuits took the Germans head-on. Hub took the wing position as Meg fastened herself to the tail of an Me-109. All of a sudden, Devine appeared, firing at her target. He missed and fired again. The German fighter started to rise. Meg pressed her gun button. Two dozen rounds ripped apart the fuselage of the Me-109, and a stream of smoke began to trail the enemy fighter. Meg crammed the stick to her left. Meg executed a four-point roll with Hub close behind. The enemy pilot pushed back his canopy and struggled out of his flaming fighter. He leaped, and in seconds, a parachute opened.

"Congratulations, Blue-three," sounded Chamberlain. "You're an ace."

Meg hummed, "Thank you, Blue Leader."

"I second that," echoed Hub.

Suddenly, Devine roared in from behind, fuming. "Damn you, Blue-three. That was my fifth bogey!"

"Blue-two, this is Blue-three. That bogey was rising. You would've been beef jerky."

"This is Blue Ladder. Knock it off, you two. They're comin' around. Stay alert!"

Meg spotted two FWs bearing down on the trailing fortress. "Bogeys at seven o'clock," Meg shouted. "Hold onto your seat." She executed a four-point roll and went into a tight, carnival-like turn.

Hub mirrored her moves.

The bomber's belly, top, and rear gunners were blazing away with .50-caliber machine guns. Tracers decorated the darkened sky. Suddenly, the lead FW exploded, narrowly colliding with the tail of the fortress. The larger flaming wreckage plummeted downward, quickly disappearing into the turbulent clouds below.

"This is Blue Leader. We're almost to the target. Get ready for a rocky ride." Chamberlain had no sooner uttered the words than black puffs appeared in his peripheral. "Hold onto your seats, gentlemen. It's gonna be a rough one."

With flak pounding at their wings, the bombardiers took over the controls to adjust their course. As the formation bombardier looked up briefly to check his map, the second bomber off the wing of the formation command ship took flak in the starboard engines. Flames began to shoot out of both, followed by panicked yelling.

The pilot worked feverishly to extinguish the flames. "I'm pulling out."

He feathered both props on the right wing then banked right and circled around. Meanwhile, the others opened their bomb bay doors. The ground briefly appeared through the clouds. More bursts of black smoke, accompanied by the turbulence of the explosions rocked the fortresses, causing them to rattle and jiggle.

The formation bombardier looked through the Norden bombsight. "Bingo!" he shouted. "I've got it. Looks like the krauts will be drinking warm beer tonight. One toast to Adolph, comin' up. Bombs away, gentlemen!"

"Spread your cheeks, Adolph," the formation commander drawled. "We've got two-point suppositories comin' your way with your name on 'em. Enjoy, butthead!"

The bombs rained as the German flak continued to pound the formation. One bomber took a hit in the port side, knocking the waist gunner backwards. He rolled back and forth, writhing and screaming with pain.

The formation commander opened his mike. "After the shock

wears off, they'll be comin' after us. Sorry we can't stick around and watch the fun. Turn it around boys. Let's get out of here."

"This is Blue Leader. Execute post-target Flight Plan Bravo, over."

As the battered bomber group began to turn around, the pursuits continued to S-turn and circle so as not to run away from the bombers that remained in their respective combat boxes for mutual support against enemy fighters.

Meg snapped her head around like a play doll, trying to spot German fighters. Suddenly, she spotted a horde of FW-190s in a light, finger-four formation. "Blue Leader, this is Blue-three. Tighten your reins. Bogeys at seven o'clock high."

"This is Blue Leader, roger. Cancel those early dinner reservations. It looks like K-rations to me."

Guns blazing, Chamberlain's squadron split the enemy formation. Hastings, Chamberlain, and Devine peeled off to the left and engaged. Several FWs broke through and headed for the trailing bombers, drawing anxious radio chatter. Meg and Hub directed their pursuits into a tight circle to head them off. Taking the lead, Hub accelerated and fired, missed, and fired again. The lead FW broke apart and exploded.

"Fantastic shooting, Blue-four," Meg wailed excitedly.

The bomber pilot radioed, "Blue-four, I'd kiss ya if you were here right now."

Looking around, two other FWs were hit by antiaircraft fire from one of the bombers and Hastings' wing guns. Two more FWs climbed then dove at the bombers. The right wing of one B-17 began to smoke, and flames erupted from both starboard engines. The nose of the bomber pointed downward, and within seconds, it descended like a wounded falcon, turning on a point.

"Come on, you guys," Chamberlain prompted. "Get out! Get out!"

Two parachutes appeared below, just as the bomber disappeared into the clouds, followed by a muffled light. It had exploded.

Devine left his wing position and banked right to pursue a lone FW. Chamberlain snarled at Devine's selfish act as he followed.

The enemy pilot executed a half-loop and rollout at the top, placing Devine in front and under him. The German pilot quickly adjusted the nose and opened fire. Two rounds penetrated Devine's stabilizer, causing a momentary lack of control. Chamberlain was ready to fire at the FW, but Devine was in the line of fire.

"Blue-two, break left!" Chamberlain ordered.

Devine turned in his seat. The FW was bearing down on him.

"Dammit, Blue-two, I said to break left," Chamberlain bellowed. "Break left!"

As Devine jammed his stick to the left, the German fired. His rounds sailed harmlessly into oblivion. Chamberlain adjusted his rudder then fired. The tracers walked into the fuselage of the FW. The pilot's head slumped against the canopy, and within seconds, his FW flopped over on its back. Gas and smoke poured out of the enemy fighter as it plunged into an uncontrolled dive, crashing into the tall trees below.

"Blue-two, this is Blue Leader. Get on my wing and stick to it. That's an order!"

Chamberlain and Devine came around and began to climb toward the beleaguered bombers where Meg, Hub, and Hastings were taking on six FW-190s that were attacking the lead bomber.

"Blue-three, Blue-four, this is Blue-one. Take the bogeys to your starboard. I'll hold off the others until Blue Leader gets back."

Meg signaled with a hand and broke right. Hub followed and pulled up alongside. Suddenly, two FWs went into a climb while the other two attacked the lead bomber.

"Blue-four, I've got two upstairs." Meg pulled back hard on the stick and charged at the ascending FWs, opening fire with her wing guns. The nearest enemy pilot broke a hard right. Her tracers narrowly missed. She gestured right then directed her Mustang into a tight left turn. Her pursuit groaned and creaked from the stress. It took every ounce of her strength to hold it in the turn.

Thinking he had shaken her from his tail, the German finally straightened out only to see Meg streaking in from the other side, her guns blazing. The rounds slammed into the FW, severing it in two. A second later, it disintegrated in mid-air.

Meg pulled up hard to avoid the fiery cloud. "Pat Reilly

showed me that trick a long time ago, sucker," Meg howled to herself. Looking back, the balance of the enemy fighters were breaking station, heading back to Germany. "Looks like we've got 'em on the run," she announced. "Let's follow them down and hit 'em on the deck, over."

"Negative, Blue-three. Get back in formation," Chamberlain ordered. "Let's get our big friends back to safety."

Meg bit her lip with frustration. "Roger, WILCO."

* * * * *

The pursuit squadron landed under the watchful eyes of Colonel Middleton. The pilots briefed crew chiefs as they assisted them out of their cockpits. Everyone was literally pumped with adrenaline. Hastings and Chamberlain were already boasting about their exploits to a civilian war correspondent.

Devine was the last to join them. He approached Meg with fire in his eyes, fists clenched tightly to his sides. "Hey, you sorry fuckin' Mick, try to steal another bogey from me like that again, and you'll be picking up your teeth with broken fingers."

The ground crew and other pilots stopped what they were doing and stared in shock.

Meg was stunned. "Look, Captain, I wasn't trying to steal anything. I know about that trick. That Gerry was maneuvering to get position on you. If I hadn't beaten him to the punch, you'd be sportin' a metal coffin."

Hastings interceded, "Why don't you cut Rye some slack, Devine? I saw the whole thing. Rye only cut in to get that kraut off your back. You should be thanking him for saving your sorry ass."

"Butt out, Lieutenant." Devine closed his eyes and took a deep breath. "Get this loud and clear, O'Reilly--"

"Reilly!" she interrupted. "It's Reilly!"

"Whatever your friggin' Mick name is," Devine continued. "I don't give a good shit who your pappy is. Cross me again, and your ass is mine." His eyes were maniac wild.

Hastings threw up his arms.

Meg stepped forward and got in Devine's face. It was everything she could do to keep from laughing. "I should've let that kraut nail ya.....Dickhead."

As the others broke into hysterical laughter, Devine spun around and stomped off toward the Debriefing Room.

Hastings gave Meg a buddy slap on the back, causing her to wince with whip-like pain. "Dickhead," he repeated, laughing harder. "It's a perfect name for a perfect prick."

"C'mon, gentlemen," Chamberlain prompted. "Let's get on over to Debriefing so we can collect our trophies."

Meg switch-stepped to fall into stride alongside Chamberlain and Hub. "Trophies?" she questioned. "For what?"

"Liquid motivation," Chamberlain explained. "We get a fifth of our favorite booze every time we get a confirmed kill."

Hub chuckled. "If word of *booze-for-bogeys* ever gets back to the States, the pulpit-pounders will be screaming for Wild Bill's scalp."

Chamberlain grinned. "I imagine they would....I like that phrase--booze-for-bogeys."

Hastings turned to the others, mimicking the British accent. "After the debriefing, what do you say that we *tottle* on over to town? I know a place where the beer is cold and the dames are hot."

Meg gave Hub a look. "Gee, John, I can hardly wait."

Chamberlain chuckled. "Ole Johnny Boy here would screw the crack of dawn if it had hair on it."

Hub caught the shocked expression on Meg's face and burst out with laughter, slapping her hard on the back. Meg forced a smile, giving Hub the evil-eye that only he could see. A belt in the mouth would have been the normal course of action.

* * * * *

A red, two-tiered bus proceeded along a narrow, brick street lined with two-story French provincial buildings. Most had shops on the ground floor and living quarters above. Era automobiles and a vast number of bicycles were being used to transport civilians and French and American military personnel. As Chamberlain was checking the front doors of the store, two American MPs cruised past slowly in a jeep, scouting for troublesome GIs.

Meg, Hub, Hastings, and Chamberlain climbed out of a jeep,

straightened their tan trousers, ties, jackets, and service caps and gazed up at the large, white 18th Century two-story flat that had been converted into a service club for military personnel. Music and smoke poured out of the open, handcrafted wooden front door. Chamberlain led the way through an iron gate and the elegant courtyard where a number of American and French military personnel and young civilian locals milled about, smoking cigarettes, engrossed in conversation.

"Definitely a step up from those service clubs in England," Hastings hummed. He gazed at the figure of one particular young French girl as they walked toward the entrance.

Chamberlain chuckled. "He's just infatuated with the language."

Hastings defended himself. "Hell, ole Bob here's just jealous, being married and all. Ain't ya, Bob?"

Hastings was the first to step inside the marble foyer. Behind him, Meg stood at ease as she surveyed the splendid decor, gazing up at the cathedral like ceiling with a crystal chandelier that rivaled the one at the Bendix Ball several years before. Through a large archway was a giant ballroom. A swing band in white jackets was playing on a stage at the far end. A trio of attractive female singers huddled around a silver microphone, singing and moving. A number of couples were dancing to "Jumpin' at the Woodside." Around the dance floor were several dozen round tables graced with fancy linen tablecloths. American soldiers and officers were talking to young French women wearing dresses that ranged from conservative printed dresses to slinky Paris fashions. Some had colorful flowers in their well-styled hair.

Meg turned to Hub. "So far, so good."

"See, I told you," Hub responded. "Just try to have a good time. You deserve it."

Meg was moderately surprised at Hub's congeniality. Could this be the same Hub she had competed against at the Transcontinental Races? He was being too nice, she thought. Then again, he had a stake in the success of this charade. Harmony was better than discord. Could it be he had grown up over this whole affair? Losing Garrett and Liz had certainly helped her own maturity.

Death and war can do that, she thought.

A well-endowed brunette in a snug cocktail dress happened by with a tray of drinks. Her petite nose, pouty lips, and dark eyes sent testosterone levels soaring.

Hastings poked Meg with an elbow. "Rye, get a load of the drop tanks on that babe. I think I'm in love."

Meg shifted from side to side like a he-man. "I've seen better."

Hub snickered. His breathing was noticeably pronounced.

Chamberlain watched the waitress's slender but athletic behind. He shook his head. "Unbelievable."

Hastings caught a second glimpse, rolling his eyes. "Yep, a definite step up in the chick department," he sighed.

The others laughed. It was killing Meg not to say something about the level of male mentality. She was waiting for Hub to blurt out his two cents worth--he didn't disappoint her.

"Yep, that's more action than two wildcats in a gunny sack."

"I thought you were into blond dames with giant headlights," she said facetiously.

Hub swiveled his head. "That just shows how wrong first impressions can be." He made a point of looking at Meg's flattened chest.

"Oh, I wouldn't say that," she countered. "I remember that horde of empty-heads hangin' all over your sorry ass during the Bendix races."

Hub leaned in close to Meg. "Jealous?"

Meg elbowed him in the ribs. "Not hardly."

Hub turned away from the others, holding his sore ribs. "That's a double-negative."

Chuckling, Meg slapped him firmly on the back. "That's what is neat about you, Hub--your ego never gives up," she uttered facetiously.

He flashed her the bird. As he turned, the waitress was standing there, smiling. He quickly dropped his hand. Meg snickered at his awkwardness.

"Would you like a drink, Lieutenant?" she asked in broken English.

"Ah, er, a four Buds," Hub answered.

Puzzled, the waitress asked, "What?"

"Budweiser beer," Hastings inserted. He then stepped closer to the waitress and whispered something in her ear.

She acknowledged his words then turned and strutted toward the bar.

Meg took out a pack of Luckys and offered cigarettes to everyone. All four lighted up, and within seconds, a heavy cloud of smoke hung in the air about them.

The waitress then returned with their drinks. Two were longneck beers that she served to Hastings and Chamberlain. The other two were drink glasses containing a dark liquid.

"What the?" Meg looked at Hastings with a skeptical eye then examined her mysterious drink. She sniffed it and jerked her head away. "Whew! Sweet Mary, mother of Jesus.....What in tarnation is this stuff?"

Chamberlain chuckled. "The elixir of the flying gods."

"Aviation fuel, of course," Hastings cooed. "It's a tradition for newbies to drink one." He held up his beer, proposing a toast. "To the United States Army Air Force."

"Here, here!" Chamberlain added.

Meg held her breath then began to guzzle.

Hub started to drink then stopped, pulling his head away, fighting the urge to heave. Chamberlain snickered.

Meg managed to finish hers, hamming it up with a rubbery, exaggerated expression. She then leaned toward Hub. "Come on, Hotshot. It's only scotch and prune juice, ya big baby. Show some balls! It'll put some hair on that boyish chest of yours."

"I am. I am!" Hub snapped. He examined the drink again.

Hastings and Chamberlain were cackling hysterically.

Hub took a deep breath, held his nose, and began to guzzle it, his eyes bulging like a frog. Finally finished, he clamped a hand over his mouth, fighting the urge to throw up.

Meg, Hastings, and Chamberlain cheered boisterously, grabbing the attention of everyone nearby. It was the first time since Garrett and Liz had perished that Meg had really laughed.

A hefty woman in a black frock waddled by the group.

Hastings looked down at her wide behind.

He nudged Meg. "Lookie at that. It's probably been 20 years since she was able to see the crack of her ass in a mirror."

Meg studied the woman's behind then giggled. Hub quickly gave her a parental look. Realizing she was risking her identity, she turned her head and covered her mouth with a hand. The elixir was affecting her emotionally. Hub was glad to see her relaxing, but not to the extent of blowing her cover.

Suddenly, the house lights dimmed, and the band began playing the introduction to a slow French tune. A beautiful brunette with long hair parted on one side, appeared center stage under an intense spotlight. She was wearing long black gloves and a black strapless evening gown, revealing her soft, youthful shoulders. The servicemen hooted and whistled as she floated in front of the microphone, bobbing their heads to get a clear view of the vibrant, statuesque figure. Her low, provocative voice had them melting where they stood.

"Now that is what I call sexy," Hastings cooed.

"Come on, Don Juan," Chamberlain prompted, "let's find someone to dance."

Hastings and Chamberlain grabbed the hand of two attractive brunettes and moved to the middle of the dance floor where they joined a number of couples dancing slowly, locked in a variety of vertical embraces. Hub, Meg, and most of the male patrons ringed the dance floor to watch the beautiful singer. Between the intoxicating effects of the elixir and the singer's sexy voice, Hub stood in a trance as the French lyrics emitted from her soft, pouty lips.

Meg slugged Hub in the upper arm with the force to maim an elephant.

Hub flinched sideways. "Hey! What was that for?"

"I thought you were into blondes," Meg snarled.

Hub massaged the wound. "Your voice, Garrett," he reminded.

"Oh, oh!" she slurred.

Hub leaned closer, whispering, "Why do you care about who I look at?" He returned his attention toward the singer. "You've reminded me often enough that you dislike me."

Meg elbowed him, this time in the rib cage.

Hub flinched backward and lost his balance, backing into a brawny Army sergeant near the edge of the dance floor. The sergeant retaliated with a shove, sending Hub sprawling onto the dance floor, forcing several couples to hop aside to avoid a collision. Irked, Hub scrambled to his feet and charged at the sergeant, wildly swinging his fists. The sergeant checked Hub's punches then cocked his arm and delivered a knockout punch to Hub's jaw. Meg winced as Hub staggered backward with a dazed look. The sergeant puffed his chest and moved forward to finish off his opponent.

Meg stepped in front of him, blocking his way. "That's enough, Sergeant."

The sergeant snickered at his boyish opponent. "Maybe you want some, too, flyboy."

As the sergeant cocked his arm to strike Meg, she took up a defensive stance, countering the powerful punch and flipping the sergeant onto his back.

"Why you punk officer," he snarled, rolling over to get to his knees. "I eat aviators for lunch."

Before the sergeant was at a full stance, Meg grabbed his hand and twisted it, forcing the sergeant back to his knees. "I forgot to tell you. I eat sergeants for breakfast."

Suddenly, one of the sergeant's comrades came at her. Meg ducked and swept his nearest knee, forcing him to drop to the floor, holding his knee in agony. Hub regrouped and stared in awe at Meg's self-defense moves. Lowering his head, he charged at the sergeant. Both went flying into a growing crowd of spectators. Two airmen righted Hub and thrust him back into the melee. Over the initial shock, liquored-up tempers prevailed.

From the middle of the large dance floor, Hastings and Chamberlain left their dance partners and began weaving through the couples to come to Meg and Hub's aid. Hastings accidentally bumped another Army sergeant with red curly hair and freckles. He immediately squared off on Hastings who dodged a jab and countered with one of his own, squashing the sergeant's nose. His opponent reached up with a hand and came away with a red hand. Looking Hastings square in the eye, the sergeant licked the blood off his fingers.

"Oh shit!" Hastings stammered.

The redhead began dancing like a boxer, trying to find an opportunity to throw a calculated punch.

Meanwhile, Chamberlain was trying to help Meg with the other two. Meg still had the big sergeant immobile on his knees, applying pressure on his wrist.

Chamberlain positioned himself between Meg and the sergeant's limping comrade who was favoring his damaged knee. "Give it a rest, sergeant."

The redhead finally landed an uppercut to Hastings' jaw then slugged him in the stomach with a combination, doubling him over. The sergeant brought up a knee, flipping Hastings over on his side. As the sergeant moved to kick him in the ribs, Chamberlain charged at the redhead, sweeping the back of his leg, flipping him over backwards. Chamberlain followed up with a bone-crushing jab.

Chamberlain grabbed Hastings by the collar and pulled him out of harm's way before retrieving Meg and Hub. As Chamberlain picked Hub off the floor, Meg gave the hefty sergeant a rabbit punch with the blade of her hand, knocking him unconscious. She spun around and joined Chamberlain who was dodging brawlers, trying to reach Hastings who was hunched over, arms folded over his stomach and moaning.

All of a sudden, they could hear police sirens.

As Meg glanced at the entrance, she spotted a face from the past.

"Rye, pay attention," Chamberlain snapped. "Give me a hand with these two. We can't afford to get arrested." He reached down and grabbed Hastings by the collar, helping him to his feet. "Out the back way, quickly. Follow me."

Meg slipped Hub's arm over her shoulder to help him walk. Together, the foursome plowed through the onrushing crowd to get outside where the MPs and the French police came to a screeching halt.

"Okay everyone, straighten up and fly right," Chamberlain ordered.

While the police raced inside to restore order, Meg, Hub,

Chamberlain, and Hastings hustled to their jeep. After depositing Hastings in the front passenger seat, Meg and Hub climbed into the back. Chamberlain started the jeep and drove away slowly.

Hub leaned toward Meg and spoke so only she would hear. "Who was that pilot by the entrance?" he slurred.

Meg's heart was beating like a war drum. "What pilot?" she whispered.

"The one that froze you," Hub snapped. "Do you know hi--?" he hiccuped. "Oh, I wish you hadn't--" he hiccuped again, "--said that." He leaned over the side and vomited, splattering the back of the jeep.

Chamberlain heard the commotion and turned his head to see. "He didn't?"

Meg nodded. "I'm afraid so."

Suddenly, Hastings leaned over the side and threw up.

"Shit!" Chamberlain bellowed.

CHAPTER 26

The pilots filed into the Briefing Room and sat.

Middleton soon made his entrance and stepped onto the wooden platform. "Okay, gentlemen. Our newbies did it again. Lieutenant Reilly got two more confirmed kills and Lieutenant Martin, one. That makes Reilly an ace. Morrison, Perry, Hastings, and Chamberlain also got one each, making Bob a double ace. Good job, men."

As everyone applauded, Middleton turned to Major Hamilton who moved over to the map to begin the briefing. "With most of the bomb group turning back yesterday, many of the targets went unscathed so we're going back to Big B."

Many of the pilots nervously stirred in their seats. Meg and Hub glanced at one another, rolling their blood-shot eyes.

Hamilton held up his hands to quiet everyone. "After the briefing, Sergeant Lindstrom will give you refresher training on contour map reading. Pay attention, gentlemen. A number of those who have been shot down or had to ditch their aircraft got captured because they were not proficient at reading a map."

The pilots moaned.

After the mission briefing, Hamilton turned the speaker's platform over to Sergeant Lindstrom. The easel near the side of the platform read: Contour Map Reading.

"At ease, gentlemen," Lindstrom said, pacing back and forth with his hands clasped behind his back. "During this block of instruction, you will become proficient at contour map reading."

He nodded at a youthful corporal who was standing by a small table. The corporal unveiled a nude female mannequin, drawing whistles and hoots.

Cackling, Hub glanced at Meg who was faking a grin. He slapped her on the back. "Great bod, huh, Rye?"

Meg pulled away. "Pay attention, Hotshot. Maybe you'll learn something about female anatomy, hopefully in the simplest of terms so that even you will understand."

He flashed her the bird.

"As you were, gentlemen," Lindstrom yelled. "By the use of this model, I will show you an easy way to identify the different types of terrain features you would encounter. First, a hilltop."

Using a white stick, the corporal pointed to the feature as the sergeant explained each, beginning with the mannequin's breasts.

"Saddle," Lindstrom continued, "is the feature between two hilltops."

The corporal pointed to the area between the mannequin's breasts.

"Next, is the ridge."

The end of the pointer was dragged along the top of the thigh.

"Like a bowl of soup, the depression is a feature in which all sides are enclosed."

The corporal pointed out the belly button.

"And finally, the valley which is much like a depression except one spills downhill. Typically, there is a stream or a river that feeds into a lake."

When the corporal pointed at the crotch, the pilots hooted, whistled, and cackled again.

Lindstrom motioned with his hands for the men to quiet. "At ease, gentlemen. We need to hurry so we can get through this. There are some simple tips to help you survive if downed behind enemy lines. One, stay off the trails and roads; instead, parallel the trails and roads. Two, follow or float on waterways to the seacoast. Three, food grows on fields near villages and waterways. Four, moving a few feet into a dense forest will conceal you. Five, dead branches on trees make good kindling for cooking; plus, they normally do not give off much smoke. And six, boil or treat all water used for drinking with iodine tablets." He paused. "You will now break up into two-man teams. My assistant will be handing out a map sheet and a grease pencil to each team. You are to identify each of the features I just mentioned."

"Hotshot, now we'll see how attentive you were," Meg said facetiously.

"It's Hub, dammit.....Hub!"

Suddenly, Major Hamilton returned. "I need to see Lieutenant Reilly." His face was somber.

Hub looked over at Meg whose face had turned to granite. "Maybe they found out 'bout our little escapade in town."

Without answering, Meg stood and shuffled along the row of seats then down the aisle. She walked up to Hamilton. "Yes, Sir. You wanted to see me?"

"Come with me, Lieutenant."

Hub felt a sudden chill as Meg and the major departed the room.

Both walked in step to the Headquarters Building. They entered and went immediately to Middleton's office.

Hamilton stuck his head in. "Colonel, Lieutenant Reilly is here."

Petrified, Meg entered and saluted. "Sir, Lieutenant Reilly reports."

Middleton looked up from a manila folder setting in front of him and returned the salute. "At ease, Lieutenant. Have a seat," he offered kindly.

Meg sat on the edge of a chair with her hands setting properly on her thighs. In one hand was her leather flying cap. "You would think that after all these years in this man's Army, I would have seen everything." He paused for a long moment. "I have a radio message in front of me from Colonel Douglass confirming your report. It was a very courageous act on the part of your sister and the other woman. Since it was a classified mission, no one will know about it. It never happened, understand, Lieutenant?"

Meg sat numb in her seat, partially from the stress, partially due to the sense of relief that her true identity had not been discovered.

"My sympathy goes out to you and your father. No man likes to see his youngsters die before he does."

"Tha.....thank you, Sir," Meg sobbed. "Meg and I were very close. This has not been easy." She looked down at her shaking hands.

"Are you going to be okay, Lieutenant?" Middleton inquired. "I think everyone would understand if you would like to hang back for a few days. Maybe I can arrange for you to contact your father."

"I need to keep busy, Colonel. Besides, I wouldn't know what to say to him at this point. Maybe in a few days."

Middleton nodded that he understood. "I didn't serve in the same unit, but I know of your father's heroics during the last war. He was one hell of a brave pilot."

"Thank you, Sir."

"I understand that your sister was a WASP," he added.

Meg's chin dropped to her chest. She nodded her head.

"Again, my sympathy to you and your family, Lieutenant." Middleton closed the file and stood. "You better get back. Your squadron is scheduled to take off in a few minutes. I know this may be of little consolation, but I just wanted you to know that you should be very proud of your unbelievable performance over the last two days. Once word of this gets back to your father, I'm sure that he will be very proud....of all of you."

Meg stood. "Thank you, Sir."

"I want you to visit the chaplain today," Middleton ordered. "I want straight heads up there, understand?"

Meg nodded. "Yes, Sir. Thank you, Sir," she sniffled.

Hub was anxiously waiting for Meg upon her return to the Briefing Room. "What happened?"

Meg remained silently gloom for what seemed like an eternity. Garrett's death was again at the top of her mind.

"Me–...Rye!" he snapped quietly. "What in the hell's goin' on? What did you tell them, dammit?"

Meg slowly turned her head. "Nothing....The colonel was merely comforting me."

*****

Chamberlain and his squadron were one of many escorting an armada of Flying Fortresses at 20,000 feet. Meg and the rest of the pursuit pilots were attentively checking the sky around them for enemy fighters. They had long since passed the border into Germany. Anxiety was festering in their every cell. It was almost noon.

"This is Blue Leader," Chamberlain announced over the radio. "We've got company at 12 o'clock high. Unload your drop tanks."

Closing one eye, Meg craned her head upward, trying to shield the sun with a hand. "There must be sixty of 'em!"

"Let's go get 'em, gentlemen," Chamberlain said calmly. "They're gonna try to go around us. Watch yourselves."

Ramming his engine at full throttle, Chamberlain began climbing, firing his guns. One of the lead FWs began smoking and plunged forward, spinning like a pinwheel into the clouds below, swallowed like a peanut by an elephant.

"Scratch one bratwurst," Chamberlain announced.

"Good shootin', Bobby," Hastings cooed.

Chamberlain strained to study the German planes from a distance. "Those aren't drop tanks they're totting, gents. Those are bombs. The krauts are gonna come in high and drop 'em on our big friends. Don't let 'em through!" He contacted the bomber formation commander. "Spread 'em out for a bit. The Gerries have got bombs, comin' at 12 o'clock high."

Devine peeled off and laid on the firing button. His rounds were missing everything.

Chamberlain was furious. "Blue-two, this is Blue Leader. Don't shoot till you've got a target. You're wasting ammo. You don't have the proper lead."

One of the FWs came at Snake Eyes from 10 o'clock high, guns chattering. The rounds walked along his fuselage, narrowly missing Devine. One cracked his canopy.

"Dammit, Blue-two!" Chamberlain screamed. "Get back in formation."

A group of three FWs came straight at Devine, trying to break through to the lead bomber. Radio chatter made it impossible to warn him.

Meg contacted Chamberlain. "This is Blue-three. We've got 'em! Stay with me, Blue-four." She peeled off.

Meg and Hub accelerated and climbed, taking the enemy trio

head-on. One of the FW-109s opened up with its four 20-mm cannon, riddling one of the lead bombers, killing both the dorsal and starboard waist gunners. Fire broke out on its starboard wing, and it began to lose altitude. Hub opened fire on the lead FW, catching the preoccupied pilot in the mid-section, breaking it in two. The FW burst into billowing flames, forcing Hub to pull up hard to avoid the debris.

Meg broke left to intercept one of the FWs trying to get a clear shot at the wounded bomber. She took a hefty lead and fired two short spurts. Smoke began to pour from the belly of the Folke-Wulf. Suddenly, it fluttered downward out of control. The German pilot managed to shove back the canopy and bail out.

"They're breaking off!" Hastings shouted.

The U.S. armada went on to Berlin, dropped its bombs, and headed back to England. Thirteen bombers had been downed by flak, but not a single bomber had been lost to the Luftwaffe. Two American pilots had died when they used their aircraft as shields against German pilots trying to ram American bombers--a sure sign that Hitler was growing desperate.

Meg downed another FW before it could ram a B-17, and Hastings rang up two more kills during the return trip. In all, it had been a successful day for Chamberlain's Blue Wings.

After the debriefing, Meg exited the Briefing Room less than pleased. Her left hand tightly clasped the neck of the Jack Daniel's bottle. Hub, Chamberlain, and Hastings were already outside, joyously waiting for her, each gripping their own trophies.

Chamberlain noticed that Meg was short one bottle. "Hey, Rye, you look like someone just stole your puppy."

"You had two kills today," Hastings noted. "Where's your other bottle?"

Meg took a deep breath, trying to control her anger. "Dickhead Devine vetoed one of my kills. My gun camera took a small piece of shrapnel."

"Where does he get off checking film?" Hastings snarled. "He's lucky to be flying."

Chamberlain's eyes were pointed darts. "He can't do that! We'll vouch for you. I saw you down the Messerschmidt that tried to ram the B-17. . . . .C'mon!"

"You guys go ahead," Hastings said. "I've got something to tend to."

The trio charged back into the Briefing Room. Standing near the back of the room was Major Hamilton getting an earful from Devine.

Chamberlain raised a hand as they approached. "Major, we need to have a word with you."

"What is it, Bob?"

Devine protested, "Wait a minute, Chamberlain. I was talking to--"

Hamilton stopped Devine with a hand.

"Sir, I saw Rye nail that second kraut," Chamberlain attested.

"Me, too," Hub chimed.

Devine glared at Meg. "Major, they're just--"

Major Hamilton cut Devine's protest short with a snarl then pointed at the case of Jack Daniel's sitting on the edge of the platform. "Congratulations, Lieutenant Reilly. Grab another bottle. You've more than earned it."

His face scarlet-red and temples pulsating, Devine stormed out of the Briefing Room.

As Meg, Hub, and Chamberlain exited, a beefy civilian photographer was waiting to take their picture. Beside him was Hastings, directing the shoot. Hastings grinned as he hustled to join Meg and the others. When the flash bulb popped, Meg dropped her chin to avoid the shot.

The photographer looked up from the viewfinder at Meg. "Hey, you weren't looking at the camera."

Meg kept walking past the photographer. "I've gotta take a leak. See you guys back at the Q."

Hastings turned to Hub and Chamberlain. "What was that all about? I thought it would be neat to get a shot of all four of us."

Meg was lying on her bunk in just a T-shirt and trousers, writing in her diary, occasionally studying several photos that she had leaned against her pillow. Three were group snapshots of her family and the WAFs, one of her mother and Amelia, one of her and Hub taken at the Bendix Ball, and one of her and Aaron at the hotel restaurant, taken the night they made love for the first time. On a night stand was a glass and a near-empty bottle of Jack Daniel's.

A knock at the door caused her to jump. She quickly stuffed the photos in the diary and slid it under the pillow.

Meg hopped off the bed. "Hold on a sec." She slipped on a uniform shirt and answered the door.

Their eyes glazed, Hastings, Chamberlain, and Hub stood side-by-side, boyishly grinning.

"We're on a mission," announced Hastings.

"We're gonna pay a visit to the nurses quarters," Hub slurred. "Wanna come?"

"It might be good for you to get out," added Chamberlain.

Meg shook her head. "Na, I'll sit this one out. I'm gonna hit the rack early. One brawl a week is quite enough for me."

* * * * *

A boisterous knock at the door brought Meg from a dead sleep to a sitting position. She rubbed her eyes, trying to get her bearings. The knock was repeated but with a fist. She turned on the small lamp sitting on the night stand. She picked up the wind-up clock and studied it. It was 3:13.

Again, a riveting knock shook the foundation.

Wearing only boxer shorts and a T-shirt, Meg shuffled to the door and opened it just enough to see who was making all the racket. A pair of black lace panties dangled just inches from her eyes.

"Hey," a familiar voice slurred, "you missed a good time, Bucko. Here's..." he hiccuped, "a present from the boys....I mean, girls."

Meg shoved them back in Hub's face, and as she tried to shut the door, he stuck a toe in the crack and pushed it open. His glassy eyes immediately examined her attire. "You look like you need to start eating more," he slurred. "Get some meat on those bones."

Meg heard shower shoes scuffling in the hall.

"Shut the damn door, Hubert," she whispered loudly. As he did, she snatched the uniform shirt off a wall hook and slipped it on. "So where are your cohorts in crime, gettin' laid?"

He turned around, wobbling. "Oh, yeah, probably," he

murmured. "Ole Johnny Boy was working this one blonde.....built like a Sherman tank. You should've--"

"All right, all right. That's more information than I asked for, Hotshot....and what about you, Hubert?" Meg almost sounded jealous.

"What do ya mean, what about me?"

"If you were having so much fun, Hotshot, why did you come back?"

Hub's face sobered. "All I could think about.....was you, Baby-face." In a real moment of passion, he grabbed Meg and kissed her hard.

At first, Meg resisted. Then, she kissed him back with equal momentum, almost pulling him through her. Hub picked her up and carried her over to the bed. They fumbled with each other's clothing, continuing to passionately kiss.

Suddenly, Meg thrust out both hands and pushed him back. "Cool your engine. We can't be doing this."

"Screw it!" Hub growled, grabbing her wrists, trying to wrestle her into his arms.

"Dammit, Hotshot. I don't love you like that."

Hub drew backward. "It's that writer friend of yours."

Meg dropped her chin, nodding.

"Well, where is he now? Has he ever told you that he loves you? I'm the one that made it possible for you to be flying in combat."

"Only because I threatened to go to the major." Meg stood and began dressing.

"When are you going to wake up girl that I'm your man?"

She studied his face to see if he was being serious. "Look, Hub, we go way back. All the girls--you're such a playboy."

"I've changed. We've changed." Hub slowly put on his shirt and regrouped his ego. "Level with me, Meg. What's behind it?"

"Behind what?"

"This insatiable passion for flying?"

Meg thought for a long moment. "My mother died when I was a little girl. You know, she was a best friend of Amelia Earhart. Together, they were breaking all kinds of records, flying anything that had wings. During their barnstorming days, she and Dad had a mock combat routine. She was the Red Baron, and he was the American war hero. He even designed her planes. Everything seemed so perfect. They were ready to take on the world. Then one day, she left us all.....for another man." There was a long silence. "I was only five at the time. For years, I blamed myself. What had I done to drive her away? Later, I blamed Dad. Eventually, I came to hate her. All those years, Dad never talked about it, not even once. He just kept flying, designing planes. It's the only thing he knows," she paused. "All my life . . . trying to fill up that big hole he kept in his heart. But he never let me in, any of us in. It was too deep." She paused. "I guess somehow, I wanted to get her attention. Flying to new heights was the closest I would ever get to her."

"I'm sorry about your mother, but I'm confused. First, you said that she died then you said that she left with another man."

Meg stared at a crack in the wall for what seemed like forever.

"Meg?" he prompted.

"They died later that day when a truck ran into their car. The news, it nearly killed Dad. I can still remember him slumped against the wall after the police came to the house. Then Amelia died, and now, he thinks he has lost me, the only other woman in his life."

"Jesus, no wonder you've been such a demon in the air," Hub stammered.

"I've never told anyone else, not even Aaron."

His faced sobered. "We're a pretty good team up there, you and me. Maybe when this is over, well..."

"How did we get into all this madness?" she asked.

Hub thought a moment. "Unknowingly, you got pushed."

"I've been thinking about that," she said. She pushed him toward the door. "Now, go to bed."

He began tickling her ribs. Meg took the challenge and wrestled with him, laughing. It was a release for both of them.

From outside her door, Devine was listening with a calculating smile.

CHAPTER 27

Meg entered Group Headquarters' outer office with a concerned face. Suddenly, Hub exited Middleton's office.

Meg and Hub shared a look.

She squinted quizzically as if to say, "What's up?"

His head down low, Hub tried to clear his thoughts.

Meg thought to herself, "Oh, oh, he spilled the beans."

The Adjutant, Louis Palin, a slender, fair-haired first lieutenant, poked his head out the colonel's door and motioned with a hand for her to enter. A serious Colonel Middleton was seated behind his desk. Sitting to one side in a folding chair was Captain Devine. Meg wanted to reach over and wipe the smug look off his face. The adjutant shut the door and took a seat on the other side of the room.

Meg walked up and saluted. "Sir, Lieutenant Reilly reports."

Middleton quickly returned her salute. "Stand at ease, Lieutenant." He paused. "Captain Devine here has just told me an incredible story. He claims he heard you and Lieutenant Martin giggling and making sexual noises all night in your room."

Meg was in disbelief. She grew to a beet-red boil. She glared at Devine. "Sir, that's ridiculous! Martin came back from a panty raid last night, half-drunk. He wanted to rub it in--what I had missed. We polished off a bottle and probably got a little loud, that's all. I assure you, Sir. There was no abnormal conduct."

"That's bull, Colonel!" Devine spouted. "They're queers. They shower together every morning.....before any of us get up. I've seen--"

Middleton held up a hand to silence Devine.

"I certainly hope not," Middleton uttered. "You and Martin are extraordinary pilots. I'd hate to lose you two, but let me make myself perfectly clear. I will not have any abnormal conduct in my unit. Am I making myself clear, Lieutenant?"

"Yes, Sir. Is that all?"

"One more thing, Lieutenant. Some magazine writer is coming here to interview aces. I understand you've been dodging the press, but now that you are an ace, you will talk to this guy. That's an order.....understand?"

"Yes, Sir," she responded nervously.

"You're dismissed, Lieutenant, for now." He paused. "Be advised, I'm obligated to check into these allegations. Now, you better get back. You've got a date in Nuremberg."

"Yes, Sir." Meg snapped to attention and saluted.

Middleton returned the salute, and Meg exited his office.

Grinding his teeth, Devine was seething with contempt. "You don't really buy that excuse, do you, Colonel?"

Middleton slammed his fist down hard on his desk. "Reilly is one smart, gutsy pilot, which is more than I can say for you. Now, get your sorry ass the hell out of my office, and not a word of this to anyone. Talk to anyone, even your mother, and I will bust you. Do you read me loud and clear, Mister?"

Flustered, Devine shot out of his seat and saluted. "Yes, Sir!"

"By the way, Captain, you've been assigned to Captain Perry's flight."

"But, Sir."

"You're dismissed, Captain," Middleton snapped. He elected not to return Devine's salute.

"Yes, Sir." Devine spun around and rushed out of the office.

Shaking his head in disgust, Middleton handed the folder to his adjutant. "They're right about Devine--he is a dickhead."

Snickering, Lieutenant Palin exited Middleton's office just as an unfamiliar face entered the building with a personnel file tucked under his arm and an Army-issued duffel bag slung over his shoulder. He lowered the bag by the strap and held out the folder for the adjutant. "Sir, I'm Lieutenant LaRocca, reporting for duty."

Palin looked at the clock on the wall. "You're too late to join today's operation. Let's get your paperwork done and get you settled in at the B.O.Q."

* * * * *

Hastings and Chamberlain were finishing a preflight check on two new P-51s when Meg and Hub arrived at the flight line in the colonel's jeep. Bright-eyed and grinning, Hastings and Chamberlain had already transferred their names and swastikas over to the new aircraft. Meg and Hub flashed a thumbs-up. It was then that Hub spotted his new Mustang. His eyes exploded.

Meg grinned. "Congratulations, Hub."

Without responding, Hub walked up to his new pursuit and ran an admiring hand over the skin of the wing. Meg grinned.

Chamberlain motioned with a finger at Meg to climb aboard. He was already settled into his cockpit when Meg arrived at his side, standing on the wing.

Chamberlain's eyes sparkled as he caressed the instrument panel and the controls as though they were the body parts of a soft, sensuous woman. "Okay, Rye, tell me everything I'll need to know in five minutes about your pappy's design."

Meg snickered, "Blue Leader, you're in for the greatest sex of your life."

"Let's not get carried away. A plane is a plane. Well, a woman is something else," he joked.

Meg looked around. "Where's Dickhead?"

"He's been assigned to a different flight," answered Chamberlain. "You're now Blue-two and Martin will be Blue-three." He paused. "What did Wild Bill want?"

"I was given a direct order not to discuss it with anyone."

Chamberlain nodded curiously. "You better get moving."

Soon, all four Mustangs were roaring down the runway.

Meg spotted Devine's Thunderbolt taxiing with his new group. He was glaring at her. She calmly placed her fingers under her chin and flipped him off. He jumped back in his seat, swearing.

* * * * *

Four bomber groups and their fighter escorts filled the sky above Germany. Meg looked down to view the landscape far below, looking for the next reference point. Glancing over at Chamberlain, she pointed downward. He nodded. It was almost time to change their course.

"This is Blue Leader. Get ready, gentlemen. Gerry should be comin' 'round the mountain most anytime now. Keep a sharp eye."

They weren't disappointed. From a dense cloud bank, six squadrons of FW-190s and Me-109s appeared.

"Herd of bogeys at 12 o'clock," Chamberlain announced calmly. "Take 'em head on."

"Just like Wyatt Earp," Hub responded.

"Watch 'em," Chamberlain warned. "They usually break and dive. Take on those who don't. We don't want to get sandwiched between, and we definitely can't let them get at our big friends."

Blue Leader's experience was right. Two-thirds of the Germans began to break and dive. Chamberlain aimed at those who did not. It was a head-on, barrel-rolling attack. The German guns flashed repeatedly like a serpent's tongue, throwing up a wall of fire at Chamberlain and his flight.

Meg and the others accelerated and adjusted their direction until each had an opponent in their sight ring. They pressed their gun buttons, unleashing the fury of two dozen Browning machine guns.

While enemy rounds narrowly missed her, Meg's tracers slammed into the nose and cockpit of her target. The Messerschmidts winged over and plunged toward earth in a fiery ball.

"I got him. I got him!" Meg whooped.

"Good shooting, Blue-two," Hastings applauded.

Chamberlain lined up another Me-109 in his sight ring and fired, peppering the wing of his foe. Again, he cut loose with another squirt, this time scoring hits on the engine cowling and propeller. The enemy bird teetered briefly then disintegrated. As they burst through the churning cloud of black smoke, the Germans were upon them, swarming like garbage fleas. The sky filled with enemy tracers. Meg instinctively realized that some were coming from behind. Her head rubbernecked, trying to get a fix. Suddenly, a tracer passed through her canopy just inches from her eyes. Meg broke a hard right and went into a tight turn, pulling until her Mustang began to shudder and vibrate. There they were--two Messerschmidts clinging to her tail. More tracers scored hits behind her canopy and starboard wing.

"I need some help here," she yelled.

"This is Blue-three. I'm on it," Hub responded. "Break left, now!"

Meg rammed her control stick to the left. Her bird responded.

Looking through his sight ring, Hub realized that he had both bogeys lined up in front of him. "Glory be." He fired a short burst to check his aim. They missed, and the closest Me-109 broke right. Hub's guns belched another burst, ripping apart the farthermost German fighter. He fired again. Chunks of the Me-109's left wing and rear stabilizer flew backward. The pilot pushed back his canopy and leaped. Soon, a parachute deployed below.

A Thunderbolt appeared out of nowhere and fired upon the descending pilot, riveting his body with bullets. The enemy pilot's body went limp. Hub was in shock as he studied the red-nosed, green-winged Thunderbolt--it was Snake Eyes.

"Devine! You rotten son of a bitch!" Hub screamed. "Damn, you!"

"This is Blue Leader. Forget him, Blue-three, and get back to our big friends on the double, out!"

Hub barreled into a tight turn and joined Meg who was already streaking toward the bomber formation. Bomber crews and fighter pilots were hysterically alerting one another about the attacking Germans. The red-nosed Mustangs wove, looped, and rolled about in aerial ballet with the Germans.

Hastings wove back and forth, trying to shake a bogey off his tail. He chopped his throttle, and the German mirrored his move. Suddenly, Hastings accelerated and climbed, looping over backwards, positioning his Mustang behind the Messerschmidts. He pressed his gun button before leveling out, riddling the German pilot who slumped forward in his seat. The Me-109 spun around then spiraled out of control into the trees. Hastings twisted his head around to check his tail--it was clear. He quickly rocketed to assist Chamberlain who was racing to beat two FWs charging at the lead bomber.

Chamberlain manipulated his control stick, trying to put one in his sight ring. He fired and missed. "Dammit!" He readjusted and fired again. Both enemy fighters pulled up and went into a steep climb. "I've gotcha now," he murmured. He accelerated as he pulled back on his joystick. "Captain Reilly, you did put together a magnificent fighter." Bright flashes emitted along both wings, tagging one of the FWs that stuttered then windmilled until it exploded.

Looking left, Hastings was now off his right wing, firing short spurts at the other FW. Together, they unleashed a windstorm of hell, chewing up the fuselage and both wings of the FW that broke in two. A large chunk hurled between them, forcing them to break in opposite directions. Both circled around to see what was left of the German attack force. The krauts were breaking contact.

"Whew! Jesus," Hastings whooped, grabbing his heart. "Man, what a chest thumper!"

Meg and Hub pulled up to Chamberlain's left to complete the finger-four formation.

"I'll tell my pappy that you like his design," Meg said appreciatively.

"Is that you, Blue-two?"

"Roger, Hell's Kiss. Looks like we've got 'em on the run."

Black puffs of smoke appeared to their front. So far, not a bomber had been shot down. The sky ahead was mostly sunny over Nuremberg. It was a perfect day for the bombardiers.

"This is Blue Leader. Hold on to your seats. We've got flak coming in. Spread 'em out."

The pursuits rolled out further to the side and started S–turning and circling so as not to outrun the slower bombers. One B-17 lost two engines when flak exploded in front of its port side wing, shattering the cockpit glass and killing the pilot. The bomber began to drop altitude with trailing flames. The co-pilot, Lieutenant Art Reed from Athens, Georgia, fought with all his football strength to pull the B-17 out of the dive.

The rest of the bombers lowered their bomb-bay doors, making final adjustments in their course, bouncing and rocking through the jaw jarring flak. Two minutes later, a half-million pounds of bombs tumbled toward Hitler's war machine. Looking down, Meg could see large gray bursts rise as the bombs pulverized concrete, tin, and wood structures. Secondary explosions were evidence that many of the bombs had found munitions plants and fuel depots.

It was the first time that Meg could see the results. She was pleased.

After the bombers made a 180-turn to head back to England and had out-distanced the flak guns, three squadrons of P-51s appeared in the horizon.

"Looks like the late shift just arrived," Chamberlain announced. "It's time to separate and head home. Look for targets of opportunity."

"Praise the lord," Meg sounded.

Like preying hawks hungry for their next meal, the squadrons peeled off and began searching the outskirts of Nuremberg for military and transportation targets. Chamberlain's Blue Flight was to locate and strafe a military airfield several miles away.

"This is Blue Leader. Target at 10 o'clock. Blue-one will go in with me. Blue-two and Blue-three, you'll come in after we make our first pass. We don't want to let the krauts get off a shot. Go for the aircraft first then the fuel dump." He pointed the nose of his new Mustang downward and accelerated.

As the features on the ground became larger and more distinct, so did the antiaircraft shells headed their way.

"We've got incoming," Chamberlain warned. "I've got the two on the runway. Take the two on the taxi area, Blue-one." He checked his airspeed: 422.

Fifty-caliber rounds kicked up the pavement and large chunks of turf as they walked into the two FWs trying to get off the runway. Chamberlain stayed on them until one exploded. He quickly broke left and climbed while Hastings polished off both FWs trying to take off.

"Like shootin' ducks at the county fair," Hastings howled.

Meg and Hub were now diving, their guns blazing. Meg silenced a gun position near the end of the runway while Hub concentrated on the fighters parked near the trees, scoring hits on two. As he and Meg pulled up to circle around, Hastings and Chamberlain were already diving again, their shells hacking apart wooden buildings, showering the air with millions of toothpicks.

Meg and Hub came around and dove again, this time for the tower and gun positions. Meg could see rescue crews and fire trucks frantically racing about. She spotted a tall hangar and opened fire. Her tracers sang along the tin roof like a hailstorm, kicking out its shuttering panels. Hub spotted a transport under a camouflage net and strafed it. It burst into flames. As he pulled up, Meg joined him.

"That's where those buggers been hiding!" Chamberlain yelled. "Four bogeys by the trees."

Four FWs were taxiing on the grass, heading for the cluttered runway. Meg jammed her stick to the left and began circling tightly. Hub followed her lead. Soon they joined Hastings and Chamberlain, and flew on line like the four Musketeers.

"This is Blue Leader. Conserve your ammo. Don't fire till you've got one in your sight ring."

All four manipulated their control sticks and rudders until they had an FW in their sight ring. Meg was the first to open fire. Her tracers slammed into the left most fighter, striking its fuel tanks. It exploded, taking out the FW to its right.

"Hey, that was mine!" Hub shouted.

"This is Blue Leader. Take mine.....But you better not miss."

Hub and Hastings shifted their aim then squeezed their gun buttons, but only Hub's guns were firing, taking out the left target.

"Blue Leader, Blue-one. Shit! I'm outta ammo!" Hastings shrieked.

"Let's take 'em home, gentlemen."

* * * * *

Chamberlain, Hastings, Hub, and Meg were barely out of their Mustangs when a group of five journalists intercepted them.

A slender correspondent in his mid-forties with a hawk-like nose stepped in front of Meg. "How was it up there, son?"

Caught off-guard, Meg tried to side-step him.

"Hey, Lieutenant. I'm talking to you."

Without stopping, Meg answered over her shoulder. "I didn't hear you. What did you say?"

"How was the action up there?"

Hub walked by and answered for her. "It was your basic turkey shoot. We all tagged a couple."

"Where's home?"

A short photographer raised his camera. Meg pivoted, facing away.

"Hey, Lieutenant, you moved," the photographer snapped. "Let me get anoth--"

Meg continued to walk briskly. "Sorry, boys, but I've gotta piss like a two-headed race horse."

Hub walked backwards, talking to them. "We'll be in deep trouble if we don't get on over to Debriefing." He spun around and caught up to Meg.

The photographer and the journalists stood there dumbfounded, scratching their heads.

"That's a first," said one.

"I'll say," the photographer agreed. "What's wrong with those two?"

Another rubbed his chin. "Usually, these hotshots are kissin' our ass to write about them. "I'm sure I've seen that face before," the photographer added.

About then, Hastings and Chamberlain strutted by and were instantly pounced on by the reporters. Hastings' war stories took their minds off Meg and Hub.

Meg and Hub entered the Briefing Room, taking seats near the front. Major Hamilton was already debriefing some of the P-47 pilots. Spirits were high. It had been a very successful day except for one P-47 shot down over the target. A commotion at the entrance caused Meg to turn out of curiosity. It was Hastings and Chamberlain, joking and shaking hands as usual. As she was turning back, she noticed that someone new was looking at her with a puzzled expression. She swallowed hard.

Hub noticed her troubled face. "For someone who just kicked ass, you sure are a sourpuss." He started to twist his neck to see who had distressed her.

"Don't look," she snapped.

"What? Who is it?"

Meg shook her head. "I've gotta get out of here before that creep recognizes me."

Hub looked her in the eye. "We're in this together. Now, level with me."

She spoke so only Hub could hear. "It's a jerk that gave me a bad time at the O-club when I first joined the WAFs. He got physical so I put him on his ass."

"If no one here suspects anything, why would he? You're Garrett Reilly for Christ sake."

Another horde of boisterous pilots charged into the room. Among them was Devine. Meg turned ever so slightly in her seat. Devine glared at her as he found his way to a seat. Right next to LaRocca.

Hub turned his head and spoke so only Meg could hear him or see his lips. "If those two are buddying up, we've got a problem, all right."

After the debriefing, Meg walked down the aisle with Hub on the heels of Hastings and Chamberlain. Hub noticed that Devine was filling LaRocca's ear.

"He reminds me of Count Dracula," Hub joked.

Meg snickered. "Now that you mention it."

"Let's go straight to chow," Hub suggested. "I don't want to get stuck eating left-over S.O.S. again."

* * * * *

A figure in a dark room with a penlight, was rifling through Meg's things. Kneeling, the intruder found a bag under the bed and rummaged through it, finding the tightly wrapped cigar box containing her prized memorabilia. Holding the pen light between his teeth, he studied the yellowed news clippings and photos of Meg, her father, and her brothers. He then spotted one of Meg and Hub at the Bendix Ball.

"Bulls-eye!"

CHAPTER 28

Meg and Hub casually scuffled down the hallway of the B.O.Q. and stopped in front of Hub's room.

Hub puffed on a cigarette. "How 'bout a nightcap?" he whispered.

"Considering the circumstances, Hub, I need some time."

He nodded. "By the way, I really admire how you've been handling all this."

"It hasn't been easy." Her face was strained and eyes sunken. "When Garrett died in front of my eyes, it was like someone reached into my chest and tore my heart out."

He wanted to pull her into a hug. "Tell me, Baby-face. Would you quit if I asked you to?"

Meg began walking toward her door. "Get some sleep."

Hub watched her until she reached her room then entered his own room, shutting the door behind him. Meg opened her door and entered the dark room. As she reached for the light switch, a hand from behind grabbed her, shutting the door with the other. The intruder tried to cup her mouth, but she countered with an elbow jab to the ribs, forcing him to double-up and stumble backward. Enraged, he tried to strike her with a blunt object, but she sensed it coming and wove her arm around his, restraining his wrist. With her other hand, she twisted his wrist, and the object dropped to the floor with a thud. Keeping a grip on his wrist, she jabbed at his face with her elbow, landing two vicious blows to the nose and throat. He stumbled backward, choking and swinging wildly with his free hand. A fist found her high cheekbone, reeling her backward onto her bunk. Dazed, she tried to shake it off and ready herself for his next move.

Suddenly, the bloodied intruder found the doorknob, opened the door, and escaped.

Badly shaken, she shut the door and locked it, bracing her shaking body against the inside of the door.

* * * * *

Meg entered the briefing room, wearing her sunglasses. She sat in the back, avoiding Hub and the others.

Hub spotted her and relocated at her side. "I didn't see you this morning."

"I'm not feeling very good."

Hub looked at her quizzically. "Why are you wearing sun glasses?"

"I've got a terrible migraine."

"I'll get you some aspirin after the briefing." Hub smiled considerately.

"Thanks. It hurts just sitting here."

Colonel Middleton entered the room and hopped on the stage. "After today's escort mission, the squadron will be returning to tactical raids until every pilot here is flying a P-51," Middleton announced. "Another transport ship just dropped anchor off England. They should be here in two or three days."

The pilots roared with approval.

"Again, Chamberlain's Blue Wings stole the show," Middleton continued. "Lieutenants Hastings and Reilly are now double-aces. Lieutenant Martin picked up three kills. He's now one shy of an ace."

Again, the pilots were boisterous with their applause.

The colonel suddenly spotted a very somber Meg. "Lieutenant Reilly, why are you wearing sunglasses in my briefing room?"

"Sh--He's got a headache, Sir," responded Hub.

Middleton missed Hub's near disastrous slip about Meg's true gender. "Did Reilly also lose his voice?" he asked in a facetious tone.

Meg sat up. "No, Sir," she barked in a husky tone.

"If you're sick, Lieutenant, report to sick call," Middle

snapped coolly, "but if you are well enough to attend my briefing then take off the shades."

"Yes, Sir!" Meg quickly took off the sunglasses, revealing the beginnings of a black eye.

The lighting was dark enough that no one noticed the shiner, including Hub. Similarly, neither Meg nor Hub could see the bruises on LaRocca's face.

After the pilots exited the briefing room, Hub double-timed it to catch Meg who was walking with a purpose. "Whew! That was a close one."

"Hub, you almost blew it."

He took a deep breath. "I know. I'm sorry. I'll go get the aspirin."

"Forget it. We don't have time."

"I'll see you upstairs." Hub's eyes followed her as she walked to Rye's Revenge.

She climbed aboard her Mustang, totally ignoring the additional four swastikas that now totaled ten. What was really bothering her? Having to look past Devine's smug look throughout the briefing. The irony of it all--LaRocca had been assigned to fly as Devine's wingman.

* * * * *

The mission deep into the heart of Germany was ordered to turn back because of bad weather over the target. Once or twice, she had spotted Snake Eyes, and off his wing, was LaRocca's Thunderbolt. Painted on the nose were a baseball cap and the words, "Brooklyn's Dodger."

After landing and shutting down their aircraft for the day, Meg and Hub circled around the other parked aircraft where Chamberlain and Hastings were surrounded by the Press Corps and the photographer that had been hounding her for the past two days. Hastings spotted Meg and Hub and pointed them out to the journalists. Three reporters moved to intercept Meg and Hub who were still wearing their flight glasses.

Meg turned to Hub. "Oh, God!" she winced. "I can't talk to those pests.....not now."

"Stick with me," he responded. "I'll get you through this. Let me do the talking."

The reporters intercepted them from the flank. One seemed less offensively aggressive. Suddenly, Meg panicked.

It was I, Aaron Masters, on assignment to interview the European Theater's aces. As far as I knew, she was Garrett Reilly, the hottest new ace. Hub had yet to recognize me from our brief meeting at the Bendix Race almost six years before.

"That's the one," the thin reporter blurted, pointing at Meg. "That's the pilot that has ten kills in four days."

I stood back, smiling. "That figures....Garrett Reilly."

Meg's face turned white. "A, er.....Hi, Mr. Masters."

With gloves on, we shook hands. I thought it odd. Garrett had never been this formal, but then he wasn't in the military when I knew him before. "Garrett, ten kills, huh?"

Meg nodded soberly. "I haven't been counting."

I looked at Hub. "I understand you got four kills in four days. How does it feel, you two, to be working as a team after all those years as competitors?"

Hub finally recognized me. "Well, I'll be. If it isn't Mr. *Aviation Life Magazine*." A hint of jealousy had crept into his eyes.

I stuck out my hand. "Hub, how are you?"

Hub shook hands. "As good as could be expected. And you?"

"Great." I looked at Garrett. "So, have you heard from Meg, lately?"

Meg was unprepared for the question. In fact, she was almost terrified. "Ah, er...no."

There was something about Garrett's voice that heightened my curiosity. "Are you okay, Garrett?"

"Affirmative," she answered. "I remember how she used to call you Brooks Brothers."

"Yeah, I kinda miss it," I confessed. "Garrett, I really love your sister."

Meg's eyes grew large, and she smiled. "I can safely say that she'll be happy to hear that."

I then realized that the other correspondents were jotting down everything we said on their notepads. I didn't want us to become part of the news. "Garrett, can we get together later today?"

"Of course," Meg said in an excited tone. Her eyes were exploding.

Hub nearly lost it with that exchange. He gave Meg a startled, yet jealous expression that only she could see.

As they moved on, one of the other correspondents addressed me. "That Reilly sure is an odd one. He's been dodging us for the past three days. Won't let his picture be taken either."

"That's his right," I growled "Don't you have even the slightest bit of compassion for what these pilots are going through? The kind of pressure they're under?"

After they had gotten out of earshot, Hub turned to Meg. "What in the hell is wrong with you? Have you gone daft?"

"No!" she snapped. "I can't deal with this right now."

Hub pulled her between two parked Thunderbolts. "What's wrong, dammit? Is it me?"

Meg pulled her arm away. "No."

"Is it Masters?"

"No, dammit!" Her eyes were sharp as daggers.

"Is it that pilot that just joined the squadron? Did he say something to you? Do something?"

Meg's expression went cold.

"That's it. Isn't it?" Hub demanded.

"It's nothing. You can't help. I've got to take care of it myself."

"What did he do to you for Christ sakes?" Hub grabbed Meg by the wrists and tried to pull her into a hug.

Meg winced loudly, and Hub quickly let go. He spotted a deep bruise on her wrist between her glove and sleeve. He then noticed the shiner. "Jesus, what the? Who did this to you?"

Without answering, she pulled away.

"I'm so sorry I ever let you do this," Hub apologized. "It's all my fault. I don't want you to do this anymore. It's too dangerous." Hub thought for a moment. His eyes narrowed like slivers. "That bastard! I'll kill him!" Suddenly, he bolted toward the B.O.Q.

Meg was frantic but managed to keep enough composure to

follow Hub.

Hub fell into a dead run. He reached the B.O.Q., opened the outside door and charged up the stairs, two steps at a time.

Meg finally caught up to him in the hallway. "Stop!"

He shook off her grasp. She lurched to grab him again as he stomped along, trying to find LaRocca's room.

"You can't do this, Hub. He knows.....and they'll--"

Hub spun around. "What do you mean, he knows?"

"Craterface knows about me, Hub, and soon they'll all know. You've got to let me handle this."

"The charade is finished.....finis!" he snapped. " I'll tell them it was all my idea. You're a civilian. They won't be able to do jack shit to you."

"Hub, they won't believe you. Besides, I have been impersonating an officer. That's a Federal offense."

Hub pulled away like a man possessed then barged into the unmarked room. He grabbed LaRocca who was trying to climb out of his bunk. Grabbing LaRocca like a wrestler, Hub picked him up and threw him across the room. His lip bleeding, LaRocca struggled to his feet then charged at Hub, growling and swinging wildly. Hub faked a left then came up hard with a right, catching LaRocca's jaw, reeling him backwards onto the bed. LaRocca sat up, shaking his head, checking his jaw with a hand. As he started to stand, Hub dove at him, pinning him on the bed, beating his face to a bloody pulp.

"How does it feel, Asshole?" Hub snarled.

LaRocca's face was crimson purple as a distraught Meg charged into the room. "No, Hub.....Jesus, you're killing him." she cried.

Hub had clamped his hands around LaRocca's throat.

Meg fought to pry Hub's hands apart. "The bastard ain't worth it!"

Finally, Hub reared back, the blood vessels in his neck throbbing, his breathing fast and intense. LaRocca coughed violently. His eyes protruded. Meg checked the hallway then shut the door.

Hub leaned into LaRocca's face. "Get this straight, you low-life bastard. If you ever touch her again, I'll kill you. If you try going to the colonel, I'll kill you! Got that?"

LaRocca didn't answer as he painfully tried to catch his breath. Hub stood and herded Meg out of the room, shutting the door as they departed.

"C'mon, let's grab some chow," Hub prompted. "I'm starved."

Meg spun him around. "You're hungry? Jesus, how can you be hungry at a time like this?"

"Fighting always makes me hungry, especially when I win."

Meg cracked a smile. "Is that a Jewish thing? Eating after a fight?"

"Seems like I remember a certain Meg Reilly crammin' down hotdogs after a good fight."

Meg briefly giggled then got serious again. "I just hope Craterface doesn't go to Wild Bill." She spotted hub's bloodied knuckles. "You need some first aid before you go anywhere. C'mon."

Hub looked at the back of both hands. "Ah, they'll be all right. A little soap and water, and they'll be as good as new."

They started walking again.

"Are you really gonna talk to Masters?" he tested.

"The colonel ordered me to," she informed him.

"Bullshit!" Hub snapped. "It's more than that. It's what he had to say about you, isn't it?"

"Maybe," Meg confessed. "I can't let him go on thinking I'm dead. He's in love with me. It's cruel. Besides, you threatened to go to Wild Bill yourself."

"I meant what I said earlier about fessin' up."

"Look, the Germans are on the run. This war can't last more than a few more weeks."

"What about Dickhead?" Hub asked. "He's LaRocca's buddy now. If he gets a hint of this, he'll certainly go to Wild Bill....We don't have the leverage on him like we do Craterface."

"Don't worry, Dickhead will hang himself, sooner or later. Besides, you heard John. His wing men have the life-expectancy of a butterfly."

Meg caught up to me while I was walking toward the Headquarters Building. She was wearing sunglasses. "Brooks Brothers! Hold up."

"Hi, Garrett. I'm glad to see you're in better spirits."

"Considering the circumstances," she paused. "C'mon, take a walk down to the flight line. I think better there."

"Okay."

"I've got somethin' to tell you, but you've got to promise to keep it to yourself."

"Normally, nothing is off the record, but considering the circumstances, I'll make an exception. By the way, I've been meaning to ask you about the name you put on the nose of your peashooter."

"Oh, that," she uttered. "Hub told my maintenance chief about dad's leg."

I nodded my approval.

We reached the quiet flight line and Meg's aircraft. Meg looked around to make sure that we were alone then faced me. Her eyes were serious. "Did you mean what you said about Meg? About loving her?" she asked in a feminine, inquisitive tone.

I know that I must have had a very confused look on my face. The question had caught me off guard. "Ah, er.....Well, of course."

"You don't seem so sure now," she stammered in a lower octave.

"What's this all about?" I asked.

Meg reached up and took off her sunglasses. "I knew that I could fool a lot of people, Aaron, but I didn't know that I could fool you." In a surprise move, she took my right hand and placed it on her chest.

Embarrassed, I jerked it away. "What the?"

"Brooks Brothers, it's me, Meg."

My mind was groping for words.

She grinned at my shocked look as she grabbed my hand again and played tug-of-war with it, trying to place it back on her breast inside her open jacket. "Dammit, Aaron Masters, it's me.....Meg.....I'm pretending to be Garrett!"

"Bu, but, why? What in the hell is going on here?" I stammered dumbly.

She leaped at me. I flinched backward, hitting the back of my head on the wing. While reacting to my wound, she managed to hug me. "Oh, I knew that you loved me, Brooks Brothers!"

Still flabbergasted, I reared backwards, hitting my head again. "Ouch!"

Finally, the slightest of smiles crossed her lips. "You meant it, didn't you?"

"Well, er, a.....Of course. I guess I always have."

Again, she leaped at me, trying to pull me through her.

I looked around for spying eyes. "Meg, how in the hell did you pull this off?"

"Aaron, you must promise to keep this confidential."

I looked at her. "What confidential?"

"Me and Nancy and Liz were in England conducting transition training on Dad's Mustang when the general ordered us to ferry much-needed Mustangs to France. Everything went well for several days. We ran into Garrett and Hub who had ironically arrived from other places. The Gerries attacked this field." Meg began to sniffle. "Major Hamilton ordered me and Liz into the air. During take-off, the krauts shot down Garrett and Liz. So I took his place. I had already cut my hair....see?" She reached up and primped what little hair was left on her head.

I shook my head with disbelief. I had just walked into the biggest story of my career and couldn't report it.

"I lowered my voice," Meg demonstrated. "Who could better pull this off than a tomboy, especially a twin? We were the same height. Same face, same eyes, same nose, same athletic abilities."

I stood there stunned, trying to manipulate my arms like a town-square statue. I finally managed to utter her name. "Meg?"

"Affirmative!" She pulled herself on her toes and generously kissed me.

I think my lips were moving. We embraced for what seemed forever. Finally able to take a breath, I asked, "Okay, kindly fill me in on the rest."

She stepped back. "It's a long stor--"

Footsteps from out of nowhere stopped her short. We both spun around, hearts racing.

CHAPTER 29

"What's this Meg stuff?" It was the slender journalist who had been dogging her.

Meg quickly put on her sunglasses and started walking away. "I'll catch you later, Mr. Masters."

"Right....thank you, Garrett." I faced the journalist. "What is it? What do you want?"

He teetered his head. "That's the second time that pilot has dodged me. Lieutenant Devine claims that Reilly and Martin are fags."

I studied the correspondent for a brief moment. "Who do you work for? What rag?"

"Why!" he asked defensively.

"Your incessant babble is insulting my intelligence."

"It's a hot lead. That lieutenant is the hottest ace in recent memory. What are you here for?"

I found myself grabbing him, pinning him against the fuselage of Meg's pursuit. "These young men are risking their lives up there," I snarled through gritted teeth. "I want my readers back home to realize that. No rubbish, no gray journalism, got it?"

The slender journalist, arms stiff down his sides and palms against the fuselage, stood in shock from the attack. "I....I got it," he stuttered. His eyes were bulging.

"If I hear that you've repeated this ridiculous tale to anyone, anyone at all, I'll crucify you. Real journalism is based on fact, not fiction, and when we suspect something, we always confirm through a second source. And we give the accused the opportunity to defend himself. I have reported on the Reillys for almost ten years, and in that time, I have gotten to know them pretty well. I can assure you that not one of them is homosexual! So get your damn facts straight before you start spoutin' off!" I pivoted about and marched off. As I rounded the last pursuit on the flight line, I glanced back--the reporter was still braced against the fuselage. Thinking back, what a macho feeling. Until that moment, I had always been a bit passive when it came to confrontations, but when that jerk said something bad about Meg, well, I guess it brought out the John Wayne in me. Had he said one more negative thing, I would have punched him.

I caught up to Meg as she entered the B.O.Q. "Would you like to join me for a drink?" I asked.

"Sure, Aaron. Where?"

"Your place or mine?" I joked.

"Where's your place?" she asked all misty-eyed.

"Here," I nodded. "The colonel said I could use the VIP room while I'm here. C'mon."

Her eyes were full-bodied as we walked down the hallway to the room at the end. I opened the door for her then entered, closing it behind me. We hugged and kissed. It was a powerful moment. It seemed like a lifetime before we stepped back.

I was the first to speak. "I have something to confide in you as well. You cannot tell anyone, absolutely no one."

Meg stopped me from saying anything by putting a finger over my lips. She then walked over to the door, checked the hallway, and closed the door. "Keep it down." She then walked over to the radio setting on a tall, slender dresser and tuned it to the Armed Forces station, giving it time to warm up before adjusting the volume. Soon, "Bugle Boy" filled the room.

I leaned close. "I've got a confession to make, too. I've been leading two lives."

She looked at me oddly. "What in the hell is that supposed to mean?"

I whispered in her ear, "I'm an agent for the Office of Strategic Services."

Her head arced like an ostrich. "What?"

"Shhhh!" I turned to look at the light coming from under the door. The coast appeared to be clear so I refocused on Meg.

Her eyes were staring. "So what is it you do? I thought you told me that you were denied military service because of your health."

"That part is true. Even General Patton tried to pull some strings. As far as he knows, I was rejected a second time."

Meg was open-mouthed. "Wow! I don't know about you, but I could use that drink 'bout now."

I reached for the bottle of Jack Daniel's setting on the nightstand and poured some into a glass. I handed it to her, and she took a couple of sips then handed it back to me. "I didn't know that you like Jack Black."

"I developed a taste for it, thanks to you." I swished the glass then smelled it before taking a sip. "Whew!"

Meg briefly snickered as she sat on the edge of the bed. "Go on, tell me."

"As I was saying, that's why I couldn't tell anyone. It could blow my cover."

"But why, Aaron?"

"Because I felt like I was just a bystander. I wanted to get more involved.....I was concerned about your opinion of me."

Her eyes turned from shocked to dreamy. She then leaned toward me and gave me a soft, long kiss, caressing my forearm with a hand. "I've always been in love with you, Brooks Brothers, and only you. Got it?"

"Blue Skies" began playing on the radio.

"I love you, Meg."

Suddenly, Meg stood and grabbed me. "C'mon. Let's dance," she giggled.

We fell into each other's arms and began to move slowly.

I reared my head backward so I could see her face. "Do you know what Confucius said about dancing?"

"No, what did Confucius say about dancing?"

"It's a vertical expression for a horizontal desire."

She laughed then kissed me passionately, devouring my face.

Before I realized it, we were lying on the bed, incredibly overwhelmed by our emotions.

Meanwhile, a dark figure carrying two metal ammo boxes, crept along the dark shadows of the flight line, looking back frequently to see if anyone was watching. He stopped at Rye's Revenge, checked the area one last time to assure his privacy then silently climbed aboard the far-side wing. He opened the panel to the wing guns and began removing some of the ammunition. He then repeated the process on the other wing then looked to see that the coast was clear before evading the same way in which he had arrived.

* * * * *

Hub intercepted Meg just outside her room. She was wearing her flight jacket.

He looked at his wristwatch. "It's almost midnight. Where in the hell have you been?" he whispered loudly.

Meg took a deep breath as she pushed by to enter her room. Hub stepped in behind her and shut the door. "Well?"

She took off her leather jacket and tossed it on the bed. "I don't care much for your tone."

Hub grabbed Meg by the arm and tried to kiss her.

She pulled away. "After what happened yesterday, Hub, I'm not exactly in the mood, understand," she said politely but firmly.

"You've been with him, haven't you?"

"If you mean Aaron Masters, yes. I had to tell him."

"What?" Hub snapped. "You told a reporter? Are you out of your friggin' mind?"

"Look, he's been a friend of the family for a long time. He promised that he would keep it between us."

Exasperated, Hub ran a hand through his hair as he groped for his next words. "Is there somethin' going on between you two?"

"We had a lot to catch up on," Meg said nonchalantly.

"I just bet you did," Hub snarled jealously.

Meg was trying to remain calm. "Look, we better get some sleep. We've got a long day tomorrow."

"You're not really serious about flying tomorrow, are you?"

She lowered her chin and took another deep breath. "Look, I've got a job to do."

"Your job's over!" Hub countered. "I don't want anything to happen to you."

"Thanks, Hub, but it's not your call. I know that you mean

well, but I must continue on in my own way. Besides, you didn't let me do anything. I blackmailed you."

"Goddammit, Meg. You and that stubborn Irish blood of yours."

Meg took a deep breath and let it out slowly. "Look, Hub, I started out to do something as Lieutenant Garrett Reilly, and I'm gonna finish it, one way or another."

"Damn! Everything was going great till that goddam Masters and that asshole LaRocca showed up." Hub turned to leave. "Go ahead and get yourself killed. But we both know that you're doing this for nobody else but yourself. Because deep down inside, that's all you've ever cared about.....tryin' to act like a man."

Meg got upset. "That's bullshit, Hub, and you know it! Now, if you don't mind, I need to get some sleep!"

As Hub opened the door, he could hear quick scuffling along the dim hallway then a door shutting quietly. He turned to Meg. "Shit! I think someone was listening outside the door."

* * * * *

Middleton was standing on the wooden platform with a pointer in his hand. "Gentlemen, I was on the horn all night with Highers. We're back to our original mission, at least for the time being. The ground crewmen have been working hard since 0500 hours to install bombs for today's tactical strikes."

The pilots glanced at one another. Some seemed puzzled; other relieved.

Middleton walked over to the wall map, and using the wooden pointer, he outlined the general target area. "As you already know, the Germans have been slowly retreating from the Bulge since the first of the year. The area east of St. Vith is one of the main routes for funneling reinforcements and supplies. It's our job to plug it up. It's a target-rich environment, gentlemen, including tanks, mechanized vehicles, and Luftwaffe airstrips. Major Hamilton will brief you on your squadron assignments. Good flying, and see you at dinner."

The pilots stood and snapped to attention as Middleton passed the wooden pointer to Hamilton on his way out.

Hamilton shouted, "As you were, gentlemen," as he stepped up to the map. Today, you'll be carrying two 500-lb. bombs. We'll be hitting targets here . . . here . . . and here," he announced, pointing at each target. "After the weather and INTEL briefing, your squadron commanders will brief you on your individual assignments."

After Hamilton finished, each of the pilots gathered around their respective squadron commander. Although Meg avoided looking at Devine or LaRocca, Hub glared at them.

The squadron commander, a mild-mannered man in his mid-twenties laid out a map sheet with military symbols and flight routes in grease pencil. "Bob, your Blue Flight and Mike's Green Flight will attack the German airfield located right here while Red Flight will hit the bridge there, and Yellow Flight will strike the ammunition depot located at the northeast corner of this road junction. Afterwards, pick targets of opportunity. Pending the fog, we take off at 0715 hours. As usual, we'll be under strict radio silence until we reach the target. Any questions, gentlemen?"

Hastings and Chamberlain were conducting preflight inspections on their aircraft when Hub and Meg arrived in a jeep, skidding to a halt. Meg hopped off the back and proceeded immediately to her plane where her crew chief was waiting to assist her.

Hub took a detour to LaRocca's P-47 farther down the flightline. "Better watch your backside out there today, LaRocca. I'm not through with you, asshole."

Devine stopped his preflight and quickly joined them.

Hub turned to Devine, growling. "That goes for you, too, Dickhead."

"I can't hear you, Jewboy." Devine sneered.

Hub flashed them the bird over his shoulder.

Soon, all 16 planes in the squadron were roaring. A somber Hub looked over at Meg.

She finally cracked a smile and returned the gesture.

A noise awoke me. I blinked my eyes several times, trying to focus on the alarm clock setting on the nightstand. It was 7:15 a.m.

I set it back down then reached for the bottle of Jack Daniel's and gargled a swallow. I then realized what time it was--Meg had left sometime during the night. Above the swing music on the radio, I could hear a tremendous roar of high-performance engines.

"Damn!" I swung my legs out of the bed, got dressed, and charged out of the B.O.Q., my shirttail flying.

I could see two Mustangs taking off with two more revving their engines on the ramp. I watched them take off, followed by the rest of the squadron. Soon, they disappeared in the horizon.

Shivering from the cold air, I returned to my room where I found a note sitting on the dresser next to the radio.

> *Dearest Aaron,*
>
> *I'm sorry I left this morning without saying a word. You were sleeping so peacefully, I didn't want to disturb you. I hope you understand. I'll catch you when we return, probably early afternoon. We can pick up where we left off.*
>
> *Love,*
>
> *Meg*

My heart filled with emotion as I read and reread the crumpled note. I've never been much on prayer, but that day, I talked to God. More than once.

* * * * *

In a finger-four formation, three squadrons of red-nosed fighters filled the sky above the landscape, flying nap-of-the-earth to avoid German radar detection. While Meg and the other pilots kept a circular watch for enemy fighters, the squadron commander looked for the last reference point where they would change course toward the general target area. Visibility had been less than a mile to this point, but the low-hanging fog was beginning to lift. Above them was a partly cloudy sky.

Five minutes from the target, Blue Flight and Green Flight peeled off to hit the airfield. Meg looked to her right rear where she spotted Devine and LaRocca's green-winged Jugs.

Chamberlain's voice broke the silence. "Blue Flight, this is Blue Leader. Let's give 'em a signature hit to remember us by."

Meg sensed the adrenaline rush. Her heart pounded with excitement as they peeled off and dipped their noses to make a west-to-east pass. It was their job to hit the field first, and as they rolled out to circle around, the Green Flight would make a pass. Until then, it was Green Flight's mission to keep airborne German planes off their backside. The runway itself was north-south oriented. Most of the buildings, tents, and the control tower were located at the southeastern side, and the parked aircraft at the southern edge.

Below, an air-raid siren began its obnoxious whine. Black puffs of smoke appeared as the antiaircraft guns began to blast away at the attacking Americans. Ground crewmen and scrambling pilots rushed toward the parked aircraft. Meg bombed a gun position near the treeline on the west side, blowing it up while Hub concentrated on another located at the northwest side. Chamberlain and Hastings zeroed in on two FWs trying to taxi to the runway. One disintegrated with a bomb. The other narrowly escaped to take off. All four Mustangs pulled up and began to circle around while the Green Flight made its pass, bombing gun emplacements at the southern end of the field and two heavily camouflaged FWs parked near the trees on the western side. Devine peeled off and went after the FW trying to take off, his rounds criss-crossing, kicking up the turf just short of and behind the moving target. Suddenly, two more FWs broke out of their concealment and made a dash for the runway just as Green Flight pulled up and began circling.

Meg adjusted her control stick, trying to fit the lead FW in her sight ring. Her finger squeezed the gun button. Streams of smoke trailed back over her wings, as her guns spit tracers at the fuselage of the FW. The enemy bird slid around like a top, skidded off the runway, and burst into flames. Meg flew overhead as it exploded; the debris narrowly missed her tail.

The terrain in her peripheral was zooming past. She checked her airspeed. It read 405. "Wow! What a rush," she murmured to herself.

"Nice shot, Blue-two," Chamberlain complimented.

Hub spotted a gasoline truck trying to run for cover at the southern end of the field. He opened fire, walking his rounds into the truck. Suddenly, it exploded, spewing ignited aviation fuel into the air. Hub kicked rudder and swung his control stick right to avoid a billowing cloud of black, fiery smoke.

"Whewwwweh!" Hub shrieked, pulling up. He swiveled his head to check for airborne bogeys.

Meg looked left. Kraut Kruncher and Hell's Kiss were zeroing on the parked fighters and transports at the southern end of the airfield.

"Bombs away!" whooped Chamberlain.

Two more FWs burst with flames. A ground crewmen began fleeing, his clothing on fire.

Meg spotted the now-moving transports. "Blue-three, Blue-two. Follow me. We've got two Juliet-Uniforms trying to make a dash for it."

Meg and Hub banked left and screamed toward the transports through heavy antiaircraft fire, blazing away with their wing guns. Meg finished them off with her remaining bomb.

"Blue Leader, Blue-two. We've got incoming yak-yak from the southwest end. How 'bout some help, over?"

"Roger, got it!" Chamberlain responded.

Meg's armor-piercing shells walked into the cockpit of the one on the left, shattering its windshield and killing its pilot. The JU-52 veered into the wing of the other transport and exploded. Jagged, twisted, screeching sections of flaming steel flung skyward. Meg and Hub both pulled back hard on their control sticks.

Hub broke squelch, "Jesus, Blue-two, how 'bout giving me a chance to nail one."

"Blue-three, this is Blue-two. What's the difference between a wingman and a puppy?"

"Don't start on me," Hub droned.

"A puppy stops whining when it grows up."

"Ha, ha," Hub snarled. "Real funny."

Meanwhile, Hastings silenced the gun position, stopping the

flow of incoming while Chamberlain took out the radar.

"Look alive, Blue-three," Meg sounded. "Two bogeys just lifted off. Looks like your big chance, Hotshot."

One of the FWs nosed up and climbed before banking right. Hub exchanged places with Meg and moved parallel to the rocketing FW. Hub turned sharply to pull behind the FW which immediately banked left. Accelerating, Hub closed on his prey. The dark outline of the low-winged FW got larger as he shoved his throttle full-open, rocketing to get within range. Hub's wing guns spurted just as the FW broke right, missing. "Damn!" he swore, again kicking rudder.

The FW stayed low, trying to outrun Hub who mirrored every twist, turn, and roll. All of a sudden, the FW was dominating his sight ring. "I love it when they stick the sausage in the bun like this." His wing guns flashed, again missing the German pilot who broke left.

"Son of a bitch!" Hub cursed. "This kraut's pretty good."

Meg shouted encouragement, "Hang in there, Blue-three. You're doing great!"

Sensing the closing danger behind him, the enemy pilot reached for the throttle and pushed. It was already fully engaged. He rubbernecked backward. Meg sensed he was about to chop his throttle.

"Fire now, Blue-three!" Meg blurted. "Trust me."

The FW writhed with each burst from Hub's wing guns. The tracers danced into the FW and pranced along its fuselage, spreading into the left wing. Pieces of the wing, fuselage, and engine cowling scattered in all directions, followed by flashes of white fire and smoke. In seconds, the nose of the FW pointed downward and crashed, bouncing like a football until it exploded. Hub roared through the tornado of smoke and pulled up.

"Are you happy now, Blue-three?" Meg joked.

"Happy as a goose in a feed bin."

"Good!" Meg zoomed past Hub to take the lead. "Follow me."

Looking around, she spotted Hastings and Chamberlain bombing the wooden sheds and outbuildings at the end of the field.

Two secondary explosions forced both of her comrades to break sharply in opposite directions to avoid the hurling debris.

Just as Blue Flight began to circle around to the left, giving way for Green Flight to make its pass, a squadron of FW-109s appeared out of the southwest.

CHAPTER 30

"Bogeys at 11 o'clock high and comin' in fast," Chamberlain warned.

"I had a hunch there were more kraut dogs coming to this here barbecue," quipped Hastings.

"Very intuitive, Blue-one," cracked Chamberlain. "Now, everybody, straighten up and fly right."

First Chamberlain and Hastings, then Meg and Hub peeled off and accelerated toward the diving Germans who were firing their 30-mm cannon. Meg could hear the plunking sound of several rounds striking her starboard wing. She instantly inspected the damage. There were several softball-size holes, but no fuel seemed to be escaping. It was then that she saw Green Flight to her right, firing. Now, the odds were only two-to-one in favor of the Germans.

An FW suddenly appeared in Chamberlain's sight ring. He immediately pressed the gun button. One of the rounds crashed through the canopy, killing the pilot. The FW went into an uncontrolled spin and careened into a treeline where both wings were sheared away before smashing against the bank of a half-frozen creek. Flaming debris belched into the air.

The Americans effectively split the German formation.

"Blue Flight, break left, break left!" Chamberlain bellowed anxiously.

Meg spotted a German ace with dozens of American and British flags painted on his fuselage. He had climbed onto Hastings' tail as though the American double-ace was a novice.

"Blue-one, bogey at your 6 o'clock. Break! Break!" Meg yelled.

Before Hastings could react, dozens of shells tore into his

fuselage. In seconds, smoke and flames erupted. Meg could see her comrade's hand trying to open the bloodied canopy. Suddenly, his hand went limp, sliding down the glass, leaving behind a red smear.

"Johnny, get out!" Chamberlain bellowed. "Get out, Johnny!"

Hastings muddled voice began to sing, "Blue skies smilin'. . . . at me, noth . . . nothing but blue skies, do I . . ." Hell's Kiss rolled over on its back and plunged like a wounded falcon into a cluster of trees, exploding on contact.

Chamberlain's stunned eyes flooded his cheeks. "Noooooo!" he cried out then slumped in his seat.

"You kraut bastards!" Hub wailed.

"Watch the language over the romeo," warned Devine. His tone was irritating.

Hub squeezed the button activating his throat mike. "Get bent, Dickhead!"

"You're time's coming," Devine countered. "You better hope that the krauts don't get their hands on you.....Jewboy!"

Chamberlain regrouped. "This is Blue Leader. Knock it off and pay attention, you two. This ain't the time or place."

Hub spotted the German ace and began circling around. Meg followed off his left wing. Suddenly, LaRocca raced in from the flank, firing his guns, causing Hub to miss the FW that suddenly broke right and went into a tight turn. Hub and LaRocca jockeyed for position to take a shot, passing over the southwestern side of the airfield at treetop level. Meg broke in the opposite direction and climbed to get altitude. LaRocca moved up even with Hub, forcing him to stay in the tight turn until his Mustang began to stall. At the last second, LaRocca kicked rudder and jammed his control stick to the left. The German ace spotted Meg coming at him, and unknowingly broke in front of Hub who was firing his guns. The tracers peppered the FW's nose and fuselage. Dark-gray smoke filled its canopy.

Suddenly, Meg spotted Hub heading for a high-tension wire. "Blue-three! Watch out for the wires. Pull up!"

As Hub snapped his head back to the front, his eyes exploded at what he saw. He instinctively jerked back on his control stick. The wire sliced off part of his rear stabilizer. Sparks showered like

Queen of Aces

giant fireworks as his Mustang began to flutter. He fought with the rudder as smoke poured from the engine cowling.

"God, no!" Meg screamed. "You're hit! Get out!"

Hub resumed stalking the German ace, again firing his guns at the FW, ripping open its fuselage like a can of Spam.

Hub struggled with his canopy, fighting to control his pursuit as he limped side-by-side with the smoking FW, both barely clearing a distant hill. Suddenly, there was a huge flash of light and a mushrooming explosion towering high into the air.

"Nooooo!" Meg screamed. She executed a visual-360 then banked toward the crash area. Tears streamed down her face. "Oh God, Hub." She glared at LaRocca who was laughing. "You did that deliberately, you ugly bastard."

"Blue-two, snap out of it and get back here now," Chamberlain commanded. "He's gone, and I've got bogeys swarmin' all over me."

Suddenly, two FWs came out of nowhere, blazing away with their 30-mm cannon, forcing Meg to break and turn.

"Blue-two, I said to get your butt over here. There's nothing we can do for Blue-three now."

"This is Blue-two, WILCO."

Crying, she went into a tight turn and dove at the enemy planes cluttering the sky about Chamberlain's Mustang. She could hear someone laughing heinously over the radio. "Devine?" she murmured. "Bastard!.....I swear I'll get you." In her peripheral, she spotted Snake Eyes and Brooklyn's Dodger holding back, as though they were waiting for something to happen.

"Break, Blue Leader. Break!" Meg snapped. Her voice was suddenly filled with new focus and determination.

She zeroed in on the lead FW that had Chamberlain in the middle of his sight. She fired two short bursts. The FW convulsed as the tracers ripped apart its tail and rear fuselage. The German pilot lost control and plunged, squashing into the ground like an accordion.

Chamberlain cheered, "Blue-two, great shootin'."

Through her tears, Meg screamed, "That's for Hub Martin, an American ace."

Meg veered to the left and quickly lined up another bogey in her sight ring and pressed the gun button. Only her left wing guns fired, but the shells managed to punctuate the FW's cowling. "What the?" She squeezed the gun button again. Again, there were only flashes from the left wing. "Impossible, I can't be out of ammo." Looking around, she spotted LaRocca's irritating smirk.

Refocusing on the wounded FW, she noticed dark fluid flowing from the engine backward along the fuselage. The FW lost speed and winged down, slamming into one of the outbuildings. Flaming chunks of metal and lumber swirled about like a Texas twister.

Chamberlain whooped with relief. "Cover my butt." He kicked rudder and jammed his stick hard to the right, trying to maneuver behind the third FW.

Meg then focused on the remaining bogey that was clinging to Chamberlain's tail. The German pilot spotted her angling from the side. He immediately banked left where Meg was waiting for him. "Tactics 101, Dumbo!" she cracked as she pressed her gun button.

Bright flashes emitted from her left wing guns. The 50-caliber tracers turned the FW into a colander. The German fighter began smoking as the pilot directed it into a tight turn. Suddenly, it flipped over and skidded into a nearby field, bounced several times, and slammed into a windbreak, igniting a flash fire. Several secondary explosions consumed the entire northeast side of the field.

"Blue-two, back me up," Chamberlain ordered. He banked right, accelerated, and zoomed upwards to get position on the other FW.

Just as Meg banked, several tracers zoomed past her canopy from behind. Snapping her head around, she caught a glimpse of a fighter some distance behind her coming on fast. She kicked rudder and shoved the control stick left only to be blocked by another fighter. It was Brooklyn's Dodger.

LaRocca made eye contact with Meg and grinned at her.

"What in the hell do you think you're doing, Craterface?"

"I told you that I'd get even," he growled. His face was crazed.

"Like hell," Meg barked. She flashed the bird at him.

Rage filled LaRocca's eyes. "You're dead, bitch!"

"We'll see about that, Craterface." Meg pulled a hard right and looked back.

Snake Eyes pulled right in an attempt to cut off her turn.

Knowing the P-47s would be sluggish, Meg instantly pulled back on the stick and went into a steep climb to put some distance between her and her American enemies. "Blue Leader, this is Blue-two. I've got two of our own trying to sandwich me like an Oreo."

Chamberlain twisted in his seat to see what Meg was talking about. "Jesus! What the hell?" He crammed his stick left and kicked rudder to bring his Mustang around. "Devine! I order you to stop.....now!"

Suddenly, two Me-109s appeared at the north end of the field at treetop level, firing their 30-mm cannon at Chamberlain. They cut short his attempt to assist Meg.

Meg peeled off and circled around. Soon, Devine and LaRocca were hot on her tail. Manipulating her rudder, Meg banked back and forth, making it hard for LaRocca to get a clean shot at her. She spotted a huge hangar still intact near the southwest end of the airfield. Both the massive front and rear doors were open.

She snickered to herself. "Okay, boys, let's see how good you are at threadin' the needle."

Now farther back and turning wider, Devine had a 45-degree shot at Rye's Revenge. Just as he fired, Meg went into a tighter turn. His rounds sailed harmlessly into the sky behind her.

LaRocca radioed Devine. "More lead, more lead!" he cracked.

"I can see that, dammit!" Devine snarled.

Meg baited them more with a series of spectacular loops and turns, causing them to miss with each volley. She laughed as they argued with each other, slowly luring them toward the hangar. She began singing intensely, "K-K-K-Katy, beautiful Ka-ty, you're the only g-g-g-girl that I adore...."

Suddenly, she could hear her father's voice. "Make your father proud. Easy now.....easy.....does it."

Meg executed a blind right turn around a tall tree then a quarter roll, narrowly splitting the doorway, one wing up, one down. She streaked through the hangar, forcing two wide-eyed, astonished mechanics in greasy overalls to dive into the corner.

"That's it.....as easy as threading a needle," she hummed.

LaRocca rounded the tree and gasped. Left without an outlet, he executed a quarter roll and followed her into the long hangar. Devine spotted the impending danger and pulled back hard on his stick, just narrowly missing the peak with the belly of his Jug. Flying over the hangar, he placed a finger over the gun button and prepared to fire at Meg when she emerged.

As Meg blasted from the hangar, she pulled back hard on the stick and spiraled upward and to the right like a soaring eagle. Upon exiting the hangar, LaRocca leveled his Jug and pulled back hard on his stick, directing his fighter into a vertical climb. Devine's face filled with horror as his propeller collided with LaRocca's tail section. Both fighters spun around, slammed into the ground, bounced several times, flipped over and over, and finally broke apart. Both burst into flames before exploding.

Meg banked to catch a glimpse of the results of her barnstorming maneuver. "I'm surprised he made it through the hangar."

The German mechanics quickly stood, looked both ways for more aircraft then frantically dashed from the rear door of the hangar like scared roosters. Pointing, they gawked at the burning Thunderbolts.

The younger, burly mechanic shielded his eyes from the sun. "Das cookoo Amerikans," he stammered dumbfoundedly.

"Ja," agreed his aging, gray-haired buddy who scratched his head.

Whipping her head in the other direction, Meg searched the immediate sky for Kraut Kruncher. Blue Leader was in the fight of his life. Both Me-109s were jockeying for a clear shot, but Chamberlain's almost instant mastery of the Mustang was keeping him one step ahead of the undertaker.

"Blue Leader, Blue-two. Hang on. I'm on my way."

"Where's Green-two and Green-three?"

"They bought the farm," she quipped. "I'm outta bullets and damn near out of petrol."

"Let's blow this pop stand," Chamberlain whooped. "Follow

me." He pulled back on his stick and rocketed upward, trying to lose his German pursuers. "Where's a cloud when you need one."

Both Me-109s mirrored his move. Meg took a deep breath and pointed the red nose of her Mustang upward. "You've still got company, Blue Leader. If I can get behind them, maybe they'll break long enough for us to get above 20,000 feet where we'll have the advantage."

Before Meg could get position behind the trailing Messerschmitt, the lead Me-109 opened fire on Chamberlain. A half-dozen rounds slammed into his fuselage just under the canopy. His Mustang slowed and began to weave, almost out of control.

"Blue Leader, are you okay?"

Chamberlain was slumped in his seat. Blood gushed from the left side of his chest with each breath. Splotches of red hindered his vision. He blinked repeatedly.

Meg accelerated and got on the tail of the trailing Messerschmitt. The young German pilot spotted her in his mirror and broke left and began circling.

Blue Leader, are you still with me?"

"I took one in the chest," he said, breathing asthmatically. "It burns," he coughed.

"Blue Leader, stick a finger in the wound."

"Finger, hell!" He coughed again. "I've got my whole damn hand in there!" The pain registered on his face with another cough. "It feels like a friggin' branding iron..... God, it burns."

"Reach into your first-aid kit, tear the cellophane wrapper off the bandage with your teeth, and place the wrapper over the wound then the bandage. You'll have to hold it on and apply pressure. That should stop the wound from sucking air and help you breathe."

He stuttered, "I don't know if--"

"Just do it!" she blurted. "No matter what happens, head for home. I'll try to keep the krauts off your tail."

Chamberlain hovered over his control stick, coughing and gurgling. "I'm not doin' so well. I think I--" Tears streamed down his face.

"Listen, Blue Leader. I don't want to hear that crap. You're gonna make it. Let's go home. Just put the pedal to the metal. Don't slow down. Don't look back."

Chamberlain struggled to apply full-throttle. He succeeded but with great pain and anguish.

"Blue Leader, you've still got one on your tail. I want you to break left so I can get his attention. If he sees me comin' at him from an angle, maybe he'll break off."

Chamberlain winced as he struggled with the stick and rudder.

"That's good, Blue Leader. Hang on."

Her plan worked. The German pilot spotted her in his peripheral and nosed down into a steep dive.

Meg shoved her stick forward and pursued the Messerschmitt. The Me-109 that had circled around, pointed its nose downward and attempted to position Meg in his sight.

"That's it," Meg said to herself. "Follow me, sucker."

She manipulated her stick and rudder to stay in a perfect line, making it impossible for the trailing Me-109 to fire without shooting down his own comrade as well.

Still diving, Meg continued to close in on the Me-109 to her front. Dangerously low in altitude, the ground was expanding fast. She was near unconsciousness from the G-force, her face stretched over her cheekbones like a monster in a horror movie.

At the last second, the lead German pilot pulled back hard on his stick to pull out of the dive. Meg quickly pulled back as well, blocking his move. He panicked and broke right, colliding with a line of tall trees.

"One down, one to go," Meg murmured to herself, twisting her neck to get a bearing on the other Messerschmitt. "Perfect!"

He was hot on her tail. With cool eyes, she crammed her stick left and kicked rudder. Rye's Revenge began weaving as she bought time to find the right situation. Dead ahead, she spotted the high-tension wire.

"That's it, Adolph." She continued singing, "When the m-m-m-moon shines o-ver the cow-shed, I'll be wait-ing at the k-k-k-kitchen door . . ." Meg accelerated toward the wire. At the last second, she pulled up hard. ". . . K-K-K-door."

The German pilot's eyes exploded when he spotted the wire. He screamed as his Messerschmitt struck the wire and spun out of control, crashed into the ground, and exploded in all directions.

She howled, "That was for Blue One."

Meg spiraled upward and accelerated to catch Chamberlain, praying that he was still airborne. Searching the sky ahead, she finally spotted a tiny silver dot several miles ahead. She opened her throttle, and after what seemed like an eternity, she pulled up alongside. His head was slumped against the canopy.

"Nap's over, Blue Leader. How ya doin'?"

"Not well," he coughed deeply, spitting up blood.

"Hang on, Blue Leader. We're almost home. Stay with me."

In ten minutes, the airfield was in sight. They began their descent, adjusting their course to make a final approach. So far, so good.

"Blue Leader, you're coming in a little fast. Back off the throttle a bit. It's a day at the beach. . . . As easy as threading a needle. Got that?"

He coughed. "I can't see very well. . . . It's all so cloudy."

"Don't go to sleep on me, Blue Leader. . . . You hear me?"

"Roger, Blue-two," he uttered faintly.

"I'm gonna be sending you cards at Christmas. . . . Drinking your ass under the table on New Years. You're gonna have tons of grandkids. Just keep those eyes of yours open!"

Chamberlain blinked several times and lifted his chin a bit.

"That's good. You're doin' good, Blue Leader. Now, lower your landing gear."

She could see Chamberlain, slumped over, reaching for the lever. Soon, his wheels were down.

Meg contacted the tower. "This is Blue-two. Blue Leader is badly wounded, and we're runnin' on fumes. Clear the runway. We'll be comin' in hot!"

On the airfield below, she could see the rescue teams and fire trucks scrambling.

Meg radioed Chamberlain. "Your wheels are down. Now, lower your flaps and move the stick to the starboard a bit.....That's good. You're comin' in fine. Keep the nose up.....That's it. That's it. . . . Easy does it."

Their wheels touched the runway, screeching on contact.

"Throttle back!" Meg shouted. "Throttle back!"

Kraut Kruncher began to veer into Rye's Revenge then straightened out. The ambulance and ground crewmen flocked toward the two Mustangs, sirens screeching, as they came to a halt.

As Meg opened her canopy, Corporal Ray was on the portside wing, assisting her out of the cockpit. She looked over at Chamberlain. Two medics were carefully lifting his bloodied body from the cockpit. Fighting tears, she jumped down and ran toward his pursuit.

"Is he gonna make it?" she shouted.

One of the crewmen looked at her as she reached the wing. "He's lost a lot of blood, Lieutenant."

Meg looked at Chamberlain as they placed his limp body on a stretcher, applying immediate first aid. As they loaded him into the waiting ambulance, several reporters flocked around her, blurting questions. She spotted me behind the others, smiling with relief.

Meg took a deep, long-awaited breath and pushed her way through the other reporters toward me just as Colonel Middleton arrived in a jeep. He hopped out before it came to a complete stop. He intercepted her before she could join me.

Wild Bill patted her heartily on the back. "That was one hell of a job, Reilly."

Meg kept staring at me as she nodded a somber thank you.

"How many krauts did you nail, Lieutenant?"

"Seven or eight," she responded, fighting the urge to cry. "I lost count. Hastings got two or three, and Hub snuffed out two before going down."

Middleton's shoulders drooped. His long face was military sober. "I'm sorry. They were good pilots."

Meg nodded. "The best."

"You better get on over to Debriefing, Lieutenant, then I want to see you at my office."

I signaled her that I would catch up to her later.

CHAPTER 31

Middleton was standing at his window, looking at the airfield when Meg, still fueled with adrenaline, arrived at his office.

He motioned at a half-empty bottle of Jack Daniel's setting on his desk as he sat. "Have a seat, Lieutenant.....Whiskey?"

"Yes, Sir!" she answered quickly.

Middleton opened a drawer, took out two short glasses, and poured two fingers in each. "What happened out there today?" He reached out with her drink.

Meg learned forward and took the glass, taking a welcomed sip, savoring it for a moment. "First, the Gerries got Hastings then.....Hub. I can't understand it."

"What's that, Lieutenant?"

"My right wing guns--they stopped working half-way through the fighting. Then my left guns stopped."

"Maybe you were pressing down on your gun button more than you realized." Middleton took a sip and leaned back. "I'm sorry about your wing man. He was one hell of a good pilot. I know you two were very close."

"Yes, Sir," she said sadly.

"Doc says Chamberlain's gonna make it," Middleton rejoiced. "If it hadn't been for that cellophane wrapper over that sucking chest wound, he wouldn't have made it. That was some quick thinking, Reilly. By the way, you haven't mentioned what happened to Devine or LaRocca. In fact, no one brought them up at Debriefing."

Meg squirmed in her seat. "We blasted 20, maybe 25 krauts out of the sky today. Things were really goin' our way. . . . Then LaRocca and Devine collided."

"Bob told me how you performed out there today, Reilly. It

was an unbelievable feat . . . that only Rye Reilly's kid could have pulled off.....out of ammo . . . low on fuel." Middleton leaned forward. "Bob recommended you for the Medal of Honor, and I plan to endorse it."

Meg was moved, nearly in tears, but instantly alarmed. With the Nation's highest award for heroism went a lot of press attention, bond drives, parades, and a likely visit to the White House.

Middleton noted her concern. "Your father was a recipient," he said, mattter-of-factly. "It must run in the genes."

For a moment, all Meg could do was nod. Clearing her throat, she finally responded. "Sir, I appreciate it, believe me, but all I did out there today was do my job. . . and try to stay alive."

"Bullshit!" Middleton countered. "If you were only trying to stay alive, you would have returned to base when you ran out of ammo. No, Reilly, what you did out there was far beyond the call of duty." He lifted his glass as a salute to her courage. "I'm honored to have had you under my command. Besides, America needs heroes. You're deserving. I know my pilots. Not even Major "Kit" Carson could have pulled off what you have in the last five days, especially today . . . real savvy."

Meg beamed. "Thank you, Sir."

Middleton sighed, pointing at the pad on his desk. "Unfortunately, I'm the one who has to write the letters to the parents and wives." He was having a difficult moment. "Only war, unfortunately, provides the opportunity for likely heroes to emerge and medals to be won.....not much else. Your dad's buddy, Eddie Rickenbacker, hit the nail on the head when he said that courage is doing what you're afraid to do; there can be no courage unless you're scared."

Meg finished her drink then studied the rim of the glass. She was having a difficult moment as well. She had been damn scared but had reached down deep, drawing from the training, guidance, and honorable values that her father had passed along. Her instincts to save Chamberlain were merely a result. She was about to make her father proud.

Middleton half-stood, grabbed the uncapped bottle, and poured her another. "Except for one thing." He sat back down, flashing a troubled expression. "I've got a major problem."

Meg reached out and grasped her drink and took a sip. "Problem?"

"Hero or not, the cat's out of the bag," he revealed. "We know who you are."

Meg tensed, gripping the arms of her chair, enough to turn her knuckles white. "Who told you about . . . all this?"

"That's not important, *Miss* Reilly. . . . The question is--how do we deal with this . . . this matter?"

Meg turned pale. "Colonel, I can explain," she said in a near-panicked voice. "After my brother and my best friend died in that raid a few days ago, all I could think about was killing the Germans who did it. Later, I told myself that I wanted to carry on his name, but I really got caught up in the thrill of the action. I guess I felt a bit guilty about loving it, but at the same time, I felt like I was fulfilling my destiny."

"You're a lot like your father from what I hear, but you're Megan Reilly, not Garrett Reilly. I know why you did this, and if I had been in your shoes and could fly like you do, I would have probably tried to do the same thing. Hell, we got an unconfirmed report the other day that one of your former WAF friends has been ferrying B-25s over the Hump in India against the Japs. So when I started hearing stories about you, I wasn't totally shocked.....I was standing at the Cleveland Airport back in '39 when you won the Bendix. All I could think about for days was how I wished my daughter was just like you." He paused to take two large swallows of the liquor. "Unfortunately, I have a war to run. Normally, we just process these youngsters in, stick 'em in a peashooter, and send them off to battle." Middleton grabbed his glass, stood, and looked out the window. "But as you admitted, you are an opportunist."

Meg raised her chin. "And a Reilly," she said proudly.

Middleton took another sip and faced her. "Impersonating an officer is a serious offense, Miss Reilly. You understand that you have put me in a very awkward position."

"In a sense, Colonel, the general created the situation along with Colonel Douglass when they had me and Nancy and Liz ferry Mustangs here."

Middleton sighed then nodded. "That's a good point, young lady. I guess that makes my job easier all of a sudden."

Meg was in tears now. "Colonel, all my life I have been trying to get accepted into your world. . . . To do that, I knew I had to fly better than a man. . . . fly in combat. But now that I've been in it, well . . . innocent, naive young men, some nothing more than teenage boys, getting maimed and killed. Dad lost a leg in the last war. I was killing him not to be a part of this one. My brother and best friend--dead; John Hastings--K.I.A. I guess I'd say. . . . It don't matter what you do to me. At least I know that a woman can do it . . . that I did it."

"That you did." Middleton was suddenly hit with a brainstorm. "And that's exactly what you are going to do, Miss Reilly."

The next moment seemed to last forever.

He leaned forward in his chair with excited eyes. "Tomorrow morning, a red-lined pursuit will be fueled. After you pack, you'll take off."

Meg moved forward on her seat. "Where to, Colonel?"

"I will clear a flight plan back to England where Colonel Douglass will arrange for transportation back to the States. You will travel under a bogus name. What you tell your family is up to you, but no one else is to know what really happened. Remember, this started out as a classified mission--it is still classified. Our records will show that Garrett Reilly was killed in action. . . . You have been successful in one regard. You have made him an ace. . . . a hero. . . posthumously. Unfortunately, you'll never get any credit for what you did in the past week. . . . Fame for freedom. . . .That's what you will have traded. Is this plan acceptable to you?"

Meg nodded her head up and down. "I got just one request, Colonel."

"Shoot!"

"Hub's Jewish. Let me take a plane to search for him. If the Gestapo gets its hands on him, they'll torture him then nail him to a cross."

"Negative!" Middleton snapped. "He knew the risks."

Meg was taken back by his apathy. "Who knows, maybe I

won't come back, and your report will be factual," she said facetiously.

"Dear God, Miss Reilly. I'm thinking about your safety, not plotting your demise. If it hadn't been for you a week ago, many of the men on this base would be sporting a wooden box. No, young lady, the general would hand my ass to me, and I don't need any more worries than I already have. . . . nor deaths on my conscience, especially a girl's." He pointed to the stack of sympathy letters.

The look on Meg's face was nondescript.

Middleton continued, "Carry on your charade tonight but not a word of this to anyone, especially to the Press Corps. As I said, what you tell your family and your sweetheart is up to you, whatever it is. They must keep it confidential." Middleton snapped to attention and saluted her out of respect. "You're one hell of a combat pilot, Miss Reilly. I really hate losing you."

Meg stood and returned his salute.

Misty-eyed, Middleton turned, picked up a case of Jack Daniel's, and set it on his desk. "Here. I had to get you out of combat before you broke the bank."

"Thank you, Colonel." She picked up the case and turned to leave.

Middleton rounded his desk to open the door for her. "Miss Reilly, after all this, do you still think that women should be allowed to fly in combat?"

Meg paused reflectively for a moment then looked Wild Bill in the eye. "No one should ever be in combat. . . . but if it has to happen then we should be fighting alongside the men."

Middleton took a deep breath and solemnly nodded. "You know what is really sad? Your friend, Liz. She deserves to be buried as a veteran."

Meg walked to her room to deposit the liquor then decided to visit Hub's room. A young sergeant was in his room, conducting an inventory of Hub's personal effects.

"Mind if I come in, Sergeant?"

He looked up from his clipboard and snapped to attention. "Not at all, Lieutenant."

"As you were, Sergeant."

He resumed his task.

She looked around. There was the usual military gear and clothing. Pinned to the wall near his bunk was a picture. She moved in for a closer look. It was the photo of her and Hub taken in front of their pursuits.

The sergeant glanced up. "I'll have to have that, Lieutenant. Regulations."

Meg fought the urge to cry as she reluctantly handed him the photo that he tossed into Hub's equipment bag.

"Thank you, Lieutenant."

On the night stand, she spotted what looked like a handwritten note. She quietly slipped it into her pocket. "Thank you, Sergeant," Meg said as she exited the room.

Meg returned to her quarters, plopped on the edge of her bed, and began reading.

So near to God, high in the sky.
Into the sun our birds ascended
First glance you were but a child, evolved First Lady of the Air.
I figured wrong. You have masterfully abounded.

A graceful bird, your wings spread wide.
And like a fool, I denied your right.
I applauded your gift, so few possess,
And so many men who have denied you flight.

I love thee angel, I've come to know.
Had I taken time to see all that you have made.
I somehow have come to understand.
That not all were calling a spade a spade.

I have looked to God, this late date,
And trust I have not waited too long.
When sunrise comes, a flash of ramparts so great.
Into thy hands where I belong.

I pray for an angel's safety.
Oh, Lord, I take off in great fear.
You have provisioned us well,
How to cope with what could be near.

Now that I know you, I am not afraid.
If you must choose, pick me then to fall from grace.
In the quest for freedom whence we pursue,
And the glory of the Queen of Aces.

I ventured to the B.O.Q. to catch up with Meg. I heard feminine sobbing coming from her room.

I looked both ways then knocked. "It's me, Aaron."

"It's unlocked."

I walked in and shut the door. "Meg, are you all right?"

"He's gone," she sobbed. "The bastards killed him. They tried to kill me, too"

"The krauts?"

She shook her head. "No. . . . LaRocca and Devine."

"What?" I asked.

After a long moment, she lay her head on my shoulder and proceeded to tell me what had happened earlier in the day. Hub had become a very important part of her life since Liz and Garrett had gotten killed. Whether coerced or not, Hub had been sharing a very deep secret with Meg. And now with Hub missing in action, there was an unfinished chapter in her life. I couldn't help but feel that some of her love belonged to him. I sensed she was holding back part of the story.

"I know Hub was arrogant, cocky, stuck on himself," she sobbed. "Sometimes, he made me so mad that I wanted to slug him, especially when he started that pregnant cigar crap.....and calling me Baby-face. Oh, that really made my blood boil...but he also had a soft side I never saw until the chips were down and team effort was essential. Oh, he fought it at first, but then grew to show me respect."

I took a deep breath. "Are you sure you weren't falling for him?"

"Not in the least," she said somewhat unconvincingly, shaking her head. "The colonel knows about everything," Meg sobbed. "I'm history. I have been ordered to quietly disappear tomorrow morning."

"So, someone blew the whistle on you, huh?"

Meg nodded. "I should have known, sooner or later, that I'd run into someone from the past."

"Who?" I asked.

"It was either Devine or LaRocca. Devine was jealous of the kills I got, and LaRocca, well I had a run-in with him at the O-club in New Castle. They killed Hub then came after me. They ended up colliding." Meg paused. Suddenly, her eyes brightened. "Why don't you come back to New Jersey with me?"

I took a deep breath and let it out slowly. It was an offer that I had to refuse. "I wish I could, but I've got a job to do then get back to London."

Meg deflated instantly. "Where are you going?"

"To meet with the Resistance...The war will be over soon. You can bet that I'll be back then."

She leaned against my shoulder, placing her face into my neck. "You be damn careful, Brooks Brothers." Meg sniffed, fighting the urge to cry. "Remember, Aaron, not a word of this to anyone; otherwise, I'll be charged with impersonating an officer."

"Your secret is safe with me," I confirmed. "How about a drink then some dinner? The colonel told me about a great French restaurant in town."

Meg squeezed me in her arms. "I've been on pins and needles since this whole thing started. Now that the cat's out of the bag, I feel like a giant weight's been lifted off my shoulders. It'll be nice to relax." She rolled her eyes upward at me. "Even if only for a night."

* * * * *

A spectacular sun appeared in the distance, and all was quiet, more than usual as Meg and I arrived at the flight line in a jeep driven by her crew chief. Most of the pursuits had already taken off for a sunrise air strike. He braked in front of a tired P-47. Meg looked up. On the fuselage under the canopy were 15 swastikas. Her eyes panned right to the name painted on the nose, "Queen of Aces." The background was a combination of a queen of spades and the ace of spades cards.

A smile grew on her face. "You know?"

Corporal Ray winked at her. "It was the Old Man's idea...It ain't no Kite, but I reckon she'll git you where ya need to go. Just keep an eye on the temperature gauge. She's been overheating."

"I understand, Corporal." Meg sat back in the passenger seat, misty-eyed, and stared at the name for what seemed forever.

In the distant eastern horizon, we could hear the faint rumbling of a pursuit. At first she shook it off as a mirage. At first, it appeared as a dot against the sun, growing larger and larger as the seconds passed, its engine coughing and sputtering. Gray smoke poured from the engine cowling. A fire truck and an ambulance, sirens screaming, raced down the runway. She strained to see the name on the nose, but the smoke was too thick.

Meg slid off the seat and began running toward the wounded Mustang as it landed and veered off the runway. It finally came to a stop in the muddy grass. A slender pilot quickly emerged from the cockpit, hopped to the ground, and began running from the smoking P-51. The pilot continued to run in Meg's direction, frequently spinning around to check on the fate of his smoldering aircraft.

"My God," she whooped. "It's you. . . . It's really you."

The pilot stopped running sideways and turned toward the raspy voice. Suddenly, Meg stopped.

It was a young pilot she had never seen before, one who had been forced to land at the nearest airfield. "Do I know you?" he asked.

Deflated, Meg fought to control her emotions. "No, I'm sorry.....I thought you were someone else.....someone I used to know."

I climbed out of the jeep as Meg returned to the flight line. "What was all that about?"

"I thought it was Hub, but it was just somebody that looked like him from a distance."

I sensed that she was holding back her true feelings for Hub. "I'm sorry about Hub. I wish there was something I could do."

Meg pulled me into a hug for what seemed like an eternity. She then walked over to the jeep and reached inside her Gladstone bag. She took out the white silk scarf Amelia had given her and positioned it around her neck. She then took out a diary and handed it to me.

"Please keep this for me," she asked.

I looked down at the tattered book with a concerned, curious look on my face. "Why?"

"If for some reason I don't make it back.....er, a, to the States.....Just trust me. There's something I must do."

"You're going after him.....aren't you?" I stammered, although I already knew the answer.

"Trust me." She pulled me into her and kissed me softly. "I love you, Aaron."

Grabbing her Gladstone bag, Meg boarded the ailing P-47. The corporal assisted her into the cockpit then hopped down. Soon, the giant engine was sputtering. He gave her a thumbs-up, and she began to taxi the half-sick bird.

I watched from the ground below. Meg managed a smile as she taxied to the runway. I smiled back. It was a terrible, empty moment for me. It was only a day before that I had found her again, and now I wasn't sure where her heart was.

Meg passed by the tower where Middleton and Hamilton stood watching from the outside deck. Sitting next to them in a wheel chair was Bob Chamberlain. They saluted her as she taxied by.

I watched with an empty heart as Meg rocketed down the runway, spiraled gracefully upward, and disappeared in the horizon.

Later that morning, Colonel Middleton summoned me to his office. "Mister Masters, Lieutenant Reilly never made it to England. I'm worried. The Thunderbolt was ready for the junk heap." He paused. "Did Reilly say anything to you about taking a detour?"

"A detour?" I dumbly repeated. A stroke-like numbness raced through my body. "I'm sorry, Colonel. I have no idea what you're getting at."

He kicked his desk. "Dammit!"

I pondered whether he had purposely given her that red-liner. It would have certainly solved his biggest problem.

"Sir, what I'm about to tell you is top secret. I must have your word that it will stay in this room."

He nodded, "Of course."

"I'm an agent for the O.S.S."

His eyes grew large.

"Secretly, I have been going behind enemy lines for the past year to help retrieve compromised agents and downed flyers."

Middleton's ears had just grown proportionately to his eyes.

"I'll need the use of your observation plane and a good pilot."

Colonel Middleton loaned me a L3 Cub, his Thompson submachine gun, and a pilot to search for Meg. Flying nap-of-the-earth to avoid enemy radar, we reached the site where Hub's plane had gone down. We found the wreckage in an open field and the charred remains of a German fighter nearby, but there was no sign of Hub. We scoured the nearby area and eventually spotted an individual in the middle of a thicket, waving his arms. We could only hope that it was not a German soldier trying to lure us into a trap.

Although the area was crawling with Germans, we landed on a nearby tank trail. I loaded a magazine into the Thompson then instructed the pilot to take off at the first sign of a German patrol.

I soon found an animal trail and negotiated the thicket. I cautiously but quickly made my way to the middle where I found Hub. He had suffered a broken leg during the crash and had painfully crawled from the wreckage to the thicket where he hid from the Germans.

His eyes nearly exploded when he spotted my face and the officer's uniform I was wearing. "Masters?" he asked, gawking.

"No time for small talk," I noted. "Let me give you a hand." I placed his arm over my shoulder and hustled toward the L3. "Have you seen any sign of a P-47 in the last hour or two?" I asked.

Hub winced from the pain of limping on the broken leg. "No, why?"

"Middleton found out about the impersonation and sent Meg back to England; however, she never made it. We thought maybe she had come after you."

His eyes tearing from the pain, he murmured. "You're the first friendlies."

Just as I lifted his injured body into the passenger seat, a

German patrol arrived in a half-track trying to block any attempt to take off.

I quickly grabbed an extra drum of ammo and two grenades. "Find her, Hub, and when you do, take good care of her."

Before Hub had a chance to say anything, I shut the door and signaled for the pilot to take off.

* * * * *

Sweaty and greasy, Rye Reilly was taking a cigarette break, leaning against the door of a large new hangar, gazing upward at an L3-B Cub circling the field.

Suddenly, a taxi pulled up to the Reilly hangar. Rye dropped his cigarette on the ground and mashed it with a boot. The passenger climbed out. He smiled then tears filled his face. Meg ran around to greet her father who gave her a bone-crushing hug. "I...I thought you had left us," Rye sniffled.

"For awhile I did, too. Oh, Dad, I still can't believe he's gone."

Rye's face flushed with tears. "No man wants to outlive his kids. Losing Gar...."

Meg pulled her father in closer. "I know, Dad. When the Gerries shot him down, all I could think about was revenge."

"That's still no reason for not contacting me. I had to go through the grief of losing my daughter only to go through it again with my son." Rye was almost limp in her arms.

Meg finally managed to utter, "I went to find Hub where he had been shot down, but the red-liner they gave me blew an oil seal, and I had to set it down. Fortunately, the French Underground got to me before the krauts did. I spent the next month trying to get back to England."

Rye was suddenly more upset. "You still haven't answered my question. Why didn't you contact me? I've been worried sick."

"It was a classified mission, Dad," Meg explained. "I had planned to write you....then Garrett got killed." Meg broke into tears. "I didn't know what to say. When I finally got back to England, Colonel Douglass told me that Aaron volunteered to find Hub. The good news--they were successful. The bad news--Aaron stayed back to keep the Germans pinned down until the plane was airborne. The pilot reported an explosion and brush fire in the area where Aaron was last seen. No one has heard from him since."

Rye held her for what seemed like an eternity. He finally spoke, "Sean is on his way back from the Pacific. I thought for a moment that you were him arriving." He broke the hug, but placed both hands on her shoulders. "You can tell me all about it later. Right now, I just want to relish you being back here....safe."

Meg eyeballed the new hangar. "It looks like you are off and running on another project. How does it feel to have some extra cash to work with?"

"C'mon," Rye said with renewed enthusiasm, "I've got something to show you."

Inside, was a sleek jet prototype. Meg walked up and caressed it with a hand. "It's beautiful, Dad. You know, the Germans have a jet. I didn't see any myself, but we heard stories. Lieutenant Drew shot down two with a Mustang."

"I was trying to get this prototype perfected just for that reason, but we're so close to winning this war, the Top Brass are dismissing the idea that we'll ever need it."

"Seems like the same BS that they were spoutin' back in '39."

Rye snickered. "Ain't that the truth." He suddenly grew a smile. "Enough shop talk, are you hungry?"

Meg's eyes lit up, and she bounced on her toes. "Yes, a Coney dog....three or four of 'em."

Rye grinned. "C'mon, I'm buying."

* * * * *

A light rain fell as the remains of Garrett's body, recovered by the Army from the crash site in France, were now to be laid to rest at Arlington National Cemetery.

Of course, the Army Air Force had covered it up that Megan Reilly had ever flown in combat during that extraordinary week.

Two months later, First Lieutenant Garrett Reilly was posthumously awarded the Medal of Honor during an emotional ceremony at the White House. In attendance were a very proud Rye Reilly wearing his own MOH, his other son, the highly decorated, six-times ace Major Sean Reilly, and Meg Reilly in her old WAF uniform. President Harry Truman placed the medal around Meg's neck who accepted the medal on behalf of her dead twin. Also in attendance was Major Bob Chamberlain who winked at Meg from his wheelchair. Little did those in the audience realize that the true recipient of the MOH was actually wearing it.

Three Months Later:

Wearing a flight jacket and khaki slacks, Meg, her eyes animated, sat on the edge of a picnic table near the airfield, talking to a group of open-mouthed, teenage girls about their future as pilots. She paused to take a bite of a Coney dog. Suddenly, the girls shifted their attention. Meg sensed someone behind her, but she did not turn, continuing to talk.

A taxi pulled to a stop, and a uniformed man climbed out of the passenger seat and positioned himself on a crutch. On his chest were several rows of ribbons. A decorated war hero. He began to whistle Blue Skies.

A curious look filled her face then she stood and turned. Meg stared at him in shock for a long moment then began to walk toward him, slowly then faster and faster. She flew into his arms.

Behind them, the kids applauded.

She pulled her head back, tears streaming, half-crying and half-smiling. "I thought you were--"

"Dead," he interrupted. "I crashed on an open field."

"But, Hub, I saw the explosion."

"That was a German fighter that went up in smoke. Anyway, with a broken leg, I crawled to a nearby thicket and camouflaged myself. I put a splint on my leg and rested till the next day. I was about to evade the area when Aaron Masters of all people arrived in a Cub. I owe him a lot. The last thing he said to me was to take good care of you. He stayed behind to cover my escape. Sometimes you just don't really know people. He was a brave man after all. I owe him my life."

* * * * *

After I had loaded Hub into the Cub, I flopped onto my stomach and began firing short spurts at the enemy gunner, trying to pin him down long enough for the L3 to take off, but it worked, and Hub was on his way to safety. My first ammo drum was soon spent. I dashed toward the thicket. The Germans gave up on the L3 and concentrated on me. Minutes later, I took a bullet in the shoulder and another in the thigh. Although writhing in pain, I managed to change drums and continue firing. Suddenly, one of the Germans tossed a "Potato Masher" at me. I rolled over enough to reach the grenade and tossed it back before it exploded, killing or wounding four German soldiers that had just entered the thicket. Using my belt and a stick, I made a tourniquet for my leg wound. As I evaded toward a nearby stream, the L3 banked just overhead then headed southwest. I tried to signal it, but smoke from the smoldering fire was blowing directly over me. I couldn't be sure if the pilot had seen me or not. Knowing the Germans would soon be hunting me with K-9 trackers, I headed for the freezing-cold water of a nearby creek.

It took me almost two weeks to make contact with the French Underground and another six weeks to heal my wounds, thanks to my former acquaintance Nicole who nursed me back to health.

By the time I had recuperated enough to travel, Germany had surrendered to the Allies. I caught a military hop to England but with Colonel Middleton gone, I couldn't get any information about Meg's status. I then read in the Stars and Stripes that Garrett Reilly had been awarded the Medal of Honor, posthumously. I located a ham radio operator and contacted Rye Reilly. He reluctantly announced that Meg had returned home and was engaged to be married. Stunned by the news, I flew back to France and asked my editor to reassign me to the Paris bureau. A year later, I was named bureau chief and married Nicole a few months later. Life was good. Then in 1948, Nicole started bleeding and was rushed to the hospital. Two days later, she died giving birth to our stillborn son. I fell into deep depression, and a liquor bottle became a permanent facial feature. I was on the brink of losing my job at the magazine when we got news that the North Koreans had crossed the 38th Parallel into South Korea.

During the first months of the war, our fighter aircraft were out-classed by the Russian MIGs, resulting in the needless death of some of America's best combat pilots. Again, America was months behind in aerial combat technology. And finally, the Top Brass visited the Reillys to get a demonstration of Rye's jet prototype.

Memorial Day, 1949:

It was a warm, sunny day, perfect for a parade in downtown Wilmington, Delaware. Auto and truck traffic was backed up for several blocks in all directions while the citizens of Wilmington and neighboring towns paid tribute to those who had fallen in combat. A dozen area marching bands, military units from neighboring New Castle Air Force Base, the local American Legion, and hundreds of veterans, including a handful of former WAFs, marched down the crowded main street lined with spectators, some in military uniform, disabled vets on crutches and wheel chairs, and families. Young children sat atop their father's shoulders while others raced about the legs of their parents, playing tag and waving hand-held flags.

I had just returned from Korea and decided to attend, hoping that Meg might be in attendance.

A squadron of P-51s buzzed over the top of the buildings in a missing-man formation, grabbing everyone's attention. I glanced up from the Press Corps convertible, my heart beating, hoping to see the Queen of Aces. I stared at the powerful machines until they disappeared from sight. As I looked down, I caught a glimpse of a tall gal with long auburn hair, wearing a leather flying jacket and sunglasses. She appeared to be about 30 years of age.

I slid off the side of the slow-moving convertible and limped to the spot where the woman had been standing, but she had disappeared. I paralleled the parade route, trying to find her without success. I finally rejoined my comrades to finish the parade but kept a vigil for the mysterious woman with long auburn hair.

That evening, I attended a banquet at the officers' club, but I couldn't get my mind off the woman I had briefly spotted during the parade. Lacking an appetite for rubbery chicken, I excused myself to take a walk down by the flight line. Moonbeams glittered off the silvery wings of the trainers and fighters as I strolled by them. Then, I spotted a dark figure slip into an open, nearby hangar.

My curiosity aroused, I quietly crept to the open door and peered inside the dark hangar. I could hear what sounded like an engine during preflight. Suddenly, the engine kicked over, and that familiar whine of a high-performance pursuit began to vibrate everything inside the hangar. As quickly as it started, the engine was shut down.

At the risk of embarrassing myself, I quickly hopped onto the wing and scaled it to the open cockpit, illuminated by the instrument panel lights. I asked, "You wouldn't know where I could get a good Coney dog 'round here, would you?"

Startled, the pilot jumped and twisted around. It was a woman. Her eyes grew large, and she shot out of the seat. "Couldn't handle the chicken, huh, Brooks Brothers?"

We lunged into feverish kissing.

Suddenly, I pulled my head back, exclaiming, "Whoa, just a second. You're a married woman."

Meg stepped out of the cockpit onto the wing. "You need to get your facts straight, Mr. Reporter. I'm not married. Never was."

"What?" I stammered. "But your father said that you were engaged."

"Hotshot had told Dad that he was planning on asking me. Anyway, after I heard that you had called, I set the record straight. Then I waited every day for months for your return. Later, I called your editor at *Aviation Life* magazine in New York, and he told me that you were in Paris and had gotten hitched. I repeat.....You, not me, got hitched."

"But I thought you loved Hub, not me."

"Negative, Brooks Brothers! Look at me, and hear me right. I never loved Hub like I love you....I have always loved you.....from the very first time I saw you.....but now you're taken."

I shook my head. "She died two years ago." I squared myself and looked back into Meg's eyes. "Megan Reilly, I love you. . . . Always did. . . . I just didn't always show it."

"At ease, Brooks Brothers," Meg ordered.

She then planted a kiss on me that I'll never forget. I picked her up in my arms.

"Where are you taking me?"

"You said nothing beats flying. I want to see how it feels to soar with an ace." I set her down in the cockpit.

We fumbled with each other's clothing, pawing at each other, full of life.

We both knew that we would never be apart again.

* * * * *

A cool breeze began to creep across the grass like a slithering snake. I raised my collar, left my book in a clear plastic case at the foot of Meg's grave marker, and struggled to stand. Most of the other visitors had already left the military cemetery. With the sun setting, I walked slowly back to my car and stared at the horizon. I missed her so, and now that my job of telling her story was done, I was ready to join her. As with Amelia, I knew the Queen of Aces was up there somewhere, soaring like an eagle.

EPILOGUE

On Thanksgiving Eve, 1977, President Jimmy Carter signed a compromise bill giving the WASPs their long-awaited veterans status which meant they could finally be buried with full military honors.

In June 1999, at the vibrant age of 80, Megan Reilly was buried at Arlington National Cemetery with full military honors next to her brothers Sean and Garrett and her father, Pat "Rye" Reilly. Someday soon, I know that I will join her. The military will bury me, as prearranged, in the same grave. But I prefer to think of it as our cockpit in the sky.

* * * * *

During World War II, 1,074 American women risked their lives daily, flying almost every type of military aircraft, including our largest bombers and fastest fighters, under some of the severest conditions, many subjecting themselves to deadly fire while towing targets.

Although unconfirmed, former WAF Director Nancy Love reportedly ferried bombers and transports over the Hump in India against the Japanese.

Former WASP Walley Funk was selected for the female astronaut program during the infamous Mercury program era. We all know that seven male candidates passed the rigorous tests; interestingly, 13 women passed the same tests. Before the woman astronaut program had a chance to develop, politics and female discrimination reared their ugly heads.....and an end to the female program.

Today, women pilot some of this country's most sophisticated combat aircraft. During the 1991 Gulf War, some female Army pilots flew helicopters in the combat zone, but none were permitted to fly an official military combat sortie. In the spring of 1999, women contributed to the liberation of the ethnic Albanians in Kosovo as combat pilots. They have finally been given the opportunity to prove themselves in combat--officially.

Hats off to all the First Ladies of the Air.